"I WANTED TO SAY THANK YOU FOR . . . COMING AND OFFERING YOUR HELP."

It was his turn to feel speechless. "I'm glad to do it."

"I know this is unusual," she said breathily. "You may think me terrible for asking."

"I won't," he said quickly.

"It's just that I've been dead in a lot of ways for a long time now," she said quietly. "I think . . ." Her gaze dropped to his lips. "I'd like to remember, or maybe to know, what a kiss feels like."

A *kiss*? He wondered if he really knew how to kiss. He'd bedded a lot of women, but a kiss? And she wanted to know what it felt like from him? "I'm not sure I'm any good at it," he admitted.

She shrugged delicately and he felt moved, almost shaken by her vulnerability. He leaned forward slowly and pressed a kiss to her lips. Her lips were soft and warm, a perfect fit for his. So this was how a kiss was supposed to feel. He hadn't known it was so sweet a thing. He pulled back slightly. "I think that's how it's done," he said softly.

"I like it," she whispered.

"I liked it, too." She rose gracefully and started from the room. She turned back to him briefly at the door, and she was so beautiful, she stole his breath.

"Good night," she said.

"'Night," he echoed. He stared at the door long after she'd shut it. He could still smell her soft scent and feel her presence. It was good. It was so much better than being alone.

Also by Jane Shoup

Down in the Valley

Published by Kensington Publishing Corporation

SPIRIT
OF THE
VALLEY

JANE SHOUP

ZEBRA BOOKS
KENSINGTON PUBLISHING CORP.
http://www.kensingtonbooks.com

The early autumn of 1882 was cooler than usual in Green Valley, Virginia, and brilliant in color. By evening, businesses—other than the saloons—had closed. Most folks were home having supper or enjoying a pipe in front of the hearth, or chatting with neighbors on front porches.

As the reverend strolled tree-lined streets, seeking inspiration for Sunday's sermon, he clearly saw the simple beauty all around the picturesque town, from the now-closed shops on Main Street to neat clapboard residences with lights glowing within. The smell of suppers cooking permeated the air overriding the scent of autumnal decomposition. Occasionally a dog barked or someone called a friendly greeting, which he returned. The chilly wind sent leaves fluttering, their fleeting flight silhouetted against the light of gas street lamps. It was all lovely, calm and peaceful, yet a feeling of pensiveness, almost a melancholy, had taken hold. It was the season. The fall of the year always made him ponder death, or rather, the brevity of life.

Stars were beginning to appear as he finished his stroll at the church. Cutting through the cemetery, the most direct route to the parsonage, he noticed a flash of color atop a shadowy, gray tombstone. A small bouquet of purple flowers. There was no need to draw closer to know whose grave they adorned. He stopped and glanced around, but no one was lurking or hurrying away. As usual, Jenny Lynn Sheffield's mourner had come and gone without being seen. A smile sprang to his lips, a sudden uplifting of his spirit, because there was something satisfying about the frequency of the occurrence. Her young life had been cut short, but she wasn't forgotten. Someone still loved her.

Ah, yes. Autumn would become winter and his seasonal sadness would be forgotten. Before he knew it, it would be spring and then hot summer. They'd all complain of the heat and wish for cooler weather again. He shoved his hands deeper into his pockets and walked on with a smile on his face.

Prologue

May 1872, Green Valley, Virginia

Sixteen-year-old Jenny Lynn Sheffield cringed at the sound of the corncob bed as she sat on the edge. The bed was probably a hundred years old, and how many people had lain there was impossible to know, but now she would be added to the list. Unless she stopped things right now. Her fists tightened as she stared at the tattered curtain in the window of the long-abandoned cabin. It fluttered from a breeze she couldn't feel. Why couldn't she feel it?

Ted had begun undressing. She could see him out of the corner of her eye. She couldn't do this. "I'm sorry," she stammered as she stood again on legs so weak they barely supported her. "I . . . I can't." She felt stiff as a board. Even her mouth wouldn't work right.

Ted looked perturbed as he stood there, his shirt partly unbuttoned, his suspenders dangling at his sides. "You promised."

Tears filled her eyes. "I thought I could," she said brokenly.

"You said you loved me," he said accusingly.

"I do, but—"

"Said you wanted to marry me."

She exhaled in exasperation. She'd never said one thing to him that wasn't true, not about her feelings.

"What?" he demanded. "I mean, you promised, and you want to marry me."

"It just . . . it feels wrong," she said weakly.

His expression softened. "How can it be wrong if I think it's right? We love each other and you want to be my wife. Right? So show me."

This wasn't an argument she could win, but nor was losing her virginity at this moment something she could do, no matter what she'd thought. It wasn't fair. She did want to marry him, but why couldn't they wait? Why did it have to be now?

He walked over to her, tipped her chin up with his finger and pressed a tender kiss to her lips. "Look. I know you're scared," he said soothingly.

She desperately sought words that would make him understand; but he didn't understand, because he reached out and untied the ribbon at the base of her long, dark braid and began to undo it in his fingers. Did he still think it was happening? "Ted," she pleaded.

"No, listen," he interrupted. "Here's the thing. If you love me, you gotta do what I say. Now, it's true that it always hurts the first time for a woman."

A woman. The words hit hard, mocking her. "I'm sorry," she whispered with a slow shake of her head. There was an abrupt change in his expression—a tightening of the facial muscles, a narrowing of the eyes. It was subtle and yet so abrupt, it stole her breath. In a moment's time, there had been a hardening of his heart she could actually feel. She'd lost him. Standing there, refusing to give herself to him, she'd just lost him. But how could she lose him by wanting to wait?

"In my world," he said without a flicker of emotion, "a promise is a promise."

A new fear seized hold of her, although it was more instinct than true understanding. She took a step away, but he yanked her right back and kissed her roughly. She turned her head and attempted to pull free. "Let go of me!"

He did. He let go of her, studied her labored breathing and flushed face for a moment, and then began to unbutton his trousers.

The confusion she felt lasted only a split second and was followed by blood chilling panic. She tried to get around him, but he grabbed her and forced her back to the bed. She cried out for him to stop, but his face was a mask of determination as he forced her down and climbed on top of her. She fought him, but he got her skirt up. "No, please," she pleaded. "I shouldn't have said—" One arm pinned her painfully, his forearm on her chest, as the other yanked at her knickers. She heard her clothing rip and he had one leg free. "Stop it," she cried. "Oh God, please—"

Her pleas made no difference. She couldn't stop him, and her innocence was lost in a stab of pain. Hot tears slid down her face and into her ears. He was still moving, still on her. Time had stopped and her life was ruined, but he was still moving. He made a strange cry and then collapsed beside her. He was breathing hard as he got off her.

She rolled onto her side and curled into a ball. She was bruised and sick to her stomach and *ruined*. Seconds passed and then she realized he was dressing. Thank God. *Just leave. Leave.* But the sound of voices—male voices—made her breath catch. She forced herself upright and tried to stand, but couldn't. She heard a voice again and was bitterly confused by it. This was an isolated parcel of her family's land. No one ever came around here. Consumed with dread, she attempted to straighten her clothing and hide what had happened, but her dizziness and badly shaking limbs made it difficult.

"Hello?" a voice called.

Jenny instantly recognized the voice of Stan Thomas, Ted's best friend. She turned to Ted with an incredulous expression, but he wasn't looking at her. In that moment, she knew. Whatever he had been pretending all these months with her, it *had* been pretending. He hadn't meant any of what he'd declared. He didn't love her. He didn't love her at all. She was a fool. Her brother, Jeremy, had been right about that. She was a stupid, stupid fool and Ted Landreth had just ruined her. She had let him ruin her. "Why is he here?" she asked in a low, trembling voice.

Ted didn't answer, nor did he look at her.

"What are you talking about . . . *share* her?" another voice said. She recognized her friend Curtis's voice.

Jenny reeled, because she'd heard the words clearly. The room was spinning madly, but she managed to stand. The realization that her knickers were still around one ankle was too much and she would have collapsed again, except that Ted was suddenly in front of her. "Hey," he said, roughly grabbing her arms.

Cold, hard disgust knotted in the pit of her belly, but it didn't stop tears from flowing down her face.

"You want to marry me, doing what I·say is part of it," he stated.

She shook her head because he was a liar. "You said you loved me."

"If I didn't think the whole world of you, would I want to share you with my friends?"

The words were monstrous. He was monstrous. How could she have been so stupid?

"Can we come in or what?" Stan called.

Ted gave her a shake. "You do what I say," he warned.

She shook her head because she wouldn't. She'd scream her head off. She'd fight him, fight them all. She'd kill them. She'd let Jeremy kill them.

The door creaked open.

"Jenny?" Curtis called worriedly.

Curtis would help her. He was her friend. "Help me," she called to him without looking away from Ted.

Ted's eyes narrowed and his jaw clenched.

"Leave her alone, Ted," Curtis said, coming into the room. "Whatever this is—"

Ted turned to glare at him. "Whatever this is, is none of your damn business if you don't want to take a turn. Just get on out of here."

The words gagged Jenny. She was going to be sick.

"There's not going to be any turns," Curtis said.

"Shoulda known not to bring you," Stan complained angrily from just inside the door. "Just clear out if you don't wanna."

"She's mine," Ted declared. "She does what I say."

"No," she exclaimed, shaking her head. "I won't!"

Curtis started toward her to help her, but stopped abruptly when he felt the gun Stan had pressed to the back of his skull.

Ted cursed as he let go of her and turned his attention to his friends. "Put it down," he ordered angrily.

"I was promised something and I'm going to get it," Stan swore.

"I said, put it down," Ted said through clenched teeth. "When did I say a damn thing about guns? Huh?"

Stan was livid, but he lowered the gun. "You promised—"

"Too bad," Ted retorted, glowering at both Curtis and Stan. "This whole thing is blown. Now let's go."

Jenny's legs gave way. She was sickeningly light-headed as

she half sat, half fell onto the floor. She kept her face turned from all of them, unable to stop the tears of mortification.

"Jenny?" Curtis said.

The others had gone, but she couldn't look at him. He was her friend and he would have helped her, but she was shamed beyond redemption. "Puh-please go."

"Will you be all right to get home?" he asked quietly, reluctant to leave her.

She nodded.

"Did he hurt you?"

She winced. "Please—"

"I'm sorry, Jenny. I'm so sorry. I didn't know."

She turned her face even farther away and held her breath at the sound of his retreating footsteps. She pressed a hand to her stomach, but she couldn't stop the wave of nausea. Moaning from the pain, she leaned over and retched before dissolving in sobs of misery.

It took time to gain enough strength to collect herself. When she left the dim confines of the cabin, the sunshine was shocking. It was a beautiful day, birds were singing. How odd. She could *see* it was a fine day, but she couldn't *feel* it. Because she was ruined. The old log cabin sat on the northwest corner of their property and she had loved it as a child, but she would never be able to set foot in there again.

She walked blindly, knowing the path by rote, stopping only when she reached the pond. Staring at the brilliantly twinkling water, she longed to have her sins washed away, but could even the best preacher pull off that feat? If she had been forced from the beginning, she'd stand a chance at redemption, but she'd gone to the cabin willingly. She'd imagined herself marrying Ted Landreth, having his children, living happily ever after. She'd been so stupid. He'd said he loved her, but he only wanted to use her, and she'd let him.

Jenny hugged herself as she walked on. When she got home, she warily stepped through the back door, praying her mother was elsewhere. She'd pulled herself together as best she could, but she felt so bruised and altered.

"Jen?" her mother called from the parlor.

Jenny stopped short. "Yes, ma'am," she said, trying to make her voice sound normal.

"What took you so long?"

"I helped Miss McCarthy," Jenny lied, clutching her schoolbooks tighter. She continued to the doorway to the parlor and saw her mother sitting in her rocking chair, mending a shirt. It was the most normal, everyday sight and it caused Jenny's shame to intensify tenfold. She turned and hurried on toward the sanctuary of her room.

"Everything all right?" her mother asked, looking up from her sewing.

"I'm not feeling very well," Jenny replied without turning back to face her mother's discerning gaze. One good look and her mother would know.

"You're probably just hungry. Dinner's about ready."

Jenny grabbed a breath and held it as fresh tears broke loose, but her room was just ahead. She made it there, stepped inside and shut the door. Backing up against the wall, she pressed her hands to her mouth to hold in the sobs that would give her away. If Mama saw her now, if she pressed for what was wrong—

"I'm starving," her brother announced, having just walked in. Which meant she'd only just missed him. She shivered at the thought of Jeremy finding out what had happened. There was no telling what he'd do to Ted Landreth.

"When's supper?" he asked.

"It's about ready. Wash up and set the table."

"Why can't Jen?" he complained.

The remorse she felt was crushing. Jenny slid down the wall, hugged her knees, and buried her face in her hands.

Jenny reluctantly went into the kitchen for supper. Her mother's back was turned and she stirred the contents of a pan on the stove. Jeremy was just sitting at his place, but she avoided his curious gaze as she sat. Roast beef and potatoes and green beans were set out.

"What's wrong with you?" he asked.

She tucked her hair behind her ear and scowled. "Nothing," she replied irritably. "I'm just not feeling well."

"Why you been crying?" he asked under his breath.

Fortunately, their pa walked in the back door, providing a moment of blessed distraction. "Mind your own business," she hissed.

He huffed. "Bet I know why."

Jenny clenched her fists tightly beneath the table and refused to look at him. Ma set down the bowl of gravy and wiped her hands on her apron before sitting. "Since you're starving to death," she said teasingly to Jeremy, "you can say the blessing."

"I'm starving, too," Rodney Sheffield said as he sat. "So bless this food we're about to receive. Amen."

"Amen," Jeremy said, reaching for the platter of roast beef.

Without question, it was the hardest meal Jenny had ever had to get through. She could barely choke down a bite, and Jeremy kept looking at her suspiciously, and her mother wanted to discuss the upcoming picnic at church. As if she could go to it. Or go anywhere. She felt cold and then hot at the thought of the humiliation to come. "I don't feel well," she said, pushing back from the table. "May I be excused?"

Her mother frowned. "You do look flushed. Go on and lie down. I'll check on you in a bit."

Jenny lay on her bed and drew the quilt over her, feeling how bruised she was. How soiled. She pretended to sleep when her mother checked on her later. She loved the roughened but tender hand that felt her forehead for fever. She loved her mother and all her family, and they loved her. And she'd ruined herself. She'd ruined everything.

Later the door opened again. "Jen?" Jeremy whispered. She didn't answer and he shut the door again.

She wasn't able to sleep at all, and she felt heavy as she rose before first light, still dressed in the crumpled clothing she'd worn yesterday. She felt so dirty and used. So damaged. She was stiff as she wrapped a shawl around herself and went outside to use the outhouse. Afterwards, she thought about returning to bed and maybe sleeping, but she began walking instead.

She ended up at the pond. Usually she avoided it, ever since the day she'd nearly drowned as a girl. Jeremy had saved her that day, and later he'd tried to teach her to swim, but her fear was too great. He'd tried to save her from Ted, too, but she hadn't listened. "He's got no integrity," her brother had stated. "It's 'cause he's never had to work a day in his life. What kind of man doesn't work a day in his life? Not one you want. You need to listen to me on this."

But she hadn't listened. She'd been unwilling to hear anything bad about Ted. Maybe it was true he hadn't had to work, she'd retorted, but neither would she, once she married him.

"Marry him?" Jeremy scoffed. "Don't even tell me you haven't noticed he's got a new girl mooning over him every few months. He promises 'em all the good life. Don't be stupid."

If only she'd listened, but she'd traded in her common sense and her integrity in the hope of marrying Ted. She had seen the way he treated other girls, and just like them, she'd thought she'd be different. Like poor Margery, whom everyone now called *easy*, and sometimes worse. And Deborah, who'd quit school after rumors started flying. And Anne, most recently. All because of Ted Landreth. All because this wasn't a town that forgot scandal and shame.

Jenny shivered at the sight of the murky, gray water as the eastern sky lightened. There was no twinkling to the water today, no beauty, but it was darkly beckoning. She looked at the place in the pond where there was no shelf, just a drop-off. The place she'd nearly drowned as a child was the very place she could drown now. Drowning probably didn't hurt, at least not more than she was already hurting, and this way they would all be spared the shame of a scandal.

She'd been known to sleepwalk when she was feverish, and her family knew she'd been sickly yesterday. Maybe they would believe that's what had happened. They'd never know she was ruined. They'd never have to know.

Once word of her death got out, Ted and Stan wouldn't utter a word about her. They wouldn't dare. She hoped they'd be good and sorry. She hoped the thought of her death would haunt them every day for the rest of their lives. If it did, maybe they wouldn't hurt anyone else.

The rooster crowed and cold tears itched as they slid down her face. She mouthed the Lord's Prayer as she took unsteady steps forward toward the right spot, toward absolution. She was sorry. She was so sorry for her sins. She stepped into the cold water and kept walking, although her body shook violently. When she felt the drop-off with her foot, she knew it was either the beginning or the end. Either the beginning of the scandal or the end of her life. She closed her eyes, extended her arms, and fell forward. As the cold water claimed her, she thought, *I'm sorry. I'm so sorry.*

Chapter One

August 18, 1883

Lester Shoemaker couldn't help his curiosity about the woman who sat opposite him in the train car between her children. Even as exhausted as she obviously was, she was lovely. Her hair was the color of sun-bleached wheat, her bone structure was delicate, and she had remarkable gray-blue eyes. She also had excellent breasts, especially for someone as slender as she was, although he'd tried to keep his gaze trained elsewhere, as a gentleman should.

As a salesman, Lester had ridden a long way on the Norfolk and Western Railway, Lexington to Richmond and back again, and he'd noticed the lady after making a trip to the smoking car to stretch his legs. The second-class accommodations where she and her children sat were crowded and uncomfortable, and so he'd discreetly invited her to join him in his compartment. With his balding head and gentle smile, he was certainly harmless looking enough. In fact, he *was* harmless—except when it came to closing a sale. The lady had hesitated, but the heat was taking a toll, and so she'd accepted.

In his compartment he'd tried to draw her into conversation, something he had a special talent for, but failed. Her children were cute things too, especially the small boy, who looked very like her, although the poor thing, who couldn't have been more than four, had a puffy black eye. As the train closed in on his destination, he tried one last time to engage her in conversation. "You folks stopping in Lexington or going on?"

"Going on," the woman replied with a polite smile.

"Ah. I hope you don't have much farther to go."

"I . . . I don't think so. Green Valley?"

"Oh, that's not far at all. Pretty town. Growing fast. I remember when it was a village of just a few hundred people. It wasn't that many years ago." She gave a tolerant smile and nod, but she wasn't a bit interested; he could tell. "Are you, uh, from Green Valley, or visiting?"

The little girl glanced at him as if suspicious of his motives, which caused him to feel a tinge of uneasiness.

"Visiting," the woman replied. "An aunt."

"Ah."

"She's not well, so—"

He murmured sympathetically. He was about to comment when the conductor called out the next stop. "That's me," he said. The train braked to a stop and he stood.

"It was kind of you to let us sit here," the woman said, moving as if to leave.

"Stay. Please. Might as well be comfortable, eh?"

She looked doubtful. "Are you certain it's all right?"

He nodded. "I'll mention it to the conductor on my way out. I travel a great deal, so they grant me some latitude."

"Thank you," she said with a sincerity that touched him. "Good day to you, sir."

"And to you all."

As Lester stepped from the train, the faces of the three individuals in his compartment stayed with him. The lovely woman who seemed haunted, the little girl who didn't seem to trust him a bit, and the small boy with the painful-looking black eye. The child had sat next to his mother, his head resting against her side the entire time. Children usually fidgeted and fussed, especially in this heat, but not those two. They had clung to their mama as if they had suffered a great loss. But that was probably it. The woman had lost her husband, the children their father. Or perhaps a beloved grandparent or even sibling. They were in mourning. He cleared his throat and hoped he hadn't pressed her too hard for conversation.

"How much farther will it be, Mama?" Rebecca asked as the train started in motion again.

Pauline Ray shook her head, not knowing the answer herself. She'd bought as much passage as she dared, and she knew they would end up in a place called Green Valley, Virginia, but that was all she knew. "Not too much farther, I think."

Rebecca looked out the window. "There's lots of hills around here. Indiana was so flat."

"It would be best if we don't mention Indiana anymore," Pauline rejoined gently.

Rebecca nodded solemnly. "It's better in here," she said, looking around the car.

"It is," Pauline agreed. "It was nice of the man." Pauline sighed tiredly, leaned her head back against the upholstered seat, and listened to the clacking of the wheels on the track. It was far better in this compartment than in the hard seats of second class. The window was cracked open, allowing a precious flow of air, warm as it was. The heat was oppressive in second class, and the smell had been even worse.

"I'm hungry," Rebecca said sheepishly.

Pauline looked at her. "There's an apple."

"I'm tired of apples," Rebecca complained.

"It's what we have left."

"Can we have something good for dinner?"

Pauline looked out the window and felt a tingling in her face as she struggled not to cry.

"An apple's fine, Mama," Rebecca said quickly. "I'm sorry."

The apology was too much and Pauline closed her eyes and felt scalding tears escape and slide down her face.

"I'm sorry, Mama."

Pauline wiped her face and shook her head. "It's not you," she whispered, looking at her daughter. "I promise. I'm just tired and I want something good for our dinner, too." Rebecca nodded but still looked remorseful. Pauline closed her stinging eyes for a moment. Freedom, safety, a new town and a new life—this had been her sole quest for so long, but exactly what she was to do when they reached their final destination was still a mystery, and she'd dragged her children into a strange new place where they knew no one.

"Here you go, Jake," Rebecca said, offering him an apple.

Jake shook his head, refusing it, and Rebecca looked at her mother as if asking what she should do. "Do you want one?" Rebecca asked, offering it to her.

Pauline took it in hand. "You want to share it?" she asked Jake.

He shook his head.

She took a bite. "It's good," she coaxed.

He shook his head again and she sighed silently and looked back out the window, wondering what Green Valley would be like. She hoped it was a good place with friendly enough people and an opportunity to make her way, because she had only thirty-three dollars and eighty-two cents left to her name. Whatever choices she'd had in her life, they were over and done with. There were none left at this point. She would have to find a cheap boarding house and a place of employment quickly. She could cook and sew well and bake better than most. There would be a place for her somewhere. She had to believe it. She had to have faith.

Chapter Two

Like most late Saturday afternoons, Jeremy Sheffield sat in The Corner Saloon, involved in a game of poker. Like many of the other men, he'd come after the half day of work. Monday through Friday were full days spent laboring in the dark, cold bowels of the earth, but Saturday was a half day. He'd washed up, but there were still smudges of coal on his neck and hands. It was imbedded under his fingernails.

Carly Jo left her room on the second floor, ready to begin her own work, and sauntered to the balcony to survey the room below. There were new faces, some with the look of prosperity about them, probably due to Gregory Howerton, who had some horse-trading shindig going on. The man had the Midas touch. His horse breeding business was as successful as his mines and his ranch. He had prize cattle, prize stallions, prize looks, and a prize wife who was a doctor, as strange as that was. Some people were just born to win.

Below, Donnie was playing the piano in his customary attire—a striped shirt, red vest, and a bowler hat. Bart Gunderson had his hand up Dora's skirt. For some reason, Bart liked to feel a girl up before going back to a room.

New men in town were always flabbergasted by the spectacle, but it got them hot and bothered, which ultimately netted more business.

Carly's gaze fell on Jeremy Sheffield playing cards with a couple regulars and some dandy she didn't recognize. Jeremy, everyone called him Shef, was expressionless, not conversing, not the least little bit interested in being sociable. That was typical, too. He was a fine-looking man, except he had the pallor of a coal miner. Six feet two, maybe six three, brown hair and fine features. But he was as lifeless as any man she'd ever known, like someone or something had sucked the life right out of him. He hadn't been that way when he was younger.

Carly remembered his sister, Jenny Lynn. Now, *she'd* been a beauty, the kind you want to hate because fate had given her the world's most perfect face and long, shiny dark hair. Unfortunately, Jenny had also been sweet as sugar, so you couldn't hate her. Life was not fair. Then again, Jenny had drowned when she was only sixteen. That should have evened things up, but in a way it didn't, because Jenny Lynn Sheffield had never gotten old or cranky or fat or wrinkled. She stayed beautiful in the minds of all those who remembered her.

It was obvious which men in the room were ranchers and which were miners. The miners were pale, but it was more than that. They moved slower and more deliberately. Ranchers were more expressive and more full of life. Miners were quiet and almost wary. Too much time spent in the dark, she guessed. Maybe that was what had so destroyed Shef's vigor. That and the deaths of his family, one by one.

As if he could sense her gaze, Shef looked up at her. She gave him a seductive smile, but he looked away without a flicker of recognition or feeling. Yes indeed. It was as if someone had sucked the life right out of him.

* * *

The dandy, a man named Chaz Morrison, dealt. "Seven card stud," he announced glibly. He'd won four of the last five hands and was feeling fine. Jeremy watched the man's hands closely. Morrison, with his stiffly starched shirt, fancy cravat, and smooth talking, had the feel of a cardsharp and, if he was, Jeremy was determined to discover it. *Look hard enough and you'll see it. Not only that, but you'll see how to beat it.*

The next hour saw a marked change in Morrison's demeanor as he lost hand after hand. He wasn't accustomed to losing, so he didn't know when to quit. "Seems I'm a little short," he finally admitted to Jeremy, who was now owed nearly fifty dollars.

Ollie White, sitting next to Morrison, looked up sharply. "Mister," he said. "Around here, a little short means a beating. And not a little one, either."

"I have the money back in my room," Morrison said nervously. "I'll just go get it and—"

"In the meantime," Jeremy said, "you can leave that fancy gold pocket watch as collateral."

"And that silver snuff box, too," Ollie suggested.

Morrison looked aghast. "I'm only staying at that boarding house on Second Street. I'll go and be back in—"

"Either leave it," Jeremy said, "or we'll go with you to get your money."

The man huffed at the implied insult. "Fine," he said, pushing back in his chair. Jeremy did likewise.

Chapter Three

The suitcase Pauline carried was awkward, the handles uncomfortable in her hand. It was because she'd crammed so many of their possessions into it. Everything that would fit. She held it in one hand and held Jake's hand in the other as they walked from the train station. Rebecca stayed close. The good news was, they'd arrived. Thirty-three dollars and change was all she had to her name, but they'd reached their final destination. Of course, the only reason it was their final destination was that she hadn't the funds to go farther.

She'd made up her mind to have faith and be optimistic, but as the sun began dipping in the western sky, a feeling of dull panic took hold. Pressure filled her chest and a sharp ache tormented her temples.

"Where are we going?" Rebecca asked worriedly.

"We'll find a place to stay," Pauline replied as calmly as she could. She noticed an elderly gentleman walking toward them. "Excuse me, sir," she said. "Do you know of a boarding house nearby?"

"Yes, ma'am. Mrs. Sherrill's place isn't even three blocks that way. It's a white clapboard place with green shutters. It's a good place run by her and her daughter."

"Thank you."

He tipped his hat and they walked on. The boarding house wasn't hard to find. It was just as described, the front porch filled with rocking chairs, most of which were occupied by people busily fanning themselves in the relentless summer heat. Pauline let go of Jake's hand to lift her skirt to walk up the steps; her son frowned accusingly, but she only had two hands. Two hands and thirty-three dollars.

They stepped inside as an auburn-haired woman walked into the foyer with a red-haired boy of perhaps two on her hip. "Hello there," the woman said pleasantly.

"Good evening," Pauline replied, setting down the suitcase and flexing her hand. "Do you have a room?"

The woman looked apologetic. "I'm sorry, but we shore don't." She cocked her hip and adjusted the boy to be more comfortable. "Normally we do, but Mr. Howerton's got some horse show going on and it's brought all sorts of folks to town."

Pauline felt like crying, but she wouldn't. It was only fatigue talking and she had to remain strong.

"I hear the hotel's full, too," the woman continued. "I'm Fiona, by the way. Fiona Jones. My mama's the proprietor, although you wouldn't know it to see her back in the kitchen right now. Are y'all just passing through?"

"No, I hope. I . . . hope to find work," Pauline stammered. *Will not cry. Will not cry.*

"Oh? Well, I guess there's more and more work all the time." She glanced at the children and flashed a warm smile. "What you might want to do for tonight is go find the Blue place. Sisters, name of Blue, that is," she added because of the expression on Pauline's face. "They put up folks sometimes, although hardly nobody knows it. They'll find room for you, and they're sweet as can be."

Pauline felt such relief, she deflated.

"All you do is go back aways," she said, gesturing with her thumb. "Three, four streets to Crooked Tree Road." Fiona broke off with a thoughtful expression. "Come to think of it, I don't know that there's a sign there anymore, but there's a big ol' crooked tree. You can't miss it. Then, after about a half mile, you'll see a long fence in both directions. Turn right and you'll see their place in no time."

Pauline nodded and picked up the suitcase again. "Thank you."

"I wish I could offer y'all some supper, but our guests have cleaned us out. Not sure we're going to be able to feed everyone we got."

Pauline tried to swallow the lump in her throat. "That's all right," she said thickly. "Thank you."

"There is Wiley's in town. That's a restaurant, but you'll be going the other way if you head to the Blues'."

Pauline flashed a weak smile and turned for the door. Tears were much too close at hand and she needed to keep moving.

"Bye, now," Fiona called.

"Bye," Rebecca said with a wave.

Fiona waved back and shifted RJ to the other hip as the trio left. She felt bad that she couldn't accommodate them. She hadn't seen a woman looking so lost and desperate since Emeline Wright, now Emeline Wright Medlin had returned to town a few years back. A clamor of pots came from the kitchen and Fiona rolled her eyes. "Let's go help Granny," she said dolefully to her son. "Before she has another hissy fit."

* * *

Jeremy followed Morrison to the front steps of the boarding house, but hesitated when a pretty lady stepped out the door with two children in her wake. He nearly reached out and offered his hand to assist her down the two steps, but she'd deftly lifted her skirt and still managed to take hold of the boy's hand. As she passed by, he noticed her anxiety. Then he registered the look of fear on the boy's face and the expression of worry and distrust on the girl's. "Ma'am," he said, tipping his hat to her.

She glanced at him with a slight nod of acknowledgment.

Once they'd passed, he realized Morrison had gone inside. He followed, but Morrison was already gone from the lobby. Jeremy hurried to the hall in time to see the man ducking into a room at the far end. Morrison shut the door behind him and Jeremy heard it lock. He quickly followed and knocked.

"Just a minute," Morrison called from inside, but then came the telltale sound of a window screeching open, meaning the son of a bitch was sneaking out the window. Jeremy considered busting the door open, but he wasn't sure the snake could pay for the damage, and he wasn't about to, so he rushed back outside, rounded the house and went in pursuit. Morrison was running away with his hat shoved down on his head and a soft-sided bag clutched in his hand. Morrison glanced behind, saw Jeremy gaining on him, then promptly tripped and went flying. Within a few seconds, Jeremy stood over him. The man had flipped onto his back with his hands in a pathetic, defensive position. "You got the money you owe me?" Jeremy demanded.

"I . . . I'm good for it, I swear," the man exclaimed.

"You're a funny one, mister," Jeremy warned.

"It's true! I have plenty of money at a bank in Roanoke. I swear it. You could go with me to get it."

"Hand over the watch and the box."

The man shook his head vigorously. "I can't. No. They have great sentimental value."

"Not to me."

"Be reasonable!"

"Reasonable? You're a damn cheat and a liar."

"I'm not lying about the money. It's in a safe deposit box at the City Bank on Third. I *swear* it. On my life."

"Then go get it and I'll trade your trinkets back for the money."

"They're not trinkets," the man objected. "I'll leave something else. I'll leave the watch, but not the snuff box."

"You'll leave them both or we'll walk over to the sheriff's office and you can explain it to him."

Grudgingly, Morrison removed the watch from his vest. "I only owe you forty-six dollars," he complained as he handed it over.

"Yeah. Only that. Doesn't seem worth a man's integrity, does it? Although some men's is worth less than others." He held out his hand. "The box."

"Just give me a moment," the man said, hovering over the small silver box. "It may seem silly," he said as he fumbled in an attempt to open the lid.

Out of patience, Jeremy reached down and snatched it from him.

"No, wait," the man cried, trying to grab it back.

"Bring me back the money you owe me and you can have it back. I'll give you three days before I pawn it."

"Fine. I will be back within three days. Just don't pawn it. Please!"

Jeremy gave him a look of disgust and started off. After several paces, he glanced behind to make sure the man wasn't drawing on him. He wasn't. In fact, he hadn't even gotten up off the ground. Jeremy was halfway back to the saloon when Morrison's last action struck him as odd.

He shook the box and there was a dull clanking sound. He stopped and opened the snuff box and dumped the snuff out. Besides snuff, two keys fell on the ground. He squatted and retrieved them, knowing that they were what Morrison had wanted. Each flat key was two inches long and had a number on it. He studied them a moment, then rose, shoved all the items into his pocket, and walked on.

Chapter Four

As Pauline and the children trudged down what they hoped was Crooked Tree Road, Pauline felt her defenses falter. It was a narrow road, wooded on one side, an empty field on the other. They might well be headed down the wrong road, and even if it was the right road, there might not be a place for them at the end of it. They were hungry; her children were hungry, and it wrenched her heart.

"Don't worry," Rebecca said soothingly, reaching up to pat her back.

The gesture was too much, and Pauline stopped short and burst into tears.

"Oh, Mama, everything will be all right," Rebecca said, stepping in front of her.

"And even if it ain't, it cain't be all that bad," a woman said. They all turned and looked at an older woman wearing men's trousers and a wide-brimmed hat walking from the woods. She carried a string with dead rabbits on it, and a large, golden-haired dog was by her side. The woman put the string over her shoulder and the carcasses hung one in front of her and two in back. "You lost?"

Rebecca looked from the woman to her dog to her mother,

who was working hard to collect herself. "I think we might be," she volunteered.

The woman gave her a cockeyed smile. "What's your name?"

"Rebecca."

"And yours?" the woman asked, looking at Jake.

"He's Jake," Rebecca supplied.

The woman pursed her lips. "And the pretty lady sobbing her heart out smack dab in the middle of our property?"

"That's my mother," Rebecca replied defensively.

"P-Pauline. And I'm s-sorry we're t-trespassing."

"I said you were on my property. I didn't say you were trespassing. Where is it you're headed?"

Pauline took a shuddering breath and set her suitcase down in order to wipe her face and hopefully recover some sort of composure.

"Goodness' sakes, Pauline," the woman said. "Whatever it is, it's likely not as awful as you're making it to be. You wanted by the law?"

Pauline shook her head. She touched her throat, unable to speak.

"You got an angry mob after you?"

Rebecca realized the woman was trying to help and that, little by little, it was working.

Pauline fumbled in her pocket for a handkerchief and wiped her nose. "We were looking for the Blues' place. H-hoping for a r-room. Fiona from the b-boarding house sent us . . . since they were f-full."

"Well, then, what luck. I'm April May Blue," the woman announced.

"Your name is April May?" Rebecca blurted.

"Shore is. And my mama thought it was the loveliest name ever given to a girl child, although she did come up with some fanciful ones."

"Like what?" Rebecca asked.

Pauline was torn between telling Rebecca not to be impertinent and being struck by the ease of conversation between them. She also needed the moments to compose herself.

"Lita Flame for one," April May said. "Mama said it come to her when she was watching my papa start a fire while she was expecting."

"Light a flame?"

"Spelled L-I-T-A. Then I had a brother named Hunter and one named Sterling. I guess those aren't too funny. Scarlet Poppy was a pretty good one, and then the baby got named Princess, though we call her Cessie. Don't know why my papa didn't up and tell Mama to name us something normal."

"Maybe he liked the names, too," Rebecca suggested.

"It's a good point, Rebecca."

"Does your dog bite?"

"Who, Sheeba, here? Naw. She's gentle as a kitten. Now, we got another dog, Wags, little mop of a thing no bigger than a minute, and she bosses poor Sheeba around something awful, but she don't bite either. I keep telling Sheeba to stand up to her, but—" The older woman shrugged and then looked at Pauline. "Why don't we head on up to the house? It's just round the bend."

Pauline nodded gratefully and bent for her suitcase.

"Here," April May said, stepping forward to take it. "Let me have it."

"Oh no," Pauline objected.

"Oh yes," April May insisted, taking it from her. "You're not one of those stubborn kinds that won't let anybody help them, are you?" Pauline nearly lost her frail grip on her self-control, and April May saw it. "I shore hope not," she said, walking on.

Rebecca did a double step to catch up with her, looking at her curiously, and the dog trooped along, paying no mind to them.

"So what brings you folks to our neck of the woods?" April May asked.

Rebecca looked at her mother, who seemed at a loss. She wished she could help, but she didn't know how to answer.

"I hope we can . . . stay," Pauline replied shakily. "I need work."

"That so?" April May looked over at Jake, who was stoically trudging along. "What about you, Jake? You need work?"

Jake frowned shyly. He didn't look at her and he didn't reply.

"He's quiet," Rebecca offered.

"I, for one, never had that proclivity," April May stated.

"Me neither," Rebecca said agreeably. They rounded a bend and saw the long fence the lady at the inn had mentioned. Across the field, deer froze in place, as if to check out the intruders. "Look, Jake," Rebecca said, pointing.

"Surely you seen deer before," April May remarked.

"Yes, but not usually so close."

"Where y'all from?"

"In—" Rebecca broke off, remembering what she was and wasn't supposed to say.

"Indiana," Pauline managed.

Rebecca looked at her and mouthed *sorry*.

If April May noticed the strain or the exchange, she didn't let on. "Here we are," she announced as they approached a sprawling two-story farm house. It was white with navy blue trim. The front door and the many flower pots on the front porch were also blue. There were chickens in the front yard, which caused Jake to look over and grin at his sister.

April May put two fingers in her mouth and made a loud whistle. "Oh, Cessie," April May called. "Brought you something."

Moments later, the screen door screeched open and another woman came out of the house, drying her hands on her pink-and-white checked apron, a small gray-and-brown terrier at her side. "You went and caught a whole family in your traps?" Cessie called playfully.

"That's right," April May called back. "That Cessie," she said to Rebecca. "She's a sharp one. Not much gets by her."

Rebecca laughed. Even Pauline smiled.

"This is Pauline, Rebecca, and Ralph," April May said when they got closer. By then the little dog had started barking.

"Jake," Rebecca corrected quickly.

April May pursed her lips thoughtfully. "I don't think I'm going to call him Jake unless he tells me to."

Rebecca knew April May was teasing again. She'd never known any grown-up who teased so much.

"Welcome," Cessie said cheerfully. She had gray-and-white hair and a still-pretty face. "You have good timing because supper's nearly ready," she said. "Are you hungry?"

"Yes, ma'am," Rebecca returned enthusiastically while Pauline nearly teared up again with relief. Whatever this place cost, it was worth it.

"Oh hush, Wags," Cessie scolded lightly.

The little dog looked up at her and stopped barking.

"Rebecca," April May said as they approached the front steps. "Why don't you and Ralph go wash up at the pump around back? There's some soap on a string and a towel on a rack. Then y'all can look around a bit before you come in for supper."

"Yes, ma'am." Rebecca led Jake off and Sheeba started to follow, until April May called the dog back. Jake kept looking back at Mama worriedly. "It's all right," Rebecca assured him. "They'll take good care of Mama. I can tell." She put an arm around his shoulders as they rounded the house. The sight of a dozen or more donkeys beyond another fence in back stopped them in their tracks.

"Can we go see them?" Jake asked.

Rebecca nodded and they went closer. As they peered in between the rails of the fence, some of the donkeys plodded toward them and they backed off a step. "We ought to wash up," Rebecca said calmly, even though her heart was suddenly beating faster. She turned and walked toward the pump, glancing back at the curious donkeys.

"Gooseberries," Jake exclaimed, pointing at the nearby bushes loaded with them. Most of them had turned red.

"We can have a few, but wash your hands first," Rebecca said sagely.

"Here, dear," Cessie said, setting a glass of red wine in front of Pauline, who was seated at the dining room table. "You sip on that."

As Cessie sat, Pauline took a drink. Because her stomach was empty, she felt it hit bottom. She took a breath, determined to calm herself. She simply didn't have the liberty of falling apart.

April May plunked herself across from Pauline, pulled the carafe to her, and poured herself a glass. "So, Pauline—"

"Give her a minute," Cessie objected in a singsong voice.

"Who you running from?" April May continued.

Cessie frowned. "Now, that is nothing but plain ol' rude."

"Your husband?" April May asked, ignoring her sister.

Pauline couldn't look at her, at either of them, but she nodded. She'd never planned to tell anyone the truth, but she didn't have the strength to lie to these women. Their warmth was like a blanket in a chilly room. She needed it. She wanted to wrap herself up in it.

"He beat you?" April May asked.

Even as Cessie huffed her disapproval, Pauline felt an unexpected sense of relief.

"He hit Jake?" April May pursued. "Gave him that black eye?"

Pauline ducked her head as fresh tears surfaced.

"April May Blue," Cessie scolded. "You are making matters worse."

"No, I am not. Face up to things and move the hell on, I always say."

"I've never once heard you say that."

"'Cause I never had the need. Now, there's the need. And that's exactly what I'm saying. You tell me I'm wrong."

"What I will say is that you go too far. But that's all I'm saying for the time being." Cessie reached over and patted Pauline's hand. "You take all the time you need, dear." She gave her sister another look of reproach, then rose gracefully and walked back into the kitchen.

"You ask me, you were right to leave him," April May declared. "Not only does a woman have the right to protect herself and her own, she ought to have the good sense to do it." She paused. "He know where you're at?"

"I don't even kn-know where I'm at."

Cessie came back and handed Pauline a fresh hanky. "You poor dear. Some men are just bad that way."

"Where were you headed?" April May persisted.

Pauline shook her head and shrugged. "Here."

"I'm not following," April May said. "You just said you didn't know where you were."

"We t-took the train for as long as we could. I didn't have a plan except to get away. I chose to go south and then east and I just went as far as we could. As f-far as I could afford. I chose this place because I liked the name. Isn't that silly?"

"Matter of fact," April May replied thoughtfully, "I think it was a wise move. And I'll tell you why. It's an awful big country, Pauline. Even if the son of a bitch does want to come after you, if you chose a direction and went someplace you didn't know, how could he guess where you're at?"

Pauline managed a deep breath. The center of her back ached, but mostly she felt stunned that she'd just admitted her darkest truth. She hadn't told anyone in all the years of her marriage, yet she'd just blurted the truth to two women she'd known for a matter of minutes. "He's despicable. But he n-never hurt either of the children before last week."

"Oh, honey," Cessie said as she sat back down. "That must have been terrible for you."

Pauline nodded. It had been a thousand times worse than any beating she'd endured, and it had just been one blow— one undeserved blow to her four-year-old son, who had done nothing to provoke his father. "I gathered all the money I'd hidden away over the years, and we ran. We just ran."

"Of course you did, dear," Cessie commiserated. "It's what any good mother would have done."

"I thought we could s-settle into a boarding house and I could find work."

"What sort of work?" Cessie asked.

Pauline shook her head. "Whatever I can get."

"What are you good at?" April May asked.

Pauline clenched her fists, digging her fingernails into her palms to ward off more tears. "B-baking. Keeping house. I could be a maid or a cook or—"

"Sip your wine, dear," Cessie soothed. "I'm going to get you a cool rag for your face. The children will be in soon and you don't want to worry them."

When Rebecca and Jake came in for supper, the table was set and the ladies were sitting around it. It was a pretty house with lots of dark furniture and pretty knickknacks, but the most enticing things were the offerings of mutton chops, thick slices of buttered bread, and bean salad. Rebecca's stomach growled. "It looks good."

"Glad you think so," Cessie replied with a warm smile. "Have a seat."

Rebecca saw that her mother's eyes were red rimmed and she looked more tired than ever before. She chose the seat next to April May and across from her mother, while Jake sat next to Mama. "Why do you have donkeys?" she asked April May.

"Why not?" April May shot back. "You don't have something against donkeys, do you?"

"No."

"Shall we say grace?" Cessie suggested.

They bowed their heads.

"Grace," April May said.

Cessie clucked her tongue in disapproval.

"Just kiddin'. Good company, good meat, good Lord, let's eat."

Rebecca and Jake giggled while Cessie sighed loudly. "Dear Lord, bless this food for the nourishment of our bodies, and thank you for our new friends. Amen."

"Amen," Pauline echoed. "And thank you," she said, looking first at Cessie and then April May.

Cessie smiled. April May gave her a nod and a wink.

"Rebecca, honey," Cessie said. "You help yourself to what you want. We don't stand on formality here."

"What about you, Chester?" April May asked Jake as Pauline put food on his plate. "You got something against donkeys?"

Jake grinned shyly and shook his head.

"That's good. As long as they don't have a problem with you, we're all fine. I'll talk to them about you after supper, although they may not have been able to form a fair opinion just yet. You didn't go and insult them or anything, did you?"

Rebecca glanced at Jake and saw that he was staring down at his plate, but smiling. He shook his head. "Do they bite?" she asked.

"Depends on what you say to them," April May replied.

"Only if they get real annoyed," Cessie said. "Naturally, that's usually directed at you-know-who here, as you can probably imagine."

"They don't bite too often," April May remarked. "'Cause they've learned I bite back."

Jake giggled.

"Hey," April May said. "Ralph here can laugh. That's good. I don't trust children who don't laugh."

Rebecca saw her mother smile and felt a sharp thrill of hope. She took a bite of tangy bean salad and wished they could just stay here.

"Fact is, we got donkeys and mules," April May said. "Did you know they're a different thing?"

"No, ma'am," Rebecca replied. "I guess I thought they were the same."

"Nope. A lot of people don't know that. Not that it makes a whole lot of difference that I can think of. But I'll tell you about them sometime if you want. More importantly, do you know the donkey song? You know, 'Sweetly sings the donkey, at the break of day,'" she sang.

"After dinner," Cessie said.

April May conceded with a shrug. "Fill your gullet and then I'll teach you. It's fun to sing. At the end, it goes, 'he-haw, he-haw, he-haw-he-haw-he-haw.'"

Cessie rolled her eyes. "Well, you've gone and sung that much, so let's just do it." With a collective breath, the sisters laughingly sang the song to the delight of their company. "All right, *now* we'll eat and we'll sing it as a round later."

"I knew that would get her," April May said. "You start singing and if there is a Blue around, we just can't help ourselves. We'll start right in, too."

"We came from a musical family," Cessie said. "It was such fun."

"Still is, as you'll see after supper," she said to Rebecca.

"I like to sing," Rebecca said.

"I had a feeling you might," April May replied.

Chapter Five

Pauline smoothed the covers over Jake. When he was sleepy, his black eye drooped; a sight that wrenched her heart. But the children had bathed and dressed in their pajamas and were tucked into the soft bed in what had been dubbed their room. "Comfortable?" Jake nodded and she kissed his forehead. "I love you."

"I love you, too," he said.

She leaned close to whisper in his ear. "I love you more."

He giggled and shook his head and she grinned at him before moving around the bed to where Rebecca lay.

"You should come to bed, too," Rebecca said.

"I will. Very soon. I just want to talk to Cessie and April May a little more."

"They're funny," Jake said sleepily.

"They are," Pauline agreed, "and they're very kind."

"And they *sang* at the table," Rebecca marveled.

Pauline sat on the edge of the bed. The truth was, she'd found the singing strange, too. It had been forbidden to sing at the table in the home where she'd grown up, and her husband, Ethan, hadn't cared for singing either. That the

Blue sisters could so readily burst into song was a little disconcerting, but also wonderful in its own way. They seemed so free.

"I liked singing with them, though," Rebecca said.

"So did I."

"Will we have to leave tomorrow?"

"No, not tomorrow."

"I wish we could stay here forever."

Pauline leaned forward and kissed her daughter. "No more worries tonight. All right? Nothing but good thoughts and sweet dreams."

Rebecca took hold of her mother's arm, unwilling to let her go just yet. "I thought the donkeys might bite."

"Don't insult them."

Rebecca was heartened to see her mother tease. "I liked hearing about them."

"I did, too. I never knew that boy donkeys are called Jack and girls called Jenny."

"Me neither. I'm going to help feed them tomorrow."

"I know."

"This is a pretty room."

Pauline nodded. "Mm-hmm."

"Kind of old-fashioned," Rebecca whispered.

Pauline looked around and then grinned. "Kind of," she whispered back.

"But I like it," Rebecca stated.

"Me too."

"Do you think you should sleep in here with us tonight?"

"I'll be right next door, and I'll leave the doors open. Unless you want me to sleep with you."

Rebecca thought about it. "It's fine if you sleep next door."

"All right."

"I still feel like we're riding in the train. Don't you?"

"A little bit." Pauline glanced at Jake, who was asleep already.

"Mama?"

"Yes?"

"You think we'll stay around here?"

"I hope so. I really do hope so."

"Me too."

"Close your eyes and go to sleep now."

"Do you think—"

"Sshh," Pauline said, gently smoothing back Rebecca's hair. "No more worries tonight."

Rebecca closed her eyes. "Don't go yet."

"No, I won't. I'll stay right here until you fall asleep," Pauline said in a hushed voice.

"Will you hum the song?"

Rather than answer, Pauline began humming Rebecca's favorite tune. Pauline didn't know where she'd heard it, nor did she know the name of it. She'd hummed it often because it was Rebecca's favorite and because humming was quiet. Singing had irritated Ethan, so she'd learned not to do it. Not that everything hadn't annoyed Ethan. Her breathing annoyed him. Her *being* annoyed him.

As Rebecca's breathing evened out, a breeze wafted in the window, making the curtains flutter. Rebecca turned on her side, asleep, but barely. Pauline stroked her daughter's hair and began the song over.

Cessie and April May were in the parlor, Cessie knitting, her needles clicking softly one against the other. April May's feet were propped on an upholstered footstool with fringe, her hands folded on her stomach. "George Mason was a wife beater," she remarked. "Remember that?"

"Yes, I do. And you remember what became of Millie Mason."

"Son of a bitch killed her deader than a nit."

Cessie's needles stopped moving as she looked up at her sister. "You know good and well that was never proved," she rejoined, "but I will say this much. He stole her spirit long before he took her life."

April May murmured agreement. Millie had been a normal girl, but George turned her into a whipped dog.

Cessie drew breath to say something, but refrained when Pauline came into the room. "The children asleep?" she asked instead.

Pauline nodded. "Yes. I don't know how to thank you both for your kindness."

"You said that already," April May reminded her.

She had, but she needed to say more. Although they thought nothing of it, it wasn't nothing—it was everything. "You've given me renewed strength to go on."

"Oh, honey," Cessie said, setting her knitting down. "We're never as alone as it sometimes feels."

"You should probably turn in," April May said to Pauline. "You look about half dead."

"April May," Cessie scolded.

"I am tired," Pauline admitted. "And I have a lot to think about. But I was hoping you could tell me about the town. Perhaps offer advice on possible employment."

"Don't need to," April May stated. "'Cause it just so happens the answer to your dilemma has already come to me."

Cessie cocked her head. "Is that so?"

"Yes, it is. And it is nothing short of brilliant. In fact, you should have thought of it, being the smarter one of the two of us. And for other reasons." She looked at Pauline. "Why don't you take a load off and I'll tell you?"

Pauline hurriedly sat.

"Well?" Cessie asked. "Pauline and I are waiting."

April May looked smug. "The upside is this. Pauline here gets herself a nice little piece of property, and she stays a neighbor, so we can keep an eye on her and the children."

Cessie looked stricken, and then she smiled despite the tears that sprang to her eyes. "Oh, of course!"

Pauline realized she was holding her breath, and released it. "I . . . don't have any money," she admitted. "N-not much money, I mean," she amended.

"That's fine because this particular piece of property isn't for sale."

"Oh, Pauline," Cessie gushed. "We'll never live this down."

Pauline was confused by the statement.

"The idea *is* brilliant," Cessie said, dabbing at her eyes. "So much so that Sister here will never let us live it down. Never, not if we live to be a hundred years old."

"How do you feel about changing your name?" April May asked Pauline mischievously.

"Oh yes," Cessie said. "You'll have to do that, although it's a pretty name. Tell her. Tell her the story."

April May nodded magnanimously. "We had a dear friend by the name of Lionel Greenway," she began. "He passed on about five years ago."

"Six," Cessie stated. "It will be six years on the fourteenth of next month."

April May gave Cessie an impatient frown. "You going to correct every sentence I make?"

"Go ahead."

"'Cause you do that. You say 'tell a story' and then I start in and you start correcting."

Cessie shook her head and gave a wave.

April May looked at Pauline. "Lionel was one of the most interesting people I ever met in my life. He was smart as a whip, always inventing things, although he liked his relaxation, too. Thing was, he was a man who kept to himself. He must have come off as more standoffish than he really was because folks called him a hermit, though he wasn't one. The thing was, he moved here late in life and most folks don't do that. You're born here, you die here."

"People do move in now," Cessie interjected, "but at the time, it was a more unusual thing. And those who did come were not warmly accepted."

"They were outsiders," April May said. "And they were treated as such. Lionel didn't care all that much, at least, not at first."

"He was a wonderful man," Cessie said warmly. "A handsome man, really. He had white hair and a neatly trimmed beard."

"Which he frequently stroked like he was some sort of wise man," April May added. "An observation I shared with him on many occasions. He'd just give me this look."

"As if to say you'd hit the nail on the head." Cessie laughed. "Oh, but he was so smart and clever and amusing. Read a lot—"

"That's mostly what he did. That and tinker with gadgets and grow grapes."

"He made wine," Cessie explained. "Wonderful wine. The wine that we had this evening, that was his."

"The *point* is," April May interrupted, looking at Pauline, "the only personal thing Lionel ever talked about was his daughter, Elizabeth."

"Elizabeth Anne Greenway," Cessie said dreamily. "It sounds like poetry. Doesn't it?"

Pauline still had no idea what they were getting at. Perhaps it should have been apparent and fatigue was making her brain soft.

April May leaned forward. "Here's the thing, and I'll just

cut right to the point. He made her up after he overheard some folks in town talking about him."

Pauline blinked. "He made her up?"

"Invented her," Cessie said. "Because of how folks were talking about him. They called him a hermit, said he'd never known love. Which was certainly not true."

"So," April May said, "he started talking about Lizzie. That's what he called her. He said his wife's name had been Cecelia and that she'd died giving birth to their child." She paused. "He couldn't win for losing because then folks started saying he was probably making her up, being the strange old bird that he was, which made him even more an object of ridicule."

Pauline felt saddened by the thought of a man fabricating a daughter to make him more acceptable to people who would never accept him.

Cessie suddenly looked close to laughter. "Until one day at the church picnic, the subject comes up and April May ups and claims we met her."

April May snorted. "People running their mouths again. I just thought I'd shut 'em up for a little while." She wagged a finger at Cessie. "But don't you dare say April May, like you didn't jump right in."

Cessie chuckled with delight at the memory. "Oh, we did have fun with it."

"Let me tell you, Pauline," April May said, "Lionel got the biggest kick out of that."

Cessie agreed. "He had us repeat the story over and over again." She looked far away and then she sobered. "The truth is, in the end, Lionel didn't have anyone but us in the world. And we didn't need the place."

"Although he offered," April May said tenderly to her sister.

"Yes, he did," Cessie said. "One day, drinking wine and

having a fine time, he came up with the idea of leaving everything to his daughter. I thought he was teasing at first, but he got more and more set on the idea. If we didn't want the place, he said, it would just sit there and wait for Lizzie to come claim it."

Pauline experienced a shiver.

"Admittedly, it's no great fortune, but—"

"It's probably eight or ten or even twelve acres of land and a right nice cottage," April May said. "Now, the place is a bit strange by ordinary standards, but it's pretty. Or it was. Restful. He designed it and had it built. Of course, it's been a while with no care, but it would be a place to start over for you and the children."

Pauline sat back, stunned at what they were suggesting.

"So, you see, dear?" Cessie said with a twinkle to her eye. "You didn't come here for no reason. The good Lord led you here. Right into our care. It was meant to be."

Pauline's eyes filled and she swallowed hard. Was it possible? Was it really possible?

April May frowned as a thought occurred to her. "Pauline, when you were in town, did you tell anyone your name?"

Pauline thought about it and then shook her head. "No."

"We love Fiona dearly, but she's got a mouth on her. So does her mother. A good heart, but a big mouth."

"No," Pauline said again, more certain as she thought about it. "I asked if there was a room, and she said no. That I should try here."

"Even if she had said a name," Cessie said to April May, "a last name wouldn't matter. Not a bit. Lizzie could have gotten married."

"Well, obviously she got married," April May said. "She has two children, doesn't she?" She looked at Pauline. "You sure you didn't say your first name?"

Pauline nodded frantically. "I'm sure."

"Good," April May said. "So, pick a new last name."

Pauline suddenly recalled neighbors from her childhood who'd seemed so happy, she'd often wished she was one of them. "Carter?"

"Carter," Cessie repeated. "You're now Mrs. Elizabeth Anne Greenway Carter. Does that sound good?"

Pauline laughed. "It sounds like . . . a miracle."

Cessie looked at April May. "You know, we're the only ones who ever did meet Lizzie here. So, Pauline stakes her claim and we back her up. Who in the world can possibly contest it?"

"If Pauline wants to, that is," April May replied.

If she wanted to? "I do! Oh yes. I do."

Cessie pressed a hand to her chest. "Oh, you just know that Lionel is tickled pink right now. Up in Heaven, looking down, tickled pink."

April May nodded in agreement. "And now that we've solved the world's problems, you should go get some rest. You look tired enough to drop in your tracks."

Even though she suddenly felt wide-awake and full of excitement, Pauline stood. "I will."

"And practice your new name," April May added. "If you want a new life, Pauline has to be no more. You'll be Elizabeth Anne Greenway Carter."

"Maybe we should have an informal baptism," Cessie suggested playfully.

"You need to think about this," April May said earnestly. "Really *think*. You do this and there's no turning back."

Didn't they realize how much she wanted this? How much she needed it? "I don't want to turn back. Not ever. This is a godsend. You," she said, looking from one sister to the other, "are a godsend."

"Maybe you're one for us," Cessie said tenderly.

"And Lionel's girl, at that," April May said to her sister with a fond smile.

Cessie welled up again.

"Get some shut-eye," April May urged. "We'll talk more in the morning."

"Good night, then," Pauline managed in a thick voice.

"'Night, Pauline," April May said. "Hey, just think. That may be the last time anyone ever says that to you."

Joy bubbled up inside Pauline, and it was only through great restraint that she didn't laugh out loud.

A half hour later, Pauline closed her eyes, hoping for sleep, but it eluded her as always. She was tired to the bone, but anxiety plagued her. Ethan was no longer present, leering, rearing his hand to strike a blow, but he *was* out there somewhere. He would search for them, and if he ever found them—

She turned onto her side and curled into a ball, wondering how he could find them when they had run blindly, ending up in a town he'd never heard of, in a state he'd have no reason to consider. But what if he searched every possible avenue she could have taken? What if he went to the depot and the stationmaster remembered seeing them?

"Stop it," she whispered. It was bad enough that he'd made her life a living hell. Why was she continuing to torture herself? If he came after them, if he found them, she'd protect herself. She'd protect Jake and Rebecca. If he came for them, she would kill him. She inhaled and exhaled deeply and purposefully. "Safe," she whispered. "You're safe."

Her excitement over the cottage had faded, because she'd never had that sort of luck. Something would happen to stop the plan, but she had April May and Cessie on her side, and that was something. She didn't feel as alone as she had for many years. They would help. They would offer beneficial advice, but the major decisions would be hers, and the first decision was that part of her meager funds would go toward the purchase of a gun. Not only that, but she would practice with it and she would use it if necessary. She would, so help her. Tears spilled over the bridge of her nose and dampened the pillow beneath her head. "Safe," she mouthed. "You're safe."

Chapter Six

Pauline woke the next morning feeling sluggish and confused, almost drugged. She'd tried to wake several times, but kept falling back asleep. This time, Jake was poised on the side of her bed, waiting, his head resting on his hands. "Are you awake?" he whispered.

She smiled and murmured a drowsy affirmative.

He grinned. "Cessie said to let you sleep, but we said you never sleep late."

"But then I did, didn't I?" she asked in a raspy voice.

He nodded, looking like he might laugh aloud. "You sound funny."

"I don't feel very funny," she replied as she struggled to sit up. She felt so strange and weighted and exhausted. She heard a strange, soft tapping and looked at the window. "It's raining?"

Jake nodded. "But it wasn't before. We fed the donkeys."

She touched his face and brushed back his soft hair, feeling guilty. "Are you all right?"

He nodded again and he certainly looked all right. "We had flapjacks and the dogs like us."

It was bolstering, how happy he seemed. "I'll get up now," she said despite the fact she could have gone right back to sleep. At the sound of a piano, she glanced at the door with a puzzled expression.

"Cessie is teaching Rebecca to play," he said. "And they play fiddle and banjo, too."

"Oh my."

"And spoons and the jaw harp," he said doubtfully. "I'll tell them you're up." He started for the door. "We're going swimming later if it stops raining."

"Oh, you are?"

He turned back and nodded. "They have a pond and April May said she can teach us in nothin' flat."

"Is she still calling you Ralph?"

He giggled as he shook his head.

"Good." By the time she rubbed her eyes and swung her legs around, Jake had gone. It was remarkable the way the children had taken to April May and Cessie, especially Jake. Pauline rose, stretched, and she'd just finished washing up when Rebecca pushed the cracked door open a little wider. "Mama?"

"Yes, I'm up."

Rebecca pushed the door open with her foot and came in carrying a highly polished teakwood tray. On it was a delicate pot of tea, a cup with a dash of milk or cream in it, a bowl of sugared mixed berries, and a slice of coffee cake.

"Oh my. Look at that."

Rebecca smiled proudly. "Cessie said this would get you started, but to take all the time you wanted."

Pauline started to take the tray, but Rebecca resisted. "I wanted to give it to you in bed."

Pauline nearly laughed. "I've never had breakfast in bed in my whole life."

"I know. That's why I want to. Please?"

Pauline shrugged and smilingly acquiesced. She propped up pillows against the headboard and got back into bed. She was still in her robe and she hadn't yet made the bed, but it still felt wrong.

"Now, you hold it for a second," Rebecca said.

Pauline took the tray.

"See, the sides come down," Rebecca said as she pulled legs from the sides of the tray. "And you can set it in front of you."

"That's clever," Pauline said as she set it in front of her. "I feel like a lady of leisure."

"I told Cessie how you drank your tea and she made it that way."

"It looks delicious."

"I want to show you something," Rebecca said. "Be right back."

As she dashed out, Pauline felt conflicted by the happiness her children were exuding. This from a good night's sleep and a few hours with Cessie and April May Blue. She was thrilled to see it and yet it made her feel blameworthy. They were children; lightheartedness should have been a given, but that wasn't what their lives had been filled with.

She filled her teacup, mulling over what she'd said about becoming a lady of leisure. It was a ridiculous notion, and yet it was possible she'd been handed a second chance on a teakwood tray. It didn't matter what the Greenway cottage looked like. If they were given a chance to start over there, near these most caring, gracious women, what more could she even wish for? Her own parents had never taken such loving care of her. For one thing, they'd been highly religious and thought to *spoil* a child promoted weakness. Duty was all that truly mattered. That's what her father had believed, and, by extension, her mother. God rest her soul, her late mother had never had a single thought that wasn't put into her head by either her own father or her husband.

As a child, Pauline had secretly believed they weren't

her real parents. Not only were they older than her friends' parents, but they'd also never doted on her as other parents did. And then there was the dream—a recurring snippet of a dream about a couple who were walking ahead of her. On a cloudy day, on a road she didn't know, they turned toward one another and looked back at her, urging her to catch up—although no words were spoken. They were a handsome, smiling couple with dark hair. They were obviously happy and in love, and they loved her, too. She felt it in the dream and always for a time after she woke.

The dream seemed so real, she'd often longed to reach out to take the hands they extended. If only she could connect with those hands. Because of the dream, she'd always suspected something had happened to her real parents, causing her to be adopted. Could the dream actually be memory, one precious memory of her real parents?

She sipped the tea and savored the moment. She was relaxed in bed with a soft rain falling outside. She was safe and her children were happy for the moment. She took a bite of berries and the flavor burst in her mouth. Was it possible they'd really been directed to this place by loving guardian angels? It was such a lovely thought.

By the time Rebecca came back in holding two photographs, Pauline had finished breakfast. The first picture, which Rebecca proudly handed over, was a grainy family portrait taken outside in front of the farmhouse. As Pauline took it in hand, Rebecca leaned close. "That's Mr. Blue," she said, pointing to the obvious patriarch. "His name was Josiah, and that's Mrs. Blue, and her name was Olivia. But they called him Sy and her Livie."

Pauline smiled, because the family was just what she would have expected. The Blue children ranged in age from nine or ten to the early twenties, and they were all attractive and vibrant looking.

"That one is Hunter," Rebecca continued. "He got struck by lightning and died."

Pauline looked at her, blinking in surprise, and Rebecca nodded.

"He was in the field when a summer storm blew up from out of nowhere."

"How terrible!"

"I know," Rebecca replied solemnly.

"You've learned a lot this morning."

"I know. I already learned a song on the piano. Just with one finger."

Pauline smiled. "That's how it starts."

"This one," she said, pointing at the second young man, who was probably sixteen in the picture, "was Sterling. He died in the war."

"Oh," Pauline breathed.

"They're all gone, except for April May and Cessie. This one is April May," Rebecca said, pointing her out.

"I can see that," Pauline said, smiling at the image of an animated young woman of twenty or so.

"She was the second oldest. Then there was Lita, that one. She just died last year. And that one is Scarlet. She died when she was having a baby and the baby died, too. Then that one is Cessie."

Cessie, the youngest, was a beautiful girl with dark hair. She and Sterling were the most comely of the family.

"Then this is her when she was older," Rebecca said, handing over the second picture.

The photograph of Cessie when she was a young woman made Pauline's skin ripple with gooseflesh. In it, Cessie's girlhood beauty had blossomed into its full promise. The hand-painted photograph showcased a young woman with soft pink cheeks and lips and deep blue, almost violet-colored eyes who was astonishingly beautiful, but that wasn't the shocking thing. The shocking thing was that she was the mother figure in Pauline's childhood dreams.

"Wasn't she pretty?" Rebecca said wistfully.

Pauline could do nothing but nod. Her throat was too tight.

Rebecca went around and sat on the bed facing her mother. "Cessie had a sweetheart named John, but he died when he was only eighteen."

"Oh, honey, I hope you didn't intrude on—"

"I didn't, Mama. She wanted to tell me. She said she hadn't talked about him in a long time, although she thinks about him every day. I saw his picture, too. She keeps it in her room on her dresser. And there's another one, too."

"Another what?"

"Picture. Of her and a man named Lionel. He was her second love."

Pauline thought back on comments made the night before. They suddenly took on new meaning.

Rebecca rose and took the pictures back in hand. "We may go swimming later, if it stops raining or even if it doesn't."

Pauline smiled. "I may go with you."

Rebecca beamed. "Really?"

"Absolutely."

"Can you swim?"

Pauline shrugged. "I wouldn't mind getting better. You think I'm too old to learn?"

"No," Rebecca replied enthusiastically before turning pensive. "Why didn't we ever go swimming before?"

Tears pricked the backs of Pauline's eyes. "We will now. That's what matters, isn't it?"

Rebecca nodded and started from the room.

"I wonder if I could see the picture of John," Pauline said.

Rebecca turned back with a smile and then dashed off, but when she returned, the photograph she carried was not familiar. Pauline had never seen or imagined the young man in the photograph. He was a fine-looking young man with sandy-colored hair and a cleft in his chin. She could well imagine how a young Cessie had fallen in love with him—but he was not the father figure in her dreams. Her dream father had wavy dark hair and dark eyes. He'd had squarish shoulders and a certain profile; she'd seen it when he'd turned to her. Now that she'd remembered the dream, it was impossible to shake the image.

Chapter Seven

The Greenway cottage, built of wood and stone, had an elaborately carved front porch, although a tangle of vines had tried to lay claim to it. Weeds in the yard were tall and saplings and undergrowth had grown wild, but there was a charm to the place that the elements could not eradicate. It seemed impossible her luck could have so changed, but Pauline wanted to believe it. "I love it."

"It will take some work," April May commented as she attempted to open the front door. It took some shoulder action because the wood floor had buckled. "But we can do it, and it will be worth it. Believe me."

"I do. I feel it, too." Pauline looked toward the top of a towering oak. Glorious green leaves waved as a breeze blew, a pair of squirrels engaged in a mad game of tag, and birdsong filled the air. The place seemed positively enchanted.

"We should go into town soon," April May said as she stepped inside. "See T. Emmett Rice about the deed. He's a lawyer, but a good man despite it. Fact is, he was one of the few who befriended Lionel."

"Oh?"

"There were a few good men. They played cards and drank too much. Lionel enjoyed those get-togethers."

Pauline followed April May, stepping inside an almost empty parlor that smelled of mildew. Dust hung thick in the air, some partially illuminated from rays of light that filtered through grimy windows.

"Part of the floor's got to be torn up," April May commented. "Moisture's ruined it. I'll tell you what else, there used to be a lot of furniture that's not here anymore. Which aggravates the life out of me."

Pauline was oblivious to the flaws. This was her new start, and a far better one than she'd dared imagine. It didn't matter if every stick of furniture had been stolen; it was a house with a roof and four walls. They'd fill it with furniture in time. April May went one way while Pauline turned down a hall and walked into a small bedroom with a bed and a chest of drawers.

"There's a little stone winery out back with a cellar underneath, and there's a bathhouse, too," April May said from the other room.

"What's a bathhouse?"

"It's made of cedar and tile and it's got a big ol' tub and a separate place where a shower of water comes down on you, because you're supposed to clean yourself *before* you go into the bath, if that don't beat all. Lionel swore that long, hot baths were good for you. It's got a pump hooked up to a wood-burning thingymajobber, and so the bathwater is hot going in. The shower, too. Lionel liked his conveniences. That's what he always said—good wine, good books, good friends, and modern conveniences are what makes life worth living."

Pauline smiled, knowing that she would have liked the

man. She walked farther down the hall and turned in to
what must have been Lionel's room. It had a wide bed and
more furniture than the parlor. There was even a book on
the bedside table. She rubbed her arms as she experienced
a shiver. The bed was beautiful, with a tall, hand-carved
walnut headboard. It was a wonder no one had carted it off.

She walked over and picked up the book, *Desperate
Remedies* by Thomas Hardy. *I know a thing or two about
desperate remedies,* she thought as she set the book back
down.

"Tell you what," April May said loudly. "When a place
has sat empty as long as this one has, there's sure to be a
surprise or two. Nests of rats, hornets, snakes, spiders.
We'll need to be mighty careful."

There were two other rooms down the hall, another
small bedroom and a study with a bookshelf full of musty-
smelling books. They were in disarray, as if they had been
rifled through. April May walked in behind her and clucked
her tongue in disapproval. "Yep, and there was a fancy desk
in here and a nice chair to go with it. Damned thieving
people. Wish I knew who snatched it."

"But it's so much more and better than I could have
dreamed of," Pauline said, turning to the older woman.
"I'm *so* glad Papa left it for me."

April May grinned. "He always knew you'd come back
sometime."

April May walked on as Pauline made her way to a bay
window flanked by heavy, plum-colored drapes. She peered
out on the badly overgrown backyard, covered walkways,
and outbuildings. It had been a lovely place and it would be
again if she had her way. "Promise," she whispered to
Lionel.

She had *thought* the name Elizabeth Anne Greenway
Carter dozens of times since she'd heard it, but, as of this

second, she was going to *be* Elizabeth Anne Greenway Carter. It was the chance, the *gift* of a lifetime. "Lizzie," she mouthed. She would dream up a whole new life story. She would keep the best of her former life, of Pauline's life—Rebecca and Jake—and recreate everything else. This would be a loving home and they would be happy here. Happy and safe. She didn't want or need anything else.

"Hey, hey," April May called from the other room. "I just found a picture of Lionel."

Pauline started from the room with a light step. She felt much freer as Lizzie Greenway Carter.

"I bet Cessie doesn't know this is here," April May said as she handed it over. "It's an old one, but that's him, a young him, with that same ol' devilish smile."

The image was of Lionel as a young man, standing against a rock ledge with a pickax in his hand. Although it was faded, its edges frayed and slightly torn, Lizzie recognized the face. *This* was the father from her dreams. Her breath caught as she stared at it.

"He was originally from South Carolina," April May said as she looked at the photograph over Lizzie's shoulder. "Then, as a young man, he went to California after gold. Found a little, lost a lot of time is what he said."

"I want to know all about him."

"He traveled a lot of places in the world, a lot more than most. Did a stint as a merchant marine, was in the war, went to the Orient, saw Paris. Cessie loved his stories. The two of them were special friends, so she got a lot more of them than I did. She'd be happy to share them if you want to hear."

"Oh, I do!"

April May took a few steps away before turning back. "He was a good man and I'm glad I knew him. You know, maybe, in the end, that's all any of us can hope to have said about us."

Pauline nodded slowly.

"Tell you what else, this place is not in as bad a shape as I feared. It's going to take a lot of work but—"

"It's going to be wonderful," Lizzie declared. "It's going to be a new life for us. I thought it wouldn't be real. That it couldn't be, but . . . I feel it, now that I'm here. That it's meant to be somehow." Her moisture-filled eyes glistened.

April May cocked her head and looked at Lizzie curiously.

"What?" Lizzie laughingly asked.

"I don't know. Maybe it's just the light in here—"

"What is it?"

"You look different. No fooling. You look a little bit different."

"Really? I'm not. I'm the same ol' Lizzie I always was."

April May guffawed and slapped her thigh. "That's the spirit!"

The two of them made their way back home along a path through the woods and it occurred to Lizzie how much more alive everything seemed here. The greens were so varied and intense in color, the chirping of birds louder. The air was hot and humid, but even that felt good. When the sun hit the tree trunks and limbs just right, the bark glowed golden and the green of the leaves was almost blinding. "Cessie mentioned John yesterday," Lizzie said. "To Rebecca. I hope my daughter wasn't prying."

"Cessie isn't going to talk about anything she doesn't want to."

"She also said Lionel was her second love."

"And so he was. I was so grateful to that man." It was a

strange enough statement that Lizzie didn't know how to respond. April May glanced at her and must have seen the question in her expression because she stopped and turned to face her. "I don't know what all was said, so I'll just tell you if you want to know."

Lizzie nodded, wanting very much to know.

"John Yardley was Cessie's sweetheart from the time they weren't but knee-high to grasshoppers," April May said. "There was no doubt in anyone's mind that they'd marry and have a long, happy life together. Probably have five or six little ones. Except for he took ill and died. We never did know what killed him."

Pauline sighed. "I'm sorry."

April May exhaled deeply. "We all were. It like to have killed our Princess. She didn't want to eat. She stopped going to school. She just wanted to sleep, and we couldn't keep her up. She stopped talking. You see her. You see her spark. She always had that, except for the year after John passed." April May paused and looked far away as she remembered. "We used to get her up, two of us, and walk her between us. She wouldn't have gone, except she was too weak to stop us. We talked at her, talked at her, showered her with love, but nothing could break through that damned melancholy. It just about killed her."

Lizzie felt tears prick the backs of her eyes.

"One day, it was summer, and the girls and I got her up and took her to the pond. 'We're going for a swim,' I said. Lita was nervous about it. So was Scarlet. Hell, so was I. Cessie's state of mind? She might have just let herself drown. But the truth is, we were losing her anyway. The most beautiful girl in the world, I mean inside and out, was wasting away before our eyes. It was killin' my mama. So I said, 'We're going for a swim,' and in we went. Her and I. Didn't even bother with taking our clothes off. I remember

Lita panicking. 'Wait,' she called. But I didn't wait. I waded in and dragged Cessie with me."

Lizzie frowned and crossed her arms, utterly caught up in the story.

"I'd taken them by surprise, so there's Scarlet and Lita watching, not knowing what the blazes to do. But it had to be done. I still remember; I turned over and floated and took Cessie with me. So we're floating and lookin' at the sky and I told her I loved her . . . more than life itself, but she had to make a choice. Live or die. Live . . . or . . . die. We wanted her to live, but the only decidin' person was her. The grieving had to end. John wouldn't have wanted it. He didn't want it." She paused and swallowed. "And then I let her go and I swam on and I swam hard. If she'd drowned herself, I think I would have had to do the same. Luckily, when I came up for air, I looked back and saw that she was making for the shore."

Tears filled April May's eyes and she laughed and blinked them free, then wiped her face. "The girls went in after her, knowing she was too weak to swim for long. When I made it back, there were the four of us, soaking wet, crying our eyes out, hugging one another. But the grief broke that day. Like a fever breaks. Cessie started getting better, although she never considered another man. And it wasn't like men didn't try. She was a real, true beauty and sweet as the day is long."

It grew silent and April May looked around. "She's one who should have married and had a whole passel of little ones."

"And then Lionel moved here," Lizzie said quietly.

"Yes, he did. Thank God. They struck up a special friendship, but she wouldn't marry him. Said they were both too set in their ways. But they'd be together for days at a time. We're not far from town, but we're out here on our own, which was a good thing. They had eight years together. Eight good years. More together than apart."

Lizzie smiled at the thought, and the two of them started to walk again.

"Years ago," April May said quietly, "maybe . . . ten or twelve years ago, a young woman drowned. Like Cessie, she was a beauty and a sweet girl. Drowned accidentally was what they said, but that girl was terrified of the water. We have a Fourth of July shindig every year and there's an hour reserved for the ladies to swim. No men allowed, although you can't really stop a boy determined to peek no matter how far around he has to go to do it. Jenny never would go in."

Lizzie looked at her, curious about what she was driving at.

"Learning about Jenny hurt my heart and gave me the shivers. I thought, that could have been Cessie all those years ago. It could have been, too. She was in enough pain. She could have breathed in a lungful of water and there would have been nothing any of us could do." She paused. "If anyone ever thought it was an easy decision to haul my baby sister out to the middle of the pond and leave her, it wasn't."

Lizzie wished she knew what to say. "You did it to save her," she said softly.

April May nodded. "But what if she hadn't chosen life? I don't know how I would have bared it. I don't know how any of us would. Nothing would have ever been the same. Not for any of us. That's for shore."

"I'm going to take a swim tonight," Cessie said as she and Lizzie cleaned the kitchen after supper.

"Do you mind if I go along?" Lizzie asked.

"Mind? I'd love it. There's just nothing like a moonlight swim."

The sound of laughter came from the other room. The low-pitched laughter of April May in harmony with the higher-pitched laughter of the children. It was such a good sound.

Cessie only had a bowl left to wash, and Lizzie had kept up with the drying, so it was time to broach the subject. "I have something strange to tell you."

Cessie looked at her. "What?"

Lizzie concentrated on the platter she was drying. "I had older parents. I was an only child, and they weren't the most loving people."

"Really?" Cessie said thoughtfully. "I'm surprised, as good a mother as you are."

Lizzie shrugged. "I did everything the opposite of them. And I love being a mother. I think that's the key to being a good parent."

Cessie nodded.

"I think, had my mother married someone else, she might have been different. More loving. But my father associated gentle and nurturing with spoiling a child, and my mother obeyed his every command and thought." She walked over and put the platter away. "I must have been about five or six when the dreams began."

"The dreams?"

"A recurring dream I would have. It lasted only seconds. It was my mother and father—not the ones I grew up with, but my *real* mother and father. My dream mother and father." Lizzie shrugged and grinned. "I really came to believe that the people who ruled my household had adopted me from these people. I reasoned my real parents must have died, maybe in an accident. A train derailment or a ship sinking. You see, the dreams were so real, I thought they must be a memory from early childhood. I can still see their faces in my mind."

"What did they look like?"

"They both had dark hair. They were very attractive. In fact, she was beautiful. The dream only lasted a few seconds, just long enough for them to turn back to look at me and extend their hands to me, but I saw them clearly."

Cessie reached for the towel and dried her hands but didn't look away from Lizzie.

"In the dream, we're outside, walking, but I've lagged behind. They turn toward each other and look back at me, urging me to catch up. They're smiling and so happy. Her hair is just to her shoulders and she wears it loose. It is dark and wavy and the wind blows some into her face. And that was it. That's all there was to it, but it was enough to convince me they were my real parents."

Cessie cocked her head thoughtfully, knowing more was coming.

"I don't know how to say this without you thinking—"

"What?" Cessie asked tenderly. "I won't think anything. Just tell me."

"The mother in my dream . . . was you," Lizzie said, finishing in a whisper. Tears filled her eyes, especially when Cessie looked stunned. "I saw the picture of you as a young woman and that's her. I mean you. You were my dream mother."

"Oh, honey," Cessie breathed, overwhelmed at the statement. She reached out and they grabbed each other's hands.

"Rebecca mentioned John, and I wondered if he was my dream father, but it wasn't him."

"No, he . . . he didn't have dark hair."

"I know who he was though," Lizzie said, reaching into her pocket for the photograph of a young Lionel. "It was him," she said, handing it to Cessie.

Cessie sucked in a breath as she looked at the photograph. She smiled first and then tears welled in her eyes. She turned and made her way to the table and sat. "He showed me this once. I wondered where it was."

Lizzie followed her and sat. "It's yours."

"Oh no. I want you to have it. After all, he was your papa," she said with a smile. "And I have him here," she said, tapping her chest. "And here," she added, pointing to her head. She looked at the picture again and then handed it back. "Tell me the dream again," she said wistfully.

"You believe me," Lizzie said wonderingly. It wasn't a question because she could see the truth in Cessie's eyes.

"Of course I do. Oh, honey, I know the power of dreams. I know how the other side reaches through to touch us and guide us. It's happened to me, too." She leaned back. "Just think of all the significance in your dream. At the time, it gave you a feeling of belonging that you needed. Now, it proves you're in the right place. That you've come home."

Lizzie took hold of Cessie's hand.

"What was I wearing?" Cessie asked.

The question was delightful, and Lizzie laughed even as she had to blink back tears.

Chapter Eight

In a coal mine known as Six, at a depth no sunlight penetrated, the blackness so dense it was palpable and disorienting, Jeremy worked with a pick and a wedge to extract the last chunks of coal from the wall without shattering it. He was lying on his side in a narrow seam, his concentration complete, and the only light came from the not quite three-inch kerosene lamp in his hat and the hat and lantern of Liam Baskerville, his helper. Liam assisted mainly by piling extracted coal into a bin, but at present he wasn't doing much more than providing company. He'd been Jeremy's partner in the mine from the beginning, almost eight years now, and he'd been a reliable one. But these days, this late in the day, Liam's vigor was shot. He started the work day well enough at six a.m., but by four, he was done for.

"My nephew started work today," Liam said. "Newest breaker boy."

"Yeah?"

"Nine years old," Liam lamented.

This caused a moment's pause. "Nine?"

"He lied," Liam said with a shrug of his bony shoulders.

"Said he was twelve. Family needs the money since William took sick."

Jeremy knew, of course, that William, Liam's brother-in-law and a fellow miner, had miner's asthma so bad he could no longer work. Liam had it too, although he hadn't fully admitted it yet. His struggle to breathe and the coughing fits made it obvious, but not as obvious as it would become as the condition progressed. Miner's asthma wasted a man down to skin and bone. It was as if a vise slowly closed around the throat so a person couldn't draw enough air into the lungs. In the end, a man had to choose between breathing and eating; they simply couldn't do both. It was a bad way to die.

But *nine* years of age. It wasn't shocking, exactly, but it was sad. Jeremy had seen the breaker boys at play on their breaks. They were the only ones with the vigor to play or fight among themselves. They were skinny, scrappy lads in filthy clothing, with coal-blackened faces and limbs, who worked for eight cents an hour. Their job was to sort rock from coal and to separate pieces of coal according to size. Most of them labored six days a week, ten hours a day. The dream of every breaker boy was to become a door boy and then a mule boy, and eventually a full-fledged miner. Jeremy took aim with his pick again and struck with precision. "Should be in school."

"Since when the hell does *should* have anything to do with anything?" Liam said tiredly. "We *should* see the sun on occasion. William's not yet fifty. He *shouldn't* look eighty and be struggling for the little bit of air he can wheeze in." He paused. "Eh, Charlie's all right. Not the smartest, but he'll make do. His brother'll look out for him best he can."

"The girls still in school?"

"No. Maura pulled Kate out this year to help at home and you know Mary's in service at Smythe House."

Jeremy nodded. There were three dynasties or moguls in these parts who owned mines, farms, ranches, and businesses, and who seemed to amass wealth exponentially: Landreth, whom they worked for; the Smythes; and Howerton. They were rich men no one liked but everyone either feared, worked for, or wanted something from. Howerton was the possible exception since he was generally respected and even genuinely liked by some, including most of his own men. Old man Landreth certainly couldn't say that.

Of course, they hadn't all led charmed lives. Landreth was a hard man who'd lost two wives and two of his four sons. Pete had died in a strange accident as a young man, when he fell off a train while engaged in drunken horseplay, and Ted had suddenly gone missing years ago; no one had ever seen or heard from him again. He'd been with a friend, Stan Thomas, who had also gone missing. It was widely suspected that they'd gone off to the city to gamble, where they'd fallen into trouble that turned fatal, but no one ever knew for sure.

For years, Landreth had owned most of the mines in the area. The one they toiled in was the sixth opened, thus its name. But then, less than a decade ago, Smythe had begun an operation that did well enough to start speculation, and in came others, including Greg Howerton. His mines had uncovered the richest veins yet, and Landreth despised him for it.

The wonder of casual observers was that Six kept a workforce at all. It was poorly constructed and Landreth paid less than the other mine owners. The majority of the workforce stayed because of indebtedness, because Landreth paid part of the wages in script that was good only for the company-owned general store or rent for company-owned

housing. He rented out hovels to his workers and overcharged
for goods at the company store, the only place his employees
and their families could get goods on credit. The deeper the
debt became, the more trapped the men became. Meanwhile, Landreth made money coming and going.

The one and only benefit of staying at Six for the long
haul was that if a man labored at the mine for twenty years,
he was awarded a pension for the next ten years. The pension was only a quarter of his usual pay, but at least it was
something. Not that many lived to enjoy the benefit.

Liam fell into another coughing fit, and when it subsided,
Jeremy said, "Why don't you go on? Get some air. It's close
enough to quitting time."

"I got this to finish," Liam said, referring to the pile of
coal not yet picked up.

"I'll get it."

Liam barked a final cough, turned his head and spat, and
then sniffed. "It's not right."

"It's nothing."

"It's not nothing, Shef. You got your job—"

"It's fine," Jeremy interrupted. "Not like you wouldn't
do it for me."

Liam conceded with a sigh that turned into another
cough. "All right, then." He rose, scooted from the seam,
and walked away slowly. When Jeremy finished the area he
was working on, he also scooted from the seam. As he
stood and stretched, he watched the small orange and
yellow lights floating toward him from the tunnel ahead.
They were the lights in other miners' hats as they came in
his direction, finished for the day.

He moved his stiff neck from side to side, then went
back in to finish. He collected the loose coal and put it in
the bin, then began setting up for one more blast. He'd set
it off just before he left, and excavate in the morning. He

bored holes and was almost finished setting the explosives when he heard the familiar clopping of mine mules and the squeak of the wheels of a loaded car on rails.

"Whatcha say, Shef?" called Timmy Wayne, the driver of the mule team. Timmy, a lanky, dark-haired boy of almost fourteen with an easy, infectious smile, walked ahead of the animals, leading them with the heavy load.

"Not much," Shef replied as he set the last explosive.

"Nope." Timmy laughed. "Never do." His face was so coal blackened that his teeth, which probably weren't all that white, shone bright in the low light.

Shef crawled back out of the hole to help dump their bin of coal into the car.

"I saw Liam. He looks done in."

"It's that time of day," Jeremy replied noncommittally.

"You ready to call it a day?"

"I was ready when I got here."

Timmy grinned. "I know whatcha mean. So, uh, whatcha doin' tonight?" The boy had a fascination with the life of single men. Coming from a near-destitute family of seven, he found it hard to imagine having no one but yourself to tend to. It was highly appealing, to his way of thinking. "Is this the night you go to the resternt?"

"I go on Fridays. Only decent meal I have all week."

"I ain't had nothing but cabbage and potatoes for a durn week, and I ain't never been to no resternt."

"Maybe I'll take you with me for your birthday. It's coming up, isn't it?"

"First of October."

Jeremy nodded. "'Kay, then. We'll go."

"You mean it?"

"'Course I mean it."

"That's right nice of you, Shef. What kind of food they have there?"

"All kinds. Beefsteak, fried chicken, ham steak. Whatever you want."

"Beefsteak. That's what I'd pick."

"How about the Friday after your birthday then?"

"Well, all righty, then," Timmy said excitedly. "If you're sure you mean it. I'd like that."

"I don't say what I don't mean."

Timmy nodded. "I'd best get on, I guess. See you tomorrow, Shef."

"See you tomorrow."

The boy walked around to the front of the mules and tugged on the reins of the lead mule. "Getty up, Stubborn. Let's finish."

"His name really Stubborn?" Jeremy asked as they started off.

"It's what I call him," Timmy said over his shoulder. "'Cause he's a sight more stubborn than the rest. Might have to get the mule lady down here to talk some sense into him."

Jeremy waited until boy and mule were a good enough distance away before he gathered his tools and then lit the fuse for the explosives. Afterwards, he walked away calmly, knowing precisely how long he had before it blew. Like all miners, he knew the right amount of explosives to use for the task at hand. Tomorrow, he'd extract the coal he'd loosened from the blast. As he walked toward the lift, the light from his hat picked up points of coal in the walls, making them glisten and shine like shards of diamonds.

He'd made it all the way to the cage when the blast happened. The men waiting for the elevator didn't bat an eye at the explosion; they were inured to a continual cacophony. Nor did anyone think it odd to see smoke from the blast, eerie and shimmering, floating toward them like a phantom mass. The elevator arrived, the weary men trudged on, and the bell was rung, signaling the hoister to raise the cage.

Once in motion, it moved surprisingly fast, the black walls flying by for more than eleven hundred feet before light assailed their senses. On this trip, twelve men emerged, each black faced, with slumped shoulders and a dour expression, squinting at the light, many of them still carrying formidable-looking tools—sledges, tamping bars, and picks. It was an everyday occurrence and yet they were a fearful sight to the uninitiated.

Chapter Nine

On Friday evening, Jeremy went into town, as was customary. He ate at Wiley's and then picked up whatever supplies he needed from the general store for the week. He came into town on Saturday afternoons too, but that was the day he gambled and drank a good deal of his pay away. He had sense enough to get the week's supplies before that.

Tonight's dinner special had been shepherd's pie, and it had been as good as usual. His usual fare during the week was beans or potatoes fried in lard with a chunk of whatever meat he'd purchased for the week. He cooked cabbage a lot, not because he liked it especially, but it was easy and it lasted. He always picked up a couple of loaves of bread from the store and ate it with most meals. Sometimes fried bacon between slices of bread was his morning and evening meal. Food wasn't something he thought about a lot; it was just what kept him going.

He left the store with his supplies in hand, setting the bell mounted over the door to tinkling, and then held the door for a woman pushing an infant in a perambulator. He started to walk on, but stopped when he noticed the lady he'd seen leaving the boarding house not quite a week ago. She was across the street, coming out of the office of T. Emmett Rice, attorney at law, with the Blue sisters. Her children followed hand in hand, but the little girl paused long enough for him to notice her stern look of disapproval. He tipped his hat to her, which did not lighten her disdain the slightest bit. It was the first thing that had amused him in a long time.

For some reason, he watched the small group walk away. There was something fascinating about the lady. The way she looked—the way she moved. He blew out a slow breath and decided maybe he'd have a drink, after all. He went first to the livery to check on his horse, and because Joseph Schultz would keep an eye on the goods he'd purchased.

In the saloon, the lighting was dim enough that he had to pause once he was in the door, to allow his eyes to adjust. "Well, hello, handsome," a young woman with light hair and painted red lips said as she sashayed toward him in barely any clothing. "You interested in being entertained?"

"No, thank you, miss," he said with exaggerated politeness as he started toward the highly polished bar. Behind it were large mirrors, framed in the same dark cherrywood as the bar.

"Oh, come on," she said, grabbing at his arm as he passed.

He turned back to her. "How old are you?"

She shimmied her body back and forth. "How old do I look?"

He considered and then shrugged. "Fifteen. Sixteen."

Her smile vanished and she huffed in insult. "Shows what you know. I'm eighteen."

She'd made an attempt to look older with face paint, but in fact it made her look younger. "Like I said before, no thank you, miss."

Her eyes narrowed and her face flushed. "Why? Don't you like girls?"

"I like girls just fine. But I only go to bed with women."

She muttered a foul word under her breath as she walked on.

He chose a spot in the center of the bar and ordered a whiskey. As he drank it, he thought about the pretty lady with the Blue sisters. It was strange that he'd seen her twice now, and the sight of her had affected him both times. There was just something about her.

"Hey there, Shef," a woman said from his side.

He knew Marie's voice before he looked at her. He stopped himself from uttering a sigh, but he felt every bit as uncomfortable at seeing her as he usually did. She was a beautiful woman with dark hair and strangely light eyes—but she'd been Jenny's friend. He could never be with her. "Hello, Marie." A moment of uncomfortable silence fell between them because it was impossible for either of them to separate memories of childhood from what they'd become.

"How are you?" she asked.

"Same as always. You?"

She shrugged one shoulder dramatically. "Well enough, I guess. 'Course, you know me. I'm always hoping someone will show up and rescue me."

It was hard not to shake his head, because he'd tried to talk her out of working in the saloon after she'd laid the choice at his feet. He downed his drink instead, then looked at the bartender and raised his glass, getting a nod in return. The comment still agitated him. "I'm pretty sure the men who come in here are looking for something other than to rescue someone," he said without looking at her.

"Guess I'd know that, wouldn't I?" she replied snappishly. Another silence fell between them and she stepped closer to him. "C'mon, Shef. Don't be like that."

"I am what I am," he said as the bartender filled his glass.

"You want to maybe go upstairs?" she asked quietly when Sam, the bartender, had moved on.

Jeremy shook his head, again avoiding eye contact.

She sighed softly, almost inaudibly. "Do you think you'll ever forget about when we were younger?"

"You want something?" Sam asked Marie as he passed by.

She nodded. "Pour me one."

He did and then walked on.

"There's things I wish I could forget," Jeremy replied. He downed the drink and then pulled out the coins to pay, placing them on the counter before he turned to her. "Sometimes I wish I could forget every damn bit of it. Just wipe it away like it never happened. I'd just be a blank slate."

"Why would you want that?"

"Be easier."

"You'd forget the happy things, too? The good things?"

"If I had to, to forget it all? Yeah."

"Betcha I could make you forget. For a while, anyway."

He shook his head slowly. He didn't want to hurt her, but he couldn't be with her, and she didn't give up easily.

"Why? Why can't we just—"

He turned to her, his eyes blazing. "Because. Because I may want to forget, but I can't."

"Your sister's gone. She's been gone a long time."

He faced front, tempted to have another drink. Or several. This wasn't a discussion worth having.

She sighed heavily. "Fine. If that's how you feel."

If that's how he felt? He'd only said so a hundred times.

"Take care," she said.

He nodded, but didn't look at her. "You too."

"I always do," she replied before walking away, looking as miserable as he felt.

"Another?" the bartender asked.

He was about to refuse when he saw T. Emmett Rice reflected in the mirror in front of him, entering the saloon. On impulse, Jeremy turned and motioned him over, getting a look of surprise in return. Still, the portly older man with an almost cherubic face came toward him without hesitation. "Yeah, one more," Jeremy said, "and what does T. Emmett Rice drink?"

"Ale or port, usually."

"Shef," Emmett said as he reached him. "How are you?"

"I'm buying. What'll you have?"

"Whatever you're having is fine."

Shef looked at the bartender, who was looking at Emmett doubtfully. "Whiskey?" he asked dolefully.

"I occasionally enjoy a glass of whiskey, Sam," Emmett stated.

The bartender shrugged and reached for a glass, then filled both men's glasses.

Jeremy waited for Sam to leave before he said, "I was curious."

"What about?"

"The lady who left your office not long ago. The one with the Blue sisters."

Emmett nodded. "Nice lady. Mrs. Carter. Used to be Greenway. She's Lionel Greenway's daughter."

Jeremy heard the word *missus* with disappointment. "The hermit?"

"The one and only."

"Why's she here now?"

"She's recently widowed."

Jeremy's interest was piqued again. "Oh?"

"She's come here to move into her father's place." Emmett picked up his glass and sipped. His mustache wriggled. "Why do you ask?"

Jeremy picked up his glass. "No reason. Just curious."

"Well, she's lovely. Just as lovely and sweet as Lionel always said."

"You hadn't met her before?"

Emmett shook his head. "They were estranged, which Lionel blamed himself for. I don't know the whole story on that. When she got news he died, she wanted to come for the funeral, but her husband wouldn't allow it. Not the nicest of men from what I gather. Fact is, he up and died without leaving her much of anything." He sipped the whiskey again, and there was another wriggle of his mustache.

Jeremy noticed Marie watching him from across the room. He pointedly faced front and took a drink.

"That place," Emmett commented, "the Greenway cottage, has gotten mighty run-down since Lionel's been gone. You know the place? Beyond the Blue farm?"

Jeremy looked at him. "I know it."

Emmett nodded. "She's got a lot of fixing up to do. Not sure how skilled she is at that sort of thing."

Jeremy's pulse picked up its pace.

"Then again," Emmett said, "she's young. I guess she's got time. And she is determined to protect those young'uns of hers. Cute things. That kind of determination in a woman gets things done. Saw it in my niece Emmy Medlin. You know her?"

He nodded. "Know who she is."

"She's not really my niece; I just think of her that way. Her uncle was my closest friend. And Lionel was a friend, too, so I'll probably start thinking of Lizzie as a niece. I'd like to see her and those little ones happy here."

Jeremy nodded, his mind churning. He finished his drink.

"You going to get a game going?" Emmett asked.

"Not unless you want to play."

Emmett chuckled. "I'm smart enough to know better.

No, I only play in real friendly games with fellas who play as poorly as I do. That way, it's fun." He picked up his glass and swirled the amber liquid, enjoying the scent that rose. It smelled a good deal better than it tasted. "If you don't mind my asking, what's got you curious about Lizzie?"

Jeremy couldn't quite frame an answer.

"No, that's okay," Emmett said quickly, waving off the question. "Sometimes there's just . . . that certain interest. It's like it's in the veins or maybe the core of a man. Though, of course, most men don't like to wax that poetic. Me, I don't mind. Folks expect a certain amount of waxing from me."

Jeremy fished out the money for the drinks and placed it on the counter. "Good seeing you."

Emmett nodded. "Thanks for the drink."

Which he'd barely touched. Jeremy reached for his hat. "See you."

"Yeah. See you, Shef."

Once Jeremy was gone, Marie walked directly to Emmett. "Hey, Emmett."

"Afternoon, Miss Marie."

"What were you and Shef talking about?" she asked, trying way too hard to sound casual.

"Aw, this and that. Nothing important."

"Not really like him to be friendly," she prodded.

He had to concede the point. "He saw a lady and asked after her, is all."

"What lady?" she asked, dropping all pretense of casualness.

"A new lady in town. Daughter of the hermit. You remember a man name of Lionel Greenway?"

She folded her arms, clearly perturbed. "Yeah. I remember him."

"His daughter recently came to town to live. Her and her kids."

She drew back. "She has children?"

He nodded. "Two of 'em. A little boy who looks just like her, and a girl. She's eight and he's just turned four."

"Why was Shef asking about her?"

He shrugged. "He was just asking. He was curious about her."

"What does she look like?"

The questioning was getting to be uncomfortable. "She's pretty," he admitted, toning down the description more than he might have. "Fairish hair."

She turned and walked away with a scowl on her face. If she had any desire to keep her feelings to herself, she was doing a poor job of it.

"So how's that whiskey?" the bartender asked with a smirk.

Emmett gave him a look. "Best I've had all week."

Sam laughed.

Marie walked back to her room and slammed the door shut. Leaning against the wall, she folded her arms tightly and fought back tears. "Damn you, Shef," she said brokenly. If only Jenny hadn't died, everything would have been different. But once she did, Jeremy began asking questions and more questions. She should have never admitted the truth, but he kept pushing. It was like he already knew Jen had been with Ted the day before she died.

Little by little, he pulled the truth from her and then he blamed her for knowing and not telling him. But Jenny had been her best friend and Jen hadn't wanted her brother to know. Marie closed her eyes with a sigh and remembered.

"Jeremy is stubborn and he's wrong about Ted," Jenny had confided as the two of them walked arm in arm from school on what turned out to be their last day together. "But he'll never admit it. Not till we're married and happy. Not for a year or two, at least."

"You're gonna have to tell your family you're getting married," Marie replied.

"But not until I graduate. The day after. That's when we're going to announce it," Jenny said happily.

"You sure he means it?" Marie asked worriedly. It wasn't that she wanted to hurt Jen, but Ted was no less flirty or obnoxious than he'd ever been. Oh, if Jenny was around, he pretended to be polite and proper, but the second she wasn't, he was the same ol' loudmouth, cocky rooster he'd always been.

Jen stopped short and turned to her, a hurt look on her face.

"I'm sorry," Marie said, "but—"

"Why is everyone against us?" Jen blurted.

"I'm not against *you*."

"Well, then you can't be against him either. I love him," she declared beseechingly.

"I just don't want you to get hurt if he . . . I don't know. Changes or something. Like he was with Anne or—"

Jen stuck her hand in the air and took a step back. "We're different! In fact, everything is going to be different tomorrow. You'll see."

Marie felt an odd pang. "What do you mean?"

Jenny turned and started off, but she was blushing. "Nothing. I can't tell you."

Marie grabbed her arm to be face-to-face with her. Jen's cheeks were crimson and there was guilt on her face. "You can't," Marie hissed, her eyes wide. She was talking about letting Ted have his way with her; she just knew it. "Not until you're married." Jen tried to walk on, but Marie wouldn't relinquish her hold.

Jen suddenly looked miserable. She whispered, "He said if I love him—"

"You make him give you a ring first and ask your daddy for your hand. Then he can't back out."

"I already told you, he's doing that the day after we graduate."

"That's only a few more weeks. So why does it have to be tomorrow?"

Jenny pulled away from her, still miserable looking. "I don't want to talk about it anymore."

"Jen," Marie said with a shake of her head.

"No, I mean it," Jenny said, walking on. After a few steps, she turned back to face Marie. "Just be my friend. All right?"

"But what if—"

"No! I'm done talking about it! One more word and I'm going to turn around and go home."

"Fine," Marie said, giving in. "I just hope it's not a big, fat mistake." They walked a good way in strained silence before Marie couldn't help herself. "Are you scared?" she asked without looking at her friend.

Silence.

"Yes," Jen admitted.

Marie reached over and took her hand and squeezed it as they continued walking.

"He does love me," Jenny said weakly. "He's already picked out a ring and everything."

"I bet it'll be the prettiest thing ever," Marie said, although she still had a bad feeling.

A sharp rap at the door made Marie jump.

"Saul says get back to it," Molly said in her nasal, girlish voice.

Marie seethed at the order. Saul owned the place and

made a lot of money, but it was never enough. Greedy bastard. "I'll be there in a minute," she called back. She took a few steps into the room, smoothing the front of her dress and composing herself, and then she turned and left the room to get back to it, as ordered.

Chapter Ten

"This afternoon," Lizzie said to Rebecca and Jake, who were on the front porch swing with her, "that meeting we had with Mr. Rice?"

Rebecca looked at her curiously. Jake had a cloth clown doll in his hand, which Cessie had uncovered, and it was taking most of his concentration.

"That was about getting a house and some land near here," Lizzie said carefully.

"Did April May and Cessie buy it for us?" Rebecca asked.

"No. Not exactly. They thought of it. They told me about it. But . . . remember that picture of a man with Cessie? She said his name was Lionel and he was her second love?"

Rebecca nodded, and Jake looked up at his mother.

"He passed away but left his house to his daughter. She . . . doesn't need it and we do, so I'm going to say I'm her." It was quiet as the children considered this. "It's what we call a white lie. Remember when we talked about that?"

Both children nodded.

"It doesn't hurt anyone if I become his daughter, and it helps us a lot."

"I'd rather live here with April May and Cessie," Rebecca stated.

"I understand, but we can't do that. Cessie and April May have been very generous, and we'll still be neighbors and the best of friends, but we can't live here. Not for always."

"I bet they wouldn't mind," Rebecca said.

"Even if they wouldn't mind, it's just not done, sweetheart. It wouldn't be right. We need our own house."

Rebecca thought about it as they swung. Jake went back to the clown doll.

"So you'll pretend you're someone else?" Rebecca asked.

"Yes. In a way. I'll still be me, of course. I'll still be your mother, but my name will be Elizabeth Anne Greenway Carter. That's what everyone will think. And your last name will be Carter, too. Rebecca Carter and Jake Carter." She paused. "Is that all right?"

Jake nodded and then looked at his mother with a guileless smile that touched her.

"Rebecca Carter," Rebecca said musingly.

"Do you want to think about it for a while?" Lizzie asked her.

"What if I said I didn't want to?" Rebecca asked earnestly.

Lizzie sighed, searching for the right answer. "What's happened," she began, "is a miracle. That we found this place, and these ladies who had a close friend who has a house near here that we can have? It's a miracle."

Rebecca looked down at the doll as she pondered. "Can I see it?" she asked Jake.

He hesitated and then handed it over. "Can I go play with the dogs?" he asked his mother.

She leaned over and kissed his head. "Yes."

He scooted off the swing and hurried into the house.

Rebecca studied the clown doll inquisitively.

"The truth is, we need this," Lizzie said. "I don't have much money left."

"I'm glad we'll live close to Cessie and April May," Rebecca said.

"I am, too. They've become very important to me."

Rebecca looked at her. "Can I see the house?"

"Of course. It needs some work and cleaning up, because no one has lived there in a long time, but it will be absolutely wonderful. I promise."

Rebecca looked back at the doll. "This is funny looking."

"Yes, it is, Miss Carter."

Rebecca grinned. "Mrs. Carter," she shot back.

"Yes, Miss Carter," Lizzie said, gently poking her in the side. "Did you call me?"

"Yes, Mrs. Carter," Rebecca said, tickling her back, which was a good excuse for Lizzie to pull her close and hug her. "I don't mind," Rebecca finally said.

"I'm so glad," Lizzie replied. "I'm so glad we found this place."

Rebecca nodded against Lizzie's breast. "Me too, Mama."

Chapter Eleven

As the sun set on the first day of September, Lizzie sat on the front porch steps and kept watch over the bonfire she'd built, probably the tenth she'd burned. She'd never worked so hard, and she felt it in every muscle in her body. They'd cleared out weeds and undergrowth, swept and scrubbed and cleaned and replaced bad floor boards.

After paying for new mattresses, basic supplies, and a used handgun, she was almost out of money, but they had a home and she had the means to protect them all in the unlikely event that Ethan found them. Their needs were small; they didn't require much to get by. She would plant a late-summer garden and she'd have a bigger, better one in the spring. April May and Cessie were giving them a few chickens and a rooster, claiming they had too many, and they'd made her promise to come for dinner a few nights a week once they were installed in the cottage. For now, they were still in residence at the Blue farm, and they'd been made to feel truly at home. She'd never felt so at home.

Lizzie had plans for the future, as well. The only bakery in town wasn't very good, so she was hoping to sell baked goods to the general stores. Of course, they had to get into the house first and she had to learn the oven, but she could picture it in her mind. She could imagine a healthy, happy life in this place. The cottage was amazing in so many ways. The bathhouse and outhouse were exceptionally built, the most exotically strange places she could have imagined. Lionel had fashioned these necessary rooms for comfort, health, even beauty.

The outhouse was a ten-by-twelve structure positioned some six yards from the house and connected by a vine-covered lattice-top walkway. The room had high, crank-out windows that allowed for light and fresh air, and the porcelain toilet bowl had a levered-trap in the bottom to seal off odors. There was also a tank of water on the wall with a nozzle that allowed a cleaning of the bowl. Rainwater that collected outside the building was somehow transferred to the tank.

Just beyond it was the bathhouse. April May had been right; there was a shower for getting clean as well as a soaking tub. The room had the same high windows for light and ventilation. At one time, there had been large potted plants in the corners. The ceramic pots and the decayed remains of the plants were still there. Eventually, she'd replace them and it would be a small oasis once again.

With less than an hour's preparation, one could have a warm shower and a hot bath. As hot as one wanted, as there were two separate nozzles that filled the tub, one with cold water and one from a tank of hot water. That was where the hour was needed. You built a fire in the small pit beneath the tank. There were actually two tanks on the wall by the tiled shower area, which had confused Lizzie at first until she'd realized the shower drew from both tanks to be pleasantly warm. It was a place of sheer luxury and she was in complete agreement with Lionel about it being good for one's health.

Beyond the bathhouse was a laundry area. The hand-cranked washing machine had an attached wringer. It had taken some experimentation, but she'd finally gotten the process down. Laundry had always been her least favorite chore, but this contraption made it dramatically easier.

The winery was a place filled with tanks, barrels, and large baskets. The cellar, what she could see of it, appeared to be filled with more barrels, but the racks that lined the walls were empty. She'd ventured part of the way down, but the stairs had decayed and, with no wine left, there was no point in risking injury. Especially when Cessie had given her several bottles of Lionel's wine.

Lizzie hugged her shawl closer as an evening breeze stirred. September's weather was far more pleasant than the late-summer heat, although she wouldn't complain about any weather. Or anything. Not even the blisters on her hands. She'd earned them for a good cause.

The light from the campfire cast eerie shadows about, but she wasn't frightened. Not in this place. It was her salvation. When the fire had burned down enough that she could leave without worry, she got back to her feet to return to the farm. They were finishing curtains tonight and she'd be hanging them tomorrow. There were countless projects to get to, but she'd take them on one at a time. *And be grateful.* "'Night, Lionel," she said with a last glance around.

At the same moment, Jeremy left the livery. After selling the family farm to pay back the bank that had held the mortgage on it, he'd removed every personal item that meant a damn and stored it all in the old cabin on the only acre he'd kept. It was the acre that contained the secrets that would see him hanged. The same secrets that damned him to the life he had now. The only living thing he'd kept was Dancer, his horse.

Once he knew what he had to do, he'd gone to Joseph Schultz, owner of the livery, and struck a deal to keep Dancer there: he would be charged nothing, and Mr. Schultz would have the use of Dancer. It was a good arrangement since Mr. Schultz was a kind man and took the care of the animals in his protection seriously. Jeremy went each week to see and ride Dancer. He often felt it was the most personal connection he had.

The temperature was pleasant as Jeremy started homeward by way of favorite residential streets. He passed couples sitting on porch swings, chatting intimately while children played. Dogs and cats stretched out on the porch steps, keeping a lookout for intruders. The smell of dinners cooking made his stomach growl and the sights and sounds made him feel lonely and isolated, but maybe that was the point. At least it made him feel something.

He usually made a specific circuit before heading back to his small rented house, but tonight he continued to Crooked Tree Road. He passed the Blue farm, where the lights glowed brightly in the encroaching darkness, and continued, curious about the Greenway cottage.

There were no lights from within the cottage, but embers glowed from a bonfire that had mostly died out. He walked over to a shovel leaning against the porch and shoveled some dirt on the embers to kill them, since there was enough of a breeze to cause a breakout fire. Setting the tool back where it had been, he looked over the cottage. The moon, just breaking free of cloud cover, didn't provide a lot of light, but it still looked like a fine place. Lizzie Greenway Carter and her children would fit well here.

Chapter Twelve

Marie accepted another glass of wine, because she was going to need it. The despair she felt was so overwhelming, she increasingly fantasized about fading away to become invisible. She ought to have been able to do it spontaneously, she'd wished for it so often. She smiled at Tucker Armstrong and Bryant Smith, just like she was supposed to, but she despised them for what they wanted. In her opinion, men who needed an audience or wanted the participation of a friend were nothing but pathetic. Unfortunately, the bottle was empty, which meant the time was at hand. At least she was half drunk as she led the way back to her room.

When it was over, after she shut the door behind them, her shaking hand stayed poised on the key. She longed to turn it, but she didn't want them to hear the click of the lock. After a few moments, she twisted it and slumped against the door.

Eyes shut, her forehead pressed to the cool wood, her thoughts of Jeremy were bitter because this was all his fault. Her becoming a whore was his fault. She'd loved him her entire life and she'd wanted to marry him more than anything. But then Jenny died, and he'd withdrawn and done nothing but work the farm. Then his mother passed and his pa began drinking his health away. They lost the farm, Mr. Sheffield hanged himself in despair, and Jeremy had gone off to work in the mine.

She hardly saw him then, and her ma had let her know in no uncertain terms that she had to get out—either get married or get a job. "Done supported you long enough, girl," her ma had declared. "There's four others behind you to raise." Her mother had once been a stunning beauty. Not only did everyone say so, but Marie could see the remnants in the now tired face. Hard work and too much childbearing had aged her, made her shoulders droop and her breasts sag. Settling for her lot in life had given her the perpetual frown lines at her mouth and the crease between her brows. It was responsible for the cool, dark shadow in her gaze.

Her ma suggested going into service as a maid, but Marie loathed the thought of waiting on other people. Her ma had declared she was too pretty for her own good and too big for her britches, but the truth was, she wanted marriage. She wanted Jeremy. So she'd tracked him down one afternoon and told him she either had to find work or a husband. When Jeremy just looked at her as if wondering why she was telling him, she blurted that she was thinking of going to work in the saloon.

He'd blinked with surprise. "What do you mean?"

She already regretted that she'd said it. She'd said it to shock him. "You know what I mean."

"You're talking about being a prostitute?"

"It's either that or be a maid."

"You can't be serious," he scoffed. "Men using you all the time? Being a maid would be a hundred times better."

She'd frowned mightily. "I'd rather be a wife. That's what I'd rather."

"Then go marry someone," he'd retorted.

The words stung.

"What about Frank?" Jeremy asked. "He's always been sweet on you."

"I don't want Frank," she practically spit. "I'd rather be a whore."

He looked at her in disbelief. "Why did you have to come tell me?"

Her eyes filled with tears. "You know why."

He shook his head slowly. "I can't marry you."

The words were terrible to hear. They made her stomach ache. "Why not?"

Silence fell between them before he answered. "I don't love you like that. I'm sorry."

They were the worst words she'd ever heard. "Then I'll go be a whore," she threatened, hoping it would spur him to action.

But he only turned and started walking away.

"I mean it," she cried.

He didn't stop or turn back, and so she'd done it. She'd become a lady of the night, although *lady* was quite the stretch. She'd become a prostitute. A whore in waiting. Forever waiting for the man she loved to realize he loved her too, waiting for him to come to her rescue. But it had never happened and it never would. At least she'd had the consolation that his family tragedies had ruined him and he was no longer capable of love. That was, until he went and took an interest in old man Greenway's daughter. A woman with children, no less. It made no sense. She drew back with a dark frown as someone quietly rapped on her door. "Who is it?" she asked warily.

"Donna."

Marie unlocked and opened the door.

"You okay?" Donna asked.

Marie shrugged.

"I'm sorry, honey," Donna commiserated. "Too bad they favor you so much."

Marie nodded in agreement. What they paid was not worth what they took out of her.

"Anyway, Walt is here and he's asking for you."

Marie sagged at the thought of returning to the floor. "I'm not coming back down tonight. I made my quota."

"Marie—"

"I know what you think," Marie replied irritably. "You don't have to say it again."

"It's not what I think; it's what I know. And what I *know* is that Walt loves you. God Almighty, let him get you the hell out of here while you still got your looks and your health. Now, get washed and dressed again, and come back down. Just spend some time with him. You don't have to come back up here."

"I hate all men right now!"

"Like the rest of us don't?" Donna countered. "Look, let me tell you something, sweetheart. That new girl, Samantha," she said, pronouncing it distinctly. "She's got intentions of landing herself a husband. Now, one of the nicest, most decent men in town wants you, but I wouldn't underestimate Miss Samantha. She's not as pretty as you are, but she's not half bad either." Donna turned on her heel and walked off. "Think about it," she called over her shoulder.

Marie stood frozen for long seconds before she shut the door again. Donna was right. She had to be smart enough to hedge her bets. She wanted Jeremy, but what if he didn't come through for her?

When she was ready and as reconciled as she'd ever be, she surveyed herself in the mirror, but even while staring into her own eyes, she thought of Jeremy. She wondered where he was and what he was doing. Probably sleeping like a dead man with no thought of her. It was a bitter thought.

* * *

She was right on both counts. Jeremy slept heavily and his dream was of childhood. Of climbing a tree with his sister close behind. Or not so close, because Jenny had stopped, afraid of climbing too high. "C'mon," he called to her.

"I'm fine here." She looked up at him. "It's nice right here."

"It's better up higher."

"I like it right here," she returned stubbornly.

Suddenly, he was beside her, and all he could see from there was the tree and the ground below. "You can't see anything," he complained.

"We could fly," she said hopefully.

He grinned, because he realized she was right. He'd forgotten for a second, but he *could* fly. Not everybody could, but he could, and he could take her with him. In fact, it seemed like he was forever rescuing her from something or other. It was mostly why he flew—that and to escape bad things, like deep, dark holes he fell into. He first needed to get a running start and then push off. It was scary, and landing was scary, but flying was the best sensation he'd ever known. "We gotta get down first."

They scrambled down the tree. He reached the ground first and didn't wait for her as he started his legs in motion. He ran full out and pushed off hard, reaching out as far as he could. Feeling himself rise in the air was incredible. The rush of the air, the exhilaration that filled his chest and tightened his stomach. The view beneath him was spectacular. Their house and barn. Neat rows of crops in the field, animals grazing. He passed over the glistening water of the pond and green meadows. Even the mountains weren't too far if he wanted to soar over them. He'd done it many times before.

He rose higher to clear some trees and then circled back to get Jen. She was waiting, looking up at him with one hand extended, one hand shielding her eyes from the sun as she watched his flight. Ma had come out from the house and was watching, too. "You be careful," she called.

He dipped to grab Jenny, but then Pa stepped out of the barn and Jeremy knew it was time to get to his chores. Dang it. If only his ma hadn't called out, Pa wouldn't have known.

He reached the ground, running until he could slow himself to a stop. Walking back to Jen, he saw his parents were already headed back inside. He started toward the barn and she fell in step beside him.

"It really is the best, isn't it?" she asked happily.

"Yeah," he agreed, thinking of the wonder and exhilaration of flight.

"I mean this," she said.

He realized she meant their life. Although it was nothing special. He glanced around the farmyard, past the chicken coop to where his horse, Dancer, looked at him from the corral. It was a fine evening and dinner smelled appetizing. He really didn't mind most of his chores any more than he minded school. "I guess so," he agreed. He wondered why he suddenly felt so happy, because nothing was any different than it ever was.

The sound of the whistle from the mine woke him as usual, but he was more reluctant than usual to rise. His dream had been sweet, although it was already fading from consciousness. He buried his face in the thin pillow, wishing he could go back to it. Of course, if wishes were horses, beggars would ride. That's what Ma would have said.

Jenny was right. Their lives had been good. He'd had a

family he loved and a home where he'd belonged. He'd had a future. The whistle blew a second time and he sighed as he sat up, rubbing his face. It had just been a dream and now it was over. He didn't have a family or a home or a life. But he did have work to get to.

Chapter Thirteen

Jeremy lifted his hand to knock on the door of the Greenway cottage, but lost his nerve. Lightning flashed in the night sky and he looked around at the wildly blowing trees. He'd chosen a lousy evening, but here he was. After thinking of little else but the very pretty Mrs. Carter for three weeks straight, it was the moment of truth. He blew out a breath and knocked. With the racket the wind was making, he had no idea if she'd hear it. After long seconds with no response, he raised his fist to knock again, but the door opened and she was standing before him, the wind buffeting her, ruffling her clothes and blowing back her hair. His heart began thudding faster.

"Yes?" she called to be heard over the wind.

"I, ah—"

He moved back as she opened the screen door to better see and hear him.

"I apologize for showing up so late in the evening," he said loudly, "but I thought you might need some help," he said, leaning forward slightly so she could hear him.

"Need some help?" she repeated, confused.

"Around here. You know T. Emmett Rice?"

She nodded.

"He . . . suggested you needed some help with the place."

She blinked in surprise and clutched at the front of her shirt to keep it from blowing open. "I'm sorry," she said, "but I'm not in a position to hire anyone, Mister . . ."

"Sheffield." He took off his hat. "Jeremy Sheffield."

The rain suddenly let loose, falling hard at an angle, bouncing off the porch floor. It had been raining off and on for two days and it didn't seem as if it was going to stop anytime soon. "Please, come in," she said, opening the screen door wider. "You'll get soaked."

He stepped inside, barely avoiding brushing against her, and the savory scent of food assailed his senses. His mind raced for what to say next, but the little girl suddenly appeared in the hall, providing a distraction.

"Go finish your supper," Mrs. Carter said to her.

"I am finished."

"Rebecca," Mrs. Carter said in a tone that apparently meant business, although the girl gave Jeremy a decidedly suspicious look before walking away. Mrs. Carter turned back to him with an apologetic expression. "I'm sorry you came on such a miserable evening." She held herself stiffly, her hands clutched tightly together.

"I don't mind bad weather. I usually work in a hole where there is no weather."

She looked puzzled.

"I work in a mine," he added.

"Oh. I see."

"Like I said, I heard you could use some help."

"I won't claim it's not true," she began slowly. "Unfortunately, I'm not in a financial position—"

It was dim enough in the small parlor that he couldn't

see her face clearly, but it was better that way. Easier. He'd come this far. "Well, ma'am, there's other ways to pay a man," he said quietly. Other than a noticeable intake of breath, she made no sound or movement. He opened his mouth to say something else, but shut it again because he hadn't meant to put it that way exactly. Or had he? "I mean to say, there's other arrangements that could be made." She still didn't respond. "Like how some people barter?"

"I . . . I'm not altogether certain what I have to barter with."

He shifted on his feet. "The food smells awful good."

She exhaled, relaxing slightly. "It's stew. Why don't we go into the kitchen," she said, stammering slightly in her nervousness. "The light is better and we have plenty to share."

"That sounds good."

"Mama," a child called from the other room. "There's another leak."

"It's this way," Mrs. Carter said. She led the way, but only made it as far as the hallway before she stopped and turned back to him with a decidedly conflicted look on her face. Because she wanted him to leave, he knew. He held a breath, waiting for the words.

"Mr. Sheffield."

She looked so uncomfortable, and he had taken her by surprise, which wasn't fair. "Would you rather I leave?" he asked quietly. "It's all right."

"I . . ." She stepped over to the lamp on the wall and turned it up before looking back at him. There was a blush on her face and her arms were folded. "I'm not sure I believe you wanted to barter for . . . food."

He struggled for a response that wouldn't frighten her away. "I didn't have any one particular thing in mind," he said, keeping his voice low. "And that's the truth. I wanted to help. I knew you couldn't pay. I'm not trying to trick you or anything."

"I didn't mean that."

"I can tell you this much," he said. "I'd never ask for more than what you'd want to give. If that's a home-cooked meal or two, I'll take it."

She considered him a moment and then uncrossed her arms. "It's this way," she said, continuing on to the kitchen. He followed, stopping just inside the kitchen door because the children were looking at him from the table. He didn't have experience with children, nor did he have the desire for any. He glanced around at the array of bowls and pans catching the drips from the ceiling.

"This is Mr. Sheffield," Mrs. Carter said. "He's offered to help us with a thing or two. Mr. Sheffield, these are my children, Rebecca and Jake."

He tipped his head to them. "Hello."

"Help with what?" Rebecca asked her mother warily.

"The roof," he said. "That'll be the first thing. Unless you like it raining in your house."

The girl was not amused.

Mrs. Carter said, "Are you both finished?"

"Yes, ma'am," Rebecca replied, still looking bleak about his presence.

"Then go play in your room."

Rebecca's eyebrows knitted. "What about dishes?"

"I'll do them later. You may be excused."

"Come on, Jake," Rebecca said grimly, getting up. Her little brother followed suit and Jeremy stepped aside to let them by.

"Please have a seat," Mrs. Carter said as she turned to the stove.

He felt awkward as he went to the empty place at the table and sat. The food smelled delicious enough that his stomach had begun growling, but he hadn't felt this out of place in as long as he could remember. Like a bull in a china shop. Or a fox in the henhouse. A wolf among sheep. Was that what he was, deep down?

When she set a steaming bowl of stew in front of him, she said, "I have cider or—"

"That'd be good. Thank you."

"Please, eat," she said before going for the pitcher.

When he took a bite, it was so hot it burned his mouth, and he had to hold his hand in front of his lips and let it cool. He was hungry, and it was better than anything he'd had in months, but he needed to remember his manners. When she set a cup of cider before him, he nodded. "It's good," he said, not quite meeting her gaze.

She smiled, sat catty-corner from him, and offered him the bread basket filled with still-warm biscuits wrapped in cloth. "I enjoy cooking."

He took one and was going to dunk it into the stew, but resisted, fearing it might be rude. Besides, these biscuits were soft, with a tantalizing scent. He took a bite and savored the taste. "Delicious."

She reached for her glass of cider. "I'm glad you like it."

"I saw you," he said. "A few weeks back. Coming out of the boarding house."

"We'd just arrived in town," she said, obviously recalling it as well.

"Then I saw you again coming out of T. Emmett Rice's office."

She looked at him, nervously waiting for more.

"This is a nice place," he offered.

"It will be when the roof stops trying to drown us," she said with a weak smile.

"What I was thinking is, I have part of Saturday and all of Sunday each week. I could pretty much do whatever you need doing."

Staring at her glass, she nodded slowly. "You said you work in a mine?"

"Yes, ma'am."

"That must be hard."

"Yes, ma'am. It is."

"Are you not too tired on your days off?"

"Tired of the mine. This sort of work would be different. It'd be good."

"Do you have a family?" she asked hesitantly.

He shook his head as he stirred the stew. "I don't have anyone." He took another bite and watched her reach for a biscuit out of the corner of his eye. She tore it in two. She set half down and tore the other half in two before nibbling on a piece of it. He took another bite of his stew and then another as she eviscerated the biscuit. Obviously, she wasn't hungry, she just needed something to do.

Rebecca stepped back into the kitchen, followed by her little brother. "There's three leaks in our room," she announced.

"There *are* three leaks," Mrs. Carter corrected. "So get bowls, please."

Rebecca looked aggravated. "The rain got on the bed."

"Get the bowls for now, please, and I'll see to it in a minute."

Rebecca flicked another suspicious glance Jeremy's way before she went to get bowls. Her little brother stayed in the doorway and then followed her back out again. Jeremy recalled the black eye on the boy the day he'd first seen them.

"Do you have tools for what you need done?" he asked. "I probably should get started on the roof at first light."

She took a moment to reply. "I think so. April May gathered a good amount of supplies and hired a boy to cut wood shingles." She paused. "Do you know April May?"

"Yes, ma'am. Known her a long time. She's a nice lady."

"She and Cessie have been a godsend." She paused before adding, "I never had family like them."

"What about your father?" When her blue-gray eyes widened in alarm, he felt bad. Emmett had mentioned she and her father had been estranged. "Sorry, I shouldn't have asked."

"No, it's fine," she said quickly. "My father and I—"

"No, I understand," he said when she faltered.

"Will you excuse me for a moment?" She pushed back in her chair and rose. "I should see about those leaks."

He started to stand, but she was already in motion. If she allowed him anywhere near her after this, he had to start remembering his damned manners.

Lizzie made it to the safety of the hall before she pressed her back to the wall with her hands crisscrossed against her chest. There was a man in her house—a handsome one, at that. Offering to help. Had she accepted?

She inhaled and blew out her breath as she moved on, attempting to look normal.

Jake played with his toy soldiers on the rug as Lizzie pushed the bed clear of the leak. Rebecca stood with her arms folded tightly, frowning. "Why is he having supper here?"

"Because he hadn't eaten," Lizzie replied lightly as she stripped off the damp bedspread and blanket underneath.

"I'm also going to invite him to spend the night in the guest room. I don't know if he will, but if he does, I expect you to remember your manners. He's going to fix our roof."

"You said we couldn't afford to pay someone," Rebecca accused.

"We can't. But he offered to help anyway."

"He's doing it just to be nice?" Rebecca's voice was filled with doubt.

Lizzie stopped and looked at her. "Sometimes people do things just to be nice."

"Cessie and April May," Rebecca said. "They're the only ones I ever knew."

"And how old are you?"

Rebecca pursed her lips.

"Let's just be grateful," Lizzie said. "And friendly. I don't think that's too much to ask."

"If you ask me, I think he's here because he *likes* you. I saw him look at you in town and I could tell."

"You saw him in town?"

"Yes. And he *stared* at you. You said it was rude to stare."

Lizzie turned away and patted the sheet, which was dry, then she picked up a folded blanket and shook it out. "Help me with this, please."

"I don't think he should stay here," Rebecca stated as she walked to the other side of the bed. She pulled the blanket straight.

"He's going to help us, Rebecca."

Jake placed a bowl on the floor to catch a leak and then adjusted it. "I think we're going to need a bigger one," he said.

"Well, we're about out of bowls," Lizzie replied. "But"—

she looked at her daughter—"we're about to have the roof fixed. And that is a very good thing. Right?"

Rebecca folded her arms again.

When Lizzie went back into the kitchen, Mr. Sheffield had washed and dried the dishes. "Oh, you didn't have to—"

"That was the best supper I've had in a long time," he said, setting the dish towel down. "It was the least I could do."

Lizzie felt warmth creep into her face and so she walked to the stove and put the kettle on to boil.

"Would you like me to start a fire?" he asked.

The rain had chilled the air and the constant drips made it seem colder. "Yes. Thank you."

He went to the hearth and laid a fire, noticing how old the wood was. It would burn fast and there wasn't much of it. He commented that unless more had been chopped, he'd need to do it soon. It wasn't until he struck a match and lit the kindling that she spoke again.

"Mr. Sheffield—" He stood and turned toward her, his expression one of concern. Because he thought she was going to dismiss him. She *felt* it and it gave her a strange sense of control.

"Ma'am?"

"We have a guest room you're welcome to use." She felt her face heat. "When you visit to . . . help."

He nodded. "That'd be good."

"It would probably be best if we keep that between ourselves," she added haltingly. "People might misunderstand."

"I wouldn't say anything," he replied earnestly. "Not ever. You have my word."

She nodded, avoiding his gaze.

"That meal was really good. Worth fixing the roof for."

The thought was so preposterous she nearly laughed, and he smiled in return. Something about his smile, about the way the lines formed at his eyes, made her heart lurch. "You needn't call me ma'am. I'm Lizzie."

He nodded. "Jeremy."

He extended his hand, offering a handshake, and she placed her hand in his. His hand was strong, the skin rough. The contact caused a tingly sensation up her spine.

"It's really nice to meet you," he said.

"It's nice to meet you, too," she managed. He released her hand and she turned away, anxious for some business to attend to. As she scalded the teapot, she heard him taking his seat again. Lightning flashed and she glanced out the window.

"It'll clear up tomorrow," he said.

"I hope so," she said without turning around. "I'm nearly out of containers to catch the leaks." She put up the dishes he'd cleaned and then poured boiling water from kettle to pot, glad for the activity.

"So, where did you come from?" he asked.

She stiffened. "The . . . Midwest." *Oh Lord.* She cringed at the sound of her voice. She tried to collect her thoughts as she set the kettle back down. "Outside Chicago." When she turned to face him, she had the distinct feeling he knew she was lying. "And you? Are you from this area?"

He nodded. "Born and bred."

She needed to get *him* talking because she was the worst fibber in the entire world. "What's it like to work in a mine?"

His expression changed. It was as if his vitality drained from him. "Dark and cold."

She wondered why he did it. The sisters had mentioned the surfeit of jobs for men. There were ranches and farms, big operations that required a lot of labor. Mining was also a big industry, but certainly not the only one.

"This dripping," he continued. "I hear it all the time."

"What do you mean?"

"It's wet deep in the earth. The walls are white sometimes."

"White?"

"Because it's so wet. I guess it's mold of some kind. It's like nothing you've ever seen."

She turned back and prepared the tray, then carried it to the table and sat. "May I ask . . . why you do it?" she asked as they both readied their tea.

"Long story," he hedged.

It was apparent he didn't want to discuss his reasons—whatever they were.

"I imagine you have a few of those," he added, glancing up at her.

Touché. "A few," she admitted.

"I grew up on a farm."

She looked at him.

"I don't know that I thought about it as a really good life at the time, but it was. I see it now."

"It was a good place to grow up?"

He nodded. "It was. It is. You won't be sorry you came here."

She smiled. "I really like the people I've met so far."

"There's some interesting ones, that's for sure."

"Besides the Blue sisters?" she asked with an affectionate smile.

"You bet. There's lots." He leaned back in his chair. For most of the next hour, he spoke of local residents, and there were some interesting characters. There was a wealthy rancher who'd married a woman doctor who'd come to town to try to save the life of a man who had been shot in the head. And his life *had* been saved. There were cowboys and professional gamblers and a clan of dark outcasts, the Lindleys, who enjoyed causing trouble.

There was a group of men who called themselves the wise men's circle, who got together to play poker once a month at Miss Julia's Teahouse, although they didn't drink tea. The group, consisting of Emmett; Jules Gunderson, the telegraph operator who had one leg shorter than the other; Joseph Schultz, the beefy man who owned the livery; and the Reverend Thompson, a rather handsome man in his forties with long white hair and a pleasant baritone voice, were some of the regulars. "I think your father used to play with them," Jeremy recalled.

She averted her gaze. "That does sound familiar," she murmured, although her tone sounded unconvincing. She had no practice at lying. Not with words, anyway. She'd deceived Ethan with every bit of money she'd managed to stash in order to get away from him, but she'd learned not to speak around him at all, unless it was absolutely necessary.

"Reverend Thompson's *friend* came and took over the church choir a while back and that caused a big controversy because his friend is a lady. She's about his age, hair about the color of yours, and they have a real *close* relationship. People know because they both live in town and she's at the parsonage at all hours. It caused a lot of talk at first. Some people even wanted to kick him from the pulpit. They didn't, though."

Cessie and April May had told her about some of the same people, but it was interesting hearing of them from another perspective. She knew the lady was named Carlotta "Lottie" Lowe and that she'd studied music in New York. She'd performed opera, and played the violin beautifully.

"Good enough to break your heart when you listen," April May had declared.

"That is the truth," Cessie had seconded. "And, honey, not only can she play, but she comes up with these songs that . . . well, they aren't even really songs. They're classical pieces by Bach and Beethoven and some others I never even heard of. But instead of them being played by an orchestra, which we don't have, she teaches the choir to sing the various parts. It's beautiful."

"Cessie and April May mentioned her," Lizzie told Jeremy. "Have you heard the choir perform?"

"Not really a churchgoer."

"I thought we'd go tomorrow with Cessie."

"You'll meet a lot of folks that way."

The fire had died down and she needed to check on the children. It probably was time to call it a night. "Shall I show you to your room?"

"Sure."

She rose and took the lead, and he followed. The door to the children's room was shut, but she heard them playing inside. She stopped outside the spare room, having lit the lamp earlier. The room had nothing but a narrow bed, a floor lamp, a chair, and a wardrobe, plus there was a small hearth and a filled wood box. "Please make yourself at home, and if there's anything you need—"

"I'll be fine."

"Then I'll see you in the morning." She quickly turned and left.

It was a good feeling to step into the children's room. Even with the bed askew, it was a cheerful room, and Jake and Rebecca had already changed into their nightclothes. She smiled to see their game. It combined most of their toys—his army men, her battered doll, blocks, and sock puppets. "Bedtime," Lizzie said as she walked over to dim one of the lamps. "Put the toys up, please."

Jake willingly complied, but Rebecca resisted, as usual.

"Remember, we're going to church with Cessie tomorrow," she reminded them. "So we'll get an early start and we'll have lunch with them."

"Will *he* come, too?" Rebecca asked.

Lizzie gave her a look of exasperation. "No. *Mr. Sheffield* is going to work on the roof. He said his supper was the best he's had in a long time and it was worth fixing the roof for. Now, come on. Into bed." They complied and Lizzie tucked Jake in first. "I don't think we should mention that Mr. Sheffield is going to stay here on occasion," she said to both. "All right?"

Jake nodded, while Rebecca pursed her lips in disapproval.

"He's doing us a great favor, but people might not understand."

"I don't understand," Rebecca murmured under her breath.

It was clearly heard, as was Lizzie's exasperated sigh. She walked around the bed, tucked her daughter in, and kissed her good night.

"Will you stay here until we go to sleep?" Rebecca asked. "Jake likes that."

Lizzie grinned. "Of course I will." She walked over to the rocking chair in the room, another gift from her guardian angels, and sat. For all Rebecca's resistance to bedtime, she dropped off to sleep nearly as quickly as Jake. The steady patter of rain helped, as did the oil lamp flickering at its lowest level.

* * *

Stepping back into the hall, Lizzie looked at the closed door to the guest room before going into her own. With the newly sewn bedspread and curtains in a floral print of sage and deep blues, fat jars of wildflowers, and a lovely painting Cessie had given her, it was finally beginning to feel like her room. It hadn't, at first. It had felt as if she were an intruder. Of course, she wasn't an intruder; she was an imposter.

All of a sudden, she felt edgy, almost caged. She turned up the lamp on her dresser and began to pace. It was astonishing that there was a man—a stranger, really—in their house. It was astonishing he'd shown up offering to help, this handsome stranger. She pressed the palms of her hands together and brought the tips of her fingers to her lips, trying to control the *feelings* coursing through her.

She stopped before the mirror above her vanity and peered at her image, wondering if she looked as different as she suddenly felt. Staring into the wavy glass, she decided she did. It was because Lizzie was so utterly different from Pauline. Pauline had been frightened every day of her life. She'd been timid and cowed, while Lizzie had the courage to begin a whole new life. In fact, to make that life exactly what she wanted and needed. She was not a child, she was a woman who would make her own way, even if that way was wildly unconventional. She was . . . "Strong," she whispered, trying out the word.

She wondered how Jeremy saw her. Ethan had never thought she was pretty. Once he'd stated she was "appealing enough for a common man," although he'd often called her twitchy. Twitchy as a rabbit. Of course, he was the one who'd made her twitchy, she thought resentfully. She shook her head and tried to force Ethan from her mind. She didn't want him there anymore. There were new things to focus on—survival, the children, the cottage.

Jeremy Sheffield.

A strange yearning filled her as she recalled Jeremy's dark silhouette in her doorway. *Well, ma'am, there's other ways to pay a man.*

She shivered and exhaled slowly. This feeling was beyond strange since she'd loathed intimacy with Ethan. She'd hated him touching her in any way. Worst of all was when he attempted to kiss her. Anything else she could block from her mind. She could close her eyes and pretend he was someone else, but a kiss was too intimate.

A kiss—

She pictured Jeremy's lips and slightly grizzled chin, and pictured her hands slipping slowly around his back. A powerful warmth emanated from her pores. For the first time she could remember, she wanted a man. A man who was not her husband.

Was it wrong? Pauline had never felt this way, but she was Lizzie now. No longer would she live with the shame Pauline had endured. She slipped her hands down her body, caressing herself. Was this what Jeremy Sheffield wanted to do? There was no doubt about it; Lizzie was brazen, maybe even shameless. She enjoyed the thought.

Jeremy's arms were folded behind his head as he stared out, lost in thought. The knock at the door surprised him. Before he could get up and put his clothes back on, the door was opened a few inches.

"May I come in?" Lizzie asked quietly.

For a moment, he gawked. Then he feared she'd come to ask him to leave. "Sure," he said as he sat, although it sounded more like a question than an answer. The door opened and Lizzie was standing before him, wearing a worn, gray cotton dressing robe. She was unclothed underneath and her hair was down. His jaw went slack. He needed to speak, to say something, but he couldn't think of a word to say.

Leaving the door open, she started forward, although she looked nervous enough to turn and bolt. His instinct was to get up, but he didn't have a stitch of clothing on. Did she want him to leave?

"May I sit a moment?" she asked.

"Of course."

She perched on the side of his bed, facing him, only a few feet away. He noticed the rise and fall of her chest as she breathed, and knew she was anxious. He couldn't stand the suspense any longer. "Do you want me to go?"

She looked taken aback. "No. I wanted to say thank you for . . . coming and offering your help."

It was his turn to feel speechless. "I'm glad to do it."

"I know this is unusual," she said breathily. "You may think me terrible for asking."

"I won't," he said quickly.

"It's just that I've been dead in a lot of ways for a long time now," she said quietly. "I think . . ." Her gaze dropped to his lips. "I'd like to remember, or maybe to know, what a kiss feels like."

A *kiss*? He wondered if he really knew how to kiss. He'd bedded a lot of women, but a kiss? And she wanted to know what it felt like from him? "I'm not sure I'm any good at it," he admitted.

She shrugged delicately and he felt moved, almost shaken by her vulnerability. He leaned forward slowly and pressed a kiss to her lips. Her lips were soft and warm, a perfect fit for his. So this was how a kiss was supposed to feel. He hadn't known it was so sweet a thing. He pulled back slightly. "I think that's how it's done," he said softly.

"I like it," she whispered.

"I liked it, too." She rose gracefully and started from the

room. She turned back to him briefly at the door, and she was so beautiful, she stole his breath.

"Good night," she said.

"'Night," he echoed. He stared at the door long after she'd shut it. He could still smell her soft scent and feel her presence. It was good. It was so much better than being alone.

Lizzie walked back to her room, stunned by the boldness she'd just exhibited. It was so completely unlike her. *No*, it was unlike Pauline—she needed to stop dwelling on the person she'd been in another life. And it *had* been another life.

She slipped off her robe, turned out the lamp, and got into bed, reliving the kiss. How peculiar that the simple touching of lips could cause so many sensations and reactions. How peculiar too, that a man was sleeping just down the hall. A man she didn't even know. Was it utterly irresponsible?

She stared at the ceiling, recalling every word that had been spoken. If her instincts could be trusted, she liked him and believed him. She trusted him. Good Lord, she'd gone to his room in a state of near undress and kissed him. A shivery thrill passed through her and she rolled onto her side and curled up.

Chapter Fourteen

Lizzie opened her eyes at the sound of the rooster crowing and reveled in the feeling of having slept well. She remembered the kiss and exhaled slowly, fighting a wave of excitement that made her stomach tighten. She sat up and it occurred to her how remarkable it was to feel so awake, so present. Poor Pauline had suffered from insomnia, but not Lizzie. Being Lizzie was better all the way around.

She washed and dressed and went to make breakfast. It was a surprise to see the fire already going. So was the fire in the stove. At the sound of a thump overhead, she realized Jeremy was already working, despite a persistent light rain.

Rebecca and Jake appeared in their nightclothes and ate a breakfast of fried eggs and toasted sourdough bread with butter and jam.

"Is it ever going to stop raining?" Rebecca complained.

"Probably not," Lizzie replied breezily. "It will rain from now on. Every day, every minute."

Jake giggled.

"Very funny," Rebecca said grumpily.

"Can we make gingerbread men today?" Jake asked. "We made gingerbread men last time it rained."

It had rained many, many times since the long-ago afternoon they'd made gingerbread men. It was funny what a child's mind clung to. "Not today," Lizzie said. "I don't have the right ingredients and we're going to go to church with Cessie. Remember?"

"Can we get the ingredients sometime?" Rebecca asked.

"Yes, we can. I look forward to baking. In fact, I hope to sell my baked goods in town. What do you think of that?"

Rebecca nodded thoughtfully. "I think it's a good idea." A second later, hammering on the roof made her look up and frown.

"I'm going to start a list of everything I need," Lizzie said. "If you'll please let me use some paper and a pencil."

Jake hopped up. "I'll get it."

"Finish your breakfast first."

"I am finished," he said as he dashed off.

"I'm finished, too," Rebecca said.

"Then get dressed and feed the chickens."

"I know," Rebecca replied testily. She got up and carried her plate and cup to the sink, sulking the entire way. Lizzie watched, disturbed by how greatly her daughter disliked Jeremy simply because he was a man, because Rebecca distrusted all men. Perhaps that distrust could be turned around in time, but what if it couldn't?

What she should have done was to find a way to escape after the first time Ethan had raised his hand to her. Rebecca had been an infant at the time. Had she left him then, Rebecca would have grown up not knowing how cruel a man could be. Of course, Jake wouldn't be here.

Lizzie got up from the table, put on her coat, and went outside. She walked around front and backed away from the house until she could see Jeremy on the roof. At least, she could see his dark coat and hat. "Mr. Sheffield?"

He looked up and took the nails from between his lips. "Thought we talked about that."

He was so handsome, the sight of him made her feel shy and self-conscious. How had she ever worked up the nerve to go to his room? "Breakfast is ready."

He nodded. "I'll come down."

As she went back inside, she was painfully aware of the pounding of her heart. When Jeremy came in, his male presence filled the room, and it was surprising how much she liked it. His company was so utterly different from Ethan's. "You got started early," she remarked as she poured him a cup of hot coffee.

"Always do." He took off his gloves, hat, and coat and accepted the cup of coffee. "Thanks. It smells good."

"Sugar and milk are on the table," she reminded him.

"I take it black."

"How do you like your eggs?"

"Any way. I'm not particular."

She fried eggs and then carried the plate to him.

"Thank you," he said.

She smiled and went to get herself a cup of coffee.

"I see you're making a grocery list," he commented.

She came back to her place and sat, glancing over the list she'd begun. Sugars, flour, baking powder, cinnamon, ginger, cream of tartar, milk, cream, and butter. "I have a plan to bake things and sell them in town," she said.

"That's a good idea."

She looked up and studied him a moment. "Do you really think so?"

"I do. I haven't tasted anything like this," he said, hefting a piece of bread. "I'd buy it every day."

It was pleasing to hear. Other than leaving Indiana, she'd never made a decision or taken action on her own. The thought of generating an income, of acquiring true independence, was thrilling. "I'm glad you think so." She paused. "We're going to church soon and Cessie mentioned staying for lunch, so I thought I'd put the stew in the oven for whenever you want it."

"Sounds good."

"We may not return until midafternoon. Do you think you'll be here when we get back?" she asked, purposely looking down at the list.

"I'll be here until dark. Or after. I mean, I could—"

She nodded rapidly and blushed hotly as she experienced the feeling again. The squeezy feeling in her stomach. She concentrated on breathing normally. *"Mm-hmm."*

"All right, then," he said.

Chapter Fifteen

The air was cooler but the weather had cleared before Lizzie and the children started for Cessie and April May's, and it was a pleasant walk along the fragrant, wooded path. Leaves, most still dark green but some beginning to change color, sparkled with raindrops. When they came upon the farmyard, they saw April May hauling a wheelbarrow out to the mules at the same moment the scent of baking ham assailed their senses from the house.

"Can we go see the donkeys?" Rebecca asked.

"Yes, but don't be long," Lizzie replied. "Cessie may be ready to leave."

The children ran off and Lizzie continued to the house. She knocked lightly as she stepped into the side door to the kitchen to see Cessie removing a pie from the oven. The scent of baked apples filled the house. "'Morning," she said.

"Good morning," Cessie said as she set the pie next to another. She looked at Lizzie. "Oh, honey. Don't you look pretty!"

Lizzie's dress was a floral print and one of only three decent dresses that she owned. "Thank you. So do you."

Cessie quickly removed her apron. "The children out back?"

"Yes, ma'am."

"They're about as taken with the mules as with Sister, and I fear one's about as good an influence as the other."

Lizzie laughed. "It smells so good in here," she said as she came farther in.

"There's not much that smells better than a baked ham," Cessie said as she pulled off a lid to stir the contents of a pot. "Unless maybe it's apple pie."

"Is there anything I can do to help?"

"No, it's done. I'll just leave everything in the oven to keep warm until we get home. You want a piece of sugared crust?"

Lizzie saw the plate Cessie had no doubt prepared for the children. She'd rolled out the bit of pie dough not used in the crust and cut fanciful shapes, then sugared and baked them. Lizzie selected a piece and tried it. *"Mmm,"* she murmured.

"You look . . . happy this morning," Cessie commented. "I was going to say bright eyed and bushy tailed, but it's more than that. You look happy."

April May walked in with her purposeful step, followed by the children. "I imagine she is," April May said slyly.

Cessie looked from April May to Lizzie, as Lizzie looked from April May to Rebecca, who looked decidedly guilty.

"I'm thinking I might just go to church myself," April May stated. "Give me two minutes to change my clothes."

"You're going to church," Cessie repeated in astonishment.

"Why not? It's an awful pretty morning and I have a feeling there might be some interesting conversation on the way."

Cessie gave her a look. "Oh, now that's a good reason to go."

"Aren't you always trying to get me to go?"

"Yes, but for the right reasons."

April May shrugged. "You know what they say. The Lord works in mysterious ways," she said as she walked off. "Don't you have something to give the children?"

"Yes, I do," Cessie said to the children. "Follow me."

Lizzie watched everyone exit and then went out to the front porch. Obviously, Rebecca had mentioned Jeremy—which she'd been planning to do herself. Not that she'd worked out exactly what she was going to say. She sat on the porch swing, knowing it was time she figured it out.

Rebecca rushed out to her with a rag doll, all guilt replaced by pure excitement. "Mama, look." The rather shapeless doll she held had a painted-on face and yellow hair. "And look," Rebecca exclaimed, tipping the doll over. The doll's skirt flipped down, revealing another figure on the opposite end, a smiling Aunt Jemima figure. "I named *her* Polly and"—she flipped back to the yellow-haired doll—"her, Daisy. Because her hair reminds me of daisies."

"Or daffodils," April May suggested as she stepped outside, having put on a skirt instead of her dungarees.

Rebecca made a face. "I never heard the name Daffodil."

"Don't mean you cain't use it. I kind of think she looks like a daffodil."

Rebecca studied the doll's face. "I'll think about it." She looked up at her mother. "Jake got a present, too. A zoetrope. Although Cessie said we could share both, if we wanted, and the zoetrope is like magic, Mama. Wait till you see it." Rebecca hugged the doll to her as she ran back inside.

April May waggled her eyebrows at Lizzie. "Mr. Sheffield, huh?"

"All right," Cessie called. "Let's go."

Lizzie quickly started toward the wagon, which was already hitched. "You heard the lady. It's time to go."

"Uh-huh," April May said as she followed.

The children rode in the back of the wagon, happily playing with their toys, while Lizzie sat between April May, who was driving, and Cessie. She'd told them about Jeremy—most of it, anyway. She'd explained that he'd shown up and offered to help after T. Emmett Rice had mentioned the state of the cottage.

"Out of the sheer goodness of his heart, huh?" April May asked.

"I'll fix him meals and send him home with food."

"Well, I'm tickled to hear it," Cessie said. "This will be good for him. Bless his heart."

Lizzie looked at her curiously.

"He's had a hard time of it," Cessie explained. "He had a wonderful family once, and then his younger sister, Jenny, drowned when she was just at the bloom of womanhood. I guess she was sixteen?"

April May nodded.

"She was a sweet girl," Cessie continued. "You don't think someone like that is going to be snatched away so suddenly, and it was a strange accident. It destroyed that family. Jeremy's mama took it so hard," she said with a slow shake of her head. "So hard. I think the shock made her sick and she was gone not even a year after. The poor father. He was trying his best, but we had a serious drought two or three years running. With the death of his daughter and then his wife, and the drought ruining crops, he started drinking. The talk was, he'd taken out a loan when the crops first failed and then . . . well, he just couldn't recuperate."

"Jeremy tried to hold everything together," April May said in an uncharacteristically solemn tone.

Cessie glanced behind to make sure the children weren't listening. "But Rodney, Jeremy's daddy, hanged himself," she whispered.

Lizzie felt sick.

"After that," April May said, "Jeremy wasn't the same. He took it so hard. Withdrew. Went to work in the mines— the worst mining operation, at that. Number Six." She shook her head. "Ought to be called six sixty-six, and that's not just my opinion; everyone says so. Hell, I been in there myself."

"Sister," Cessie scolded. "Language. And on a Sunday when the children can hear you."

"I beg everyone's pardon," April May said loudly. "You too, God."

Rebecca giggled and Cessie shook her head and sighed in exasperation. "I think it seems like a mighty good step," Cessie said a moment later. "That he's willing to reach out and help you and the children. It'll be good for him."

"I hope so," Lizzie said quietly. "I like him."

"I like him, too," April May said. "Always have. Just out of curiosity, what'cha know about coal mines?"

"Nothing, really. He said it was dark and cold."

"That's an understatement," April May said wryly.

"Sister goes down there sometimes to rescue the mules they can't do anything with. They call her the mule lady."

"Dark and cold doesn't even begin to tell the story," April May said with a grim shake of her head.

The church service was short and the choir was wonderful, both of which Lizzie appreciated. They were walking

out when she was tapped on the shoulder, and turned to see
Fiona.

"'Member me? Fiona Jones."

"Yes, of course. The boarding house."

"Hello, Fiona, dear," Cessie said, patting her arm as she
walked by. Jake held Cessie's hand and Rebecca followed,
still holding her doll. April May had exited early and was
chatting with someone in the courtyard.

"Hey, Cessie." Fiona grinned at Lizzie when Cessie and
the children had walked on. "She looks like the grandmother she always should have been."

"They're wonderful. I'm so grateful you sent us that way."

"Funny how things work out. Hey, listen, I was wondering if you want to head out to the Martin farm with me next
week and visit my friend Em Medlin. You'll like her. In fact,
you kind of remind me of her. Might be a nice diversion
from working on the cottage."

So, everyone in town knew she was installed in the
cottage. My, but it *was* a small town.

"The kids can go too, of course. We'll have lunch and
spend a few hours visiting, jaw jacking. My aunt Doll lives
there, too. It's always a real nice time."

"I'd like that," Lizzie replied enthusiastically. Ethan had
kept her cut off from other people, but she was in control
now, and it would be wonderful having a friend or two.

"We shoot for Tuesday if it's not raining. Start about ten
thirty? That sound good?"

Lizzie nodded. "Yes. Can I bring something?"

"Oh Lord, no. Bring food into Doll's kitchen? She cooks
for the outfit."

"C'mon, Fiona," a man said as he approached with a
fussy two-year-old. "Let's get."

"That's my husband, Wayne, and our fusspot, who is

needing a nap in a big way. I'll see you Tuesday," she said with a gentle squeeze to Lizzie's arm. "I'll pick you up."

Lizzie nodded again and Fiona followed after her husband and son, greeting others as she went. Lizzie followed too, returning the smiles and nods of those who watched with unabashed interest. She saw no hostility or even reserve; it was more avid curiosity and perhaps even a little shame. *You should feel shame*, she thought, *if you treated Papa poorly.* It took a moment to realize that she felt indignant on behalf of a man she'd never even met, and then it occurred to her how much Lionel would have enjoyed that.

Chapter Sixteen

"Mama, wait," Rebecca complained. "Why are you walking so fast?"

Lizzie made herself slow down. "Am I?"

"Yes!"

It was true. In her eagerness to get back to the cottage, she'd adopted a too brisk pace despite her hands being full. Cessie had insisted she bring ham and a pie back for Jeremy. It was just that everything had taken longer than expected. Church, visiting after church, the ride back, and then lunch. Not that it all hadn't been nice. It had. Very nice. But she couldn't help her eagerness to get back home. "Sorry."

Jake stuck his zoetrope to his eye as he walked.

"Play with that when you get home," Lizzie rejoined. "I don't want you to trip and fall."

He dropped it to his side with a half pout. "I wouldn't fall."

"Honey, this isn't level ground. You might easily catch your foot and fall. And break your toy."

Rebecca was turning her doll over and over, black face

to white and back again. "Do you think he'll still be there?" she asked without looking at her mother.

"He said he would," Lizzie replied. "That's why Cessie sent these things."

"'Sweetly sings the donkey,'" Jake began to sing.

Lizzie joined in the song and then Rebecca did, too. When the cottage came into view, Jeremy was nowhere to be seen. He was not on the roof and there were no sounds of work being done. Lizzie's dismay was immediate and acute. The instant she heard the chopping of wood, her heart leapt, although it was followed by an inner warning that she shouldn't have been *that* disappointed, or *this* relieved.

They entered the house through the front door and the children went to change their clothes. Lizzie hurried to the kitchen, set the food down, and then went to find Jeremy. He was around back, cutting wood shingles. He saw her and stopped, although his gaze flicked over her appreciatively.

"We're back," Lizzie said needlessly.

"How was it?"

"It was very enjoyable. Cessie sent some food for you. For later in the week."

He looked puzzled for a moment. "So she, uh, knows about—"

"That you're helping," Lizzie said.

He brushed his hands off. "That was nice of her."

Lizzie wondered if she should add something more, something about how the subject had come up when they'd both agreed to keep it private.

"We're out of shingles, so I cut some more," he said.

The *we* in the sentence sent a thrill pulsing through her, but he looked tired. "You should stop for the day. Please."

He nodded slowly, looking let down. Did he think she was dismissing him? Asking him to leave?

"I'm almost at a stopping point. It won't be finished today, but I got the major leaks fixed."

"April May sent a deck of cards," Lizzie said with a shy smile, anxious to convey she wasn't asking him to leave. "She asked if I had one, I said no, so she sent one. Although I don't know any card games." The smile that transformed his face proved she'd been right.

"You don't play poker?" he teased.

"I couldn't play a game of poker if my life depended on it."

"I can teach you. If you want."

Her smile broadened and she nodded before starting back to the house.

The fire in the hearth crackled as Lizzie set her dish towel aside and turned back to watch the construction of the house of cards in progress. It was Rebecca's turn, and she was moving slowly and carefully to place two cards. The parallel struck Lizzie. Rebecca's approach to the game was similar to her approach to Jeremy. Distrustful, wary, aware everything could suddenly crumble before her with the lightest touch. But maybe Rebecca had the right idea, and it was she who was wrong.

How queer it was that, only a few days ago, she couldn't have been convinced a man would show up and turn her head. She'd had no idea that one's heart rate could increase from attraction. From fear, yes—but from attraction? She'd had no idea. Jeremy made her feel something she couldn't define exactly, but she liked it. Still, she'd only just met him—and here he was in her home with her children. Not only that, but she'd kissed him. She'd gone to his room dressed in a robe, her hair loose—he must have thought the same of her morals—and she'd kissed him. And, worse, she wanted to do it again.

Rebecca placed the cards successfully and began backing away, but then they toppled. A collective *aw* was uttered all around and Lizzie was quick to smile sympathetically, although she circumspectly watched Rebecca for her reaction. "It's time for bed anyway," she said.

Rebecca pouted. "Oh, Mama, just one more game."

The words were good to hear. "No, ma'am," was the answer anyway. "Another time. It's past eight, so go get ready for bed."

As usual, Jake popped up and went cheerfully while Rebecca went grudgingly. Lizzie sat back down as Jeremy got the cards back in order. "That was a good idea," she said. "They enjoyed it."

"You want to play another round of five card stud?"

He'd written down the hands in the order of how they ranked, and they'd played for matchsticks. "For matchsticks again?"

"Sure," he replied lightly. "Then maybe the winner gets something else."

The muscles in her stomach tightened. "Like what?" she asked as she rose again to get the pile of matchsticks.

"Oh, I don't know. What do you want?"

"It was your idea," she hedged as she came back to the table. She sat and divided the matchsticks. "What sort of thing were you talking about?"

"How 'bout a . . . kiss," he said quietly.

She hoped she looked calmer than she was feeling. She couldn't even look directly at him. "Deal."

"You mean 'it's a deal'?"

"I mean deal the cards, Mr. Sheffield."

He grinned and shuffled. "I'll do that, Miz Carter."

His utterance of the name was a reminder that, to some degree, this was make-believe. *She* was make-believe. Or was she? The funny thing was that she felt like Lizzie Greenway Carter as much as she'd ever felt like Pauline Ray. She had more of a sense of belonging here in Green Valley than she'd ever had in her entire life.

He began dealing. "You didn't say what you wanted if you win."

She picked up her cards without reply, but a smile played on her lips.

"Oh, I see," he said. "You want to think about it awhile. Is that it?"

She shrugged lightly and studied her cards. "Did you say four aces was a good hand?" she asked musingly. His smile was instant and glorious. It made her heart race. Oh yes. A heart rate could increase from sheer attraction.

"I think the lady likes to bluff. Although it might be worth losing just to find out what you want." He paused. "How many cards for you?"

Her gaze met his. "One, please."

He slid one over. "I sure hope it's not the fifth ace."

She laughed.

"Dealer takes two." He studied his cards a moment and then looked at her. "What's your bet?" She pushed two matchsticks in.

"I'll see your bet. Call."

She laid down her cards one at a time. An ace of spades. A three of diamonds. A six of hearts. A nine of hearts and a jack of clubs.

He blew out a breath. "Hard to beat that."

"I know. It's so pretty and colorful," she teased along

with him. When had Pauline ever teased? Never. But she wasn't Pauline anymore. She was Elizabeth Anne Greenway Carter. This wasn't make-believe. She was really sitting here in her kitchen in her home that had belonged to her father, with this handsome man who was helping her and who made her heart beat fast. She had excellent instincts and she frequently laughed.

"I fold," he said, tossing his hand face down. "What'd you win?"

"I'm still thinking about that." She began to rise. "But, for now, I should check on the chil—" She broke off as she made a mad swipe for his cards, scooping them up and backing away as he laughingly grabbed after them. He had two sevens. She gave him a look. "You can't fold after you bet, and you don't quit with a winning hand. Or did I misunderstand that?"

"Okay," he conceded. "I win."

"Are you going to tuck us in?" Rebecca asked from the doorway.

"I'll be right there," Lizzie said calmly, despite the excitement she felt. She set the cards down. "Did you say good night to Mr. Sheffield?"

"Good night," Rebecca said sullenly as she turned away.

"'Night," he returned, as if he hadn't noticed her tone.

Lizzie held back a smile as she shook her head at him, then left to see to the children.

Thirty minutes later, Lizzie walked back into an empty kitchen. She'd indulged the children with two stories, so perhaps she'd taken a little longer than expected, but she was disappointed to see that he'd gone to bed. Although he had worked hard every day for a week, so she was being utterly unfair. She packed a basket full of things for him to take, turned out the wall lamp, and went to her room, but she'd only removed her shoes when there was a light knock on the door.

It was him, of course. "I just wanted to say good night," he said quietly so as to not disturb the children.

"I thought you'd gone to bed," she replied just as softly.

"No. I was outside. I'm going to my room now."

If only she'd noticed he was outside. They could have played longer. "There's a basket in the kitchen for you. Don't forget it tomorrow."

"I won't."

"It's small enough pay," she said sheepishly.

"I liked being here. I even liked building the house of cards."

She smiled, grateful for the sentiment.

"Well, good night," he said, stepping back.

"Your bet," she said impulsively. "I mean . . . you won the bet."

He stepped closer, but not all the way to her. He nodded slowly and then he leaned in and pressed a kiss to her cheek. The whiskers on his chin were rough, but they merely tickled, as gentle as the touch was. "I'll see you next week."

All she could do was nod. Her heart was in her throat.

Chapter Seventeen

September 17, Indianapolis, Indiana

Charles Ray was tallying columns in a ledger, but he couldn't get the same sum twice in a row. He was standing at the counter of the cooper shop, slumped over the book and getting more frustrated by the minute, when a middle-aged woman walked in. She wasn't an attractive woman. She was solidly built, her hair dark, her face plain, her lips and eyes both on the smallish side. He straightened and set his pencil aside, weary of calculations. He'd been adding one column for what seemed like an hour and it always netted a different sum. "Yes, ma'am?"

"Is Mr. Ray available to speak with?" she inquired.

"I am Mr. Ray."

"Mr. Ethan Ray?"

He hesitated because he loathed when everyone assumed Ethan was the man in charge. "Charles. Ethan is my brother, and we're partners in this establishment. Can I help you?"

"No, sir. It's a personal matter. Is Mr. Ethan Ray here?"

"He's here."

"Would you get him, please?"

Her expression hadn't changed one iota, which was to say she remained utterly expressionless. He wondered how much her expression would change if he smacked her upside the head. "Who can I say is calling?"

"Cynthia Perkins," she supplied. "From the Pinkerton Agency."

He drew back in surprise. "Pinkerton? As in detectives?"

"If you'd be so kind as to get your brother," she said curtly.

For several seconds he didn't budge, but she continued to peer at him until finally he relented. He found his brother overseeing the loading of a wagon. "Ethan," he called.

Ethan looked over at him with his typical scowl. "What?"

"Someone here to see you. A woman."

The loading was completed and the workers tipped their hats to the brothers before climbing on the wagon and driving away. Ethan wiped his hands on his apron as he walked closer. "Who is it?"

"From the Pinkerton Agency," Charles replied.

Ethan looked irritated. "I thought you said it was a *woman*."

"That's right. Name's Cynthia Perkins and she's one cold fish."

Ethan moved past his brother and walked into the small lobby, and Charles followed.

Cynthia looked around the shop as she waited. It was neat, sparsely decorated, and smelled of wood. It was interesting to observe the brothers walking in together. There was a resemblance between them, but the differences were clear to see, too. Ethan was the younger, but the leader. They both had thinning brown hair, although neither man was older than his midthirties. Neither was particularly attractive, but Ethan was the more attractive of the two. There was an arrogance about both of them, and there was something in their expressions, or something just beyond, that spoke of quick anger and an innate sense of entitlement.

Ethan stopped in front of her but didn't offer his hand. "I'm Ethan Ray."

"Cynthia Perkins from the Pinkerton Agency. I've come in response to your inquiry."

"I asked for a *detective*," he stated coldly.

"And here I am."

"A woman?" Ethan scoffed.

She didn't bat an eye because she'd heard it all before.

"Since when are there *women* detectives?"

"Since nearly the beginning, sir. Have you never heard of Kate Warne?"

"No. Who's she?"

"She was one of the best. Mr. Pinkerton relied heavily on her and claimed she never let him down. Nor have I, as a point of fact. Is there somewhere we could talk in private?"

He studied her a moment, flummoxed and agitated and not the least bit concerned with concealing his feelings. "And if I insist on a man for the job?"

"There are none currently available, but I'll certainly return to the office and report it, if that's your wish. Of course, with every day that passes, the trail grows colder."

"What experience do you have?" he challenged.

She smiled, but barely. "I should not have been sent had I lacked the necessary experience."

He huffed his displeasure, but led the way toward a private office. Charles, she noticed, didn't particularly care for this arrangement. She followed Ethan to a small office

where he motioned to a chair. She walked over and sat, and
only then did he round his desk and sit.

"So, how do we do this? What do you need to know?"

"I need facts. Details such as the date your wife left."

"It was a month ago. August seventeenth. A Friday."

"And you've heard nothing at all since?"

"No."

"Do you have a photograph of her and the children I
can use?"

"I have a picture of Pauline. It's ten years old, but it still
looks like her."

"I'll need it, but you'll get it back. I can write you a
receipt for it, if you wish."

He leaned forward menacingly. "It's not my wish." His
forearms rested on the table and his fists were clenched.
"I don't give a damn about it. Use it and then burn it, for all
I care. But find her."

"How old are the children?"

"Rebecca is eight. Jake is four."

"Did your wife leave any sort of letter or—"

"No. Nothing."

"Do you have any idea what mode of transportation she
employed?"

"No, I do not, but she didn't have any money, so I don't
see how she could have gone at all, much less stayed gone.
Which means somebody's got to be helping her. I'll tell you
one thing, when I do find out—" He left the rest of it
unsaid, but his malevolent scowl spoke volumes.

"Does she have family she might go to?"

"No. She was an only child and her folks were older.
They're long dead. There's no one. Don't you think I've
racked my brain for where she might be?"

"Where was she from originally?"

"Here! We're both from here."

"What about close friends?"

"Something wrong with your hearing? There is no one! I didn't allow her to waste time with worthless, gossiping females."

He was abrasive in the extreme, but certainly not the first she'd dealt with. Cynthia Perkins opened a small handbag, pulled out an envelope, and handed it to him. "It's our policy to establish our fees in advance. We have set hourly, daily, and weekly fees, whichever best works to your benefit, plus you'll pay all pertinent expenses I incur."

He narrowed his eyes and then opened the envelope and took out the form. Looking it over, he huffed in disgust. "I can't afford this."

"Those are our rates, sir, and they are non-negotiable. You should already have been informed of them."

"Well, that's when I thought a *man* was—"

"As I told you, sir—"

"I want a guarantee of some sort," he interrupted.

"A guarantee is not possible, but you know our reputation."

"Where will you even start? I'm not just going to throw away good money."

"I'll speak with neighbors and—"

"Like hell you will. I forbid it. You hear me? No one needs to know my business."

"That makes it considerably more difficult. I will have to note that limitation in the report."

"You saying you can't do anything?"

"No, I am not saying that. If I'm not allowed to speak with neighbors, family, or friends, I'll begin by going to the livery and the depot to see if someone remembers seeing your wife and children."

"No names. Don't give anybody any names. You got that?"

"I understand."

Ethan began scribbling on the form. "I will not pay for any services beyond six weeks." He handed the signed contract back to her. "Find her in that time or I'll find someone else."

She glanced over what he'd written and then put the contract back into her bag. "Her picture?"

Ethan pulled open a bottom drawer of the desk and took out a framed picture. He removed the daguerreotype from the frame and handed it to her.

Cynthia stood. "I'll be in touch regarding my progress."

"You do that."

"I can see myself out," she said, starting from the room.

He sat back in his chair, flabbergasted. "A goddamn woman detective," he muttered under his breath.

Chapter Eighteen

Lizzie sat in the front of the wagon holding RJ, Fiona's son, while Fiona drove. In the back, Rebecca and Jake sat looking out, their elbows perched on the side of the wagon and their chins resting on their forearms. The sky was nearly cloudless and the autumnal countryside was beautiful and colorful, with rolling hills and mountains in the distance no matter which way you looked. Indiana was different, flat land with what seemed miles of sky. It had been a pleasant ride.

"So Em moved here when she was twelve," Fiona said. She had effortlessly gone from one subject to another, oftentimes asking and then answering her own questions, although Lizzie didn't mind. Fiona was nothing if not entertaining.

"'Cause her folks passed. It was her uncle, Ben Martin, who went and fetched her and it started a real good, real close relationship. Unfortunately," Fiona said, stretching the word out, "Ben had a wife who had kind of a mean streak. I don't know. Em was only a kid, but Amy Martin, Ben's wife, resented her for showing up at all. And worse than her was Jimmy, Em's cousin. Mean as the day is long. The type that likes to torment anyone he can get away with tormenting. Well, he got Em in his sights. Made up an ugly story about her having a *thing* with the Lindleys. You know who they are?"

"I heard," Lizzie replied. They were a clan that lived nearby who were practically outlaws.

"Em's pretty as can be, so there was probably some jealousy involved too, but when she got to school, Jimmy had already poisoned everyone against her. They chanted things, said awful things, treated her like she had the pox." Fiona sighed. "You know I was never one to torment, but it will bother me until my dying day that I didn't try to stop it either. None of us did. Nobody befriended her."

Lizzie looked away, thinking that she and Em really did have some things in common.

"So, later Em goes off to college and . . . I don't remember exactly how it happened, but she got the attention of this rich, powerful man who owned a big hotel. He was not a nice man. In fact, he"—Fiona paused and glanced at Lizzie—"he kept her prisoner in his fancy hotel," she whispered. "For almost a year," she said in her regular voice. "And let's just say . . . he did what he wanted to with her," she finished in another whisper before nodding meaningfully. "Including, among other things, beating her black and blue from time to time."

Another thing she and Em had in common.

"Somehow, Em escaped. Now, you can't tell her I told you all this. I wouldn't tell most people, you know. But we're all going to be the best of friends, I just know it."

Lizzie smiled and nodded, hoping it was true.

"So she escaped and she got herself back home. I was the first to see her once she got here. She stayed at our

place and borrowed a dress so she could look presentable
to her uncle. 'Course, she didn't know her uncle had had a
fit of apoplexy while she was gone. Did I say she was gone
a couple of years? A long time. By the time she returned,
she was prettier than ever. You know, if I described her—
brown hair, brown eyes—she wouldn't sound that special,
but she is. You are, too. Nature was just better to some of us
than others."

"Oh, Fiona," Lizzie said.

"No, no, no. I'm not feeling sorry for myself. I may have
hated my red hair when I was a kid, but I'm fine with it
now. I'm content with my lot. Especially after growing
close with Em and learning all she's been through. Her
story does have a happy ending, though."

Lizzie shifted RJ, who was beginning to squirm.

"Hey, little man," Fiona said sharply, "we're almost
there, so you just rein in your wild horses."

Lizzie heard Rebecca giggle. She turned to look and
Rebecca was smiling, having heard the admonition. Lizzie
smiled at her and Rebecca winked back, which was funny
to see. April May had certainly been an influence on her
child.

"Em got home, and Ben was so happy to see her. Amy
was gone by then; she died before Em left," Fiona said,
speaking more rapidly. "And Em met this man. Tommy
Medlin. Oh, honey, Tommy is one bee-u-tiful man, so
handsome everybody used to call him Pretty Boy. He's got
dark hair, these blue, blue eyes, and he's sweet as can be,
besides. Oh, and just wait till you see the two of them together. You've never seen two people more in love. Least, I
haven't." She lifted her chin. "See over there? That's the
Triple H, Mr. Howerton's ranch."

Lizzie looked over the green, well-manicured grounds

with the long, white fence that went on for as far as she could see. Cattle were grazing in a field and cowboys rode among them.

"Cowboys!" Rebecca exclaimed. Both children were watching the cowboys with rapt fascination.

"Unfortunately, Ben had another fit and died," Fiona continued. "Em was devastated and flat broke—"

Broke. The third common factor, Lizzie thought.

"Then, in stepped Tommy and offered her his life savings. Not asking anything in return. See, he already loved her by then. He'd already rescued her from some other men who tried to hurt her. Well, she agreed to take his money, but only if he'd become her partner in the farm. She'd own half, he'd own half. Just business, right? Only they went and fell in love." Fiona turned onto a long driveway. "And here we are."

Lizzie saw the Welcome to the Martin-Medlin Farm sign, warmed by the happy ending. The Martin-Medlin farm was impressive, too. There was a neat farmhouse, barns, and a long building that Fiona explained was the bunkhouse and dining hall. The fields were deep green and thriving. A woman in her early twenties walked out of the house and waved. She was lovely from a distance and the closer they got, the lovelier she became.

"Hey, Emmy," Fiona called.

Lizzie felt a twinge of nerves. She hadn't had many friends in her life. What if these women didn't like her? What if they sensed there was something different about her, something unlikable?

Fiona stopped the wagon. "Emeline, meet Lizzie and vice versa."

"Hello," Em said as she reached up and took RJ. "And welcome. I'm so pleased to meet you."

"It's nice to meet you, too," Lizzie returned, rising. By the time Lizzie had climbed down, Fiona had already jumped down and helped Jake and Rebecca from the wagon. It felt extraordinary to be with women her own age, mothers who looked out for one another's children. She'd never experienced the like.

"This is Rebecca and Jake," Fiona said to Emeline.

"Nice to meet you," Em said to the children.

"Very nice to meet you, ma'am," Rebecca replied politely. Jake ducked his head and halfway hid behind his sister.

"Where's Caty-bug?" Fiona asked as they started toward the bunkhouse.

"Where do you think?"

"You mean if I had three guesses and the first two didn't count? I'd probably say she's in the arms of a lady I know, name of Doll."

Em looked at Lizzie. "Doll complains that Caty is going to be spoiled because she's held all the time, but I've no sooner put her down than she picks her up. Before Caty even fusses, by the way."

Lizzie grinned.

"May we go see the cat?" Rebecca asked.

"Of course you can," Em replied.

Lizzie looked and saw a gray cat sunning herself on the verandah of the bunkhouse.

"Her name is Queen Pritoria," Em added.

The name delighted Rebecca, who giggled. "Queen Pritoria?"

"Or Pritty, for short," Em replied. "It's silly, I know."

"Wood named her," Fiona stated as she took RJ from Em. "And he is silly."

Rebecca and Jake went one way to see the cat, and the ladies continued around the back of the bunkhouse.

"You gotta go potty?" Fiona asked her son, who shook his head.

"Best not be having no accidents," Fiona said. "You tell Mama when you have to go. Hear me?"

"How do you like it in Green Valley so far?" Em asked Lizzie.

"Very much."

They rounded the back of the longhouse and Em pulled open the screen door for the others. Lizzie stepped into a kitchen and dining hall. A short, stout lady with a reddened but pleasant face stood at a table, salting a platter of sliced tomatoes as she held a dark-haired infant in her arms. There was a savory scent in the air, and a good deal of food had been prepared.

"Hey, Doll," Fiona said. "Meet Lizzie."

Doll set the salt down and came closer. "Nice to meet you, honey," she said, extending her hand. "Welcome to town."

"Thank you. It's nice to meet you, Doll." She looked at the blue-eyed babe, the prettiest she'd ever seen. "She's beautiful. How old?"

"Almost eleven months," Em replied.

"Not quite walking yet," Doll said, "but trying hard. Pulling up on everything."

"On those rare occasions we put her down," Em added wryly.

Doll reached out and popped Em on the behind, which made Em jump and all of them laugh.

"That was a little dig at me," Doll told Lizzie. "Where's your young'uns?"

"Around front. They saw the cat."

"The queen, you mean," Doll said with a nod. "She thinks she's a queen, too," she said, handing the baby to Lizzie.

Em looked apologetic. "I'll take her."

"I'd love to hold her," Lizzie admitted.

"Her name is Catherine," Em said with a proud smile.

"But you call her Caty," Lizzie said lightly. "Hello, Caty."

Doll scooped up RJ, who squealed with displeasure. "Well, at least give your old aunt Doll a kiss."

RJ resisted, so Doll set him down. "Be that way, then. But don't forget, you owe me one."

"What's for lunch?" Fiona asked. "It smells good."

"Bubble and squeak with onion gravy and the last of the tomatoes. Have a seat. Y'all want something to drink? We've got apple cider, buttermilk—"

"No, I'm good for now," Fiona said as she walked to one of the many tables and sat on the accompanying bench.

"I'm fine, as well," Lizzie replied. "Thank you." She followed Em around the table and they both sat. It was a pleasant, well-lit room thanks to the many windows. A few were open and provided a flow of air.

"We'll get you set up before the men come in," Doll said. "Every day they come in like a swarm of locusts, convinced they're about to perish from starvation, despite the hearty breakfast they ate not even five hours past."

"On second thought," Fiona said, getting back up, "I will have some cider. Does it have a kick to it?"

"The cider with a kick is over there. Can't be letting the men have that at noontime," Doll said as she went back to the stove.

Fiona went to the right pitcher, poured a glass, and tasted it. "*Mmm*, that is good."

"Pour the girls one, too," Doll said.

Fiona did and carried them back to the table.

"So, tell us everything about you," Doll said to Lizzie.

"Doll," Em laughingly scolded.

"Oh, Pauline," Doll said, "it's not like we won't find out anyway. Right?"

The use of her real name startled Lizzie. A moment later, she realized the others were staring at her, taken aback by her reaction. She hadn't just imagined that, had she? Doll had called her Pauline. "D-did you just call me Pauline?"

"No, honey," Doll said apologetically, setting her spoon aside. "I said please in a silly way."

"You all right?" Fiona asked worriedly.

Lizzie nodded but she had no voice. She felt so foolish and so exposed. These women were nothing but friendly and hospitable, and now they would think she was strange. "I'm sorry, I—"

"It's all right," Em quickly assured her.

"It is," Fiona seconded. "Really. No matter what you're running from."

Lizzie didn't know what to say. Doll sat next to Fiona and looked sympathetic.

"I don't know if I mentioned it," Fiona said with a discreet wink, "but it was about two years past when Em walked into the boarding house looking for a room. Even though this was her home."

Em nodded to confirm the truth of it.

"She seemed jumpy and exhausted, like she'd been running for her life."

"And I was," Em said quietly. "From a terrible man."

How well Lizzie understood that. Although she couldn't say so.

"The day you come in, I got the exact same feeling about

you. I guess it's one of the reasons I wanted you to meet Em. I feel like we'll all be good friends, but also it's just nice to see that sometimes people do get to live happily ever after, and Em here is living, breathing proof of it."

Lizzie felt tears prick the backs of her eyes because it felt like they knew. Knew and accepted her anyway.

"We probably will find out everything about you," Doll said, "'cause we are a nosy bunch, but in your time is just fine. We won't push. But just know we're here and we'll be on your side. I can promise you that."

Lizzie was grateful and touched, but she couldn't say so. Even if she'd had the words, her children were coming in. "This is Rebecca and Jake," she said thickly.

"Hello, Rebecca and Jake," Doll said cheerfully, turning to them.

"Hello. There are a bunch of men coming this way," Rebecca reported.

Doll nodded. "They'll be wanting their dinner, but I'll get y'all's first."

"I can help," Rebecca volunteered.

"Well, now that's an offer I'll accept," Doll said enthusiastically.

Two hours later, they headed back home, each with a small crate of fresh vegetables and a ball of goat cheese. It had been a wonderful day, and Lizzie felt light and happy. When the men had come in, the banter started and never stopped, despite the fact that they were hungry and went right to filling their plates and eating. They were priming the tobacco crop, which meant pulling the leaves at the bottom of the plants. It was the first step of the harvest.

Even though they had big appetites, they took the time

to spar and laugh, and Doll could hold her own among them. Lizzie had never experienced anything like that easy camaraderie. Neither had her children, who watched with unabashed delight.

Wood, the foreman, was a man in his fifties and he was kind and witty. He'd known just the right amount to tease with Jake and Rebecca. Another of the men, Hawk, was part Indian, and proudly owned it, even amidst ribbing from one of the others, named Malcolm. They'd all been discussing the merits of a cigarette-rolling machine; apparently one had been invented.

"It could go and change the whole industry," Wood said. He looked at Lizzie. "Right now, companies can't keep up with demand 'cause hand rolling is slow. A person can do, like, less than ten an hour by hand rolling. But this fella, Bonsack, went and made this machine that can roll two hundred a minute." This caused a general scoffing, which didn't bother Wood in the least. "It's what I read. I recommend you fellas try it sometime."

"How—" Jeffrey started.

"How do you read?" Malcolm interrupted. "Well, first you pick up a book."

"Ha, ha," Jeffrey said with a sour look.

"Usually," Malcolm said, "it's Hawk here who says *how*, only he means *hi*," he finished with a big wave.

"That joke never gets old," Hawk said with a bored lift of his brow.

"Just no way a machine can roll two hundred cigarettes a minute," Jeffrey said, getting back to the point.

"Not only can it," Wood stated, "but the man who invented it won that contest put on by a cigarette company out of Richmond, and he won seventy-five *thousand* dollars."

The conversation went on and on, and it was entertaining to observe. So were the Medlins. Baby Catherine favored her father, who was breathtakingly handsome, but the truly beautiful thing to witness was Tommy and Emeline. The love between them filled the room. The way they looked at one another, the way he touched her. He took the baby and held her the entire time he was there, and it was clear how much he adored her. Never had Ethan looked at his children that way. It was also clear that there was no other woman in the world for Tommy. Em was his world and he was hers. Never, ever had she felt that for Ethan. She hadn't experienced even a fraction of that emotion. But could she? With the right man? With Jeremy?

She tried to push the thought away, but another took its place. After a day of glorious weather, with such gregarious people, who clearly cared for one another and worked hard together, it made the contrast of Jeremy's existence—in a dark, cold mine—hurtful to think about. Why did he do it? When there was work on a farm or a ranch in the fresh air and sunshine, why would anyone subject himself to working in a mine?

"Today was fun, Mama," Rebecca said from the back. "Can we go back again?"

"Oh, we'll go back lots," Fiona answered.

"Thank you for taking us under your wing," Lizzie said.

Fiona smiled and jutted her crooked arms out. "I got big wings. Happy to have you."

Chapter Nineteen

It was on a cloudy Thursday afternoon that Jeremy trudged out of the mine's lift behind a half dozen men. Liam had managed to position himself to get off the lift first, which was why he saw his eldest nephew, Errol, waiting right away. Jeremy knew what the news was by the boy's stance and drawn face. The others knew too, and murmured words of sympathy as they passed. William's death had been inevitable; it was only a question of when.

Liam looked at Jeremy and gave a grim nod.

"I'm sorry," Jeremy said. He looked at Errol. "I'm sorry for your loss."

The boy nodded in acknowledgment but didn't meet Jeremy's gaze.

"We'll bury him tomorrow," Liam said.

"What time?"

"Afternoon," Liam said.

"Three," Errol said with downcast eyes. "Mama said three."

Liam walked away with his nephew. Several paces away,

he put a protective arm around the boy's shoulders and they conferred quietly. Jeremy watched, saddened by the inevitable end of a life spent in the mines. It was a bleak legacy.

When he got back to his house, he sat heavily at his table. For a while, he was too tired and depressed to move. When he did, it was to reach for a bottle of whiskey and the glass he'd used the day before. He poured a drink and downed it. He poured another and downed it. Then he sat back and watched the daylight growing fainter.

The following day, Jeremy stood in the back of the group gathered for William Baskerville's funeral. It was a dour-looking crowd of a few dozen people. What could anyone say other than it had been a hard life and an even harder death? A wife and children were left behind, and their lives were hard. They weren't going to get any easier, either.

When the service ended, mourners headed back to their homes in the mining camp, a place known as the patch, but Jeremy stayed behind. He stood with his head slightly lowered, hands clasped together in front of him, lost in a mire of thoughts. It occurred to him that he didn't recall one thing that had been said at the service. Not one single word. He hated funerals. At Jenny's funeral, he and his father had anchored his mother between them. The pastor had spoken of a light being extinguished too soon, but he'd been more focused on keeping his mother upright than listening to the words of supposed consolation.

At his mother's funeral, he stood shoulder to shoulder with his father. He remembered the looks of sorrow and softly spoken murmurings of sympathy over what they'd had to endure. The pastor had spoken carefully, mentioning a mother's love often. It was true, she had been a loving mother, but Jeremy hadn't felt love from her at the end; he'd felt a void. He'd felt emptiness. Jenny's death had shattered her mind, body, and spirit.

At his father's funeral, he'd stood alone and numb. At least, he'd started out alone. By the end of the service, he realized he was flanked by Miss McCarthy, his old school-teacher, on one side, and T. Emmett Rice on the other. Miss McCarthy had taken hold of his arm and Emmett had a hand on his shoulder.

Jeremy turned and made his way through the cemetery to the row where his parents and sister were buried, because what he needed was a reckoning. He needed to be finished with the past, if that was possible.

He stopped before his mother's gravestone first. "Sorry it's been so long," he said quietly, although he was alone in the cemetery. The pastor kept the cemetery in good condition, mostly using the labor of adolescents who'd gotten into mischief and had a debt to pay to society, but Jeremy wished he had flowers to lay before her grave.

He stepped past Jenny's grave to his father's, wondering if he'd paid enough for his sins, but he still heard his father's voice in his head. *A life for a life, Son.* What a mistake telling him had been. Jeremy had thought the knowledge that he'd exacted justice for Jenny would bring his father some sort of satisfaction. Instead, it had torn them apart. *That's the way of it! A life for a life.*

Jeremy had argued that it was *their* fault, Ted Landreth's and Stan Thomas's. That Jenny was dead because of them, but his father wouldn't listen.

"I've lost a daughter and a wife," Rodney Sheffield had ranted. "You think I can bear to see my son hanged for exacting revenge? Revenge for a crime that can't even be proved? Must never be proved. Would you have us drag your sister's name through the mud? For the love of God, Son. A *Landreth*. They won't stop looking for him until he's found. Until they know. And then the law will say what it's always said. A life for a life!"

"They won't be found," Jeremy stated, but his father was through listening. He turned his back on his son and walked away. Soon, he'd crawl back into a bottle. And why not? In a short time, he'd lost pretty much everything. His only daughter and then his wife, and the farm would probably have to be sold, too. It was only the two of them left, and their relationship was crumbling.

It was later that night when his father didn't come in to dinner that Jeremy went in search and found him in the barn.

Hanging.

Dead.

It wasn't a sight that would ever leave him, however much he wished it.

Maybe that's what he deserved, because if he hadn't admitted killing Ted Landreth, his father wouldn't have snapped. Jeremy had accepted his punishment and sentenced himself to a life of hard labor in Six. His question now was, did he owe the rest of his life? Was eight years long enough, or did he owe dying there? The quick death of a cave-in or the hard death of black lung.

He closed his eyes and sighed heavily. He'd been foolish to think he'd arrive at any sort of reckoning. All that was here was a reminder of the deaths of his family. At least his father's death had been quick. He'd wrapped a noose around his neck and stepped off the loft. His neck had snapped, his death instant.

His mother, on the other hand, had lingered and suffered,

using more and more laudanum to help with the pain of grief, growing thinner and weaker until her heart gave out. Or so the doctor had said. It would have been bad enough to lose Jenny to an accident, but in washing her body for burial, the truth of what she'd been through became apparent.

If Ruth Sheffield hadn't cried out, causing Jeremy to come rushing in to the kitchen where Jenny's body lay on the table, he wouldn't have known. But he did see. He saw the bruises on her arms and wrists and neck, and instantly he knew. And his mother knew. He could still picture her hovering over her daughter's body, sobbing, as the truth tore her up inside.

No one in his family had ever once discussed it, but the abuse Jenny had suffered took on a presence of its own, and it was the loudest specter in the house. He knew when his father had been told. He knew when either of his parents were thinking about it, especially his mother. He saw it in her eyes every day until they went vacant, in part due to doses of laudanum.

Jeremy opened his eyes and looked at his sister's grave. He'd loved her. He still loved her. He'd always wanted to protect her, but she'd made bad choices that had gotten her hurt. The hard truth was, he'd been angry with her a long time. He hadn't actually admitted it, not even to himself, but it was time he faced it. He'd warned her about Landreth. Warned her and warned her, and she'd ignored him. It was pointless to be angry at her when she was gone, but her death had ruined everything. It had destroyed every one of them.

But he still loved her, and he knew how much she would have hated hurting anyone, most especially her family. In fact, she'd probably died to keep the truth from coming out. That would have been like her. Damn it, he didn't want to be mad at her anymore. But it could have been different. *You should have known that you could come to me and I would have taken care of it. You should have known. You didn't have to go and do it. Why did you? It ruined everything. You ruined everything, Jen.*

He swallowed hard, trying to rid himself of the painful lump in his throat, but it wouldn't subside. He shook his head. If nothing else changed today, this would change. He was going to admit he'd been angry with her and he was going to forgive her. She hadn't meant to get hurt. She'd believed in the wrong man, and she'd only been sixteen at the time. Sixteen.

I'm sorry, Jenny. I love you and I forgive you. I know you didn't mean for any of it to happen.

He felt the soft touch of a woman's hand on his back and knew it was Lizzie. It surprised him that he knew who it was without seeing her and also that she'd approached so quietly. He tried to compose his face as he turned, but when he did, no one was there. He shivered from the strangeness because it had been such a physical touch. He looked back to Jenny's gravestone and tears blurred his vision. He cleared his throat and wiped his face, sniffing hard.

A new realization suddenly seized him, and he turned back to his father's grave, but what he saw was the past. What he saw was the moment his father learned the truth about what Jeremy had done. He'd gotten angry, of course, and gone on and on about a life for a life and about not being able to bear seeing his only son hanged. Because, in his mind, some sort of celestial debt was owed.

Jeremy reeled because he'd always thought his father's suicide was meant to punish him. It was an act of desperation and heartbreak, yes, but he'd believed it had also been meant to punish him. *But it hadn't been.* Instead, it was a drunken, misguided pact with the universe. It was Rodney Sheffield saying, *If a life is owed for the Landreth boy, here I am. I give mine. Leave my boy be.* It had been an act of love. He didn't fully understand how he knew this now; he just knew. Jeremy unsteadily made his way to the nearest bench and sat, and this time, he cried without shame.

Chapter Twenty

It was dark, well after nine, when Jeremy reached the cottage. After leaving the cemetery, he'd gone to the saloon for a couple of drinks before going on to Wiley's for supper. Lizzie wouldn't be expecting to see him tonight, so he wasn't going to put her out. He wouldn't ask for anything but a bed so that he'd be able to get an early start. Liam was taking the day off and so would he. That was a day and a half of work missed this week, and old man Landreth wouldn't pay a dime for an hour not spent working, not even for a funeral, but Jeremy was beyond caring.

His time at the cemetery hadn't provided the peace of mind he longed for, but it felt like he'd made a start. The truth was that he'd been caught up in a quest for atonement for years—even if he'd never called it that or realized it was that. Maybe, just maybe, he had paid enough. He was about half drunk now, so he'd have to sleep on it and see how things looked in the morning, but it was a good thought.

He walked around to the side door to the kitchen and knocked lightly, but there was no answer. A light burned inside, so Lizzie wasn't asleep. Or if she was, she'd accidentally left the lamp on. He hesitated and then opened the door and stepped into the kitchen lit by the fire burning in the hearth and one wall lamp. He decided to write a note and then make his way to bed, but as soon as he made a move to do it, Jake appeared in the doorway. The boy looked half asleep as he cowered. He'd been crying. "What's the matter, Jake?"

Rather than answer, Jake looked around for his mother.

Jeremy started toward Jake, but the child jerked back, frightened. Jeremy halted abruptly because scaring Jake had startled him. On instinct, he squatted to be at eye level with the child. "It's okay," he said gently. "Your mama's not here, but she may be in her room."

Jake considered him warily and then shook his head.

"Maybe in the outhouse." He paused. "Did you have a bad dream?"

The boy nodded.

Jeremy caught a whiff of urine and noticed that Jake's pajama bottoms were wet. This was beyond his realm of experience, but he had to say or do something. For one thing, Jake knew he'd noticed. "You know, wetting the bed happens sometimes after a bad dream," Jeremy said. Jake quivered, and it did something piercing to Jeremy's heart. "It's all right," he assured the boy before rising. "Is Rebecca asleep?"

Jake nodded jerkily.

"Well, how about we get you in some dry clothes and get you back to bed?"

Jake didn't back away, so Jeremy rose and started forward slowly. He reached the boy, held out his hand, and Jake took hold of it before glancing up at him. Jeremy's heart experienced yet another piercing stab of some sort. Whatever it was, it was sharp enough to rob him of breath.

The two of them walked back toward the room Jake shared with Rebecca, passing Lizzie's room along the way. The door was open and the room empty, so she was probably in the outhouse or the bathhouse. They entered the children's room, where Rebecca was curled on her side, fast asleep. "Where's your clothes?" Jeremy asked quietly, letting go of his hand.

Jake went to a chest and opened the bottom drawer.

Jeremy felt totally out of his element. "Put on something dry, all right?"

Jake obeyed and Jeremy walked over to the bed and saw the wet spot. He glanced back at Jake, who was bent over dressing. He looked so small, hunched over like that. So helpless and innocent. Jeremy thought back on the black eye Jake had come to town with, and then of the way the child had drawn back when he'd started toward him. Who was it that had put that fear into him? "I'll be right back," he said quietly.

Jeremy went to the wardrobe at the end of the hallway where Lizzie kept towels and blankets, and retrieved a couple of towels before going back into the room. Jake stood at the bed, looking abashed and uncertain. Jeremy doubled one towel over the wet spot and then put the second on top of it. "It's a little trick," he said with a wink. "Come on." He lifted Jake up and put him down on top of the towels. "We can change the bedclothes in the morning. How's that sound?"

Jake nodded.

Jake turned on his side and got settled and Jeremy covered him up after making sure the top cover wasn't wet. Again, he squatted to be eye level with the boy, suddenly reluctant to leave him. "You want to tell me about the dream?"

Jake didn't move or speak.

"That's okay," Jeremy assured him. "I'll see you in—"

"A bad man was after us," Jake said.

Jeremy's breath caught. He hadn't been altogether certain Jake *could* speak. He hadn't heard his voice even once. "Is that right?"

"He hurt Mama," Jake said, "and he was looking for Rebecca and me. I couldn't run away."

"That sounds scary, but it was just a dream. No one is hurting your mama or Rebecca or you."

"Or you?"

Jeremy smiled despite the sudden ache in his chest. "Or me." Jake's small, warm hand reached out and covered Jeremy's hand resting on the bed, and the ache intensified.

"I wish we had a dog," Jake said sleepily. "Our neighbors had a dog and it barked if anyone came around. Except not if he knew you."

"What was the dog's name?"

"Blackie."

"What color was he?"

Jake grinned. "Black."

"Having a dog might not be a bad idea," Jeremy said after a brief pause. "Of course, you'd have to take care of it."

Jake's eyes grew round. "I'd take care of it," he pledged.

"How 'bout if I talk to your mama about it?"

Jake nodded and smiled, excited by the prospect.

"Think you can go to sleep now?"

Jake closed his eyes at once.

"That was fast," Jeremy teased.

Jake kept grinning, but kept his eyes closed.

"I wish it worked like that for me. I'd say, 'Jeremy, go to sleep now,' and I'd be out, just like that." He pulled his hand from Jake's grip and touched the boy's hair. "Good night, Jake."

"'Night," Jake whispered.

Jeremy stepped back into the kitchen just as Lizzie walked in the back door wearing her worn-out robe. Her hair was wet, her face pink from the heat of a bath. She stopped short when she saw him.

"I knocked, but—"

"I wasn't expecting you," she said haltingly, folding her arms in front of her, apparently uncomfortable at her lack of dress.

"Sorry for just walking in."

"No, it's fine," she said, shutting the door behind her.

"Someone died," he blurted, taking her by surprise once again. "Someone from the mine."

She looked stunned. "I'm sorry."

"It's better that he passed. Black lung is a hard way to go."

Clearly, she didn't know what to say.

"I thought I'd take tomorrow off and get an early start here."

"I'll go put on some clothes," she said as she started forward.

"Jake woke," he said when she was almost even with him.

She stopped and looked at him with alarm.

"I'd just stepped inside and he was there. Looking for you. He'd had a bad dream. He'd, uh, wet the bed."

She cringed. "I'll see to him."

"I already did." For the second time, she seemed staggered and he wondered if she was displeased. "I put towels over the wet spot and he got into dry clothes. I figured it was best to change the bedclothes tomorrow."

"Yes," she murmured. "You're right. Thank you."

He was getting an odd feeling from her, as if she wasn't sure how she felt about him helping her boy. Of course, he had come in uninvited. "When I first saw him, he was standing in the doorway and I could tell he'd been crying. I started toward him and he jerked back, like he was afraid of me."

Lizzie dropped her gaze.

"He said a—"

Her eyes locked on his. "He spoke to you?"

He nodded. "Once he was in bed."

"What did he say?"

"He'd dreamt a bad man was after you and Rebecca and him. He said he couldn't get away." He paused, wondering if she'd say something, but she didn't. "Is there anything you want to tell me?"

She hesitated and then shook her head.

"I'd help if I could," he said. "I hope you know that."

She averted her gaze again. "It was just a dream."

"Was it?" She lifted her chin and met his gaze, but he could sense that a wall of defense had come up.

"We've probably all had that dream. Someone big and mean after us. After the people we love."

He nodded slowly even though he knew she wasn't telling the truth. At least, not the whole truth. She was definitely a woman with secrets, not that she was the only person in the room with secrets. "He wants a dog."

She blinked in surprise. "A dog?"

"Like your neighbors had. A dog who'll bark when strangers come around."

She paled as she gripped the front of her robe tighter. "He told you about our neighbors?"

He noted her reaction. "Just that they had a dog who barked when strangers came around," he replied calmly.

"Oh."

"You can talk to me, you know," he said carefully. "Whatever your secrets are, I've got worse."

"You can't really know that, can you?" she asked darkly.

"I do know that," he stated without hesitation.

The light from the flickering lamp illuminated some inner struggle on her face. "Perhaps one day you'll share your secrets and I'll share mine," she replied guardedly.

Fat chance, he thought. If he shared his, she'd boot him out of their lives so fast, his head would spin. She wouldn't want him anywhere near her kids. She turned and went after the shawl on the back of her chair, and he had a queer feeling that she'd just issued an invitation, and he'd missed the chance.

She wrapped the shawl around her. "Would you care for a glass of wine?"

He wasn't a wine drinker, but he wanted more time with her. "That would be nice." As she went for it, he pulled back a chair and sat. She carried back an open bottle and two glasses. She poured and then sat. "I guess you probably know a lot about wine," he said.

"Not really."

He took a drink. It was a red wine, dark and fruity, but not as sweet as he'd expected. He took another sip, trying to decide if he liked it.

"Thank you for taking care of Jake."

He looked at her. "I didn't mind."

She smiled and seemed to relax a little.

"You know, getting a dog isn't a bad idea," he continued. "I could look around for one."

"It's nice of you to offer," she said less than enthusiastically as she swirled her wine and watched the liquid cling to the sides of the glass.

"Lizzie?"

Reluctantly, she looked up and met his gaze.

"Is there a bad man after you?"

"I certainly hope not," she replied, attempting to sound light. "I know a very good man is helping us out."

He frowned, because the statement put him in his place. "I'm not a very good man. Maybe I could have been. I don't know. But I'm not. I just care about you and the kids."

She cocked her head, disturbed by the statement. "Why do you work in the mine?"

The question took him by surprise. How bizarre it was that he'd asked about her secrets and then she'd hit on his. "We went from getting a dog to why I work the mine?" he asked, to buy a moment.

"A few days ago, we went to a farm. Fiona, from the boarding house, took us to meet her aunt and her friend Emeline."

He sat back and watched her. He had no idea what she was getting at, but she was so pretty, all clean and red faced and wet haired from a bath. It was strangely intimate.

"It was a lovely day," she said. "When the men came back for the noonday meal, it was . . . enjoyable. Everyone there works hard, you can tell, but they enjoy each other's company, too. They seem to enjoy their lives. And on the way back home, I kept thinking of you in the mine. I wondered why you do it. Why not work on a ranch or a farm, especially when you know the life?"

"There was a reason for going to work in the mine."

"Was it *not* to work on the land? To do something different after—"

He half expected her to say *after the murder*, but she didn't. She just let the half-spoken statement hang in the air. "Why don't we get back to the bad man?"

Her expression grew wary. "Jeremy—"

"I'd rather know what I'm up against. If I'm up against something."

She frowned. "You're not."

Again, he felt put in his place. She was shutting him out. Out of what, he didn't know exactly, but she was definitely shutting him out. "Maybe you'll trust me enough someday."

"Maybe when you trust me enough to confide in me."

"The difference is, I want to know to help protect you," he retorted.

Confusion flickered on her face. "Maybe I feel the same."

He almost scoffed, the thought was so absurd. "You want to protect me?"

She was suddenly angry enough that her eyes flashed. "Maybe I do. I'm not sure you're doing a very good job of it."

She meant it, and for the third time that night, he felt his heart lurch. "How did Jake get that black eye he had when you first came to town?"

She looked away.

"Lizzie?"

She sighed. "A bad man," she admitted quietly.

"A bad man who may come after you?"

She looked at him warily. "I don't know how he could possibly find us."

"In the place your father lived and died?" he asked incredulously. She blushed, because there was something else she was hiding. "Why don't you just say what you're not telling me?"

It was the wrong thing to say, or maybe the right thing to say, because a tear slipped down her face. She quickly wiped it away.

"Nothing you say will ever leave this house," he pledged. "I just need to know to . . . to be able to protect you."

"I've told you," she said guardedly.

"You're not telling me the whole truth."

"Have you told me the whole truth?"

So, they'd reached an impasse. He couldn't tell her and she wasn't willing to share more than she already had. At least he knew there was a man responsible for the pain and damage. It couldn't be anybody too close to her, because then he would have known where her father lived. Maybe after her husband died, another man came into the picture, one who didn't care for her children. He picked up his glass and took another drink, wondering how to diffuse the tension that had crept between them. "Did you get your baking supplies this week?"

"All that I could," she replied stiffly.

"What do you still need?"

She shook her head. "I'll start with what I have. I'll begin with simple breads and work my way up to cakes and candies."

"I'll help if you tell me what you need."

She pulled her shawl tighter. "Our arrangement is set and . . . I don't think we should get money involved."

The words stung. "I wasn't talking about our arrangement. I wasn't talking about a new one either. I was just talking about helping. I eat your food, don't I? Drink your wine? We didn't have a specific *arrangement* for that."

She studied him a moment, as if confused again. "I should check on the children. They might—"

"Go. Check on them. I should go to bed, anyway." He pushed back in his chair and stood. "Thank you for the wine," he said before turning away. He started to the guest room. The *guest* room. That's all he was, a temporary guest, and he shouldn't forget it.

Chapter Twenty-One

The next afternoon, Lizzie walked toward Jeremy, who was plowing a garden spot. She felt a mixture of guilt and bewilderment for many reasons. For one thing, she knew she'd hurt his feelings by refusing his offer to help purchase baking supplies, although it certainly hadn't been her intention. She'd tried to smooth things over this morning, but he'd remained cool and distant. For another thing, it suddenly felt as if they'd known each other a year and not just a few days. How did he know what he knew about her? At least, he seemed to know. He also seemed to care—sincerely care—or was she imagining that? "Water," she called, holding up a glass.

He looked over at her and halted his horse with a "Ho!"

She went to him, stepping high over the furrowed earth, which wasn't too difficult because she'd put on a pair of men's overalls April May had given her. They felt strange on her, as if she was wearing too many clothes, but she was planning on getting dirty. Jeremy looked quizzically at her clothing, accepted the glass of water, and downed it. "I'm going to help," she stated. "You take a break and—"

"No."

"Don't be stubborn. You've already broken up the dirt, so it won't be so hard now."

"You ever plowed before?"

"I have not, but I'm looking forward to it."

"It's no work for a woman. No matter how she dresses." He handed the glass back. "I'd take more water, though."

"Then you go get it and let me do this. I want to help."

He gave her a look. "There's so much to do around here, we won't have it done in a year."

The words were thrilling.

"You have baking to do, don't you?"

"You mean after I get you more water like the helpless woman I am?"

He scoffed. "I never said that and I never thought it."

She turned and started away, but turned back when she realized he hadn't begun plowing again. Just as she'd suspected, he was staring at her. And grinning. That gave her a thrill, too. "What?"

"It's not a sight you see every day," he said. "Just thought I'd enjoy it."

She rolled her eyes and started back so quickly that she tripped and fell. "Are you okay?" he called, but she could hear the laughter in his voice. She got up and turned back to him. She couldn't be offended, since teasing and talking was so much better than silence and hurt feelings. "I suppose you think I'm going to rinse the dirt from your glass before I refill it?"

"I'm not thinking anything. I'll take the water, dirt and all. Happily."

When she returned with a clean cup and a filled pitcher, he halted the horse again and drank his fill. "Tell you what. You can do one row," he said, barely keeping a straight face.

"So you can laugh at me? I don't think so."

"Oh! So now you refuse to help."

"That's right. I'm going to go find my own project. A new project."

"What project?"

She shrugged. "I've never gone all the way down into the cellar."

His grin disappeared and he shook his head. "No, you're not. Those steps are rotted."

"So, I'll fix them," she replied breezily.

"Do not go down there," he said sternly.

Her eyes widened with surprise because he was serious.

"Let me fix the steps first," he continued. "I mean it. You fall through and you'll break your leg or worse."

Why was her heart beating like mad? "All right. Fine."

He nodded, satisfied that she acquiesced. "Maybe tonight we can work on a list of things to get done and we'll prioritize them. So be thinking about that."

She didn't want to show how much she was feeling, so she pursed her lips and looked at the plow and the horse. "I really can do a row."

He handed the glass back. "I was kidding."

She took the glass from him, and decided to take the plunge. "I didn't mean to hurt your feelings last night."

"You didn't," he replied quickly. Too quickly.

Had the wall come right back up between them or was she imagining it? She didn't know what else she could say and so she turned and started back to the house.

"Lizzie," he called when she was clear of the furrowed ground.

She turned back. "Yes?"

"The offer I made . . . it still stands."

Tears pricked the backs of her eyes and she looked away quickly.

"No strings attached," he said, "other than to taste some of the stuff you make."

She nodded but couldn't look at him, and he didn't stop her again when she walked on.

As the sun set, Jeremy brushed down his horse, a chestnut stallion that stood sixteen hands high, with a reddish-blond mane. The plowing had been hard work and the horse was as sweaty as he was. Not that he minded. He was tired, but he felt alive in a way a man was supposed to feel alive.

He noticed Rebecca slowly coming closer. She was wearing a pair of overalls made of sturdy blue fabric with a pink patch in the middle that had her name embroidered upon it. The clothing was obviously the influence of the Blue sisters. April May frequently wore such garments, while Cessie, who'd likely done the sewing, was as feminine as could be. Cessie had a pretty face and liked lace and frills. Cessie and April May, while close to each other, were at opposite ends of the spectrum in their tastes. As he recalled, the other girls in the family had fallen somewhere in between.

The Blues were a funny, gregarious family, full of life and laughter—but April May was *funny* in a different sort of way. He knew this because of a time the two of them had been together after managing to rescue a mule from the mine.

Sometimes mules went mad from the dark dankness beneath the surface of the earth. Usually the madness manifested itself when the animal exited the mine, transporting a load. The light and the air triggered a need so deep that no one could get it to go back inside, not by coercing, pulling, or beating. On this occasion, they'd actually gotten a mule back to its confines within the depths of the mine, but then it went crazy. It brayed, cried mournfully, and went in circles, rearing and kicking, driving off the other mules. Finally, it just lay down to die. Try as they might, they couldn't get the animal up. No one wanted to haul a mule carcass from the mine, so the mule lady had been summoned, and she'd gotten it up using soothing talk and treats. Jeremy had helped, walking ahead of her and the mule, with a lamp.

Once outside, the beast of burden broke free of them and ran, braying joyfully. It was shocking to see. Not only was the mule nowhere close to dead, it wanted life and light and air. Jeremy should have gone right back to work, but he'd lingered. He'd always liked April May Blue, odd as she was. She was honest to a fault—that was how his mother had once put it. She spoke her mind and didn't care what anyone thought of it.

"You ever want to do that?" April May asked him as she watched the mule with that cockeyed smile of hers.

"What?"

"Break free and run in circles. Scream 'I am alive, damn you all.'"

He grinned. "Is that what it's saying?"

"Oh yeah. He'll settle down before long, but for now he wants us to know. I . . . am . . . alive. Damn you all very much for stickin' me in that stinkin' hole." She looked at Jeremy. "Of course, you stuck yourself there, so maybe you don't feel the inclination."

It was true. He had stuck himself there and he wasn't asking anybody to feel sorry for him. The mule finally came to a standstill and was lifting and lowering his head, as if to better feel the sunshine. Or maybe adjusting to the brightness of day. It was overcast, but it was painfully bright in comparison to below. "No one could get him to budge an inch," Jeremy commented.

"Yeah, well, I promised him the right thing. Freedom. We all want freedom."

It was an odd comment. "You don't think most people are free?"

She chortled. "Most people are anything but free. It's just that we're bound by different things. Working somewhere we don't want to in order to put food in our mouths. Fear. Bad marriages. Obligation."

"You seem pretty free."

"I'm probably freer than most," she acknowledged. "In some ways. Or maybe not," she mused. "Maybe less."

He had no idea what she was getting at. "I bet most people think they're free."

"Most people don't analyze too closely, probably because they don't want to face certain truths."

Then maybe he was freer than most. He'd faced the truths and was paying the debt he owed. "What freedom would you want that you don't have?" he asked, desirous of keeping the discussion about her and not himself.

"The freedom of love, I guess. That special, sacred bond."

It was strange to think of her in love, but then again, most people wanted that. Or needed it. Not him, of course, but other folks. His guess was that she was just so different, men didn't see her the way a man saw a woman he wanted to marry. That was sad, because she was a really good lady.

"Well, I best get my new friend on home," she said, starting toward the mule.

He wanted to say something more—something that would let her know how well he thought of her. "It was his loss," he called when she was halfway to the mule.

She turned back to him, curious about the statement.

"If there was someone special," he said, "and he was too blind to see what all you offer, it was his loss."

She smiled, touched by the sentiment. "I appreciate that. Although, just between you and me, it was *her* loss," she said with a wink. She turned and started toward the mule again, which was a good thing, since Jeremy's jaw had dropped.

"What's his name?" Rebecca asked from a safe distance.

"Dancer."

"Why'd you name him that?"

This was the first time she'd struck up a conversation with him, which was oddly pleasing. He shrugged. "He does this prancy thing sometimes, kinda like a dance," he said as he kept brushing. "I named him a long time ago."

"How long have you had him?"

"Almost twenty years, I guess."

She came a little closer, moving slowly, her hands shoved into her pockets.

"Do you like horses?" he asked.

"I like donkeys. They're smaller."

"More stubborn, too. Horses are friendlier. They get to know you and they want to please you."

Her expression turned doubtful.

"It's true," he said, moving around to the other side of the horse.

"April May says mules aren't as stubborn as people say. They just want what they want."

He grinned because he could well imagine her saying just that. "She's probably right."

"Did you know that donkeys and mules are different?"

"Is that so?" he asked thoughtfully.

She nodded. "Mules are bigger. They come from a horse and a donkey. The horse was the mother."

Jeremy murmured his interest. "They're strong," Jeremy said. "That's why they're used in mines to haul heavy loads."

"They don't like that," Rebecca stated matter of factly.

"I don't imagine they do," he agreed.

"Were you scared to get up on him at first?" she asked, looking at Dancer.

"Nah. Not that I remember. We had a farm, so we always had horses."

"Do you still have the farm?"

"No. I only have this piece of ground that nobody else wanted."

"Why didn't they want it?"

He stopped for a moment and looked over at her. "Truthfully, I didn't offer it. It had this old cabin on it that some of my ancestors lived in a long time ago, so I kept it." He paused. "You know what an ancestor is?"

She nodded. "Family that lived a long time ago."

"I bet you did good in school."

"I was top of my grade," she replied proudly. "The last day of every month, Miss Jamison, our teacher, wrote the names of the top students in every grade and it always said 'second grade, Rebecca Ray—'" She broke off suddenly with a startled, almost frightened expression.

He blinked in surprise at the reaction. "That's something," he said calmly, wondering what had so spooked her. "I never did that well."

She studied the ground around her, looking miserable. It felt like they'd made a little progress, but then she'd taken a big step back. *Second grade, Rebecca Ray. Rebecca Ray Carter.* What had spooked her? "How do you think Jake will do?" he asked.

"He's not going to like it. He won't want to speak up."

He tossed the brush aside and reached into his pocket for the pick. "He might surprise you," he said as he picked up Dancer's front hoof and started cleaning it. He noticed Rebecca come around so she could watch what he was doing. She still kept her distance, but it interested her.

"He thinks he likes you," she said. It was almost spoken like a challenge.

"I like him, too," he said without looking up.

She hesitated. "Do you like me?"

He dropped the leg and looked at her. "Sure, I do."

Silence.

"If I pet him, would he bite me?"

"No. He'd just look at you. Wonder about you."

"How do you know?"

"'Cause I know him. I told you, I've had him a long time. We know each other's mind."

She came forward, reached out tentatively and touched the horse, which then turned its head to look at her. She stepped back.

"He won't bite. I promise."

"I bet if he stepped on my foot, he'd break it."

"Yeah. You've got a little foot and he's got a lot of weight. So don't let him step on your foot."

"Shouldn't he be in a barn?" Rebecca asked, as she rounded the stallion in front, keeping enough distance. The horse continued to watch her.

"He's all right in the open. He likes it. He's in a barn some of the time."

"On your land?"

"No. I board him. Where I live most of the time, there's no room for him. He stays at the livery in town." He paused. "Would you like to ride him?"

"No, thank you."

"You sure? I could put you on him and walk him around. He wouldn't take off running or anything."

She considered. "Maybe sometime I will."

"All right. You tell me when." He walked over and put the brush in his saddle bag and set it aside. "I'm going to go get cleaned up for supper."

"Are you going to take a bath?"

"I am."

"You know, you have to wash first."

He nodded. "I know. Your mother showed me how it works."

"Rebecca," Lizzie called.

"I have to go now," Rebecca stated coolly before walking off.

Jeremy watched her go. She wasn't nearly as open to him as Jake, but she wasn't as closed off as she had been either. It felt like a victory of sorts. He was still grinning about it as he finished his chores and started toward the bathhouse.

Chapter Twenty-Two

By the time Jeremy climbed out of the tub, he felt limp. The entire bathing experience was an odd affair. He'd never experienced a continual shower of warm water. There was hair wash in a bottle, and two kinds of soap hanging on a string over the tile floor of the shower area. He'd chosen one with a pleasing sandalwood essence. Of course, then he'd soaked in the tub and probably washed the pleasant scent off, but the hot water had worked magic on his sore back and shoulders.

He dried with one of the towels rolled in a basket, and put on clean clothing. A fresh-smelling man's robe hung on a hook and Lizzie had told him to use it when and if he liked, but it seemed too odd. He didn't bother with shoes, and walked barefoot back to the house, where Lizzie was working on a supper that smelled like heaven. It was fried pork of some kind and he didn't know what else.

"Just leave those on the porch," she said, looking at his dirty clothes. "I'll wash them tomorrow."

"You don't have to—"

"I'm glad to do it. I do little enough for you," she said as she turned back to dinner preparations.

For a moment, he was at a loss for the right thing to do,

but then he went back to the porch and left his dirty clothes in a pile before going back inside.

"From now on, leave them in the laundry house and I'll get them back to you," she said nonchalantly.

The words caused a thrill that he tried to disguise. "Can I help?"

"You can have a glass of wine and keep me company."

He blew out a breath. "I don't know. That's asking a lot."

She laughed and poured wine into two fancy crystal goblets. "We're down to the last few bottles, so we should enjoy it."

"I'll bet when your father passed, this place got cleaned out of most of the wine that was left."

"I understand quite a bit was taken."

"What smells so good?"

"Pork chops." She carried both glasses with her and handed him one. "Smoked by none other than Miss April May Blue. Is there anything the woman can't do?"

He grinned and raised his glass. "To the amazing Miss Blue. In fact, to both of them." She smiled back at him, touched her glass to his, and it made a clear pinging sound that he'd remember for a long time. They sipped, and the wine tasted good to him. "These are pretty glasses."

"I found them in the back of a cupboard. On their side, wrapped in flannel, behind a pot of lard. Thank goodness," she said, starting back to her preparations. "Otherwise they would have been taken too, I'm sure."

As he took another drink, he realized how much easier it had become between them. Natural. Almost like he belonged here. If only he was that lucky.

"Did you enjoy your bath?"

"I can't believe how much I liked it. I never would have guessed."

"I know. Lionel was definitely on to something."

"You called him Lionel?"

She froze for an instant. "I know," she said after a moment's pause. "It's strange, isn't it? I didn't always call him that. But . . . sometimes," she finished weakly.

He noticed the tension in her body. "Did Jake and Rebecca know their grandfather?"

"No." She turned and went back to her dinner preparations. "Unfortunately. No."

He wanted to ask more, but he heard the kids approaching. Instead, he walked to the table and sat. The instant the kids appeared, Jake smiled to see him, while Rebecca went right to setting the table as if she didn't see him there. So much for the progress he thought they'd made. "You want some help with that?" he asked her.

"No," she replied without looking at him. "Thank you," she added stiffly. She placed cloth napkins in a neat folded rectangle at each place and then placed a fork on top of each. "Did you wash before you got in the tub?"

Lizzie looked at her, aghast at the impertinence, and the look was not lost on Rebecca.

"I did," he said easily, hoping to diffuse the strain in the air. "I like that contraption. What about you, Jake? You like it?"

Jake nodded.

"You should answer when someone asks you a question," Lizzie reminded him gently.

"Yes, sir," Jake replied, his gaze dropping.

Lizzie was meaning to help, but she wasn't. She handed Rebecca a plate filled with cut-up meat, and Rebecca carried it to her brother before returning for hers.

"Do you want to fill your plate over here?" Lizzie asked Jeremy.

"Sure," he said, rising again.

"I can cut up my own meat, Mama," Rebecca stated.

"All right," Lizzie agreed. "I guess I'm just used to doing it."

"But since Pa—" Rebecca began and then broke off. "But since I'm older now."

"I agree," Lizzie said. "You are old enough."

Jeremy had been filling his plate, but he heard the dialogue with puzzled interest.

It was a fine supper, as usual, followed by apple turnovers with a drizzled white icing on top. "Why don't I do dishes," he said when supper was over. "You can go have a bath—"

"No," she said, rising. She picked up several dishes and carried them to the sink.

Jeremy noticed Rebecca studying him quizzically.

"Papa says—," Rebecca began, before breaking off again and looking at her mother.

Jeremy looked, too. Although Lizzie's back was to them, she'd frozen.

"He died," Rebecca said quickly to Jeremy.

"I know," he said quietly. "I'm sorry. But what did he used to say?"

"That doing dishes was a woman's work."

"Maybe he thought men weren't smart enough to figure out how to do it."

Jake giggled, and even Rebecca grinned after losing a diligent struggle not to.

"But I know how to do them," he continued. "I grew up doing them with my sister and I do my own dishes now."

Lizzie turned around. "Why don't you two go get ready for your baths," she said to the children, "and you should go relax," she said to Jeremy. "Please. You've worked hard today."

He wasn't sure if he was being dismissed or she was merely being polite. Her smile seemed real enough and there was a blush to her cheeks. Of course, she was used to

doing things herself, although he would have been happy
to help. More than happy. He stood, accepting the dismissal.
"Thank you for supper."

"You're welcome."

Jeremy went to the study and looked over the book selection on the shelves. He picked out a few of the volumes
on wine-making and made himself comfortable, first lighting a fire in the hearth and then turning on lamps to read
by. One book was more interesting than the others and soon
he went in search of paper and a pen and began making
notes.

Jake was the first to join him. He came in smelling clean
and wearing his pajamas, and plunked himself down in
front of the hearth with a wooden puzzle, which he dumped
out unceremoniously before beginning the process of
putting it back together.

Rebecca looked in the room and then left, but soon
returned with her own paper and pencils. She sat at the
table in the room and began to draw. "We're going to church
tomorrow," she said after a few minutes.

"That's nice," Jeremy returned.

"Do you ever go to church?"

"Used to. Not so much anymore."

"What are you reading?"

"About making wine."

She thought about it. "Why do grown-ups like wine?"

He looked up at her. "Not all of them do, but some do.
They think it tastes good."

"Do you think so?"

He nodded. "I didn't used to, but now I do."

"Are you going to try to make it?"

"I don't know anything about it yet. That's why I was reading."

It grew quiet again, but it was a comfortable quiet. He went back to reading, Rebecca went back to drawing, and Jake continued laboring on the puzzle. Lizzie disturbed the silence a little after eight when she came in and told the children it was bedtime.

"I'm not tired," Rebecca complained.

Lizzie sighed with exasperation. "That's what you say every night, no matter how tired you are. Now, scoot."

The children trudged rather than scooted out, and Lizzie gave him a look before following them, although the look wasn't easily read. In fact, he had no idea what was going through her head. He was aware when, after seeing the children to bed, she retired to her room. He gave it a few minutes, wondering if she'd come back and join him, but she didn't. He took his book, turned off the lamps, and went to his room.

The soft knock on the door later surprised him as much as it had the first night, although this time he was sitting atop the bed reading, still wearing his shirt and pants. He set the book aside once more. "Come in."

The door opened and she stood there in her robe again. "May I?" she asked softly.

"Of course."

She shut the door and came toward him slowly. "I'm sorry, I . . . I've never done anything like this before."

She was trembling, so reaching out and taking her hand was pure instinct. "What?"

"This," she said. "Us."

He pulled her closer and she sat facing him. "Are you having second thoughts?" he asked reluctantly, fearing the answer.

She shook her head slowly.

The relief he felt was overwhelming. "I'm glad."

"I'm glad you're here," she admitted, blushing as she said it. "I like you being here."

He squeezed her hand gently. "I like it, too."

"That kiss you won," she said quietly.

"You want to take that back?" he teased. She smiled and ducked her head, but he tipped her face back up with a finger until her gaze met his. She shook her head and her eyes glistened. His gaze raked over her flushed face and rested on her lips before he leaned forward to kiss her. First her lips, and then her warm cheeks, and then her lips again. Her eyes were closed, her breath coming fast. She clutched his arms, followed his movements, matched his pace. Again, he pressed a soft kiss to her cheek and along her jaw.

"Jeremy," she whispered.

"What?" he whispered back. He kissed the side of her neck, and then her earlobe, and felt her jerk slightly, followed by the softest of sighs. It was an intoxicating reaction. This was the same woman who'd claimed she'd felt dead. Well, so had he, and for probably a lot longer than she. But no more. Or, at least, not tonight. His hand stroked her breasts and her nipples strained toward him. He teased one between finger and thumb and her lips parted in a gasp. It was the perfect opening and he took it, pressing his mouth to hers for a deeper, thrusting kiss. Her hand closed around the back of his neck and an intense tremor went through him. He wanted to take her, but he also wanted to suffer this strange ecstasy of longing, too.

She pulled away and stood. For a moment, he feared she would leave, but she slipped her robe down a bit, revealing bare shoulders. He got up as well, and unbuttoned his shirt. He could smell her feminine heat and it caused his pulse to pound. He pushed her hair back and caressed her shoulder.

How had he never noticed how lovely a woman's shoulders were?

She was trembling but she let the robe slip lower, and he relished each inch of skin. He ran his fingers over her arms and it seemed to him that he'd never touched skin before. She let the robe fall fully and she stole his breath, she was so beautiful. He pulled her into his arms and kissed her hungrily, aware of the surreal quality of the moment.

He took off his pants and gently eased her onto the bed. "Tell me how you like it."

"I've never liked it," she admitted in a low voice. "This is a new experience."

The words were gratifying, but more than that, he saw her desire. He wanted her badly, but, just as badly, he wanted to please her. He kissed her until she was kissing him back, offering her tongue and writhing with need. When he entered her, her breath caught and she pushed against his chest. "Should I stop?"

She shook her head.

He moved slowly until he realized she was moving with him, her body no longer resisting his. Her hands were splayed open on his back, and he could feel the tension in them. He began to move faster and she moaned. Her hands slipped down his back to his buttocks, feeling the movement. He buried his face in her hair, struggling to maintain control, but when she cried out and her body jerked with release, it sent him spiraling into an orgasm that left him gasping.

When he curled beside her, he was slightly dizzy. He reached for her hand and held it in his, watching as her chest heaved. There was a sheen of perspiration on both of them. He wanted to say something, but what? He wanted to thank her, but what if she took it wrong? As an insult?

That's when he noticed the tears in her eyes. "What's the matter?" he asked softly.

"N-nothing."

She rose up on an elbow, as if preparing to leave, but he couldn't let her go. Not like that. "Did I hurt you?"

She wiped her eyes and sniffed. "No. I swear."

"Then what is it?"

She shrugged. "I liked it," she admitted in a tremulous voice.

He didn't understand. If it was true, why was that upsetting?

"I never liked it before."

He stroked her hair. "I never liked it so much before."

She looked at him quizzically. "Really?"

He nodded. "Swear."

She relaxed and allowed him to pull her close. He liked the feeling of holding her like that, their bodies warm, slightly sweaty, sticking together after making love. He listened to her breathing and hoped she'd stay. He was just beginning to drop off when she pulled away. "Don't go," he said in a husky voice.

She hesitated, but then rose. "I have to," she whispered. She grabbed her robe and slipped from the room without looking back. Once he was alone, it felt as if she'd taken all the warmth of the room with her. For a time, he watched the door, hoping it would open again, but it didn't and he finally gave in to sleep.

Chapter Twenty-Three

Jeremy rose and dressed before sunup. He saw the light in the kitchen, but it was still a surprise to see Lizzie up and working. She had a large bowl in hand and was stirring a thick batter. He cleared his throat to warn her, but he startled her anyway. "Sorry."

She smiled, embarrassed. "I just . . . I didn't hear you. You're up early."

"I'm usually up now. Why are you up so early?"

She shrugged and blushed as she looked back down at the batter. "Do you want something to eat?"

"Not right now. Don't let me disturb you."

She blinked. "You're not," she said earnestly.

"I can wait. I think I'll get started."

"But it's dark."

He grinned. "That's not dark," he said, jutting his thumb toward the door. Her expression turned almost mournful, which gave him a strange feeling.

"I wish you didn't have to work in the mine."

"I may not . . . always," he replied slowly. "I've been thinking about it. I've been thinking about a lot of things." He moved closer. "There's something I've been wondering. Replaying in my mind."

"What?"

He hesitated a moment. "What's Rebecca's middle name?"

She gave him a bemused look. "Aileen. Why?"

"Aileen," he repeated.

She nodded. "After her grandmother on her father's side. Why do you ask?"

"Rebecca Aileen . . . Ray?"

She took a sharp breath, but couldn't seem to utter a word. She shook her head and looked away from him before walking over to set down the bowl. "How did you know?" she asked in a low voice.

He felt a chill run up his spine.

She turned to face him, clearly alarmed and upset. "How did you know our name?"

He'd hit on something—but he didn't have a full picture yet. He stepped to her, trying to choose his words carefully. "I care about you," he ventured carefully. She still had a worried, almost frightened look on her face. What had he uncovered? "I don't have much to offer, but . . . I'd marry you." It looked as though she'd stopped breathing. "I'd take care of you and the kids." She squeezed her eyes shut, as if in pain, and his heart plummeted.

She looked at him again. "You've sworn never to tell," she said in a low, almost dead-sounding voice.

The words needled him, especially after she'd made it apparent she wouldn't consider marrying him. "Yeah, I've sworn it. I still swear it. What are you getting at?"

"You asked about the bad man."

He frowned in confusion. "I remember."

"It's him."

He shook his head, not following. "Who?"

"My husband. The father of my children."

The words rocked him, but he tried to look impassive because he wanted her to keep talking. She'd lied; she'd been lying all along, but he remembered the talk about the bad man. And Jake's bad dream. And Jake's black eye. He felt anger take hold, turn cold and harden in his gut. "He hurt you?"

Her chin trembled. She nodded.

"And the kids?"

Her eyes filled. "I never thought he'd do that. I never thought he would hurt either of them."

"But he did?"

"He hit Jake the one time. That's when I knew I had to leave. I couldn't live with that."

"But it was okay for him to hurt you?" he demanded angrily.

"I certainly didn't know it would be like that, at first. And then, I . . . I didn't think I had a choice."

Jeremy cocked his head, sensing a problem with this story. "Why has he not shown up here?" He paused, but she didn't answer. "I remember you saying he wouldn't know where to find you, but that doesn't make any sense."

She looked down, her face filled with shame.

He took hold of her arms. "Lizzie, look at me." He waited until she did. "I'll protect you," he pledged. "No matter what, but tell me the truth."

She bit on her bottom lip as some inner struggle raged.

"Do you believe me?" he asked, unwittingly tightening his grip.

A soft sigh signified a conclusion or maybe a decision. "Yes."

"Well, then?"

"Lionel Greenway was not my father," she admitted slowly.

He didn't understand yet. "Go on."

"It was by sheer, dumb luck that I ended up here. Or

fate. Maybe fate. Not only here, but at the doorstep of April May and Cessie."

"I thought you'd met them before."

"You don't understand. I'm really not who I've claimed to be. I mean, I've become her, but I didn't start out as her. I had never been to this town before the evening you first saw me. I didn't know Lionel when he was alive," she said haltingly.

"Uh-huh," he muttered under his breath as he let go of her.

"I was desperate. I had nowhere to go when I left. I just ran. Took my children and ran."

"From where?"

"Indiana. We took trains, first in one direction, then in another. I used most of the money I'd saved in secret. Ethan never allowed me to have my own money, so I'd stashed some each week for months. For years."

"Ethan," Jeremy repeated as if the word tasted bad.

She nodded. And waited.

He took a few steps away, stopped and grabbed the back of his neck. Seconds ticked by before he turned back to face her. "You're saying there's no reason for you to be here. No way for him to track you down."

She nodded slightly and then shrugged. "I don't know how he would," she replied weakly.

"And your name's not really Carter. It's Ray."

"Was. My name *was* Pauline Ray."

Her name was Pauline. Not Elizabeth. Not Lizzie. He felt strangely vulnerable and more than a little betrayed. "All those times I called you Lizzie."

"Because I am now! I left Pauline Ray behind and I became Elizabeth Anne Greenway Carter. I even feel like Lionel was my father. I know that must sound crazy, but it's true."

"Is Ethan the reason you don't want to marry me?"

She looked distressed. Tears escaped, but she wiped them away and looked at him stoically.

"Tell me."

She folded her arms tightly. "Th-that is a reason, I suppose," she stammered miserably.

"You're Lizzie Carter, right?"

She frowned in puzzlement as she considered the question, but then she nodded. "Yes."

"And your husband, Mr. Carter, he passed. That's what I heard."

She hesitated and then nodded.

"He's not the reason, is he? Ethan, I mean."

She shook her head slowly. "He's dead to me," she admitted quietly.

"Then why?"

She looked pained. "It's not been long enough. You haven't really let me know you yet."

"At least you always knew my real name," he reminded her bitterly.

"But, Jeremy, what if you change your mind?"

What if *he* changed *his* mind? He took several moments to answer, because almost everything out of her mouth was a surprise. "I won't."

"I can't leave again," she said in a choked voice. "This was my second chance. There won't be another."

Was it that she didn't think he'd made an earnest offer? "You won't have to. I'd take care of you. I'd be the husband you deserve."

"Please," she pleaded. "Please, don't insist. If you do, I'll give in. But I don't want to take that step right now. And it has nothing to do with loving you."

He was so stunned by the words that silence filled the room. A thick, emotion-filled silence. "I've never asked

anyone to marry me," he said quietly. "I never thought I
would." He watched as she ducked her head, either hurt or
maybe touched by the words. If only he could come up with
the right words to make her understand. "You say you've
become someone else. Well . . . so have I! I haven't given
a damn about anything or anybody for the longest time. Not
until you. Maybe it hasn't been enough time, but I knew
after an hour with you. Maybe even before that. All of a
sudden, I want to live again. I want to love you and take
care of you. I want a family. I want *this* family."

"You *want* to love me," she repeated, disturbed by the
words. She studied him, trying to discern the meaning in
the words and perhaps beyond the words. "Why do you work
in the mine?"

He was taken aback by the change of subject. "I'll quit.
I'll leave it. I'll find something else."

She shook her head, because that wasn't the question
she'd asked. "I told you a secret that would ruin me if it
got out."

"And I told you it won't get out. Not by me. Even if you
kicked me out tonight and never looked at me again, I
would never want to see you hurt. Don't you know that?"

"I do, because I trust you. So, maybe you can trust me
in return and answer my question. Why did you go to work
in the mine?"

"Why do you keep asking?" he demanded angrily.

"Because! There's something you're not telling me. You
claim you care enough about me to want to marry me."

"Love you enough," he corrected.

The words silenced her. "That's not what you said," she
finally replied.

"I'm not good with words, Lizzie. Pauline," he corrected
bitterly.

She stiffened. "Don't call me that."

He didn't understand, but it was clear that she was serious.

"It's like a slap in the face. Don't you understand? I left her behind. I left that life behind. And I've shared everything with you," she said thickly. "I've told you everything."

He sighed. "I went into the mines after my father died. After my whole family had gone. I felt dead . . . and so I went into the ground."

The words sank in and her expression turned sorrowful. "You have to know they wouldn't have wanted that."

He nodded slowly. "I know," he said quietly.

She walked over and sat, looking exhausted. It looked like she was done talking, and maybe they had said enough. He couldn't believe how much had been said. "I'll be outside."

Lizzie rose to finish her cake, although it took an inordinate amount of will and strength. Having completed the task, she went back to her room and stretched out on her bed, covering herself with a blanket. What had she been thinking, confiding her every secret to him? It was almost as if he had some sort of power over her. Because he was handsome. And he cared. He cared enough that he'd asked to marry her. *Love you enough*, the memory of his voice echoed. She exhaled slowly and hugged the blanket tighter.

Chapter Twenty-Four

Lizzie's angst grew as she and the children walked the path to the Blue home that morning. What if she was wrong about trusting Jeremy? Not only had she put herself at risk, but her children and April May and Cessie, as well. She needed to forego church and speak with him again. She had to make him understand how much was at risk. Hopefully, Cessie would take the children and April May wouldn't ask too many questions. She had a way of ferreting out the truth.

Cessie was delighted to take charge of the children and April May was checking traps, so Lizzie made a clean getaway after pleading a sudden stomachache. Rebecca gave her a suspicious look, but said nothing.

"I'll walk them home this afternoon," Cessie said cheerfully. "You just feel better."

Lizzie started home at a brisk pace, although her steps slowed as she got closer. When she stepped into the clearing, the view of the home she'd inherited and loved so much hit with a strange impact. She loved it, and she wanted to stay for the rest of her life. She also wanted Jeremy in her life, although it *was* too soon to think of marriage. What would people think of such a rash decision?

She needed to be accepted here first. Folks hadn't accepted her father—and he wouldn't want that kind of life for her. She didn't want to be an outcast.

She heard the sounds of hammering and started forward again. She didn't know exactly what she would say, but she had to make him understand. The sound was coming from the winery, where Jeremy was rebuilding the cellar steps. She looked down the treacherously steep staircase. "You were worried about me breaking my neck going down there," she said.

He looked up at her in surprise and had to remove the nail held between his lips before speaking. "Your neck is worth more than mine."

"Is that so?" she asked wryly.

"Thought you were going to church."

"Cessie took the children. I . . . we need to talk," she said haltingly.

With the light behind her creating a halo effect, she looked truly angelic, especially dressed up for church. "I'll come up," he said. "I came down here on a whim, and then got sidetracked looking around to see what it was going to take to repair these steps."

"No, that's all right. I'll come down," she said, already taking the first step.

He tossed the hammer aside and held up a hand to assist her, staying ready should she fall into his arms.

"It's so dark down here," she commented when she reached him.

"This isn't dark," he rejoined.

"I suppose not. Not like you're used to. May we sit?"

"Sure, but—" He tugged off his coat and laid it on the step for her to sit on. "So you don't get your dress dirty."

"Thank you."

She sat on the second step and he sat next to her, shoulder to shoulder. "You feeling uneasy about what you told me?"

"It's not that I don't trust you—"

"You sure about that?" She shifted to better meet his gaze and, even in the dim light, he saw the intensity in her eyes.

"Yes, I am! I knew I could trust you. I know I can trust you. But having shared what I did—"

She had a point, and his conscience was weighed down by his secret. How could he keep getting more and more deeply involved without telling her the truth?

"It's not only me at risk," she continued. "It's the children and April May and Cessie. Who only wanted to help me."

"Two men," he said quietly, "are dead because of me." He heard her breath catch. "The truth about me is a whole lot worse than the truth about you, but I'll tell you and then you'll have something on me."

Her jaw went lax for a moment; then she clamped it shut, angry. "I don't want something on you! Is that honestly what you think I want?"

He shook his head. "I didn't say it right. But it's only fair that you know, since I asked to come into this family. Not that you would have agreed, but—"

"I will agree," she interrupted. "When it's been long enough that everyone won't be shocked. I want to marry you. But I don't want us to be . . . judged. I want us to be accepted. That's my hesitation. And maybe that makes me a terrible person, since I am . . . married to Ethan." She finished the statement as if the words had a bad taste. "And yet I'm not afraid of God's judgment. I'm afraid of people's." She paused. "I love it here. I want us to stay and be happy the rest of our lives. A lot of these same people didn't accept my father."

"Your father," he said quietly.

"I know," she said with a bemused smile. "Maybe I'm not making any sense, but I do feel like Lionel's my father. And here I am, concerned with public opinion when I'm suggesting bigamy. Which is not only a sin, but a crime. But I'm speaking my heart. What I truly feel. I feel like I've buried my old self, my old life. I don't feel married. I wouldn't feel any conflict about marrying you, because Pauline Ray doesn't exist anymore."

"I wouldn't feel any conflict about marrying you, either," he said. "But bigamy wouldn't be my worst crime. You need to hear this." He got to his feet and crossed to the shelves that lined one of the walls. The ceiling was low, only inches above his head, but it wasn't as tight as what he was used to. Keeping his back to her, he sought for the right place to begin. He'd kept the truth locked away for so long, it didn't want to come out. "My sister, Jenny, fell in love with this rich man's son, who always did what he wanted and got away with it. He used girls. Ruined them. I warned her. Over and over again," he said with a shake of his head. "I warned her about Ted Landreth."

"Landreth?"

He turned to face her and nodded. "His father owns the mine I work in. Like I said, it's a rich family. Not known for being good people, either." He hated this story. "One day, Jenny came home. I don't know; she wasn't right. She seemed real upset, but trying to hold it in. She left the dinner table without touching her food and went to bed. Then the next morning we found her—"

"I know," she said, although it came out as a whisper. She cleared her throat. "I know she drowned."

"On purpose."

Lizzie's eyes widened.

"I believe she took her own life."

Lizzie rubbed her arms against a sudden chill.

"I found her. I pulled her out of the pond."

"I'm so sorry," Lizzie said with a shake of her head.

"It was a terrible day, one of the worst ever. My mother took it upon herself to . . . prepare Jenny. She could have waited for a neighbor to help, but I think she suspected something wasn't right. But when Jen was stripped of the wet clothes, my mother cried out. I went in and I saw."

Lizzie's face was a mask of tension and empathy.

"She'd been handled roughly," he said haltingly. "That's all we knew. But I had a pretty good idea who'd done it. The thing is, a weasel like Ted Landreth would never take responsibility, no matter what he'd done. He'd never had to, not for anything, and he wouldn't be starting now."

"What did you do?" she said just above a whisper.

"I went to the only decent friend of his I knew. His name was Curtis Powell, and I found out from him what happened."

"You're saying you found out what happened to Jenny?"

He nodded reluctantly. "Curtis said another friend of theirs, Stan Thomas, pulled him aside one day and offered him a bit of *fun* that involved lying with a woman, and not a whore, either."

Lizzie cringed.

"Not rape," Jeremy continued. "Stan said the girl would be willing. Curtis didn't get the full gist and he didn't know where they were going when they started off this one day." He paused. "The day before Jenny died."

Lizzie pressed her fisted hands to her lips.

"Ted had a head start, Stan said. Ted always had a head start he said, and he laughed when he said it."

"Oh, my God," Lizzie breathed.

"Curtis figured out where they were going before they got there. It was an abandoned cabin on the edge of *our* land.

By then, he was going because it was Jen. Not to hurt her, because he'd always been sweet on her. More to make sure she was okay. But she wasn't. Right as they got there, Stan admitted it was Jenny and said the plan was to share her."

Lizzie exhaled as she bowed her head, pained by the words.

"They went inside and it was obvious she'd been hurt. He said she was white as a ghost, obviously sick to her stomach. And she looked like she'd been manhandled. He didn't remember exactly what was said, something about sharing her, but she was saying no. Real upset. Curtis told Ted to leave her alone, but Stan was not about to give up what had been promised, so he drew a gun on Curtis."

Lizzie's eyes widened.

"Ted made Stan put down the gun and then the two of them left, but Curtis was pretty sure Ted had already hurt her."

"Oh, Jeremy."

"Curtis followed them to be sure they didn't circle back, and because Jenny wanted him to leave. Begged him to. He was going to come calling the next day to make sure she was all right, but there was no next day."

Lizzie's eyes filled with tears and spilled over. She shook her head, exhaled shakily, and wiped her face. "It's so terrible."

"I know." Jeremy came back to the step and sat again. "It took some time, but I came up with a plan, and Curtis helped. After what happened to Jenny, he wouldn't have anything more to do with Stan or Ted."

"What was the plan?"

"What we wanted was for Ted to admit he'd hurt Jenny. Of course, the only way he'd do that was if he felt safe enough. If he was bragging about it."

Lizzie hugged his arm for support.

"There was a new circuit judge in town and his son was someone Curtis had become friends with. His name was Alex Corry, and he agreed to help us. So, this poker game was arranged, a night of drinking and playing cards. Guess where Ted suggested they go for the game?"

"The cabin?"

He nodded. "In a way, it made it easier for me, 'cause I was outside listening. No way they would have said anything if I was there. But since I knew the place—"

Her grip tightened on his arm.

"So, they were all drinking, except Curtis and Alex had watered theirs down. Alex was real clever the way he went about drawing Stan and Ted out. He told them he could find out what women in the county were in trouble for this reason or for that, his father being the judge and all, and that maybe they could take advantage of the knowledge."

"Take advantage," she repeated with a curl of disgust on her lips.

He nodded. "Use the knowledge to—"

"To do whatever they wanted," she interjected, with distaste. "I understand."

"They thought he was one of them once he said that, and he just kept egging them on. When Curtis left to relieve himself, Ted and Stan said Curtis shouldn't be a part of the plan, that he'd just ruin it. Alex asked what they meant and he got the whole story."

Jeremy looked away and swiped at his eyes. He didn't want to give in to the rage of emotion tearing at his insides, but he'd kept the truth to himself for so long. Sharing it now made it fresh again. Lizzie put her arm around him protectively. "The truth is, she went to the cabin willingly to be with Ted," he continued in a thick voice, "because he said he loved her and wanted to marry her. I'd already learned that much from a friend of hers. But once she was there, she changed her mind. Or tried to. Alex asked Ted what he meant by that and the son of a bitch said he changed it back for her."

Lizzie shuddered.

"Then Alex said, 'so you raped her,' and Ted said he didn't think it could be called rape because she'd said she would."

"You must have been sick to your stomach," Lizzie commiserated.

He nodded. "And it got worse. Stan said he would have had her too, except for damned Curtis. Then Curtis stepped back in and Alex stood up and said he was ready to go. He'd heard what he needed to. Up until then, he'd been acting half drunk, but suddenly he was stone cold sober. So, Ted got all alarmed. He demanded to know what the hell that meant, and Alex said, 'I'm going to go back and tell my father exactly what you did. I don't know what they can do to you legally, but pretty soon the whole town will know what you really are.'"

Jeremy shook his head. "He wasn't supposed to do that. But he did and the rest of it happened so fast."

"What happened?"

"Ted yelled, 'The hell you will,' and he stood, drew a gun, and fired. He blew Alex backwards into a wall."

"Oh, dear God!"

"Then he aimed at Curtis, but I was firing by then. There was one window in the cabin, and I shot through it and killed them both. Ted and Stan. I killed them."

She took a shaky breath and then another.

"Luckily, Alex wasn't dead," he said.

"He wasn't?"

Jeremy shook his head. "The bullet went into his shoulder. Curtis took him into town to the doctor."

"How did they explain?"

"They claimed someone shot out of nowhere. This hellion named Abel Lindley had been on the warpath about some disputed territory. He's part of this crazy family, so everyone believed he did it, although it couldn't be proved."

"And Ted and Stan?" she asked reluctantly.

"They disappeared, never to be seen again." He paused. "If you mean what really happened, I dropped their bodies down an old well shaft near the cabin." She nodded very slightly and then hugged him close. He felt the solidarity and knew they were bound for life. More than any ring or words of passion could do. He was so grateful for it, he couldn't speak for several moments. "Curtis and Alex started the rumor that Ted had been talking about going into the city to try out some gambling trick he'd learned. That's the thing about a small town. Start a whisper and it becomes a wildfire. The rumor started; people believed it. Especially when no one could find either Ted or Stan. And a lot of men were hired to look for them. Eventually, everyone assumed they'd gotten themselves tangled up with the wrong gamblers and killed."

"All that talk about not being a good man," she said. "That's what it was about?"

He nodded.

"You shot those men in the defense of others."

"I doubt a judge would see it that way."

"It's what it was! It's just lucky that Alex lived."

"I don't know, Lizzie," he said with a slow shake of his head. "I think I would have killed them no matter what. Once Curtis and Alex were gone. I think I would have."

"You don't know that. You can't possibly know that."

Except he did know that. But did he really want to convince her he was a killer at heart? This place was her second chance, and she was his second chance. "So you can live with knowing all that?"

"Of course I can."

"And you're really going to marry me?"

"Are you really going to marry me?" she echoed.

"Nothing in the whole world would make me happier, Elizabeth Greenway Carter."

She leaned in to press a soft kiss to his lips. "Me too," she whispered.

He smiled and stood. "I want to show you something interesting I discovered." He walked over to the wall and knocked.

"If someone knocks back, I'm going to jump to the top of these steps."

"Point is, if that was wood backed by earth, it wouldn't sound hollow."

Her puzzlement cleared and she rose and walked to him, intrigued.

"It opens," he said. "Here." He pointed to two vertical seams. "You have to take off this center section of shelves," he said, starting to do it.

She grabbed his arm, stopping him. "Wait."

He looked at her and she looked disturbed all of a sudden. "What's wrong?"

"Why did you go to work in his father's mine?"

He hesitated a few moments. "I killed two men. Maybe three, including my own father. He took his own life once he learned what I'd done. I thought knowing might give him some peace, but it worked just the opposite. He kept saying 'a life for a life.'"

"Oh, Jeremy."

"It's true. He thought I was damned, that I'd be hanged, and he couldn't take it. So he—"

"You did *not* kill your father!"

"I know that now," he said quietly. "Too much grief broke him. He was drinking at the time—"

"But at the time, you thought . . . you had all this blood on your hands, so you—"

"I thought justice would be done if I died in the mine."

Tears shone in her eyes, but more than anything, she looked angry. "How completely, utterly *stupid* of you!"

Tears escaped and slid down her face, and she started to turn away, but he grabbed her back. "Lizzie—"

"What?" she demanded, refusing to look at him.

"I didn't mean to upset you. You just had to know."

She swallowed hard and wiped her face, then looked at him. "So now I know. You've been punishing yourself all these years." It was silent for several seconds. "Just tell me you'll stop," she said beseechingly.

He studied her a moment and then nodded.

"So what's behind the wall?" she asked, granting him a reprieve.

He turned, swiping at his nose and eyes discreetly, knowing she'd changed the subject for his sake. He removed the four center shelves and then swung a three-foot section of the wall open to reveal another room, although it was dark inside. "It's full of wine."

"Is it really? And we found it today, of all days."

He grinned. "Yeah. The day of our beginning. Our real beginning. No more secrets."

"No more secrets," she echoed solemnly.

He felt the lifting of a long-held weight; held so long, in fact, it made him feel giddy to be unburdened of it. "What do you think? Is it too early to open one?"

She laughed. "No." She reached out and cupped his face and her smile turned wistful. "I love you."

He wrapped her in his arms and kissed her. "I love you."

Chapter Twenty-Five

Marie glowered as someone else mentioned the change that had come over Shef. Why couldn't everyone just mind their own damned business? Was there nothing else in the whole world to talk about?

"What's the matter, Marie?" Walt asked, walking up to where she stood at the edge of the bar.

"Nothing."

"You look mad as a wet hen."

"Well, I'm not."

"Well, good, 'cause it's too fine a day to be unhappy. And a Sunday, besides."

"Everybody just talking about everybody else," she complained. "That's all. It gets on my nerves."

"Who they talking about?"

She shook her head. "No one. Never mind."

"Must be someone."

She folded her arms. "You heard anything about the woman who came to town? Mrs. Carter, used to be Greenway?"

"Yeah, sure. The hermit's daughter. I haven't seen her, but I hear she's real nice."

"And pretty as everything," Marie added bitterly.

"She can't be near as pretty as you are."

Marie rolled her eyes. Apparently, she was to Shef.

"I wish I could make you smile, Marie," Walt said wistfully.

"I'm fine," she said.

"You don't seem fine."

"Well, I am, so stop saying that."

"Okay. You want to go upstairs?"

A sigh escaped her before she could stop it and a hurt look crossed his face.

"You know what?" he said. "Don't do me any favors." She drew breath to respond, but he continued. "It may come as news to you, but there's girls here who actually like my company."

She felt a prickling of panic. Donna had warned her enough times about Walt losing interest. "I like your company."

"You don't act like it."

"Oh, come on, Walt," Marie said, taking his arm. "You know you're my special guy."

"Since when?"

Marie pouted. "Since always."

"I know what got you so dad-blamed bothered about Mrs. Carter," he accused, his expression hardening as the truth dawned on him. "It's Shef, ain't it? The two of them have struck up some sort of thing, and you've still got a sweet spot for him."

"I do not. It's got nothing to do with him. I just don't like people talking about other people. That's all. Besides, I don't think they're together. Where'd you hear that?"

He pulled his arm from her grip with a shake of his head.

She noticed Samantha watching them from across the room, and a renewed sense of panic took hold. Vultures were waiting to move in on her territory. "Look, never mind about Shef and whatever that lady's name is," Marie said as she maneuvered close. She teasingly kissed his grizzled cheek. "Let's you and me go upstairs and get more comfortable."

He sulked. "You sure you want that? I ain't Jeremy Sheffield, after all."

"Walt." She pouted. "Come on. I don't want to talk about him. I haven't had a sweet spot for him since we were kids."

Walt gave her a wry look. "I've seen you when he's around."

She took hold of his hand. "Whaddaya say you give me a chance to prove you're wrong?" she all but purred.

"I don't think you can prove I'm wrong, but we can go upstairs."

Marie smiled like she was the happiest girl in the world, and it wasn't that much of an act, because she was relieved. It would have been humiliating if Walt had walked off and gone over to Samantha. She made sure her rival was still watching, and then led Walt away, walking with a pronounced swagger.

Chapter Twenty-Six

It was near quitting time when Jeremy finally broached the subject with Liam. He was lying on his back working on a vein overhead because the seam they were in was only three feet tall by some twelve feet long.

"Quitting?" Liam repeated. He was propped against the side of the seam, spent from the day's work and a recent coughing fit. He watched Jeremy's lamp bob as he nodded. It was silent for a few minutes as both men pondered the next steps. Liam needed a new partner or he would be let go, and he wasn't in the prime of youth or in the best of health. "What will you do?"

"Not sure yet. Maybe become a farmhand. I don't know. I just can't stay here anymore."

"I know what you mean." Another silence fell between them before Liam asked, "When were you thinking?"

"When we find you a new partner."

Liam barked a laugh, although there was no amusement in it. "I thought you said you wanted out."

Jeremy felt like shit. He didn't want to leave Liam in a bind, but he needed to get out of this hellhole. He cared enough that he'd shown up today, and he'd keep showing up until they found some solution for Liam—but they both had to be realistic, too. He could give it a week or two, maybe a month, but he couldn't stay indefinitely. Damn it, Liam was his partner in the mine and his friend, but he'd never been assigned as Liam's keeper. "Maybe you could find work outside this place, too."

"It's a good thought," Liam replied dryly. Then he coughed. "I'm only something like six weeks from pension."

Jeremy froze. He felt a little sick to his stomach all of a sudden. "You are?"

Liam nodded. "Never thought I'd take it. Never figured I could make ends meet on a quarter pay, but it beats nothing." He paused. "Wonder if I could find someone to hook up with for the month and a half."

Jeremy barely held back a sigh of fatigue and depression. He knew the same as Liam that no one else would take him on. Which meant Jeremy would have to stay. For the sake of a pension, he would have to stay. "I can stick it out that long."

"You don't hafta," Liam objected. Then he coughed.

Damned pension, Jeremy thought. The only reason they offered it was because most men didn't make it twenty years in the mine. If a man did, he sure as hell didn't make it much longer. They heard a mule team coming, pulling an almost full train of carts behind it. It sounded different when it was a heavy load. "Whatcha say, fellas?" a voice called.

"Not much," Shef answered, glad for the diversion.

"Nope. Never do."

"How are you, Timmy Wayne?" Liam asked as he slowly scooted out of the seam.

Jeremy also followed because he needed to stretch.

Timmy made it into their shallow pool of light. "Any better and I'd be twins," the boy said with a grin.

Liam grinned back. "That's a good one."

"About that birthday of yours," Shef said as he rotated a stiff shoulder.

"I thought you forgot," Timmy said.

"Nope."

"You sure you wanna do that, Shef?"

"I said so, didn't I?"

"Yep. So you did."

"So, this Friday after work?"

"Yes, sir. I'd like that a lot. Think we can go back to the patch after, so I can change into clean clothes?"

"That's what we'll do," Jeremy said as he bent to help Liam dump their bin of coal into the cart.

"Say, Timmy," Liam said after they'd finished the task. "You know of anybody looking for a laborer?"

Jeremy looked at Liam, but Liam wouldn't meet his gaze.

"Can't say I do," Timmy replied as he stepped back and wiped his hands on the sides of his trousers. "If I did, I'd try to convince 'em to bring me on. I'm ready."

Liam clapped him on the shoulder. "You'll get there."

"Why you ask?" Timmy inquired.

Liam shrugged. "Curious."

"They'd take on more miners," Timmy said. "But you gotta have two years' experience and pass a test on explosives and such. It's a written test, too," he said dejectedly.

"Not so good at written tests?" Liam asked.

"No, sir. Readin' and writin' is not my strong suit. Not by a long shot. I never did take much to book learnin'."

"It was the same with me," Liam said.

"Well, I'd best get. I'll see you Friday, Shef, if not before." Timmy led the mules onward until darkness swallowed them whole.

"You gonna blast again?" Liam asked, still avoiding his gaze.

"I don't think so. I'm just going to pick up." He started back into the hole.

"Shef—"

Jeremy turned and looked at him. Even with only the whites of Liam's eyes gleaming clearly in the light of Jeremy's lamp, Jeremy could tell it was important. "Yeah?"

"You can't worry about me."

The words caught Jeremy off guard, and a flood of emotion kept him silent.

"You've been carrying your weight and some of mine too, and it's time we . . . I don't know, face up to the light of day and move on accordingly." He paused. "It's a funny thing for one miner to say to another, isn't it? Face up to the light of day."

"That's what I'm looking forward to," Jeremy said thickly. "I want to hold my face up to the light of the day and breathe fresh air."

Liam nodded.

"But I'm not going to leave you in the lurch with six weeks to go till pension. Six weeks in Six. I've done a hell of a lot longer than that. I can make it six more weeks."

"I'm not asking, Shef."

"I know. I'm offering." He paused. "The only thing is, I don't want to work the half day on Saturday anymore. But you can pick up someone else to work with for that."

Liam nodded and then looked off. Only the quivering of his chin gave away the emotion he was fighting. "You mind if I head on out?" he asked in a shaky voice.

Jeremy shook his head. The lump in his throat was painful. "No," he managed. Liam gave a weak salute and started off, but Jeremy didn't hurry to finish his final task.

Liam needed a little while alone, and so did he. Down the tunnel some distance away, small orange lights bobbed and swayed as tired men trudged toward him. He couldn't see anything but the lights from the lamps in hats, and yet he sensed the weariness of the men beneath. He understood completely. He felt it, too.

Chapter Twenty-Seven

Friday, October 5

Lizzie swatted at an insect that buzzed near her ear and then went back to pruning the vines. She'd walked the children over to Cessie and April May's this morning, determined to begin reclaiming the vines, and she'd been at it all day. The books on wine making stated fall was the time to plant. "It'd be nice if you'd guide me," she murmured. "Don't let me tear out anything I shouldn't."

Not only was it easy to imagine Lionel with her, it was a comfort. Today he would have brought a chair, two glasses, and a bottle of wine. He would have worn a big-brimmed hat and supervised in his witty, almost cavalier manner. He'd possessed wisdom and humor, intelligence and humility. She knew this. She also knew that he was pleased she was there. How, exactly, she had come to possess this knowledge, she didn't fully understand, but she knew it in her heart.

She couldn't dally too much longer, because she needed to get cleaned up and join the others for dinner. Jeremy had sent a note to let her know he was taking a young friend from the mine to dinner and that he would be

coming over later. She couldn't wait to see him. In fact, her
senses suddenly and overwhelmingly flooded. She blew out
a breath and crossed her arms over her chest, aching with
desire. Never had she experienced anything like what he
made her feel. Many years ago, Ethan had seemed a good
man and a sensible choice, and her father had approved of
him, but her husband had never made her feel special or
sensual or beautiful, the way Jeremy did.

As it turned out, Ethan had not proved to be either a
good man or a sensible choice, but she'd made her bed by
marrying him. It would have probably remained that way,
despite her fantasies of escaping, except that he'd hit Jake.
That one blow meant that he could no longer be trusted not
to hurt their children.

She would never forget the memory of that night and the
way Jake had cowered on the floor after being knocked
down. Horrified, she'd rushed toward him as Ethan reared
back to hit her. For some reason, he'd refrained that time.
Instead, he'd spewed vile words and stormed from the
house. She'd pulled Jake into her arms, rocked him, and
cried. Hating Ethan. Hating herself. Rebecca had joined
them on the floor, the three of them hurting. Frightened.
Crying.

When the tears finally stopped and the self-hatred
abated, a cold, bitter finality set in. She put the children to
bed and went to her hiding place, a loose floorboard in the
keeping room. She withdrew and counted the money she'd
secretly squirreled away for the last seven-and-a-half years.
Ethan was so tight-fisted; she'd borne many blows because
of occasionally overspending. Of course, never once had
she actually overspent. She'd simply claimed she had in
order to save. Kneeling in the keeping room, she'd felt sick
to her stomach, wondering how they'd be able to begin a
new life with just over seventy dollars to their names.

But you did it, she imagined Lionel saying as he raised his glass to her.

I couldn't have without you, she thought.

I'm delighted at the way it turned out. We showed them all, didn't we?

She stood and stretched. "It still seems like a dream sometimes."

But it's not, he reminded her. The thought made her smile as she started back for the house, removing her work gloves as she went.

Chapter Twenty-Eight

Jeremy and Timmy Wayne walked together back to Jeremy's two-room shack amidst the other cheaply constructed, wooden, tin-roofed shacks rented to miners and their families. Company-owned housing for miners was known as a patch and, in this patch, the rows of houses looked pretty much alike. Most had two bedrooms and a kitchen. In the backyard were privies, sheds, and clotheslines. Inside was as stark and plain as the outside. The floors were wooden, the walls unadorned. The kitchens had a small table with crudely made chairs or benches, a coal stove, and a cupboard. They were lit by oil lamps and there was no running water.

Jeremy's house was on the outer row, the last row built. Most houses lined a dirt road and faced other homes, but his row faced outward, toward the mine. Their small backyards abutted other backyards. The separateness hadn't bothered Jeremy, but, looking around, Timmy Wayne found it strange. "But at least," the boy said, "you got it all to yourself. We sleep four to a bed."

While Jeremy washed up and changed his clothes, Timmy Wayne hurried home to do the same. When he returned, a three-legged dog trailed behind. "Stay, Tripod," Timmy commanded.

"I didn't know you had a dog," Jeremy commented.

"Ain't my dog. He just likes me. It ain't nobody's dog, poor thing. Look how skinny it is."

Which was true, although the light brown mutt had a sweet face. He'd wanted to find a dog for Jake, but this wasn't what he'd had in mind. Still, the dog had obeyed Timmy's command. Jeremy squatted and called to the dog and he came, although more reticent than exuberant.

"He's kind of skittish," Timmy Wayne said, bending down to pet the dog on the opposite side. "He's had some rough treatment. You can tell."

"Doesn't belong to anybody, huh?"

"No. You should take him. He's a good dog, 'cept he don't never bark."

That was two strikes against the mutt, except that Jeremy already felt a fondness for the pathetic pooch with the adorable face. Maybe it was the attachment of one stray to another, or maybe it was that he loathed the thought of anyone mistreating a helpless animal. He didn't know how Tripod had lost the leg, but he'd been hurt by another dog. He could see scars from teeth on his muzzle and there was some bad scarring on his head and the back of his neck. "Who named him Tripod?"

"That's just what I call him on account of him having three legs."

Jeremy stood. "I know a little boy who might like him."

Timmy Wayne stood, too. "It would be good for Tripod to have a home and regular food to eat. I ain't been able to give him much."

Jeremy nodded and then shrugged. "We'll see if he'll follow. Then we'll just see."

"Oh, he'll follow."

* * *

After dinner at Wiley's, a meal that Timmy Wayne had proclaimed to be the best he'd ever "et," Timmy went back home, while Jeremy started toward the livery for his horse. The dog seemed torn, but stayed with Jeremy when beckoned. Of course, he'd been fed plenty of scraps from the restaurant, probably the best meal the dog had ever "et." Jeremy hoped Jake and Rebecca would take to him, because, one way or the other, he couldn't very well turn his back on the creature now.

He passed the Blue farm, which glowed from lights within. The smoke curling from the chimney was a cozy sight that made Jeremy anxious to reach the cottage. At the sound of barking, he looked and saw the Blues' dogs tearing toward them. Tripod heard too, and cowered. "Some watchdog," Jeremy muttered. He stopped the horse, poised to get down if he needed to. However, the Blues' dogs got close, and barked a stern warning but didn't do more than that. "Come on," Jeremy called to Tripod, who hopped along, glancing back nervously.

It wasn't late when he reached the cottage, not even nine o'clock, but the house was quiet when he stepped in the back door. There was a glass of wine poured and the light of the fire caught in the glass. He walked down the hall, noticing Lizzie's bedroom door was standing open. He cleared his throat before reaching it so he wouldn't startle her, but when he stopped in the doorway, it was apparent she'd been expecting him. Dressed in her robe, she was sitting in bed with her knees drawn up and a book on her lap. Her hair was loose and a glass of wine was on the bedside table. In the glow of the firelight, the room looked mighty inviting. More than inviting, it looked like a haven. "Hello," she said.

"It was so quiet, I didn't know if you'd be sleeping."

She shook her head. "Reading. Waiting for you."

The words made him smile. "I'll get cleaned up."

"I poured you a glass of wine, if you want it."

"I saw. Thanks. I'll just set my stuff down," he said before walking to his room and setting his bag down. "Um," he said upon stopping back in her doorway. It didn't look like she'd moved a muscle. "I found a dog. A stray."

"Oh?"

"He's not perfect, but the kids might like him. I guess we'll see in the morning." He thought about mentioning the three legs, but that could be left until tomorrow.

"All right."

He drank the glass of wine in the kitchen, then filled a bowl of water for Tripod. The dog jumped up to see him, but looked wary. Jeremy petted his head. "It'll be all right," he said soothingly. He set the bowl down. "Go to sleep. You'll meet everybody in the morning."

Lizzie leaned forward and hugged her legs. It had been an enlightening evening, starting with an after-dinner discussion as the ladies cleaned and put away dinner dishes. Cessie had broached the subject of school and Lizzie knew right away that Rebecca had put her up to it.

Between Cessie's gentle, prodding way and April May's straightforward manner, they had got her to face the truth—that the only reason she hadn't started Rebecca in school here was fear, and not a reasonable fear at that. To have Rebecca gone for much of the day and away from her protection was frightening.

"But, honey," Cessie said, "she'll be at the schoolhouse. It's perfectly safe."

"I planned on letting her start soon."

"Well, that's good," April May said. "What about Monday?"

Lizzie concentrated on the platter she was drying. As ridiculous as it was, she felt tears prick the backs of her eyes.

"Here's what I think," April May said as she pulled out a chair and sat. "When you know fear is stopping you from doing something that you should do or you really want to do, deep down, you just look the devil in the eye and you say, 'I am not going to let this damn fear stop me.'"

Cessie nodded. "She's right, although the curse words aren't necessary. If you can just see that it's nothing but worry—"

"And, Lordy, Lizzie," April May interrupted. "Rebecca is tough as nails. I fear for anyone who gets in her way."

Lizzie had laughed and turned to them. "Next week then," she said. "I'll get her started next week."

The decision felt right. She'd privately acknowledged how much she'd allowed fear to imprison the woman she had been. Elizabeth Greenway Carter was not going to follow that same path. Whether it was proper or not, she was so, so glad that Jeremy was here. She wanted him in ways she hadn't known were possible. She wanted his touch, his kiss, his concern, his counsel, and his passion. She wanted him inside her. She wanted him to hold her afterwards. She wanted their softly spoken conversations. She wanted to tell him about her day and she wanted to know about his.

No more fear, she thought as she settled back against the pillows.

Jeremy dried off after his bath and slipped on the waiting bathrobe. The robe that had belonged to the hermit. It didn't feel as odd as he'd thought it would. As he hurried back to the house, the air felt colder than before and the paving stones beneath his feet were cold and slippery. He let the dog onto the screened-in porch and propped the door open with a broom. "See you in the morning," he said before going inside.

Lizzie had gone back to reading, but she set her book aside as he slipped off the robe and got into bed. He turned on his side to face her and she scooted close. "How was dinner?"

Jeremy smiled. "Timmy liked it a lot. He'd never been to a restaurant."

She cocked her head. "Never?"

"Never. People in the patch are poor. Really poor."

"The patch?"

"The mining camp. Part of how people are paid is in script. Most people, anyway. That's one thing I stood firm on. Only cash for pay."

"What's script?"

"It's good for the company store or rent, only the rent is too high, especially for the places they live in, and the company charges twice what everything is worth at the store. Miners and their families have no choice about it, though, since that's all script is good for."

"Why don't they all demand cash for pay, too?"

"Not everybody can. When I signed on, they needed miners. But the man I work with, Liam, is a laborer, like a helper. He helps load the coal I dig out. He didn't have a choice." He paused before adding, "Problem is, no one is paid enough, especially not men like Liam, so they have to buy on credit. Only place you can do that is the company store, which charges even more when it's on credit."

She nodded thoughtfully. "How old is Timmy?"

"Just turned fourteen."

She sighed quietly and then reached over to press a kiss to his lips. "I'm glad you're here."

"I'm glad I'm here, too."

The fire crackled in the hearth. "Rebecca's going to start school next week."

"That's good. She'll like that."

"I know."

He suddenly grew serious. "I want you to know something. I see your face all the time. When I'm in the dark and I'm working, my hands are doing what they do, but in my mind I see you, and it gets me through the day."

Her eyes glistened. "I'll be so glad when you're done with that place."

"Me too. Six weeks."

She gave him a quizzical look. "Why—"

"Liam's due for a pension in six weeks. I gotta stick it out."

She leaned in and kissed his lips. "You're a good man," she whispered when she pulled back.

He woke a few hours later. They'd made love with hunger and vigor and fallen asleep tangled up in each other's arms. Now he had to relieve himself, so he got up. She moaned softly as he did, a good sound, and muttered something unintelligible. He got up and went outside to pass his water, and the dog woke and watched him with curiosity.

Going back inside, he opted to go to his room. As tired as he was, he might sleep until morning, and he didn't want to put her in an awkward position if the children woke first. The bed felt cold to climb into and he had second thoughts, but he curled up, warmed up slowly, and drifted back into a deep sleep.

Chapter Twenty-Nine

Jeremy woke again, confused at the bright light slanting in the window. It was later than he ever slept, which was disconcerting. By the time he opened his bedroom door, dressed and ready for the day, he smelled bacon. He walked into the kitchen and saw a covered plate, but no one was around. He stepped outside and saw Lizzie, Rebecca, and Jake playing with the dog. Lizzie flashed a bright smile, Rebecca laughed at the dog's antics, and Jake noticed Jeremy. "He's ours?" the boy called hopefully.

"He sure is. If you want him."

"We do," Jake exclaimed.

"Can we name him?" Rebecca asked, shielding her eyes from the morning glare.

"I already named him," Jake announced. "Lucky."

Lizzie beamed. "I think that's an excellent name for him."

Rebecca made a face. "No, it's not. How lucky is it to have three legs?"

"He just found a family to love him, didn't he?" Lizzie asked.

The dog looked at Jeremy—and Jeremy knew exactly

what he was thinking. That the two of them had that in common.

Rebecca considered. "I guess."

Lizzie started for the house. "I'll make you some eggs," she said to Jeremy. When she reached him, she glanced back at the children, who were involved with Lucky, and pressed a kiss to his cheek. "Thank you," she said softly. "He's perfect."

Jeremy laughed softly that a three-legged dog could be thought perfect.

The kitchen smelled of gingerbread when Jeremy stepped back into the room in the late afternoon, having just cleaned up after a day spent clearing a space for a barn. He'd gone into town to price out lumber and assistance in building the structure, and a plan was now in place. Since he would be here full-time in the winter, he would need the barn. It was a wonderful thought. A cold rain had blown up, which shut down work for the day, but that was fine with him.

Lizzie's back was to him as she coated chicken and put it into a skillet to fry, which added a rich and spicy aroma to the air. Rebecca was setting the table as rain began to beat down on the roof. "It smells good in here," he commented. "Can I help?"

"No," Lizzie replied without turning around. "But thank you anyway."

"Rebecca?" he asked.

Rebecca shook her head. "No, thank you."

"Which ones did you do?" Jeremy asked, nodding at the plates of gingerbread men.

Rebecca walked over and pointed them out. "That one, that one, and that one. Jake did that one." She looked up and gave him a wry look. "He wanted to know if we could make a gingerbread dog next time."

Jeremy grinned. "Good question. Do we actually get to eat those cookies? They look too pretty to eat."

Rebecca turned and leaned against the table. "We eat them."

"But not till after dinner," Lizzie added.

The chicken was sizzling, and the aroma made his mouth water. "Do you know how to play checkers, Rebecca?"

"Yes, but we don't have a checkers game."

"We should get one."

She mulled it over a moment. "That would be good."

"That's what we'll do, then."

She looked at him questioningly and then turned to her mother. "Can I go play now?"

"Yes, you may."

Jeremy watched Rebecca exit the room, then crossed to Lizzie. Placing his hands on her hips, he leaned around and pressed a soft kiss to her temple. "I think I'm making progress there," he said quietly.

She smiled and nodded. "You are."

More than anything, he wanted to express his joy in the simple moment. He wanted to say he was exactly where he wanted to be. Then, as if she understood his thoughts, she looked at him, pressed a soft kiss to his lips, and her expression was so tender his eyes misted over. He let go of her and walked away quickly, wrinkling his nose. He sniffed discreetly as he poured them each a glass of wine. He walked back and handed her the glass, then watched as she sipped, set the glass down, and turned the chicken in the pan. "Lizzie?"

"Yes?"

"I don't say it enough, but you're the best thing in my life. You, the kids, this place."

She turned to him, smiling warmly. "We've made it a nice home, haven't we?"

"You've made it a really nice home."

She drew breath to say something, but Jake beckoned from the other room. "Jeremy, you've gotta see this! Lucky learned a trick."

Jeremy grinned as he set his glass aside. "Excuse me, ma'am, but I've got to go see a trick now."

"Go." She laughed. "By all means, go."

Chapter Thirty

Cynthia Perkins stepped off the train in Green Valley, Virginia, and followed other passengers toward town. She was content to walk at a leisurely pace through the picturesque streets festooned in late-autumn splendor. Neat clapboard homes had well-used porches and whitewashed picket fences with ornate gates. She could certainly understand choosing to live here—but how and why had Pauline chosen it, if indeed she had?

She'd had success following Pauline Ray's trail, starting with a station attendant at the depot in Indianapolis who'd reported that Pauline and the children had gone southward. "Into Kentucky. Maybe Tennessee," he'd pondered thoughtfully. "I want to say Louisville."

She thanked him and followed the lead. There had been more dead ends than hits, but she'd eventually picked up the trail and followed it well into Virginia, where it went cold until she sent queries to local newspapers and telegraph offices, along with Pauline's photograph.

The effort paid off when a salesman by the name of Lester Shoemaker recognized Pauline from having ridden with her and the children, although they'd continued beyond his destination. Pauline, however, had shared she was going to Green Valley because of an elderly relative who was ill. Ethan Ray had claimed she had no family, but perhaps Pauline hadn't told him everything. Or perhaps she'd told Shoemaker a falsehood. No matter. If Pauline and the children were not here in Green Valley, she would continue on to as many towns as she possibly could for the short time left in her contract with Ethan Ray. She didn't care one bit about the man; he was an ill-tempered, small-minded bully, but she had a record of success to consider, not to mention the reputation of the agency.

The church, at the end of Main, was on the small side but lovely, with an impressive steeple that enclosed a belfry. As she strolled past, she found herself wishing the bells would toll. The cemetery next to it was well tended and quite beautiful with towering trees. There were benches placed throughout that issued a silent invitation to sit and contemplate her thoughts and actions. Instead, she walked into town. It was apparent that Green Valley's growth was recent and rather dramatic, since many of the buildings looked new. Only Main Street and Market Street had older buildings.

She started at a hotel, where she asked the proprietor if he knew Pauline Ray. Initially, he gave an open, honest, "No, ma'am," but then she showed him the photograph. He still claimed not to recognize Pauline, but now he was lying. That meant Pauline was or had been in the vicinity, using an assumed name. Confident she was on the right track, Cynthia went to the dress shop and spoke with the proprietor. Cynthia instinctively knew when people were being disingenuous, and the shopkeeper was being truthful when she declared she did not know Pauline Ray. Yet again, a glimpse of the photograph made the woman withdraw into suspicious silence. "Don't know that she does look familiar," the woman hedged. "Couldn't say. I see a lot of ladies, you know."

"I'm sure you do," Cynthia replied impassively.

The shopkeeper at the dry goods store claimed not to know her, but Cynthia knew he wasn't telling the truth either. She fared no better at the newspaper or the cobbler's shop. For someone who had not been in town long, Pauline Ray seemed to have earned loyalty among the townspeople, which was strange for a town this size. Small towns tended to be wary of newcomers.

Cynthia crossed over to the jail to speak with the sheriff, although she didn't expect anything to come of it since Pauline would have wanted to avoid the authorities.

One deputy was on duty. Slunk down in his chair, relaxed, his fingers interlaced on his stomach, he snapped to attention when she walked in. "Yes, ma'am?" he said, sitting up straight. "Help you?"

"I hope so. I'm looking for this woman."

He glanced at the photograph in her hand and then looked back at Cynthia. "Why?"

"We're kin," she said, trying a different approach.

He cocked his head, slightly suspicious. "That so?"

"Cousins," she continued. "Unfortunately, there was a falling out within the family, but I'm hoping to make amends. After all, it wasn't her fault or mine. It's time we let bygones be bygones."

"Was one of your folks kin to Lionel, then?"

Cynthia smiled, relieved for partial confirmation, even if she didn't fully understand it. "That's right. My father. They were brothers."

His face cleared because he believed her. "Miz Carter's

there. At the Greenway place. I don't know if you know this or not, but her husband passed on."

Cynthia's expression grew somber. "I did know, yes. It's one of the reasons I wanted to reach out to her . . . and the children, of course. I haven't seen them since they were babies. I suppose Rebecca must be eight by now. And Jake would be four or five."

"Yes, ma'am. Well, that's where you'll find her."

"Can you direct me? I was a child when I was last here."

"Sure thing. It's past the Blue farm. Here, I'll draw you a map. It's not too far at all."

"Thank you. I really am grateful."

"You bet," he said as he reached for pencil and paper and began drawing a map. "Mrs. Carter is a nice lady."

Cynthia murmured her agreement.

He handed her the map. "I hope you can fix your, uh, estrangement. I get the feeling Mrs. Carter's had a real hard time of it. I think things are just starting to work out for her."

"That's good to hear. Thank you."

"You're welcome, ma'am. Tell her Ellis says hello. And Shef too, if you see him."

"Chef?"

"Jeremy Sheffield. A good man. He's helping her out some and we're all pretty sure they're sparkin'," he said with a silly grin.

"Ah. I will. Thank you again."

Cynthia left the office feeling more conflicted than victorious. *It's a job*, she reminded herself. *It's a job and success matters*. She headed to the livery to rent a horse and wagon and drive out to the Greenway place. If she saw Pauline Ray in person, she'd send a telegram to her office and to Ethan Ray and she would be finished with the assignment.

Shef. She mulled over the name and wondered how big a role this Shef played in Pauline's new life.

Lizzie placed the last of the eggs in her basket and started back to the house, but stopped when she saw a wagon headed toward her with a woman driver. Shielding her eyes from the afternoon glare, she waited. "Hello," she called, when the woman got close.

"Afternoon," the woman said as she braked to a stop. "Is this the Blue place?"

"No, but you're close. It's not even a mile that way. Actually, you passed it."

"Ah. Well, thank you," the woman said. "I suppose I was distracted. This is such beautiful country."

"It is," Lizzie agreed with a smile.

The woman nodded and turned the wagon around. As she rode back to town, the conflict Cynthia felt surprised her. She should have been nothing but pleased because, after all, she'd performed her assigned task well and met with success. But Pauline Ray was exceptionally lovely and Ethan Ray was a controlling, bad-tempered man who had probably driven her away. Still, her business was her job, which she had performed admirably. Everyone would be pleased with the results. Everyone except Pauline and possibly the children.

Cynthia turned the horse and wagon back in at the livery and walked to the telegraph office. Two men were present, one older, one younger, though the younger man was headed to the back room when she walked in.

"Help you, ma'am?" the telegraph operator asked as he came forward. One of his legs was shorter than the other, so he had an odd gait.

"I need to send a telegram to Mr. Ethan Ray in Indianapolis."

The man picked up a tablet and began scribbling in cryptic symbols. "Your name?"

"Perkins. Cynthia."

"Go ahead."

"Subject located," she said, watching his face. "Stop. Green Valley, Virginia. Stop. Going by name of Carter."

The man glanced up sharply, then looked back down, his face reddening.

"Will find at Greenway cottage, east of town," Cynthia continued. "Stop."

"Is that all?" he asked stiffly.

She realized the man didn't particularly care for his job right this minute. She also knew, as he did, that he had to send the message and keep it confidential. "Yes."

"Three dollars," he said, giving her a hard look.

She also realized she was being overcharged, but she didn't care. Ethan Ray would be paying the bill. She handed over the money. "I'll be needing a receipt."

He grabbed a receipt book, wrote it out, and handed her the receipt. "Mind me asking why you're poking your nose in other people's business?"

She folded the receipt and put it into her reticule. It was a Friday afternoon, her job was completed, and she had a train to catch. "I do, actually. Good day."

Chapter Thirty-One

It was late when Bart Gunderson leaned across the table toward Marie. She looked like a goddess in her low-cut red dress. He couldn't keep his eyes off her cleavage. "Got something to tell you," he said, slurring his words. As usual, he'd had too much whiskey.

"What's that?"

"I could get in trouble. Lose my job."

She almost rolled her eyes, knowing, as she did, he worked for his uncle. Jules Gunderson, the telegraph operator, was a good man. Too bad for him Bart was so worthless. She felt for Jules, getting stuck with him. "Then why would you tell me?"

He shrugged. "I'm thinking you want to know."

She reached for the bottle of whiskey and refilled his glass. "And why would you think that?" The drunker he was, the less he'd be able to perform, and that worked for her.

"It's about Mrs. Carter." He watched closely for a change in her expression.

"So, what is it?" she asked after a brief hesitation.

"I know something about her. Something damaging," he said, stretching out the word.

She sat back, wondering if he was just angling for her favor or if he really had information worth knowing. "What?"

"It'll cost you."

She reached for her glass and sipped. "What do you want?"

"A blow job."

She leaned forward, disgusted with him. "I can't be working deals under the table," she hissed. "I'll get into trouble."

"We'll go about it secret-like," he replied with a shrug. "I'll leave and go around and you can let me in the back."

She thought about it and decided he must have something worth trading. He looked too smug not to. "We'll have to get away from each other for a while or it won't fool anyone."

He grinned. "Quarter of an hour do?"

She sat back again, her eyes blazing. "It better be worth it."

"Put it like this. If Shef finds out what I know, my guess is he'll hightail it. So, you tell me. Worth it?"

Marie got to her feet, but as soon as she went to walk past him, he tried to put a hand under her dress.

"Don't push it," she warned in a low voice.

"Oh, but that's exactly what I'm going to do, sweetheart," he said, gloating. "I'm going to push it every way that it can be pushed."

Disgusted to her very core, she walked off. Glancing at Saul, who was involved in conversation, she slipped outside for some air and space and a smoke to hopefully cool her agitation. There were times she felt she couldn't take one more minute of her life, and this was one of them.

* * *

At the same moment, Jeremy's hand hovered over the surface of Lizzie's stomach, feeling the heat emanating from her skin.

"What are you doing?" she murmured.

"Feeling you. Watching you breathe. It's nice."

She was covered in a fine sheen of sweat, from lovemaking that had left them both spent and lethargic. "I doubt it's that nice," she said sleepily.

"No, it is. The little hairs on your stomach. You almost can't see them. The way these muscles move," he said, touching lightly and making her smile.

"That tickles."

"I like this time . . . after," he said mischievously. "I like noticing little things." He looked into her eyes as he caressed her face with the backs of his fingers. "The expressions on your face. Figuring out what's going on in your mind."

She turned toward him and looked deeply into his eyes. "What am I thinking now?" she asked in a sultry voice.

"Don't go using that voice on me, woman, or we will start all over again."

She laughed softly. "I don't think I have it in me."

"Oh, we'll find it."

She reached for his hand and kissed it. "I've never been this happy."

"Me either," he whispered.

"Mrs. Carter . . . isn't really Mrs. Carter," Bart said, still breathless from his reward. Although she'd kind of cheated. She hadn't taken off her clothes. In fact, she hadn't done anything except undo his trousers, release him and go to work on him. It hadn't been all mouth. She'd used her hand, too.

"What's that supposed to mean?"

"This stranger, a woman, comes in today wanting to send a telegram to a man in Indianapolis, Indiana," he said with a waggle to his head. "The message was this. Subject found. Going by the name of Carter. Stop. You'll find her at the Greenway place. Stop."

"*Going* by the name of Carter?"

"Yeah. Meaning whoever Mrs. Carter is, she ain't. You get my drift? She's wanted by someone in Indianapolis, Indiana." He paused. "Makes you wonder if Shef knows who he's mixed up with."

Her heart did a painful flip-flop. She started to turn away from him, but he grabbed her arm.

"Honey, you only just whetted my appetite. Now, I told you I want—"

She jerked away from him. "I don't care what you want. A deal's a deal and I did what I agreed to."

"Yeah, well, your boss man doesn't know that, does he? And you want to keep it that way, I'm thinking."

She crossed her arms, looking confused. "Maybe I'm wrong, but, uh, isn't it against some rule to pass on what's in those telegrams?"

His expression went from smug to slightly ill. "No need to get all bitchy about it."

She glared, allowing him to see the disgust she felt for him. "Fasten your britches up and get the hell out of my room, Bart. And go the back way out because you were never here."

An hour before dawn, Jeremy pulled his arm from around Lizzie and turned over. When he touched something warm on the other side of him, he opened his eyes in confusion and saw Jake lying beside him. At first, the boy looked asleep, but then his eyes opened. "I had a bad dream again," Jake whispered.

"It's okay," Jeremy whispered back, patting the boy's chest lightly. Lizzie was still fast asleep on his other side. The plan had been for him to be gone by morning so the children wouldn't know. *So much for that plan*, he thought wryly.

"I didn't wet the bed," Jake added.

"That's good."

"Are we still going to go to town tomorrow?" Jake whispered.

Jeremy nodded. "Mm-hmm."

Jake closed his eyes. "I don't like bad dreams," he murmured.

Jeremy tugged the covers around the boy and kissed his head. "Everything is all right now."

"I know," Jake murmured sleepily.

If any two words had ever been sweeter or more meaningful, Jeremy couldn't think of them. Lizzie shifted and draped an arm around his waist and Jeremy experienced the most profound contentment he'd ever known.

Chapter Thirty-Two

In Adams' General Store the next afternoon, Rebecca and Jake ogled the tall jars of candy on the counter, whispering about which looked best. Lizzie's shopping was nearly completed and Jeremy's items were stacked on the counter. He walked over and stood behind the children. "You ready to go?"

They looked up at him and nodded.

"I don't think so," he said. He looked up and waved over the shopkeeper. "Not until you pick out some candy."

The way their faces lit up was a sight to behold.

"How many do we get?" Jake asked excitedly.

"Jake," Rebecca hissed.

"No, it's a good question," Jeremy said. "If you don't ask, how are you going to know?"

Jake beamed. Rebecca made a face.

"What do you think?" Jeremy asked.

"Five?" Jake asked.

Rebecca shrugged.

Jeremy looked at the patiently waiting shopkeeper. "They'll each fill up one of those," he said, pointing at the colorful paper candy bags.

Jake and Rebecca's eyes grew wide in wonder.

"As long," Jeremy added quickly, looking at Jake and then Rebecca, "as you don't eat it all at once. You go and get sick from eating all that and—"

"We won't," Jake said.

"We promise," Rebecca said solemnly.

"What will it be, little ones?" the shopkeeper asked, leaning on the counter with a patient smile.

As Jeremy walked away, he wondered if he looked as happy as he felt. Mrs. Daniels, a middle-aged widow he'd known all his life, smiled warmly at him, having enjoyed the scene, he supposed. He tipped his hat to her and continued on to Lizzie, who was fretting over bolts of fabric.

"Do you like this one," she asked him, holding up a patterned fabric, crimson with small white and yellow flowers, "or this one?"

"What for?"

"A dress. I'm making school clothes for Rebecca."

"I like both. Get both." He leaned close. "We've got the money," he said softly.

She looked away, embarrassed at how her body had reacted from his low voice and the tickle of his warm breath on her ear.

"I love it when you blush," he whispered. She gave him a look of objection and turned farther away from him. He chuckled before turning to catch the shopkeeper's eye. "She'll take these."

"Jeremy," Lizzie said again, clearly uncomfortable.

"And get some for yourself."

Lizzie bit her bottom lip.

"I want you to. Get what you want."

"Can we walk around the square?" Rebecca asked.

Jeremy glanced down at her and experienced a jolt of surprise that she'd addressed the question to him. He glanced at Lizzie, who smiled and nodded—again, at him.

"Sure," he said to Rebecca. "Just keep an eye on your brother."

"I will."

Jeremy watched them leave, excitedly clutching their bags of candy. He was on top of the world, until he noticed Marie staring at him from across the store. Tension tightened his gut, but he calmly tipped his head to her and looked away. "I'm going to step outside," he said to Lizzie.

"I won't be long," she said.

"Take your time. Pick out something nice." The smile she gave him, full of gratitude and love, warmed his heart. It didn't take much to make her happy. Then again, it didn't take much to make him happy either. Her smile alone did it. Seeing the kids thrilled by candy and a couple minutes of freedom. Rebecca asking his permission like he was her pa.

He walked out of the store somewhat reluctantly, knowing Marie would follow. The way she was watching him, she had something to say.

Rather than follow, Marie wandered toward Mrs. Carter, watching her discreetly. Striking was the first word that came to Marie's mind. She was more striking than beautiful. Mrs. Carter caught her staring and smiled politely. "Having a hard time deciding," she said.

Marie blinked at the smile and the blue-gray eyes which held such warmth. On second thought, she was pretty. Very pretty. "What's it for?" Marie asked.

"School clothes for my daughter."

Marie looked over the selection and ran a hand over a bright striped pattern of pinks, red, and orange. "I like this one."

Lizzie moved closer to see it. "That is nice," she said.

Marie was surprised by how close Mrs. Carter had gotten to her. They'd almost touched. Most ladies kept their distance as if she might have something catching. "It's bright and fun."

"It is."

Against her will, Marie liked Mrs. Carter. She wandered off and pretended to be interested in some talcum powder that smelled of lavender.

"Help you?" Mrs. Adams, the shopkeeper's wife, asked her coldly.

"No, thank you," Marie said with exaggerated sweetness. She meandered on, taking her good, sweet time, until she heard Mrs. Adams behind her. "You do know what she is?" the old biddy asked. Marie tensed and listened closely for Mrs. Carter's answer.

"I didn't think you knew," Mrs. Adams said a moment later. "You being new in town. After all, a decent woman might not know."

"I'll take two yards of each of these and three of the others," Mrs. Carter said coolly.

Marie sucked in her bottom lip to keep from smiling. Mrs. Carter had been nothing but polite, and she'd still put that nasty old bitch in her place.

Mrs. Adams sniffed. "All right."

Marie glanced at Mrs. Carter again. She didn't catch her eye, but she clearly saw what had so attracted Jeremy. What a strange feeling to know the lady was possibly in some sort of trouble and didn't even know it. *I could tell her. Warn her.* Then again, if she didn't, Mrs. Carter would probably be gone soon and Jeremy would be alone again.

Marie started for the door, patently ignoring a hostile look or two directed her way from the fine Christian ladies of Green Valley. Outside, she crossed over to Jeremy, who was leaning against a post. "She seems very nice," she said.

"She is."

"I can see you . . . care."

He nodded.

Marie hesitated and then decided to risk it. "Do you love her?"

"Yes."

The quickness and sincerity of the answer shook her. She looked away from him, shaken so badly she felt dizzy. She didn't mean to say it, but she did. "I've loved you all my life."

"I wish you well, Marie. I hope you know that. I wish you'd made some different choices . . . for your sake. It was always for your sake."

She hated the words and she hated herself for nearly bawling. "I wish I hadn't waited for you."

"I wish that, too."

It was pathetic; she was pathetic, but she couldn't help asking. "If it wasn't for her, would there be a chance?"

"No," he said with a sad expression and a shake of his head.

Heartsick, in fact, feeling sick to her stomach, she stepped back, turned, and walked away from him.

Chapter Thirty-Three

Jeremy scooted from the seam he'd been working in and stretched as he looked for Timmy or whatever driver was going to show up. Liam had gone for a rest break some time ago, but he wouldn't be coming back this late. Jeremy's left shoulder was sore, so he massaged and rotated it until a deafening explosion and a shaking of the earth around him made it difficult to remain upright. Rock walls and ceilings began collapsing with a terrible booming roar and a noxious odor permeated the air. He was used to explosions, they all were, but nothing like this. This was a death quake.

He ducked back into the seam he'd been working and fumbled for the cloth he wore as a mask after blasting. He held it to his face, knowing that certain gases in a mine could kill a man but quick. Of course, so could tons of rock, but he couldn't fight against that. He went for the ground cover he sometimes used, to cordon off the area from the fumes, but the earth was shaking so, he could hardly move. He finally got the cover and maneuvered to the entrance of the seam. He was coughing and fighting nausea as he found a shelf at the top wide enough to support a steel wedge. He lifted the cover in place, making, in effect, a curtain, and placed the wedge to hold it. He found another place a wedge would fit and lodged it in. His pick held one side in place, his tamping bar the other. It wasn't a perfect seal, but it was the best he could do.

He scooted back to the far side and waited, his heart beating unmercifully. The irony was painful. He'd sentenced himself to die in this mine years ago, and only now had it happened. Now, when he'd decided to get out and live. When he'd found happiness with Lizzie. Did it mean this was the end he truly deserved? The seam suddenly felt like his coffin.

Chapter Thirty-Four

T. Emmett Rice looked up from his desk at the sound of continually ringing church bells. He rose and stepped from his office and saw he wasn't the only one who was confounded.

"Explosion at Number Six," someone called. The cry came from a miner who'd been at his labor today; face and body were covered with soot. "We need help!"

People were already mobilized. Emmett locked his office door and hurried to the livery for a horse. He wasn't sure if the sound of the bells would carry to Howerton's place or to Tommy and Em's, and they would want to know. Every able-bodied man would be needed, and the Triple H had a lot of them. So did the Martin-Medlin farm.

"How bad is it?" he asked Joseph Schultz, the brawny owner of the livery. "Do you know?"

Mr. Schultz had a substantial enough handlebar mustache that his upper lip was hidden. "Bad," he answered as he readied a horse for Emmett. "Only a few men had come off the shift."

"Do we know what happened?"

"An explosion and a raging fire. That's all we know."

He handed the reins to Emmett. "You know they did a slapdash job of building that place."

Emmett mounted and rode out. He was not even halfway to the Triple H when he encountered a bunch of Howerton's men riding in, with Sam Blake, the foreman, in the lead. "What are the bells ringing for?" one of the men called.

"There's been an explosion at Number Six," Emmett replied, reining in his horse as the others were doing. "A fire, too. I was riding out to tell you fellas and Tommy's men. I wasn't sure if you'd hear the bells."

Sam Blake looked grim. Somewhere between forty and fifty years of age, Sam had a strong jaw, a watchful gaze, and a cool head. He wielded power over the men through respect and authority granted by Mr. Howerton, who relied on him heavily. "Stop in and tell Mr. Howerton, will you?"

"I will."

"Tell him we're going on to see what we can do," Sam said, already spurring on his horse.

The group rode on in one direction, Emmett in another.

Rebecca looked out the window as April May and Cessie drove up, looking upset. She'd been seated at the table by the window in their bedroom, practicing her penmanship, but she popped up and hurried to the front door to let them in. Jake came right behind her, as usual. Cessie and April May had gone in through the kitchen, and by the time she got there, they were saying something to her mother, who looked upset, too. Rebecca had a terrible fear that Papa had found them.

"Jeremy's mine," her mother uttered.

April May nodded. She too looked near tears, and April May never looked near tears.

"Is that why the bells are ringing?" Rebecca asked. "Because there was an accident at Jeremy's mine?"

"Yes, honey," Cessie answered. "It's to call out to folks to come help and to pray. You and Jake get some things together. You'll come to our house."

"What about Mama?"

April May answered. "Your mama and I are gonna go see what we can do to help."

Lizzie seemed too stunned to move.

"Get your coat and hat and gloves," April May said to Lizzie. "It's going to get cold."

Lizzie nodded rigidly, then turned and left the room, looking unsteady.

"Is Jeremy stuck down in the mine?" Rebecca asked worriedly.

"We don't know that yet," April May replied. "But if he is, he'll need help, and if he's not, he'll be helping and we'll help, too."

"Get your things, honey," Cessie urged. "You too, Jake."

Rebecca and Jake turned and went to their room with heavy hearts. Rebecca's eyes filled because she wished she'd been nicer to Jeremy.

"Is Jeremy going to die?" Jake fretted.

"Shut up, Jake," she said, wiping her eyes so he wouldn't see.

"You're not supposed to say shut up."

"Just get your pajamas and leave me alone!"

Chapter Thirty-Five

"Oh, my God," Charity Howerton said under her breath as the mine came into view. Her hand unwittingly tightened on her husband's leg. She was a physician trained in the city of Philadelphia and used to crises, injury, and death, but she had not happened upon many disasters, certainly none of this magnitude. Whatever explosion had occurred, it had been big and it had caused a chain reaction. Smoke billowed from the opening where the lift had been and from the smoldering remains of the breaker, the several-story structure above the mine where coal was sorted.

Gregory couldn't tear his eyes from it. This mine's breaker had been smaller than the ones at his mines, which housed some hundred or so workers at a time—but how much smaller? Could any of them have survived? He'd built a fire escape on each of the six levels of his breaker, but he knew damn well that Landreth hadn't. This one had been built directly above a main shaft, not away from the mine as most owners chose to do. It was likely it had gone up like a powder keg.

He thought he'd been prepared, but this was much worse than he'd imagined. A crowd had already amassed, many of them the frantic family members of miners, and there was a terrible smell in the air, a combination of sulfur, smoke, and death. "Be careful," he said before climbing down.

Charity followed and hurried to get to the wounded, clutching her medical bag. She saw badly burned boys and broke into a run to get to them. The burns looked fatal. The skin, where there was skin, was black and red. Clothing had burned away, as had hair. Their own families might not have known them at first painful glance.

Gregory walked over to join his men, who were engaged in a heated conversation with Darnell Landreth, a hard-hearted son of a bitch if Howerton had ever seen one.

"—what kind of loss this will be?" old man Landreth was saying.

For a moment, Gregory thought he meant in terms of life. Then Sam turned to him, his face full of disgust. "Worried about the goddamned cost."

Landreth glared at Howerton accusingly, resenting his presence. There was no great love between any of the mine owners, but the two of them had a particularly mutual dislike.

"You have any goddamn idea how dangerous it is, going into a mine full of firedamp?" Landreth demanded, directing the question to Sam. "It's not like anyone can be saved."

"You don't know that," Sam shot back.

"Thirty years in this business," Landreth retorted furiously, "says I do know that."

"We will damn well try."

Landreth scoffed. "Not unless I say—"

"You think you can stop us?"

Howerton shouldered in. "You don't want to take this position," he warned Landreth. His voice was dispassionate, but his eyes held contempt.

"Why don't you mind your own damn business,

Howerton? Case you don't know it, this could happen to you same as it happened to me."

"It didn't happen to you," Sam cut in, "you son of a bitch. It happened to the men down there."

"If it's the cost you're worried about—" Howerton started.

Landreth threw up his hand in disgust. "Do what you want, but it's on you. And I mean all of it. These people die here today trying to be heroes when ain't no one can be saved, and it's on you."

"Look around," Howerton replied angrily. "Men are dying. Right now. Right over there," he said, jabbing a finger toward the chaos, "and down there," he exclaimed, pointing straight down. "While we stand here arguing about trying to save them or not."

Landreth shook his head and walked away, and his men followed.

Sam was livid. "You were despised before this, Landreth," he called after the man. "I wouldn't count on sticking around too long after."

Landreth turned back, red faced in his fury. "That a threat?"

"A prediction. I got a pretty good talent at predicting."

"Forget him," Howerton said to Sam as he looked over the scene. "Let's get to work." It was mayhem and they were running out of daylight. "Anyone with medical experience should be helping my wife."

Already, people were approaching Howerton and his men.

"We'll need a new lift," Howerton said. "Or at least a platform that can be used. Who can do that?"

Several men spoke up, and then began gravitating toward one another.

"We'll need supplies," Sam said. "Bud, you and Lynn ride into town."

Bud Vincent and Lynn Green, hands from the Triple H, nodded.

"Anything you think we might need," Howerton said. "Wood, rope, nails. Tell them to put it on my tab."

"There might be more than one lift." A familiar voice spoke up from behind. Howerton and Sam turned to face Tommy Medlin and his men, who had just arrived. It was Tommy who had spoken. Greg nodded, relieved that Tommy was there. No one was harder working and no one was luckier—or maybe more charmed. Tommy had survived a gunshot wound to the head and he'd ended up with the woman of his dreams.

"Who knows this mine?" Howerton asked.

"Willie Giest," a man replied. "I'll find him. I saw him earlier."

"It's not going to be easy," a black-faced coal miner said in a hoarse voice. Telltale streaks and smears down his face told of tears shed and wiped away. "The gas is bad. Real bad."

Howerton nodded. "Landreth is an ass, but he made a point," he stated. "Anyone who helps with this could die in the effort. I think you all know that, but it has to be said and it has to be faced."

"Plus there's cave-ins," another man said. "It may be hopeless."

"It may be," Sam agreed, "but five years ago at Rascal Pass, you remember that?" Most men nodded. It hadn't been nearly the disaster this was, but nine men had been lost in a cave-in and it had taken three days to reach the bodies. "We lost them all, but some of the bodies were still warm. Remember?"

"Yes, sir," someone replied. "Remember it well. It was a hard pill to swallow."

"Here's Willie," someone said, and the crowd parted.

Willie Giest was a small, wiry man in his late forties,

although he looked older. Given the soot on his face, hands, and clothing, he'd spent time in the coal mines on this day. He was visibly upset, trembling violently.

"We need a plan of attack," Howerton said to Willie. "And you know the mine better than anyone, right?"

Willie nodded. "But the men, they're all over. A mile down. Two."

"Are there other lifts?" Tommy asked.

"There's only one other from the surface, though we don't hardly use it no more."

Sam laid a hand on Willie's shoulder. "We need the best three or four places to dig, and we need you to point them out."

"Want I should fetch a map?" another miner asked Willie.

Willie nodded and started off in the same direction, and several men followed, including Sam. Tommy started to go as well, but Howerton stopped him. "We need a ground operation," he said. "Set it up."

Tommy's gaze sharpened. Howerton had been his boss and he had become a friend in the time since, but it didn't set right with him not to dig with the others.

"We need a medical tent," Howerton continued. "Ask Charity what she needs. And we'll need another area set up for food and drink. This'll likely go on for days."

"Food and drink," April May Blue said as she joined them. "What else?"

"Construction materials in one place," Howerton continued, still addressing Tommy. "And then get them started on the lift and whatever else is needed. Once we've got a plan from Willie, direct the men where to go."

"Except I should be digging, too," Tommy said.

"If this doesn't work," Howerton said, waving a finger around the area. "That won't work like it needs to. We've got to have organization. I'll handle it over there, you handle it over here, and then we'll go to the next thing that needs doing." Howerton turned and walked off without waiting for a response.

"How many are down there?" April May asked.

Tommy shook his head. "I don't know."

April May turned to speak to Lizzie, but she'd walked off. No doubt hoping to see Jeremy among the men helping. "I'll see to getting tents from the reverend and I'll handle the food and drink part."

Tommy nodded. He saw Bud and Lynn were mounting up to ride into town. "Barrels," he called. "We're going to need barrels for water."

The men nodded and rode out.

April May had gone in one direction while Lizzie kept moving forward. As she walked, she tried to shake herself from her stupor, but the sight before her was so shocking. It looked like a smoky, bloody battlefield. Women wailed before a row of corpses. They were hard to look at, although she looked at each body there to make sure Jeremy was not among them. Some were sickening to see, especially the charred remains of boys. The families of the deceased knelt over the bodies, sobbing in agony. She'd never imagined a more terrible sight. She couldn't even fully take it in. It was like being trapped in a nightmare.

"Can you help?" a lady called to her.

The woman speaking was striking, with fair hair. Lizzie moved closer, but had to swallow down bile at the sight of white bone protruding from a man's badly torn and broken leg. He was lying flat on his back, squirming and moaning in pain.

"Hold his shoulders," the woman said. "I've given him all the morphine I can spare."

Lizzie dropped to her knees and did as bidden. The man's eyes were on the woman tending him, fear etched heavily on his face.

"Try and lie still for me," the woman said to him before she began pushing the bone back into the leg. Lizzie squeezed her eyes shut and held his shaking shoulders with all her might as he did a closed-mouth scream.

"Good," the woman said. "Will you hand me that roll of bandage?"

Lizzie quickly handed it over.

"And that splint."

Lizzie handed it over and watched the woman deftly splint the leg. She'd rarely felt so inadequate.

"Hold him again," the woman said quietly to Lizzie. "I've got to clean the wound, Joe, but then the worst of it will be over." He nodded and she reached for a bottle of something and poured it over the wound. It bubbled white where it made contact and the man cried out. "It's over! It's over now," she said as she began bandaging the leg.

"Thanks, Doc," the man said weakly when she was finished.

The woman stood, wiping her bloodied hands on her apron. Lizzie hadn't yet made it back to her feet. "I'm Charity Howerton."

"Elizabeth Carter. Lizzie."

"Do you have family in the mine?"

"I have . . . someone. Yes."

"I'm sorry. I know how difficult this must be. But if you can help—"

"I can," Lizzie said.

Charity walked to her bag and picked up a bottle. "This is chloroform. I've doused some rags that are being held close to the mouth and nose of some of the more severely wounded. If you'd go around and moisten the cloths again, that would be greatly helpful. Make sure whoever is holding it isn't too close. If they are, they'll faint."

Lizzie got to her feet and took the bottle.

"Then if you can, come back," Charity said as she hurried off to tend to someone else.

Willie directed men to the best places to burrow down to reach the tunnels, assuming they were intact. As the sun began setting, casting everything in an eerie pink, digging began, along with construction of a crude platform that could be lowered into the main shaft on ropes.

Lizzie knelt by a woman cradling a man's head in her lap. His shirt was torn open and covered in blood; a gash tore his middle from sternum to hip. Rags had been used to try to stop the bleeding. Her hand was on top of the wound to keep it closed. "Will the doctor be here soon?" the woman asked. "He's lost so much blood."

"I'm sure she will," Lizzie replied. "Here, let me—" she said, holding out the bottle.

"She said to keep pressure on the wound, but it feels wrong," the woman said as Lizzie doused her cloth. "I can feel his blood pushing against my hand. Like a heartbeat."

That seemed right to Lizzie and she said so. Fortunately, an older man with a doctor's bag knelt on the woman's other side. "Let me see," he said.

"Oh, thank God," the woman cried. "Help him, Doc."

"He'll be all right," the doctor calmly assured her. "You just keep that rag near his nose and he'll keep sleeping while we sew him back up."

"His own pick cut him open in the explosion."

Lizzie bit on her bottom lip as she rose and moved on. She was nauseated by the thought of it, by the sights all around her, and by the acrid stench in the air. She hadn't gone far when she stopped short at the sight of a burned boy who lay staring up sightlessly. Dead. He'd probably died alone and in utter agony. His remains were a pitiful sight—his skin blackened and blistered pink by flames. His scalp was burned—one ear had burned off completely.

"Miss! I need it," a woman cried.

Lizzie tore her eyes from the boy and saw the woman who'd called to her. She also had a horribly burned boy propped against her. Half his face was unrecognizable.

"Please," the woman said. "I don't want him to wake like this."

Lizzie hurried to the woman, nearly tripping over her own feet in her rush. She poured more chloroform in her cloth with a badly shaking hand.

"God bless you," the woman said. The tears fell in a steady stream down her face and her nose ran, and she unceremoniously wiped her face with her sleeve. She placed the cloth inches from her boy's mouth and nose.

Lizzie squatted before her, wishing she could do something more to help. "Is he your son?"

The woman nodded. "My Andrew. Fifteen years old." She looked up at Lizzie. "Why did this have to happen?"

"I don't know." Lizzie's eyes filled. "I'm so sorry."

"Lizzie," Charity called urgently.

Lizzie saw her pointing to someone else in need and rose to her feet. She had a job to do.

Chapter Thirty-Six

The first two volunteers to go into the hole were miners, one who had not worked that day and who had a brother still unaccounted for, and one who'd left early, feeling ill. It was the smell, he said. They'd drilled into something bad, he reported. "We plugged it and I went to the surface for air and to find Willie or Jim to tell them."

From his account, the approximate place of the explosion became clear to Willie, who adjusted the sites where they were digging. The second lift wouldn't operate because it kept hitting rock, so their hopes were all riding on the makeshift platform. A dozen men lowered it slowly while listening for the men on the lift to yell when they came to an opening.

"It seems wrong, them wearing flames in their hats," someone commented. "I mean the place blew. What's to say it won't blow again?"

"Shut it," someone growled. "That ain't helpin'."

Lower and lower the platform went. They'd lowered a hundred feet of rope, at least.

"Shouldn't they be there by now?" Sam asked Willie.

"Way might have been blocked," Willie said with a

shake of his head. "That blast, the way everything shook, no telling how many cave-ins there were."

Lower and lower. They'd gone two hundred feet. Two hundred and fifty. Three hundred.

Howerton walked to the edge and looked down, but the dark had swallowed everything except two faint lights. "You all right in there?" he shouted.

Silence.

"Can you hear me?" he yelled. "Potts, Flagg! Can you hear me?"

Silence.

Howerton stuck up his hand. "Pull them up."

"And . . . heave, ho," the lead man chanted. Each *heave* was a pull, each *ho* a hand moving forward to grab the rope, until the platform came back into view with the men lying on it, unconscious. They were quickly pulled off and Charity and Doc Simmons moved in to tend them. The men were white-faced, their breathing shallow, but Charity looked at her husband with a solemn nod, meaning they would revive. "No one can go down there yet," she said regretfully.

Within minutes, smelling salts revived the men, although they were disoriented. It was now fully dark, the only light coming from a campfire some twenty-five yards away. Even the cloudy sky seemed pitted against them. There was probably no getting to the survivors tonight—if indeed there were any survivors. Still, few people were willing to leave and so a second and then a third campfire were started and people settled in around them. Blankets were passed around and a hearty stew was served by cooks from the Triple H, the Martin-Medlin farm, and others. Even cooks from Wiley's. Men continued digging by torchlight, Tommy among them.

Many of the dead had been taken home in anguished

processions. There were sixteen casualties so far, including all but one of the breaker boys on duty, and he was so badly burned, it was only a matter of time. The wooden breaker, the crudely constructed structure the boys toiled in, had been directly above the initial explosion. With only one egress, there had been no chance of escape, and nine boys between the ages of ten and fifteen had burned alive.

The other seven deceased had been on the lift at the time of the explosion. The force of the blast was of such magnitude, four of the men died upon impact. The others had succumbed to blood loss. Five men on the lift had survived, although one was still unconscious.

As it grew late, Charity Howerton settled next to her husband to rest. She was exhausted, but she doubted the night would bring much sleep. It wasn't the sound of the men working; that had become mere background noise. Nor was it being uncomfortable, because she was weary enough to sleep despite it. It was the spirits of the dead still hovering among them. Gregory's presence was a comfort. He was the strongest, most caring man she knew, much more so than people knew. Now, beneath the blanket, he discreetly massaged her back in the places he knew she needed it.

At another fire, April May stroked Lizzie's hair after coaxing her to lie down and get some rest. Lizzie couldn't stop thinking of the boys who'd died. They'd been children. And the pain they'd endured. Tears filled her eyes and she shut them and squeezed the bridge of her nose. There was too much pain and sorrow in the world and too much injustice.

"Tomorrow is another day, you know," April May said quietly. "We have to have faith."

Spoken like Cessie, Lizzie thought. Her heart felt wrenched in a dozen different ways. There was too much sorrow, it was true, but there was also love and compassion and kindness. One only had to look at the people who'd come to help rescue the miners. Many of them didn't know anyone below. They just wanted to help and were willing to risk their lives to do it. And Cessie and April May. They had become family, dearer to her than anyone other than her children and Jeremy. "He asked me to marry him," she said softly.

"He did?" April May said, knowing full well she meant Jeremy. She chuckled. "Well, good for him."

"I said it was too soon."

"It was quick. 'Course, that doesn't necessarily mean too soon."

"I love him."

"I know, honey. We figured that out a little while back." Lizzie sat up. "What if he's—"

"If the worst has happened, we'll have to face it. But not till then. Not until then."

Lizzie nodded and hugged her blanket closer.

Tommy stared at the second lift. They'd gotten it to go down ten or twelve yards, but then it got hung up. "You think there's a way to get underneath it?" he asked the men around him.

"If we could get the cage out," someone said.

"That's a good idea," Wood seconded.

With agreement and general excitement, the men worked to hoist, maneuver and disengage the cage from the shaft so it would be out of their way. The effort drew the attention of several men working in other places, who came over to assist. Once the car was outside the shaft, men wearing lit miners' hats were lowered into the shaft on rope lariats to see what could be done. The lights from the hats illuminated black walls and tin guide panels for the wire ropes.

The air felt cooler as they went lower and it smelled damp, but not noxious like the other lift shaft. The lifts were at least a quarter mile apart, the second farther from the site of the explosion.

The blockage, when they reached it, was not complete. Some of the rock was moveable. They shouted the news up to the surface and were almost instantly rewarded by the sound of banging, not from above, but from below. They joyfully shouted up the news and banged back with the picks they carried.

Jeremy's light barely registered. He knew it was because there was less air now. He closed his eyes, aware that death loomed. It wasn't so bad. He'd simply go to sleep and not wake up. It wasn't so bad, except he wouldn't have a life with Lizzie.

Elizabeth, he mouthed, like a prayer.

It didn't matter that her name had been something different. She was Lizzie now. She was his Lizzie now. She would have been his wife.

He floated in darkness and yet was weighted down by it. His father was there, trying to explain something to him. *A life for a life,* the older man said sadly. *There was never any choice but this.*

Jeremy looked away and saw Jenny admiring the gold pocket watch he'd won from Morrison. "It's time," she said tenderly, looking up at him.

He didn't want it to be time. "I just found her."

Jenny held up one of the strange-looking keys he'd found in the snuff box. "If you do it right, you can turn back time," she said as she popped open the watch and found the keyhole.

He frowned in confusion, because he hadn't realized

there was a keyhole in the watch. How could there be a keyhole? And turn back time? That wasn't really possible. Was it?

"It is," she assured him. "That's how I came back."

He was trying to understand the message in her words, because there was a message, but banging started and it was distracting.

"Maybe you should let them in," Jenny suggested, as she went back to directing her full attention to the watch and key.

"She's right," their father said as he stepped into a pool of light. "Go," he said with a gesture beyond where Jeremy stood. "You say you want to live, so go."

A confused Jeremy turned to see what they were talking about and jerked awake, blinking into the vast darkness. He struggled to sit up, fighting against dizziness and disorientation. But there *was* banging. And shouting.

"Hey," men called. "We're here! We're here!"

This was not a dream. Others were alive and had air enough to shout. He began working out the logistics of where he was and where the voices were coming from. With his air supply all but depleted, he had nothing to lose, and so he moved to the curtain, tore it off, and crawled toward the noise. With every movement, he thought *Lizzie*. He thought her name, he thought of her face, he thought of lying next to her again. She was worth the effort, worth the pain.

Lizzie.

It was an awkward operation—the platform they'd built for the main lift had been moved to the secondary one, and men went back and forth, loading all the rock they could onto the lift, which was then hoisted to the surface to be unloaded. Each trip was powered by a line of men, until horses were brought to speed up the process. Even so, the rock had to be unloaded in a bucket brigade formation, but hearing the voices of men below had lent the rescuers stamina and resolve. Those who weren't working had drawn close, to watch and step in when needed.

Below, trapped miners were also working to remove the blockage. Six men, fortunate to have been far enough from the explosion to survive, had congregated and worked their way to the back lift, only to find it blocked by a cave-in. Al Trachenburg, Zach Rogers, Benjamin Daly, Clifton Worrell, John Dix, and Davey Hounshel wasted no time in getting to work on the rock. Being sealed off at both ends as they were, they knew there was a limit to the air supply, not to mention their meager water supply. They knew their only hope was to get the shaft cleared.

It was after midnight when a wide enough opening had been created that the miners could scramble through, one at a time. With the appearance of each freed man, there were tears of joy, relief, sorrow, and cries of gratitude.

"Did you see anyone else down there?" someone asked the first man up when he'd caught his breath. "Or hear anything? Besides your group?"

Zach shook his head. "We were cut off," he replied. "Cave-ins on both sides. Knew the lift was our only hope."

As the doctors tended each man, Lizzie stood nearby, hugging herself for warmth. She was cold through and through, mostly from fear. She felt each and every second ticking by like a small eternity.

"It's still the best place to dig in and make a new start," Hawk said. "They squeezed out, we can squeeze in and tunnel from there."

There were nods of agreement before new volunteers started down, but no more survivors were found. By the early hours of morning, the operation stopped in order for everyone to get much-needed rest.

Jeremy's light was gone. The lamp had run out of fuel, either oil or oxygen or both. He'd come to a massive obstruction caused by a cave-in, but he lacked the strength to search for an opening. He'd reached a wall, figuratively and literally. There had been sound from the far side, but it had gone silent. Men had been there but must have moved on, leaving him to die.

He collapsed against the seemingly impenetrable blockage and felt a tickle of air on his cheek. Frantically, he twisted around and put his mouth and nose near the soft flow, cupping his hand around it. *Air.* He drew it in to his starved lungs as best he could. It was difficult not to let panic take over, but he wanted to live. That meant staying calm and hoping against hope that someone was looking for him. *Please, please God*, let someone be looking.

Chapter Thirty-Seven

The sky grayed as dawn approached and people stirred to life. Cooking and tasks began. A volunteer went down the main shaft and came back up fully conscious, although nauseated by the odor. With renewed enthusiasm, rescue efforts began anew.

Victory and defeat came one after another. Men were found—but all were dead, having suffocated. Shortly afterward a survivor was found, although he was unconscious. Slowly, tunnels were made and men were pulled out with cuts, bruises, and broken bones. Some had been crushed. More men were dead than alive, but the hope of survivors drove the effort.

At ground level, corpses were laid out one next to another in a long row. Among them was a thin boy of fourteen named Timmy Wayne.

"Lizzie," April May called with great urgency.

Lizzie stood from cleaning a man's open sores and looked around to see where April May was motioning. Charity and Doc Simmons hovered over a man they'd just pulled from the second lift. Lizzie's heart gave a painful lurch and she started forward, breaking into a run midway. She couldn't yet see the man because so many people surrounded him, but she knew they'd found Jeremy. She felt it. *Please, God, let him be alive.*

She pushed through the group and dropped to her knees at his side. Her jaw went lax and she uttered a terrible sound because, after all the waiting and worrying and praying, he was dead. He was deathly pale, covered in gray ash and soot, his eyes slightly open. Then his eyes moved—his gaze fastened on hers. She gasped, blinked tears away, and saw his chest move. She cried out and threw herself over him. "You're alive, you're alive, you're alive." She couldn't stop saying it.

Jeremy felt hot tears slide from his eyes and trail down the sides of his face. His fingers circled her waist.

Lizzie pulled back to look at him more closely. He was conscious, breathing, no broken bones or head injury that she could see. She took his face in her hands. "Thank God. Oh, thank God."

He looked around at the many faces around him, most of whom had tears in their eyes, and knew it was a good day to be alive.

Chapter Thirty-Eight

Jeremy didn't understand why he was so weak, but when he was helped to his feet, he nearly collapsed. With the aid of a man on each side of him, he walked toward April May's wagon, but he came to a halt at the sight of the devastation before him. There was no more breaker. Nothing but a smoldering, blackened pile of debris. He saw the row of corpses. "How many?" he asked in a raspy voice.

"We don't know yet," one of the men said sorrowfully. "But it's bad."

They urged him on and he went. He didn't want to get a closer look at the dead. He didn't have the strength for it. Lizzie was at his side, watching him worriedly, and he focused on her instead. She loved him and he loved her. He'd survived. That's all he would think about for the moment.

He was helped into the wagon and Lizzie followed and placed a blanket over his lap. April May climbed into the driver's seat, then reached over and kissed his cheek. "Welcome back," she said. As she turned the wagon around, he stared at the rescue operation and the obliteration of Number Six. He was staring right at it and he still didn't comprehend it. Lizzie had an arm around him, but it was apparent she didn't know what to say. None of them did. "How many made it out alive?" he asked, breaking the silence.

"A dozen or more so far," April May replied hesitantly. "And hopefully there'll be more."

A dozen. There were at least sixty men per shift, not to mention the breaker boys. "Did any of the boys from the breaker make it out?"

"No," Lizzie replied quietly. "I'm so sorry." She hugged him closer.

"You'll be coming to our house," April May said. "Until you recover."

Lizzie leaned forward to look at April May with a puzzled frown. "He can stay—"

"At our place," April May interrupted. "People are going to be checking on him and y'all don't need any sort of controversy just as you start a life together."

Maybe the statement shouldn't have surprised him, but it did. To hear it stated out loud as if it was a simple fact that everyone knew? Jeremy looked at Lizzie and tears were pooled in her eyes.

"That is, if you still want to marry me," she said.

If. She'd said if. He didn't know whether to laugh or cry. "You know I do."

April May slung an arm around his shoulders. "Oh, my boy. The good Lord has plans for you. That's what I think."

What a thought that was. The sky was suddenly bluer than he'd ever seen it. Leaves on the trees were nothing short of glorious in reds and golds and oranges. Had they been that colorful before? He could feel the love and concern that surrounded him.

When they drove up the long driveway of the Blues' farm, Rebecca and Jake, who had been sitting on the front porch with Lucky, jumped up and came running. Jeremy had only just made it down from the wagon when a crying

Rebecca launched herself into his arms. Deeply surprised and touched, he dropped to a knee and held her tightly. "I'm all right," he assured her.

"We th-thought you died."

Jake reached him and Jeremy opened his other arm to allow him into the embrace. They'd be filthy afterwards, but no one seemed to care. "Everything is all right." Even Lucky, Wags, and Sheeba wanted in. April May had her arm around Lizzie, watching, and Cessie was hurrying to join them. Like the others, she was crying and laughing at the same time.

Chapter Thirty-Nine

"Tommy?" Em murmured. She sat up from a restless sleep and looked around, sensing he'd just been there. He'd been working in the rescue effort, as had the rest of the crew, as well as Doll. Doll had returned and shared her experience, including the way the men were pushing themselves. That wasn't a surprise to Em. She knew her husband.

She rose and stepped out into the parlor, noticing the light from the nursery in the loft. She went upstairs and looked in the baby's room, where Tommy was silhouetted against the backdrop of the window. He was holding the baby, rocking her gently. Em crossed the room, pressed herself to his back and wrapped her arms around him, content to move with his motion and say nothing.

"I almost went to work in the mine," he said quietly.

She reached up and stroked the base of his neck.

"It's why my brother and I came to Green Valley."

"I know."

"Those men didn't do anything wrong. They were just in the wrong place at the wrong time."

The toll the last two days had taken on him was evident. "You're exhausted."

He nodded. "But all I wanted was to get home and hold her. And you."

"Come get some sleep."

He shifted the baby to his chest and pressed a kiss to her soft, dark curls, then laid her back down in her crib. Em massaged his shoulders and felt the tension and the weariness in his muscles. He turned to her and wrapped her in his arms, and she realized it was going to be a while before they slept. He had a need more pressing than rest.

Chapter Forty

Cessie walked into the kitchen and put an apron on, then glanced out the kitchen window, blinking in surprise to see Jeremy standing at the fence watching the mules. It was early, not even seven in the morning. She made coffee and sliced some of the coffee cake Lizzie had made the night before. It was delicious, made with cinnamon and brown sugar and walnuts. She put on a coat and walked out with a steaming mug of coffee and a plate of cake. "'Morning," she called.

He turned to her. "Good morning."

She reached him and handed him the coffee. "Brought you some breakfast. I'll make you some oats or sausage and eggs, whatever your heart desires, but I thought you might enjoy this first." She set the small plate on the fence post.

"Thank you."

"I didn't expect you'd be up so early."

"I'm going to help at the mine today. Do whatever I can."

Cessie frowned worriedly. "Are you well enough for that?"

"I'm all right."

She gave him a look.

"I've gotta help."

She nodded slowly. "I understand. I'm not sure Lizzie will."

"Is she here?"

"No. They went home."

"Well, dang if it ain't a party," April May called.

Jeremy and Cessie glanced back at her as she walked toward them.

"Eggs and sausage, then," Cessie said to Jeremy. "You'll need your strength."

"That would be good. Thank you."

She patted his arm and started back to the house.

"No need to run off just because I showed up," April May said, passing her. "Although I am famished."

"It'll be ready soon," Cessie replied.

April May reached him and lifted her mug to him. "You're up and about awful early."

"I'm going to the mine to help."

"Yeah. Figured you might be. I'll go, too." She looked out at the mules and sipped her coffee. "You remember that fella?" she said, pointing at one.

"I do," he said, although, in truth, it looked no different from the others.

"Moe. That's what I named him."

"Oh yeah?"

"Yep. Named him that because no matter what you give him, he wants mo'."

Jeremy grinned.

"It's one fine morning, ain't it?" April May said, looking around.

He nodded. "I couldn't wait to get outside."

"I'll bet. I can't even imagine what it was like down there, and I've been in the mine."

He looked out at the mountains in the distance. "This was different," he said quietly.

"You know you don't ever have to go down there again. But that doesn't mean the nightmares won't come."

He nodded and she reached over to squeeze his arm before starting back to the house.

Lizzie stared at the vines, wondering what more to prune. They were intricate and very green. Very alive. The fact was, she couldn't decide where to cut because she was having trouble concentrating—and she was having trouble concentrating because she was frustrated. April May meant well, but Jeremy should be here, where she could take care of him.

"Just tell her so," Lionel said.

Lizzie turned to face him where he sat on his favorite chair, a wide-brimmed hat on his head to block the sun from his face. He had a glass of wine in hand, and a bottle rested on the table next to a pipe that was still smoking. The fragrance of it reached her and it was surprisingly pleasing. "You're here," she remarked.

"Of course. Where else would I be?"

She felt confusion, which quickly became panic. If Lionel had come back, did she have to leave?

He waved off the notion, although she hadn't spoken it aloud. "Come sit and have some wine. You worry too much."

It was true. If she hadn't worried about what other people thought, she would have agreed to marry Jeremy when he'd asked. She could have insisted he leave the mine, and then he wouldn't have come close to dying in that terrible place.

"You shouldn't fret so much, Lizzie," Lionel said, lifting his glass to her. The red wine caught the afternoon light and shone like a ruby.

She woke with a gasp, the image fresh in her mind's eye. She looked around the moonlight-dappled room, aware that the scent of a pipe was in the air. It quickly faded, but it *had* been there. She stared at the ceiling, her eyes wide, her skin covered in goose bumps. She wasn't frightened as much as startled and energized. "You're right," she whispered. Less worrying. More action.

More living.

Rebecca walked into the kitchen, blinking in surprise at the table filled with muffins. She looked decidedly grumpy. "Jake wet the bed again," she said disgustedly. "It got on me."

Lizzie turned and handed her a plate. "Fortunately," she replied calmly, "we have a wonderful bathhouse where you can clean up before school. In the meantime, why don't you pick out your breakfast?"

Rebecca surveyed the choices. Apple cinnamon, honey bran, and blueberry. "Why did you make so many?"

"I'm going to offer them to the stores."

"Today?" Rebecca asked as she picked out a blueberry muffin with crumbly brown sugar on top.

Lizzie nodded and sat with a cup of tea. She reached for a muffin. "No more putting it off. All they can do is tell me no if they don't want them, right?" She took a sip of her tea and added another spoonful of sugar to it.

"I don't want to sleep with Jake anymore," Rebecca complained irritably. She bit into her muffin, but continued to frown.

Lizzie set her spoon on her saucer with a soft sigh. "It's a very important job, being an older sister. I hope you realize that. Jake's had a difficult time with . . . everything. It's been scary. That's why he sometimes wets the bed." She paused. "I think you know how much he loves you. He takes everything you say to heart. So please, don't make him feel worse than he already does."

Rebecca made a face, but her mother had gotten through to her. "I just wish I could have my own room," she muttered.

"You will. One day soon." Rebecca looked at her suspiciously and Lizzie nodded. "I promise."

Rebecca went back to eating. "Jake wishes you'd marry Jeremy," she said moments later without looking up. In fact, she was studying her muffin intently, as if counting each blueberry.

"I want that, too," Lizzie replied carefully.

Rebecca looked at her. "Do you love him?"

Lizzie nodded. "I do." As Rebecca considered the reply, Lizzie rose. "I forgot to get your milk," she said as she went to the icebox.

"Would I have to call him papa?"

"No," Lizzie replied evenly. "No one will make you. That would be up to you."

Rebecca shrugged. "Jake would like it."

Lizzie walked back with the glass of milk and sat. "I'd like to know how you feel."

"Mama?"

"Yes?"

"Did Papa always hit you?"

It took Lizzie a few moments to find her voice. "No," she said softly with a shake of her head.

"Did you love him?"

"To be perfectly honest, I've wondered that, too."

"How do you not know?"

"Well, I was young when we met and a lot changed over the time we were married." She looked far away for a moment. "I feel like I was someone else then."

Rebecca grinned. "Because you were."

Lizzie laughed, but her smile slowly vanished. "May I ask you something?"

Rebecca nodded.

"Do you think about your father?"

Seconds of silence ticked by. "Yes."

"Do you miss him?"

Rebecca's expression darkened before she shook her head resolutely. "I will *never* miss him."

Lizzie felt stunned by the virulence of the answer.

Rebecca's face suddenly fell. "I'm sorry, Mama."

"It's all right," Lizzie assured her.

"Do you think I'm a bad person?"

"Oh, honey." Lizzie grabbed her up and pulled her close. "No! Oh, no. You're strong and such a good big sister and the most wonderful daughter." Rebecca was clinging and crying—not at all like her, and so Lizzie held her even tighter. "It sometimes scares me how wonderful you and Jake are. How much I love you. I feel I haven't done anything good enough in life to deserve you."

Rebecca shook her head. "That's not true."

"I'll stop thinking it, then." Lizzie pressed a kiss to her head. "And you never, ever entertain that thought again. You are a good person. Loving and strong and smart. I wouldn't change anything about you. I love you so much."

"I love you, too," Rebecca said brokenly.

Lizzie held her until the tension relaxed from her child's body. "You have a new dress to wear today."

Rebecca sat up with a grin on her face. "You finished it?"

Lizzie nodded. "It's in my room."

Rebecca popped up and hurried from the room, passing a sleepy-looking Jake, who'd put on clothes, although they were crooked. He looked abashed. Actually, Lucky did, too. He'd followed Jake in, as usual, since he'd taken to sleeping in their room. She hoped she didn't have one of his messes to clean up, as well. "Come have some breakfast," she said. "Then I thought I'd start some laundry, wash all our bed clothes today, and then we'll walk Rebecca to school. What do you think of that?"

He nodded soberly and then walked to the table. "That's a lot," he said as he looked over the array of muffins.

"I know," she said as she got up to fetch him a plate and a glass of milk. "We're going to the stores in town to see if they want them."

"Mama?"

Lizzie turned to him.

"Is Jeremy coming home soon?"

Lizzie smiled. "I'm going to have that very discussion with him today. Tell him that we want him to come home."

Jake nodded. "Lucky misses him."

Rebecca handed Jake his plate and set his glass of milk on the table. "C'mon, Lucky," she called, as she crossed to the door to let him out. The dog hopped out obediently, and the sight tugged on Lizzie's heartstrings. "Good boy," she said as she opened the screen door for him.

The morning was cold, but beautiful. The deep red leaves on the trees particularly stood out, and she was reminded of the red of Lionel's wine in her dream. She was suddenly filled with so much gratitude, she couldn't hold it in. "I love this place," she whispered, knowing somehow that he understood her. *I love it and I'm going to live my life here as it's best for us. No more fear.* It was funny how much the dream experience had affected her. That's what she was thinking as she opened the door again for Lucky and followed him back inside.

Jake had nearly finished a blueberry muffin. He had a smear of blueberry at both sides of his mouth. "I'm going to start the water for laundry. Would you mind getting your bed covers and putting them in the tub when you're finished?"

His eyes widened momentarily and he shook his head.

Rebecca came into the room in her new dress. Lizzie had known it would fit; Rebecca had tried it on enough times as Lizzie sewed, but it looked wonderful, and Rebecca was obviously delighted with it. "I love it," Lizzie said.

"Me too." Rebecca whirled about and then did an elaborate curtsy.

Lucky let out a strange-sounding whine, which was all the noise he ever made, and his tail wagged. "And Lucky loves it, too," Lizzie said. They all laughed.

"Marie," Heidi said, shaking her awake.

Marie turned and blinked in confusion. It was early—too early.

"Walt's here," Heidi said. "He wants to see you for a minute."

"Wha—" Marie croaked. "What time is it?"

"Seven. In the morning," she added, when Marie continued to look baffled.

Marie sat, huffing her displeasure, but the event was strange enough that she was awake. Heidi was still in her robe, but she looked wide-awake and refreshed. Marie knew damn well she herself looked anything but.

"Happy birthday, by the way," Heidi said with a smile as she started out.

It *was* her birthday. "How did you know?"

"Walt said so." Heidi turned back at the door. "Why do you think he's here?"

Of course. Walt would remember. He would be one of only a few that would. Marie got up to make herself decent.

That had been her mother's expression. *Come on, girl*, she'd said in the early mornings Marie had always loathed. *Get up and make yourself decent*. Of course, now there was an undeniable irony to the phrase, since she would never truly be decent again.

"Can we stop in and say good morning?" Rebecca asked as they approached the Blues'.

"That was my plan exactly."

Lizzie watched the children run ahead. They dashed into the house, although they were back out before she reached them.

"Jeremy's not here," Rebecca called.

Cessie came right behind them, shielding her eyes from the brightness of the morning. Lizzie reached her, frowning with worry.

"He went to help," Cessie told her.

Lizzie's heart dropped. Surely, though, he wouldn't go back down into the mine. He wouldn't put himself in that kind of danger again. Would he?

"He felt well enough?" Lizzie said, because she had to say something.

Cessie nodded. "He did. He had a good breakfast. Oh, honey, he feels the need to help. You can understand that. And he'll be careful."

Lizzie turned away, trying to guard her expression. The children didn't need any more to worry about. "Well, we're off to town," she said, trying to sound upbeat.

"I heard."

"Do you need anything?"

"Not a thing, but stop by afterwards and tell me how it went."

"I will," Lizzie answered as she started off.

"Jake," Cessie called. "Do you want to stay with me?"

Jake looked at his mother hopefully.

"It's all right," she assured him. "If you want to stay."

He nodded and hurried toward Sheeba, who was lazing about on the front porch.

"We'll have some lunch ready when you get back," Cessie called.

Chapter Forty-One

Marie found it surprisingly enjoyable to walk arm in arm with Walt. He'd brought her flowers and a box of candy and asked for the pleasure of a walk. For someone who had never enjoyed mornings, the experience felt like a revelation. The light of morning painted the world a different color than it would be later. Shopkeepers were busy opening their shops and people were already going at their daily tasks, taking no notice of her. Of course, she was wearing a coat and had a clean face, and her hair was pulled back into a simple twist. No one seemed to recognize her, not that anyone was looking twice. They assumed she was decent, that she was one of them. It felt good.

"I got something to tell you," Walt said, looking straight ahead.

She looked at him. "What?"

He halted, sighed softly, and then turned toward her, finally looking into her eyes.

She tensed, because it was bad news of some sort. Had he met someone else and really only come to tell her good-bye?

"I'm leaving," he stated.

Her jaw went lax. She really had done it. She's squandered her best opportunity for a normal life. He'd offered and she'd refused.

"My cousin Jeb moved off to Baltimore a few years ago and started a hardware store. He did all right with it, but he had stiff competition from a store that had been there a long time. Well, now the man who owns the store has offered to sell it to him. It's a bigger, better place, and if I go in with him, we could buy it and run it together."

She felt sick to her stomach. He'd come to say happy birthday and good-bye.

"I'm sick of scratching out a living," he continued. "Do you know, every year the price I get for a bushel of corn goes down? I work morning to night, and I only cleared a hundred and sixty dollars last year." He paused. "I like the idea of being a shopkeeper. You open your shop at eight and close it at six. You take Sundays off. Jeb and I talked about it and we'll each take one other day off, as well. I think it would be a real good life. Better than this one."

She couldn't think of a thing to say. She sincerely liked him and wanted the best for him, but she'd never imagined he wouldn't be here. That he wouldn't be available when and if she decided she wanted him. Which was arrogance on her part, pure and simple.

"My brother will give me a fair price for my land," he said, "so there's really nothin' to hold me back." He looked at her searchingly and sadly. "Aw, Marie. You're breaking my heart, the way you look."

She turned away, blinking back tears. Who would ever want her now? No one as decent and kind and good as Walt.

"You won't even consider going?"

She turned back to him with a gasp, her eyes wide.

"What?" he asked, surprised by her reaction. "You know I want you to."

"You . . . still want to marry me?"

"Do I still want that? It's all I been wanting for the last how many years? Are you crazy?"

Her limbs suddenly felt weak and words failed her. Or maybe she didn't want to admit what she thought. If he hadn't considered that he was too good for her, she didn't want to put the thought in his head.

"I don't want to be a dog chasing my tail, but—"

She shook her head. "You're not," she said thickly.

"Then you'll think about it? And maybe we can have supper tonight? You ought to be able to get off work for supper on your own dang birthday."

She felt light-headed—as if she'd been granted the reprieve of a lifetime. "I'd like that."

He smiled back, excitement beginning to shine in his hazel eyes. "I, uh, reckon I best get on for now. You want I should walk you back?"

"No, thank you. I think I'll walk for a while."

"All right then." He leaned in and kissed her cheek. "I'll see you tonight. Birthday girl," he added with a silly grin. He stepped back and walked away with a definite bounce in his step.

He still wanted her. *Thank God.*

Even before they'd reached the schoolhouse, Rebecca saw a friend waiting and bid her mother a good day before running ahead. Midway there, she turned back to wave, and it was a moment that would be etched in Lizzie's mind. Rebecca, with the striped skirt of her new dress peeking from beneath her coat, and a smile of sheer happiness on her face. Lizzie smiled and waved back.

This general store was owned by the Dugans, and it was the closest stop. There were already a half dozen customers milling about when she stepped inside. "Help you?" the proprietor asked as he pointedly looked at the box in her hand. He was around thirty years of age, a small man with receding hair and sharp features. He'd never struck her as particularly helpful.

"I bake," she said when she reached the counter. "I was hoping you might have an interest in selling my wares."

"What do you bake?"

"All sorts of things. Cakes, breads, cookies." She set the box on the counter and the aroma of the muffins wafted out. "I made muffins this morning. Would you care for one?"

He shrugged. "Why not?"

She opened the box. "Blueberry?"

"I like blueberry," he said, eyeing the contents of the box. "How much you thinking?"

She handed a muffin to him and watched him bite into it. "I was thinking thirty-six cents a dozen," she said quietly. "I thought you could mark them up to five cents apiece and you'd make twenty-four cents profit per dozen." She handed him a handwritten list of goods she could make, the price she was asking, the suggested retail amount and the profit. "I made this list."

Curtis Dugan glanced at it dispassionately. "Cut your prices in half and I'm interested."

It took self-restraint not to show the offense she felt. She'd priced everything out in order to make a modest profit, not nearly the profit he would make for simply reselling her hard work. "Mr. Dugan, prices are what they are. A five-pound bag of flour is fifteen cents. The same amount of sugar is thirty-five cents. A pound of butter is twenty-six cents."

"Yeah, I know prices," he scoffed.

"My point is, by the time I put a loaf of bread before you, or muffins or a cake or a dozen cookies, there is a cost involved. If I can't exceed that cost, there's no point in trying to sell my goods."

"Just saying you're asking too much."

"I can't take less unless you're willing to cut the prices of the ingredients by half."

He smirked. "Not likely."

She felt shaken, but he seemed immovable and so she closed the box, tipped her head to him, and left the store. Outside, she kept her chin high as she walked, but she only had enough vigor to make it to the empty bench between the barber shop and the cobbler. Mr. and Mrs. Adams owned the other general store, but Mrs. Adams had been decidedly cool the last time she'd left the store. Would the lady be willing to work with her now? If not, where else could she go?

Marie sat in the cemetery with her eyes closed as the church bells clanged eight times. Usually she slept right through the morning chimes, but she loved the sound of them. She opened her eyes and inhaled the autumn-scented morning air, watching as gravediggers went about their task across the cemetery. Already there were a dozen graves dug, and there would be more. Many more.

It was a strange realization that as she turned another year older, mere children were being put into the ground because they'd taken up the wrong profession. She too had taken up the wrong profession, but she wouldn't be in it much longer. Walt was a good man, and she was fortunate that he wanted to marry her. She would marry him and she'd try hard to make him glad he'd chosen her.

The younger Marie who had pined so long for Jeremy seemed a different person altogether, a more foolish, naïve, and, in truth, manipulative young woman. She'd once been told she was too beautiful for her own good and she saw the truth of it now. Which was ironic since her looks were beginning to fade. Or was it just her unhappiness that made it seem so? She rose and began the walk back home. Except it wasn't a home. It was a brothel. But soon she'd have a home of her very own.

When she saw Lizzie Carter sitting on a bench on Main Street, she came to a halt. How strange to see her today, when her life had just taken such a startling turn. Did it mean something? Something like she should warn Lizzie about the possible danger she might be in? She started toward her because she knew the answer. She'd known it for some time. Warning her was the right thing to do. "Good morning," she said as she drew close.

Lizzie looked up and blinked in surprise to see the very person who'd caused Mrs. Adams to turn unfriendly. The woman looked different today. She didn't look like a prostitute at all. "'Morning," she returned.

"May I?" the woman asked when she reached her.

"Of course."

She sat, although she kept all the distance it was possible to keep on the bench. They both started to say something at the same moment and then laughed.

"Go ahead," the dark-haired beauty urged. Lizzie didn't know her name.

"The fabric that you pointed out that day—" Lizzie began.

Marie nodded.

"I made my daughter a dress from it and she wore it today to school."

Marie smiled. "I'll bet it's nice to have a little girl."

"It is," Lizzie replied. "I have a young son, as well, and it's just as wonderful."

"I'm Marie, by the way. Or did Jeremy tell you?"

Lizzie's smile slipped a bit at the odd question. She shook her head. "I'm Elizabeth Carter, but everyone calls me Lizzie."

"Looks like you made a purchase already this morning," Marie observed, as if trying for conversation.

"No," Lizzie said, running a hand over the top of the box. "Just the opposite. I was hoping to sell some baked goods. Would you care for one?" she asked as she opened the lid.

"Those look good."

"Please." Lizzie brought the box closer.

Marie chose one. "Thank you."

"I might as well, too," Lizzie said as she picked up one. "I don't think anyone's going to be interested. Mr. Dugan certainly wasn't. He'd allow me to *give* them to him but not sell them at a fair price."

"He's an ass," Marie stated with a curl to her lip.

Lizzie laughed at the blunt statement and they each took a bite.

"That is so good," Marie said when she'd swallowed. "What you should do is go to the bakery. The man who used to run it is hardly able to do anything anymore. He had one of those fits that left him so he can't move or talk right. His boy is trying to run the place, but he's young and he just doesn't have a talent for it. Mr. Alford's wife helps but—"

This was all news to Lizzie. "Thank you. Maybe I will call on them. You don't think that would be insulting?"

"No. Not at all. I think they'd be glad for it. Thing is, Curtis Dugan's a cheap, mean-hearted little fool. If he had taken on your stuff, he could have put the bakery out of business. And what did he have to do except ring it up?"

"I had the same thought. Well, not the first part. I didn't know about the baker."

"They're pretty nice folks," Marie said with a light shrug. "The wife won't look at me much, but that's nothing new. Mr. Alford was always real polite though. I was real sorry to hear about him taking sick."

Lizzie nodded slowly. Marie was puzzling. She was beautiful and she looked so perfectly normal this morning, not like when they'd met in the store. That day, it had been abundantly clear what she did for a living. Why had she chosen a life of prostitution instead of getting married? She must have had many suitors.

"How's Jeremy?" Marie asked.

"He's . . . well. Well enough to have gone back to help with the rescue operation."

"They don't think anybody else is left alive," Marie said, looking out. "But I get him wanting to help."

Lizzie nodded slowly. She understood, too. She would have preferred him to rest and recuperate, but she understood.

"What I was wanting to say," Marie continued, "I should have said before."

Lizzie looked at her and was baffled by the angst in Marie's expression and the tension in her posture.

"I know about someone named Ray who's looking for you," Marie said with a shamed expression.

Lizzie's breath caught.

"I think he may know where you're at. I liked you right away in the store that day, and I should have told you then. I should have warned you."

Lizzie's eyes filled, the words were so shocking. Her skin suddenly felt painfully chilled.

"It's just"—Marie looked away—"Jeremy. I don't think right around him, and I know I haven't acted right. I'm really sorry."

Lizzie felt as if she couldn't breathe. Ethan knew where

she was and Jeremy had betrayed her. He'd sworn he wouldn't tell what she'd confided, and then he had told Marie. Why? She'd opened her home to him and given him everything she had to give. He'd said he loved her. He'd said he would never betray her trust. He'd said he would never tell.

"If there's anything I can do," Marie added weakly, "I will. Today is my birthday," she said with a sheepish smile.

Lizzie swallowed hard. She felt ill and remarkably strange, as if this wasn't really happening. As if it was a bizarre nightmare.

"And I've decided everything will be different from today on," Marie continued. "I'll be different."

Lizzie couldn't think straight. Was this woman, this prostitute, really sitting there calmly telling her Jeremy had betrayed her and then telling her it was her birthday?

"I'm sorry I upset you. Is this Mr. Ray dangerous to you?"

Lizzie couldn't tell up from down. Was the question real, or an implied threat? She was so stupid. So stupid to have trusted Jeremy. "H-how do you know Jeremy?"

The question seemed to surprise Marie. "I've known him all my life. I would have done anything for him."

When had he done it? When had he betrayed her? "That day in the store," she said as she realized. "You were there and . . . did Jeremy t-talk to you that day? Did he . . . did he tell you?"

"About you, you mean?" Marie asked.

Lizzie nodded, afraid of the confirmation she felt coming. "Yes."

Lizzie clutched her hands tightly together and stared out. The rug had just been yanked from beneath her feet, but she had to know what was being said. Or threatened. It was more than just her life on the line. "What is it you want?" she asked weakly.

Marie looked out at the street and lifted her chin. "I'm going to get married and start living a normal life."

So this was about staking a claim on Jeremy? Well, Marie could have him. He'd shattered her heart in a million pieces, betrayed her trust and the trust of her children. It would have been better if he'd died in the mine. A split second after the thought, she cringed with shame. She didn't mean it, and the fact that she'd thought it shook her to her core. She handed the box of muffins to Marie, conceding the beauty's victory. "Happy birthday," she said in a low voice. She managed to rise to her feet and walk away. Wisely, Marie didn't stop her or say anything else.

Marie was perplexed by the last moments of the exchange, but Lizzie had been terribly upset about the news concerning Mr. Ray. Meaning he must be a thoroughly rotten apple. But she'd warned Mrs. Carter that he knew about her, and she had Jeremy to protect her. She'd be all right.

She rose and started to the bakery to offer Mrs. Carter's muffins to the Alfords. It was her birthday and everything had changed for her, and she was going to be changed, too. She was going to be giving and grateful for a chance at a new life as Mrs. Walter Davis. Once they were in Baltimore, no one would even know she'd been a whore. She'd just be a wife and maybe a mother one day. It was a wonderful prospect.

Chapter Forty-Two

Cessie looked up from her task of sweeping the front porch when she saw Lizzie coming down the driveway. Sensing something was wrong, she propped the broom against the wall and went to meet her. The closer she got, the more concerned she became. Lizzie was deathly pale. "What is wrong?"

Lizzie shook her head. "I don't feel well."

Cessie stepped closer to feel her forehead. There was no fever, but she was obviously ill. "I'm going to put you straight to bed."

"I'm going home. I want to go home."

"Then I'll walk you there and stay with you."

"No. Please. I just need to rest."

Cessie didn't like it. "Then at least let me keep the children. Jake has built a rather magnificent fort in the backyard and he's ordered the dogs to stand watch and keep intruders out."

Lizzie fought the urge to fall into Cessie's arms and blurt the truth about her colossal blunder. Her children were happy here, and it was possible they were going to have to go on the run again. All the way here, she'd thought about what Marie had said, but the words had become hopelessly jumbled in her mind. Had she said that Ethan knew where she was, or was she merely threatening to tell him? She had to find out, but for the moment she lacked the strength. Jeremy's betrayal had sapped her strength. All she knew was that she'd foolishly destroyed her one and only God-given second chance.

"Lizzie?" Cessie said gently.

"Of course, yes. They can stay," she said, pulling away. "Thank you."

"Oh, honey. You're sure you won't stay, too?"

Lizzie shook her head but kept moving. She didn't dare look at Cessie again or she'd lose all control.

"I'll check on you later," Cessie called.

Once in the privacy of the woods, Lizzie lost her frail grip on self-control and sobbed without any attempt at restraint. She made it home and got into bed, not even bothering to remove her shoes. The crying spell sapped her, and despite her misery, she fell asleep, waking again when it was early evening. She rose, disoriented, and went into the kitchen, where the fire had been built up. A covered plate of food was on the table next to a note that simply said everything was fine with the children—and to rest until she felt better. Her hand, still clutching the note, fell to the side of her body as if it were weighted. She felt completely alone. Even Lionel had abandoned her. And why not? She'd destroyed the gift he'd given. She'd destroyed her second chance.

She pulled back the cover and looked at the dinner Cessie had prepared, slices of ham and deviled eggs. So she could eat without having to bother warming everything. Lizzie covered the plate again and went back to bed.

She woke again when it was dark, and puzzled over the fact that she was still wearing her shoes and clothing. She sat, blinking in a thick daze until a rush of resentment filled her.

She got up and went to lock the doors. Cessie or April May had been back and left more food and built up the fires, but they wouldn't come again this late. Jeremy might try, not knowing what she'd learned, and she'd be damned if she'd let him back in the house.

She went around and twisted the key in every door, something she'd never bothered to do before. Stepping back from the front door, she pictured his face once he realized she'd locked him out. Would he suspect the reason right away? Surely it would cross his mind. Would he feel bad at that point? Would he panic? Would he regret the life he'd surrendered? She hoped so.

Chapter Forty-Three

Seventeen more bodies were taken from the mine. Ten men were still missing, buried under rock and earth, but there were no tunnels unexplored and no possible survivors left. It was a quiet, somber group that lingered as corpses were either taken away by grieving kin or, if the miner had no family, placed in a wagon to be taken to the small mine cemetery behind the patch.

Jeremy and April May were silent for most of the trip back home. All he knew was that he needed to see Lizzie. He needed to take a bath, see the children, and hold Lizzie. Tomorrow he was taking a trip to Roanoke. With no job and not a great deal of savings, he needed all the money he could get his hands on, and Morrison still owed him. It was strange that the man hadn't come back after throwing such a fit about his belongings. After his dream—or had it been a hallucination?—Jeremy hadn't been able to stop thinking about the watch. "I'm going to take a trip to Roanoke tomorrow," he said. "A man there owes me some money."

April May nodded but didn't comment.

"And I'm going to go see Lizzie if she's not at the house."

"Don't blame you." There was silence before she added, "Today was hard."

It had been hard. Liam was gone. Almost every miner he knew was gone. Timmy had been killed, as had every single boy in the breaker and even a twelve-year-old girl working the door in the mine. He hadn't realized any girls worked there. He hadn't seen her body—it had been pulled from the mine the day before—but he'd heard the description of her small body lying among the men's.

As it turned out, Lizzie wasn't at the Blues'. Cessie explained she was feeling unwell, so Jeremy set off to check on her. The locked doors he encountered were strange, and he considered crawling through a window, but decided against it. She wasn't feeling well, perhaps because of the mental and physical strain of the days before, so he'd let her sleep.

He found a stack of clean clothes in the laundry room and bathed before checking the doors one last time, knocking lightly. The knock wasn't answered, so he headed back to the Blues'.

Jeremy woke early and went to the cottage first thing, but the doors were still locked and his knock wasn't answered. He went around to her bedroom window, and the crack in the curtains allowed him to see her sleeping. He was disappointed because he so wanted to talk to her, but he would let her be. Obviously, she needed sleep. He would have liked to have touched her face, smoothed back her hair, and told her he loved her, but it would have to wait.

He returned to the Blues', had breakfast, and walked Rebecca to school before returning to his small house in the patch to collect what he needed before embarking on the trip to Roanoke. Looking around, he found the anonymity of the place disquieting. There was nothing personal, nothing homey. He'd be glad never to see the place again. He packed a small, worn satchel with basic necessities in case he had to spend the night in the city, including his gun and holster. He resented the train fare he'd have to spend, and he'd damn well collect it in addition to what Morrison owed him, but if he was lucky enough to find the man quickly, this would be a one-day trip. Roanoke was only a little over an hour away by train.

Lizzie rose feeling weak and sluggish. She forced herself up and into the kitchen and ate slices of sourdough bread and drank strong tea until she felt some life return. The mind took longer to bring around. First things first. She unlocked the doors and stripped her bed. She went to the laundry house and saw his dirty clothing in the basket. So, he had been there. She'd been right to lock the doors.

She put her sheets in the wash basin, filled it with hot water, and added soap. Her intention had been to agitate it a few times and then let it soak, but the effort of working the handle that forced the paddle around felt satisfying. Frowning darkly as she pondered the circumstances, she came to an understanding. The fact was, she'd felt like a victim most of her life, but she hadn't been one since she'd found this place and these people. She would *not* give it up. Not this home, not Cessie and April May, not her children's happiness. Not Lucky. Not Lionel. Not anything.

If Ethan found her, she would demand a divorce and she would refuse to return with him. And if he attacked her or attempted to harm her children ever again, she would kill him. She was not a victim. She would *not* be a victim. By the grace of God, she'd become Elizabeth Anne Greenway Carter, and Lizzie Carter was a strong and capable woman who could protect herself and those she loved.

Feeling better, she stepped back and shook out her arms. The grief of Jeremy's betrayal lingered just below the surface, and she had to keep it that way. She couldn't think of him now. She was strong, but she wasn't that strong.

Chapter Forty-Four

Roanoke was a city of nearly sixteen thousand people. It was disconcerting. Jeremy walked street after street until he found the sheriff's office and went in to inquire after Morrison.

"Do I know Chaz Morrison?" The sheriff repeated the question slowly and with a droll expression. He hadn't bothered to rise from his desk or even to sit up straight, which rubbed Jeremy the wrong way. "Who's asking?"

"My name is Jeremy Sheffield. I'm from Green Valley and Morrison owes me money."

"Correction, he *owed* you money. Past tense, since he went and got hisself shot between the eyes a couple months back."

Jeremy gawked. "He's dead?"

"You ever know anyone to get shot between the eyes and not be dead?"

It wasn't worth a reply and so Jeremy didn't attempt one.

"Look," the sheriff said, "it's a shame you got a bad debt on your hands, but you got lots of company, if that's any consolation. I've had at least a dozen men come looking for him for the same reason." The sheriff shrugged. He was a fleshy man with bags and dark circles under his eyes.

"Morrison was a scoundrel. No two ways about it. He was a card cheat and not a very good one, which is why he went and got hisself shot." He glanced at Jeremy's holstered pistol. "Maybe you had something similar in mind."

"No, sir. I just wanted the money he owed me."

"Well," the man said with a shrug. "Fact is, we couldn't even hang the man who did it, he took off so fast. Not that anyone lost a lot of sleep over that."

Jeremy looked toward the street and sighed.

"Hope he didn't get you for too much."

Jeremy nodded his thanks and walked out to the street, feeling invisible in the bustling town. He'd counted on getting his money, but at least he had the watch and the silver snuff box. They were worth something. He began looking for a pawn shop or a jeweler, but the sight of a bank made him stop short as he remembered the keys and Morrison's claim that he had a safe deposit box in the bank on Third. What if it was true? Jeremy pulled out the silver snuff box and let the keys fall into his hand. Each one was numbered. It was worth a try.

The City Bank of Roanoke on Third Street was an elegant place with high ceilings and arched windows. As Jeremy walked to one of the sharply dressed men who manned partially barred stations, he wondered how much the place had cost to build and exactly who had paid for it. What exactly was the point of putting a lot of money into building a fancy bank? Behind the clerks were offices made with dark wood, the occupants of which would occasionally look out upon the floor. Jeremy felt nervous. He felt like a criminal. Was he doing something criminal?

"May I help you, sir?" the clerk asked.

"I need to get into safe deposit box one fifty-four," Jeremy replied without a flicker of expression.

"Certainly." The man pulled out a ledger and read through a few pages of entries. "The name?"

"Morrison."

"Very good, sir."

"Also," Jeremy said, "box eighty-one."

The man looked at the ledger again and flipped a page, then nodded once more before setting the book back down. "If you'll follow me."

Jeremy did his best to remain expressionless as he followed the man. They walked through the bank and entered a long room full of brass squares that ran the length of the walls. The banker found eighty-one and pulled the long rectangular box from the wall. They then walked to one of several curtained-off sections, although they were the only two people in the room. In the space was a table where the man set the box. Jeremy waited for the man to retrieve the second box and leave before he tried a key. His hand was actually shaking and he blew out a breath to calm himself.

Inside the first box were ten-dollar and fifty-dollar bank notes, as well as silver certificates. Jeremy held one up and read. "This certifies that there have been deposited with the Treasurer of the U.S. at Washington, D.C., payable at his office to the bearer on demand, 1000 silver dollars. This certificate is receivable for customs, taxes, and all public dues and when so received may be reissued."

It was worth a thousand dollars? A *thousand* dollars. His heart was pounding. He swallowed hard and fingered through the other silver certificates, then looked up and around to make sure he was still alone in the room. This was Morrison's cache, and he'd gotten possession of it because the man had cheated him, been caught and forced to give up his valuables. And then Morrison was killed when caught cheating again. It gave Jeremy a chill up his spine.

He opened the second box and found much the same, although there were also IOUs, a few gold certificates, and pieces of jewelry: a woman's diamond pin, shaped like a bow, and a man's gold cufflinks. The bow pin was all white diamonds, or what looked like diamonds, on a black setting, except for the single central gem of pale pink. It was exceptionally feminine, something Lizzie would like even if it wasn't made of real gems.

He licked his lips as he shoved the contents of both boxes into his satchel, forcing it all to fit. He had to gather his composure before locking the boxes again and leaving, nodding to the banker, who nodded in return.

Back on the street, he felt conspicuous and light-headed as he walked. Had he just committed a crime? Was it theft? He was in possession of something that wasn't his. At least, it was never supposed to have been his. He went into a restaurant and was seated in a private booth, which he was glad for. He needed to think and he needed a drink.

The waiter appeared and handed him a menu while casting a discerning eye over him, as if determining whether he could pay for his meal. If only he had any notion of how ridiculous that was.

"May I get you something to drink, sir?"

"I'll take a glass of wine. Your best-selling wine." The waiter inclined his head and left, and Jeremy rolled his shoulders discreetly and stretched his stiff neck. He picked up the menu, but couldn't concentrate on it. How much money had he just taken? Would anyone come after him? How could they? He had the keys to the boxes he'd asked for. He'd been given them by the man who owned the box. The man who'd stolen and cheated for years.

The waiter was back with the wine, both the bottle and a glass. He showed the wine label, as if Jeremy could concentrate on that, and then poured a small amount, saying, "This is ten-year-old Gruaud-Larose."

Jeremy picked it up and sipped. "It's good."

The waiter poured more into his glass and set the bottle on the table, then gestured to the menu. "Have you decided? May I say, the veal and the lamb are excellent. Both served with potatoes au gratin and a vegetable medley."

"I'll take the veal."

"Very good," the man said with a bow of his head. "I'll bring a basket of bread."

As the man walked away, Jeremy sipped the wine again, fascinated by the rich, complex layers of flavor. It felt as if he was playing a part, and maybe he was. Only a few days ago, he'd been close to death a mile below the surface of the earth, and today he was sitting in a fine restaurant in the city next to a bag containing a fortune. The only problem was that it wasn't his money.

Chapter Forty-Five

Marie's head was slightly turned as she sat at her vanity braiding her hair slowly and methodically. Her face was clean and her clothes were new, purchased yesterday as a birthday gift to herself. She wore a simple white shirtwaist with a slim gray ribbon-bow around the neck and a black-and-gray striped skirt.

At this time of afternoon, she ought to have been getting dressed for work, but everything was about to be different. No—everything was already different, because the night before, she'd told Walt she would marry him. They wouldn't leave for Baltimore until the first of December, but she couldn't do this anymore. She couldn't be a whore, not for one more day.

She'd thought about going to Saul and telling him—but he was known to go crazy when a girl left, even one who had the right to go, as she did. She'd told her closest friends and she would leave Saul a note explaining, but she was clearing out this afternoon, hopefully without seeing him. She'd packed what she needed and she was going to Walt's to surprise him. First, though, she was going to see Lizzie Carter.

Not only had the Alfords been pleased by the muffins

and purchased them, they wanted whatever Mrs. Carter was willing to bake. They were also interested in her teaching their son, young Clay Alford, about baking, and were willing to pay her for it. Marie had money to pass on to Lizzie, and also possibly hope.

She stood and smoothed her skirt, pleased by how respectable she looked. Maybe she'd even stop in to see her mother and younger brothers and sister before she left. They'd not spoken in ages, but it would be good to show them what she'd become. At least, what she was about to become.

On the way back home in mid-afternoon, Jeremy sat on the train, lost in thought. After his meal, he'd gone to the newspaper in Roanoke and struck up a conversation with the editor, a man named James Page. The affable man had joked about calling the newspaper *Page's Pages*. Instead, he'd gone with the more dignified *Roanoke Daily News*. Not only was Page able to produce Morrison's obituary, which Jeremy had requested, he'd known the man's family.

"Charles was his father's heartbreak," Page confided. "He was probably sixty, or not even, when he passed, but looked ten years older. All from Charles's scandals," he said with a shake of his head.

"Charles had no family left when he was killed?" Jeremy asked, glancing over the brief article.

"No. Probably a good thing."

Fortunately, the seat next to Jeremy was unoccupied. His new satchel, a large one, sat on the seat next to him and his hand rested atop it. Inside was the money—a still uncounted sum—and gifts for Lizzie and the children.

For Lizzie, he'd purchased a crimson silk robe and a wedding ring, although he'd had to guess at the size. If it needed adjustment, they would come back together. In fact, they would anyway. They'd stay at the best hotel and eat at the finest restaurants and try all the wines.

Except it's not your money.

He tried to shrug off the thought as he looked out the window. For Rebecca, he'd gotten a tote bag made of canvas, leather, and fabric for transporting her schoolwork back and forth. It was the perfect size, and he'd added a pad of paper bordered with daisies and a pencil bag full of pencils and an eraser.

For Jake, he'd purchased pots of modeling clay and a baseball. There hadn't been bats small enough for him, but Jeremy would make him one. By the time he started school, he would be ready to keep up. At least at recess.

Buying the gifts had been a great joy and he'd looked forward to giving them. He still did, only . . .

He looked down at his impressive new satchel, highly polished leather with brass buckles. Inside it was his smaller satchel with the money. How much, he didn't know, but it was enough to provide security for a long, long time. Except it wasn't his money. He didn't know who it belonged to. Maybe no one, but it had only fallen into his hands by a twist of fate and because of a cheat. A cheat who'd tried to cheat him. But that didn't make it his money. Forty-three dollars was his, plus extra for the trouble of the train trip, but he'd spent more than that already. So, what was he to do with the rest of it?

Spend it? Hoard it? Use it wisely? Why shouldn't he? Most people would. He wondered if most people would feel so conflicted about it.

Marie felt giddy as she turned onto Main, because she'd snuck away from Saul's without detection. There would be no confrontation and there would be no going back. All she had to her name were the possessions and small amount of cash in the travel bag she carried. She'd left all her risqué clothing, face paint, and accoutrements behind for her friends, as she had no need of them any longer. She'd left the vile tonics, her womb veil, her long-handled sponge, and the ingredients for her after-intercourse douche behind.

When she reached the church, she stopped briefly. In Baltimore, they'd find a friendly church and they'd go on Sundays. In a few years, she could picture her fair-haired young son clutching the hand of his father while she held her dark-haired infant daughter in her arms. Her son would look like his father and her baby girl would look like her. Only her little girl would be smarter and much better cared for than she'd ever been. Her children would never know what she'd been. They would only know her as their sweet, gentle mama.

She meandered through the cemetery to Jenny's grave and stopped, wondering how different things would have turned out had she not drowned.

Jeremy stopped in the shade of an ancient oak because, across the cemetery, Marie was standing at his family's gravesite. He'd been planning on going there himself, but he didn't want to encounter her. Instead he turned and headed toward Emmett's office.

Marie walked on until she saw the train station to her right. The train was there, and passengers were boarding while others, having just arrived, dispersed. A few walked away, stiff and distracted with the business at hand, while others strolled with loved ones, all bright smiles and happy chatter. She watched people waving good-bye to whoever was behind the small gray windows of the smoke-belching train.

"Excuse me, ma'am," a man said, stopping before her. "Are you from this area?"

He thought she was a lady and so she smiled a serene, restrained smile. "I am."

"Can you direct me to the Greenway cottage?" he asked.

Her smiled slipped and her heart began to hammer. It was he. It was the man Lizzie was afraid of. "It's that direction," she replied, trying to sound calm and natural despite the fact that she was telling an out-and-out lie.

He blinked. "Where's the town?"

"In that direction." She pointed.

"I thought the Greenway cottage was east of town. That's what I was told."

She shrugged lightly. "I can't tell one direction from another, but I've lived here all my life. The Greenway place is maybe a mile that way."

He looked aggravated, but tipped his hat to her and walked on. Going toward town. She lifted her skirt slightly and hurried to warn Lizzie.

Rebecca saw Jeremy and ran for him. She reached him and hugged him, which was a wonderful feeling. "What are you still doing in town this late?" he asked.

"We practiced for the Christmas pageant after school. Did you just get back?"

"I just got off the train. I'm going to go see Mr. Rice for a little while, but will you tell your mama I'll be there soon?"

She grinned, nodded happily, and hurried off, full of purpose.

* * *

Marie reached the crooked tree, and hurried over to stash her bag behind it since she'd be able to walk faster without it. She set it down behind the tree where it wasn't noticeable, then turned and found herself face-to-face with a livid-looking Mr. Ray.

"I guess you know my wife?" he asked accusingly.

"N-no," she stammered.

"Liar," he said, giving her a vicious shove backwards.

Her foot caught on a raised root and she was propelled backwards without control. Her head hit the trunk of the tree and she lay stunned. Mr. Ray stepped into view, glaring down at her, and then turned and walked away. She tried to sit up, but only made it a matter of inches. She felt warm blood seeping down the back of her neck. She tried to get up, but she couldn't. Everything was strange, slanted and moving slowly. So skewed. So very skewed.

"Jeremy," Emmett said, rising from his desk and extending his hand.

Jeremy shook it. "May I have a few minutes of your time?"

"I've got an appointment in a quarter of an hour, but you can have until then."

Jeremy sat, but was suddenly at a loss for words.

"Something wrong?" Emmett asked gently. "I mean, something other than the obvious. I know what you've been through."

Jeremy sighed. "When I was in the mine, trapped—"

Emmett nodded.

"I thought of something. I had . . . sort of a dream, and I remembered this man who owed me money. He was a gambler. He lost several hands and ended up owing me nearly fifty dollars. This was in August."

Emmett nodded again, all ears.

"The man claimed he had the money back in his room, but he didn't. Then he said he'd bring it back, but I didn't trust him, of course."

"Understandable."

"So, in the meantime, I kept his watch and this silver snuff box. He wanted them back real bad. Begged me not to pawn them. He said they had sentimental value. The man's name was Morrison. Charles Morrison. He swore he'd get the money to me in three days, but he didn't."

"The man owes you money," Emmett said, "says he'll get it to you in a matter of days. In the meantime, you hold some of his valuables for collateral."

Jeremy nodded. "But he didn't return. So this morning I took the train to Roanoke to find him, because he said the money was there in the bank."

"Sounds like a man who talks a lot and means very little of it," Emmett said.

"Yeah, only he did have money in the bank." He leaned over and opened his satchel and pulled out the smaller one from within. He handed that to Emmett, who took it with a bemused expression until he looked inside. He looked up at Jeremy sharply.

"When I got to Roanoke, I went to the sheriff first. He told me Morrison had been shot and killed. I saw his obituary. Morrison died not a week after he left here."

"That would explain his failure to reappear. If he'd ever had the intention."

"Oh, he would have come back, because there were keys hidden in the snuff box I took from him."

"Keys?"

Jeremy nodded. "I didn't understand what they were for

at first, but then it all came together when I left the sheriff's office and started thinking about the bank. Morrison said he had the money in a safety deposit box."

"Ah, the key was to the box."

"Keys. To the boxes. Yes. So I found the bank and asked for the boxes and they were filled with that," he said, nodding at the satchel. "I took it."

"Did you claim to be Morrison?"

"No. I said I wanted to get inside a safety deposit box. The banker asked what number and I told him. I knew because it was on the key. Then he looked it up in a ledger book and asked me the name. I said Morrison. I didn't say I was Morrison."

Emmett pondered. "He asked what name was on this account and you told him."

Jeremy nodded.

Emmett glanced in the bag again. "How much is it?"

Jeremy shook his head. "I didn't count it."

Emmett looked regretful. "If Morrison has family—"

"He doesn't. I made sure."

"So, why have you come to me?"

"It's not my money," he said, knowing full well how foolish the predicament was. He'd gone after the money, collected it, and there it was. But he couldn't keep it. He'd spent too many years paying for one crime to go and commit another. It felt like a test, and he wasn't about to fail when he had everything to look forward to right now. He would find another way to survive. "I guess I came for your advice about what to do with it. What's the right thing to do?"

Emmett leaned back. "Did this Morrison have debts that you know of?"

"He was a card cheat. The sheriff said a dozen men had showed up looking to collect."

Emmett pondered a few moments. "But he had no family and there's probably no way of tracking down who's owed what."

Jeremy nodded.

Emmett shrugged. "Seems to me this is a stroke of great good fortune."

"Have I done something illegal?" Jeremy asked worriedly.

"Morrison gave you the snuff box as collateral. He told you he had money in the bank. In fact, he told you the specific bank?"

Jeremy nodded. "Yes, sir. He wanted me to go with him instead of handing over the watch and the box."

"But you weren't in a position to go, so he gave you the snuff box with the keys inside and told you about the bank."

"He didn't like that I was keeping it. He didn't like it at all. Like I said, he begged me not to pawn it."

"You didn't do anything illegal, Jeremy. Far as I can see, the money is yours."

"The one thing I do know," Jeremy rejoined, "is that it's not mine."

Emmett considered in silence. "Give me a day or two to think about it?"

"I appreciate it," Jeremy said. He rose and offered his hand and Emmett shook it with a firm grasp.

Chapter Forty-Six

Lizzie opened the back screened-porch door and swept the dirt out, then tackled the steps. Finishing, she noticed Jake heading back to the fort he'd made, his hands full of toy soldiers. Lucky dutifully followed. She smiled to herself as she set the broom aside, and then went back inside to check the applesauce cake that was baking.

She peeked inside the oven and knew the cake was done. She reached for a hand towel as Lucky started barking, which startled her, because he never barked. He sounded agitated, which made her concerned for Jake. She grabbed the hot pan and quickly set it atop the counter, then turned to go see what the ruckus was about.

Blinding pain was the next thing she experienced, followed by a surprised awareness that she was on the floor. Lucky was close by, barking ferociously. *What in the world had happened?* Frightened for Jake, she struggled to rise, which was when she saw Ethan hovering above her, his face enraged, his eyes bulging.

"Stupid bitch," he seethed. "You have any idea how much this stunt of yours cost me?"

She saw his fist fly but could not react fast enough. She nearly cried out at the blow, but the thought of Jake made her bite the sound back. Drawing on all her strength, she lunged at Ethan, clawing at his face. There was a momentary pause after she made contact, and then she felt herself being dragged upwards by her hair. Dizzy from the blows she'd received, she couldn't stand, nor did she need to. Ethan slammed her head into the corner of the table.

"Four times four is sixteen," Rebecca chanted as she kicked a pinecone along while she walked home. She was nearly home and was looking forward to telling Mama that Jeremy would be there soon. It was fun to have news to tell. "Four times five is twenty. Four times six—"

She jerked to a halt with a gasp as something flew at her from the brush ahead. It was Jake, and he was crying, his face white with fear as he threw himself into her arms. She could barely breathe for the fear that gripped her. "What's the matter?"

He made a choking sound. "Pa-pa-pa."

"Pa?" she repeated incredulously. "He's here?"

He nodded jerkily. His breathing was strange and wheezy.

"He's here?" she asked again, not wanting to believe it. "He found us?"

Jake kept nodding. "I th-think—"

"What, Jake?"

"He killed Mama," Jake whispered.

Rebecca's stomach clenched, but she couldn't be sick. "I've got to go get Jeremy. He's in town. You stay here."

"No," Jake screamed, grabbing hold of her for dear life.

"Jake, stop it!" She tried to shake him loose, but he wouldn't budge. "We have to help Mama. Let go! I'm going to go home and—"

"No! He'll kill you, too," Jake cried.

"No, he won't." She tried to reason. "I won't even let him see me. Now, let go of me!" With a violent thrust, she shook free of him and broke into a run toward home, because riding Dancer was the fastest way to get to Jeremy. She knew Jake was following, but she couldn't wait for him. When she reached their property, he was still right behind her. Somehow, he'd kept up even though she was a much faster runner. She crouched and looked around, but there was no sign of her pa. A dog was barking madly, which confused her. "Is that Lucky?" she asked Jake.

Jake nodded.

If he was barking at her father, that meant he was around the house. Or in it. "I have to get to Dancer," she said. "You stay here."

She made a dash for the barn and Jake followed, hot on her heels. She went to Dancer and opened his stall. He merely looked at her curiously. She didn't have time to saddle him, because Pa might see her any moment. Jake had to be wrong about Pa killing Mama, *he had to*, but if he was hurting her, they couldn't make him stop. Only Jeremy could make him stop. Or April May with her gun. Either way, they had to get to someone fast.

Shaking from fear and adrenalin, her muscles so stiff she couldn't move easily, she climbed the slats of the stall and got on Dancer's back and Jake scrambled on right behind her. She grabbed the mane and kicked the sides of the horse. "Hang on, Jake!"

Jeremy heard a horse approaching. It made him curious, but in no way was he prepared for the shock of seeing Dancer come into view with Rebecca and Jake hanging on for dear life, Rebecca clutching Dancer's mane, and Jake clutching Rebecca, both of them clearly terrified. They'd only ever ridden with him leading the horse. He dropped his bag and helped stop the horse, then pulled Jake off. The boy didn't look well and his small body was shaking. "What's happened?" he asked, directing the question to Rebecca.

"My father is here," Rebecca cried. "He found us."

He set Jake down, but the boy's legs gave way and he fell to the ground.

"Go to the Blues'," Jeremy said urgently as he got Rebecca down. She dropped to Jake's side protectively as Jeremy mounted Dancer and rode out. Cold, sick fear gripped him, making it hard to breathe. When he got close to the cottage and heard a man yelling for the children, he stopped Dancer, dismounted, and ran the rest of the distance on foot, suddenly fearful of what Ethan Ray might do to Lizzie if he saw him coming. The commotion of the man's yelling and a dog's barking enabled Jeremy to circle around and enter the house without being heard.

Blood was the first thing he saw when he went into the kitchen. Lizzie was on the floor, lying perfectly still. He reached her and gathered her up in his arms. Her face was cut, swollen and already bruising, but she was alive. The sound of Ethan Ray's voice was closer now and it brought an icy calmness over Jeremy. He laid Lizzie back down, got to his feet, and moved backwards, flattening himself against the wall.

A man of medium build came into the kitchen and moved close to Lizzie's body, his fists clenched at his sides. Jeremy stepped out, allowed the man to see him, and then swung his fist into the man's cheek, crushing bone. An incredulous Ethan staggered backwards and hit the counter. "Nobody hurts my family," Jeremy said.

Ethan got his feet under him and glared malevolently. "That's *my* wife, you son of a bitch, and I have every right—"

The *right*? Had he really just said that? Jeremy lunged for the man.

Chapter Forty-Seven

April May rounded the cottage carefully, shotgun in hand, and entered the house through the front door. Moving quietly, she made her way into the kitchen, where Lizzie lay on the floor, pale and much too still. There was a pillow beneath her head and a cover draped over her. Lucky was standing beside her whimpering. The older woman's stomach ached with tension as she hurried to her, knelt, and touched the side of Lizzie's neck to make sure of a pulse. She exhaled with relief to feel it.

Ethan, that son of a jackal, had done a number on her. Her face was swollen and bloody, blood had seeped from one ear and matted in her hair, but glancing around the room at the toppled furniture and broken dishes, she knew the amount of blood on the floor could not be from Lizzie alone. It just couldn't be.

April May heard a man's voice and looked out the open back door before rising and striding to the door, gun at the ready.

Jeremy and Ethan were in the yard. Ethan was on the ground but trying to rise. Jeremy was standing over him with clenched fists at his sides. Jeremy's back was to her, so she didn't know what blows he'd sustained, but it was evident Ethan Ray had taken a good deal of punishment. Ray glowered at Jeremy as he made it to his knees.

"I'm here," April May said quietly.

Jeremy turned his head slightly at the sound of her voice, which was the distraction Ethan needed. He drew his gun. Before April May could cry out in warning, Jeremy drew and fired a split second before Ethan's gun went off.

Ethan jerked and fell back with a yell while Jeremy remained on his feet. April May dashed out to make sure he wasn't hit. He wasn't. Ethan's gun was on the ground and he was writhing in pain. Jeremy stared at the man with loathing in his eyes, as if he wanted to do nothing more than shoot him again. And maybe again and again. "You got him," she said.

He slowly lowered his gun. "Lizzie—"

"I'll see to her. She'll be all right. You best see to him."

They stepped closer to the man, close enough to see he'd taken the bullet in the torso.

"Can't breathe," Ray grunted.

"Get him to the doc," April May said dispassionately.

"So he can come back here and hurt her again?" Jeremy asked, scowling down at the injured man.

"He tried to kill her and he tried to kill you, too. At the very least, he's going to jail. And Lizzie can divorce him before he goes off to jail."

Jeremy considered a few moments and then holstered his gun. He whistled for Dancer, who came running.

"Want me to watch him while you saddle up?" April May asked, still watching Ethan suspiciously.

"No. Don't need to." He hauled Ethan Ray up and over his shoulder before unceremoniously hoisting him over the horse. Ignoring the stream of grunted complaints and obscenities, Jeremy mounted behind the man and looked at April May, needing to say something more.

"I'll take care of her," she pledged.

He nodded meaningfully and rode away.

Lizzie had come to and was attempting to rise when April May got back inside. "Ho, there. Stay down a minute."

"Jake," Lizzie moaned. "Where's Jake?"

"The children are fine, but you are damn sure not, my girl, so lie still." April May set the shotgun aside and grabbed towels, stepping over puddles of blood on the floor. She dampened a towel and went back to Lizzie.

"Ethan. He's here."

"I know, honey. The children told us."

Lizzie frowned in confusion. "What? How—"

"Lucky sensed him sneaking around and started growling," April May explained as she gently pressed the towel to the cut on Lizzie's cheek. "Animals sense danger. They sense evil, too. Because of Lucky, Jake saw Ethan and ducked into his fort. Then when Ethan went into the house, Jake ran for you. He climbed up and looked in the kitchen window and . . . saw you on the floor."

"Oh no."

"It's all right. The little man did just what he should have done. He ran and got Rebecca, who was coming home, and the two of them lit out after Jeremy."

"Jeremy?"

"He was close, headed home from town, and he told the children to come to us." Lizzie looked close to passing out again and April May hesitated, wondering whether it was better to let her be or to keep her awake. "I'm going to get you some wine."

"Jeremy?" Lizzie murmured again.

April May got up and fetched a glass of wine, then helped

Lizzie to sit, propping her against the cupboard before bringing the glass to her lips and urging her to drink.

"Where?" Lizzie said weakly, pushing the glass away.

"The children are at our house. They're safe. I'm not so sure about Ethan."

"Wha . . . what do you mean?"

"Take a drink."

Lizzie took a swallow.

"Jeremy got here, saw what Ethan had done, and they fought. Ethan got the worst of it, which is just as it ought to be. He drew on Jeremy, but Jeremy shot first. I was a witness to that part. Anyway, Jeremy has taken him into town. He'll go to the doctor first and to the sheriff second. I'm not a hundred percent sure Ethan will live, but if he does, he ought to be going off to jail."

"Lizzie!" a woman called from outside.

April May didn't recognize the voice, and Lizzie looked every bit as perplexed. April May set the glass aside and hurried out the back door as Marie rounded the house. The dark-haired beauty looked shaky on her feet and one shoulder was covered in blood. "Lord have mercy," April May exclaimed as she hurried toward her. "What happened to you?"

"It was that Mr. Ray."

April May wrapped an arm around her and felt how unsteady she was. A good, strong wind would knock her over. "We know," she replied grimly. "He's been here."

Marie made a whimper and started to cry. "It's all my fault."

April May had no idea what she was talking about, but there would be time enough to work out the details. She helped Marie inside and into a chair, and examined her head. "Ethan Ray did this to you?"

Marie looked at Lizzie with an expression of profound regret. "I was coming to warn you."

April May went for another towel, wet it, and brought it back to clean Marie's wound and determine whether stitches would be needed. Fortunately, though there was quite a lump, the bleeding had mostly stopped. She fetched a glass of wine and brought it to the girl. "Drink. And then tell me how the Sam Hill you know about Ethan Ray." Marie cringed at a sudden pain and swayed. April May braced her. "Steady, there. Come on now, drink."

Marie drank and leaned against April May, dizzy and weak. "Some woman came to town a few weeks ago," Marie said. "Looking for Lizzie. I don't know who she was."

April May glanced at Lizzie, who was watching Marie with bafflement and great intensity.

"The woman . . . sent a telegram," Marie said. "It said—" She closed her eyes, trying to recall exactly what had been relayed. "'Subject located. Going by name of Carter. You'll find her at the Greenway place east of town.'" She opened her eyes and tears rolled down her face as she straightened in her chair. "Someone who was in the telegraph office that day told me," she said brokenly.

"That fool Bart," April May said accusingly, stepping back from Marie. "Wasn't it?"

Marie nodded slowly.

"That boy's not worth a diddly squat."

"I should have told you right away," Marie said to Lizzie. "I should have told Jeremy."

Although pain was throbbing in Lizzie's head, a strange elation surged, making it difficult to breathe. He hadn't betrayed her. Jeremy hadn't betrayed her. But hadn't Marie claimed he had? "You said . . . Jeremy told you about me."

"That he loved you," Marie said. "I saw the way he looked at you, so I asked him. And he told me. I felt crushed inside.

I wanted to hate him. I wanted to hate you. I really didn't. It's just that I—"

"You've been in love with Jeremy your whole life," April May said with surprising gentleness.

Lizzie squeezed her eyes shut because what she'd thought was shameful. Jeremy hadn't betrayed her. He would never betray her, but how quickly she'd believed it.

"Where did he go?" Marie asked dazedly. "Did he take the children?"

"No," April May replied. "Jeremy got here and Ethan ended up shot. Jeremy's taken him to town. He's not dead, although I wish I'd shot him dead. A snake in the grass like that—"

Lizzie opened her eyes, horrified by the sudden fear of Ethan somehow getting the better of Jeremy.

"Now, you listen to me," April May said, seeing Lizzie's expression. "Jeremy will be all right. He's a man who knows how to take care of himself."

"You don't understand," Lizzie said. "Ethan is—"

"He's a damn coward who beats on a woman and doesn't think a thing of hitting his own child. I know exactly what he is."

Lizzie began crying. "I d-didn't see him. If only I'd seen him. I . . . I b-bought a gun."

"Shh," April May said, going to her. She got down on the floor and wrapped her arms around Lizzie. "It's going to be all right. You'll see. We're going to get you cleaned up and into bed." Lizzie clung to her, trembling, so April May held her, patting gently. "Everything is going to be all right. You weren't sent here and given the protection of people who love you for no reason. Isn't that right, Marie?"

Marie rose and came to join them on the floor, also crying, and so April May wrapped an arm around her, too. *"Shh*, now. We're all going to be all right."

* * *

Jeremy rode back to the cottage feeling strange and numb. Ethan Ray was dead. He'd died before Jeremy reached town. The sheriff had listened to Jeremy's story and taken possession of the body, and he'd told Jeremy to go. "For now," he'd said grimly.

Everything had happened so fast, it was hard to wrap his head around it. Ethan was dead, and judging from the accusing look on the sheriff's face, he was probably going to be arrested, tried, and hanged. Because he'd killed before. Because he was a murderer. He wasn't a family man, he was a *murderer*. When the noose went around his neck, would he have any final words to utter? "Shouldn't have hurt her," he muttered.

Jenny's sixteen-year-old face filled his mind and tears suddenly rolled down his face. *Damn the tears. Let them come*, he thought angrily. And damn Ted Landreth and Stan Thomas. They'd gotten what they'd deserved. And damn Ethan Ray. He'd gotten what he deserved, too. No, he wouldn't have any final words. He didn't regret anything except that he wouldn't have a life with Lizzie and the kids.

A memory rushed back at him so sharp and so clear, his breath caught and he stiffened enough that Dancer halted. *The lake on a misty, gray morning. He'd gone looking for Jenny when she wasn't in her room. She wasn't in the outhouse and she wasn't in the yard or on the porch. He yelled her name and went in search, then froze abruptly when he saw something in the water. In one terrible second, he recognized it was a woman with dark hair, and he rushed into the water, knowing it was his sister. On the bank, he held her lifeless body and cried as he had never*

*cried before. Over and over again he called her name. She
was gone, long gone, but he couldn't stop saying her name.*

He shook his head, trying to clear his mind of the
painful memory. He wiped his face with both hands and
rode on.

Chapter Forty-Eight

Lizzie woke in the pitch dark, mentally and emotionally dulled from the beating, wine, and the headache powder she'd consumed. She'd been in so much pain earlier, she hadn't expected to sleep, but she had. Now, disoriented and laden with fear, she began to rise until a wave of nausea engulfed her and she had to wait for it to pass. When it did, she lit the lamp and got up. One hand outstretched, pausing often to catch her breath, she made her way to the children's room, but they weren't there. *Because they are with Cessie and April May*, she remembered. They were safe. Unless Ethan was still lurking somewhere.

She noticed the light from the kitchen. Her heart began beating harder as she made her way there. Just as she'd hoped and prayed, Jeremy was sitting in his place with his back to her. A piece of paper and pencil were in front of him, as if he was prepared to write a letter. "You're here," she uttered.

"I killed him," he stated in a flat voice without turning to look at her.

She exhaled with relief and continued to the table. She pulled back a chair and sat, but Jeremy wasn't looking at her. He was staring straight ahead, glassy eyed and expressionless. She felt shaken in a different way, and certainly not because Ethan was dead. Perhaps she'd be damned to hell for it, but it was a great relief. If he weren't dead, she would be. It was only a question of when. The fear she felt was because of the way Jeremy looked. Somehow she'd lost him. He'd saved her, but was lost because of it. "I'm sorry," she said in a shaky whisper. "It was my fault."

He looked at her and cringed to see her face, but then his expression grew angry. "Why do you say that? None of it was your fault. Men . . . stinking, rotten, violent men. It's *their* fault! A man hurt you, so he's to blame. I just killed the son of a bitch, so I'm to blame. *You* are not to blame. And Jenny wasn't to blame, although I was angry at her for a long time." He bowed his head. "Oh God, Lizzie, I have to go."

She gripped the table and yet she still reeled. "What do you mean, *go*?" she asked breathlessly. "Go where?"

"Doesn't matter," he muttered.

She shook her head, even though it hurt, and she clutched his hand. "No! I won't let you go."

He looked at her with remorse. "It'll be better for everyone."

"That's not true. Please. I'm sorry for what happened. I thought . . . I'd have some warning. I bought a gun. I was going to protect myself and the children, but . . . I didn't know he was there until—"

He withdrew his hand from her grip. "You're going to be fine now. He can't hurt you anymore."

Panic clawed her insides. "I won't be fine if you leave!"

"I don't belong here."

His calmness made her feel like screaming. "Yes, you do. We were happy."

"The truth is, I'm a murderer. You want a murderer around your children?"

"You are not a murderer, and I want *you*. I love you!" Pain filled his eyes, but it was better than emptiness. Better than his determination to leave. "Please, love me enough to stay."

"Don't you get it? It's because I love you that I have to go. I don't want you or the kids to have to live with seeing me hanged. I know you. You'll blame yourself."

"You won't be hanged," she pleaded. "It was self-defense. April May saw it."

He shook his head. "Everyone knows she'd say or do anything to protect you. I can't put you or the kids through it."

She was getting nowhere. His mind was made up. She was going to lose him. "I'll follow you," she declared. "We'll follow you wherever you go."

"Stop it, Lizzie. Just stop it."

"I will," she swore. "I won't let you go."

"Your face," he said, grieving.

She knew she looked atrocious. She'd seen herself in the mirror earlier.

"C'mon," he said, rising. "You need to go lie down."

"No." If she went back to sleep now, he'd be gone when she awoke. The only man she'd ever loved or ever would love would be gone. "You want to convince me you're not a good man, but you're the man who showed up on a rainy evening offering to help me."

"Because I couldn't get you out of my mind, not from the first time I saw you. I wanted to make love to you. More than anything. It's all I thought about. Don't go thinking I'm noble for showing up here."

He was slipping away. "You're the man who got Jake back to sleep after his nightmare. The man he felt safe enough to talk to."

Jeremy flinched. "Don't do that."

"The man who found Lucky for the kids. And who was

so patient with Rebecca, even when she was unspeakably rude."

"She had reason."

"Yes, but *you* weren't the reason. I love you. I want to spend the rest of my life with you." She reached for his hand and kissed it.

"Lizzie, stop."

"I love you," she said, looking up at him.

"You shouldn't."

There was so much pain in his face. "I know how you see yourself, but it's not how I see you. I see a man with honor and strength and passion, a man who'd give his life to protect his family. To protect us. I want that protection. I want it for me, for Rebecca, Jake, and for all the children we will have."

He bowed his head and a shaky breath escaped him.

"Don't you want me? Don't you want our children?"

"Lizzie," he breathed.

She placed her hands on the sides of his face, loving him so much it hurt. "Look at me. Please. I want you to see what I feel."

He looked at her. "Just think about what it would do to the kids if—"

She cut off his words by pressing a kiss to his lips. Pulling back, she said, "We are going to be fine. We're going to have a life together."

He pulled her into his arms and they clung to one another with all their might. "It's all I want," he murmured. "It's all I want."

Chapter Forty-Nine

Jeremy walked to the Blues' the next morning with a sense of peace he hadn't known in years. The decision was made; he was marrying Lizzie, and together they would make their way. It was possible he would be arrested and tried, but he had shot Ray in self-defense. For now, he'd have faith. Faith in the love he'd found and faith in the truth. He'd lived without hope for a lot of years, but hope and faith felt good. The bakery, as it turned out, wanted Lizzie's baked goods and her expertise, and she was glad about it. She had to heal first, but she was ready for the venture.

As for him, his old life was gone. In fact, his old lives were gone. The men at the mine, some of them good friends, were gone. Even Marie was going, getting married to Walt Davis. He was glad for that. In the end, she'd tried to do the right thing, but the fact that she'd known Ethan Ray had been told of Lizzie's whereabouts and had not warned him was hard to forgive. What if he hadn't made the afternoon train? What if he hadn't reached Lizzie in time? Had he known Ray had been alerted, he never would have left her in the first place. He didn't wish Marie ill, but he was glad she was leaving.

Once Lizzie was better, he'd find a job. Anything out of doors would suit. He also wanted to try his hand at wine making.

The morning was cold, with a pale sky that promised snow. The light wind that whistled through the barren trees smelled like snow, and he was ready for it. He retrieved his satchel from the place he'd dropped it and continued on to get the children. He heard a horse approaching just before Emmett came into view, riding toward him. The older man lifted his hand in greeting. "I think I got a good solution," Emmett said as he came close.

"What's that?"

Emmett reached him and dismounted. "Landreth wants to sell the Six."

Jeremy was stunned by the implied suggestion.

"Howerton offered to buy it, but Landreth said he'd rot in hell first. He hates Smythe just about as much. Truth is, he'll let it go for a lot less to anyone other than his former competitors."

"What are you saying?"

"The mine is going to be bought and restarted. There's just too much money in coal for that not to happen. And Six was a productive mine. What if—"

Jeremy shook his head. "Oh no."

"Now, just hear me out. Someone could buy the mine and run it right. Build it safer, not that a mine can ever be completely safe. We both know better. But he could treat the miners fairly. Pay them better. Pay them in cash. Have medical care available. Better housing."

Jeremy's expression slowly changed as he considered what Emmett was saying.

"Not only that, but the man who did that could make sure children didn't work. That they went to school. I've got this theory that workers who are treated better will be better workers." He paused, but Jeremy didn't say anything. "I can try to broker a deal. Keep your name out of it, if you want."

"The families that lost someone should be helped," Jeremy said.

Emmett nodded. "Why don't you let me see what I can arrange? About buying the place. Rebuilding. Compensating the families of the lost miners."

Jeremy didn't know what to say. Emmett was still acting as if this was Jeremy's money. "I think it's a good plan, but it's not my money. I trust you to do what's right. I like the plan."

"Okay, then. I'll see what I can find out and report back," Emmett said with a smile that made his face seem even rounder than usual. He mounted again. "You know, sometimes folks are given a second chance for a reason."

A second chance? Jeremy shifted on his feet. "Did you hear about Ethan Ray?" he asked.

"In a town this size? What do you think?"

"You think they'll arrest me?"

"For what? He drew on you and you had to shoot him. That's what I heard. That's not a crime."

"You're sure?"

"The law is my business. I'm sure."

Jeremy felt himself deflate with relief.

"How's Lizzie?" Emmett asked.

"She'll be fine."

"With a man like you to look out for her? You bet she will. Give her my best?"

"I will. Thank you, Emmett. For everything."

"You bet." Ethan tipped his hat to Jeremy and rode back toward town.

* * *

Jeremy walked in the side door to the kitchen of the farmhouse and heard group singing from the parlor. *"Do Lord, oh, do Lord, oh, do remember me."* He set his bag down and walked on. Before he reached the parlor, the song had morphed into *"It's me, it's me, it's me, oh Lord, standing in the need of prayer."*

Rebecca was seated next to April May, who had her arm wrapped around the girl, and Cessie held Jake, who was dressed in an old-fashioned nightshirt that was too big for him. A blanket was draped over their laps. April May's hair was bound loosely and Cessie, still wearing a dressing robe, wore her hair loose. A fire was burning in the hearth and all three dogs were stretched out in front of it.

The singing stopped and they all looked at him expectantly, half fearful. He smiled to relieve their anxiety and he felt the collective sigh of relief. "Ready to go home?" he asked the children. "Your Mama's anxious to see you."

Jake started crying and buried his face against Cessie's shoulder. Cessie held him tighter and kissed his head.

"I told you she was fine," April May said tenderly. "A little banged up is all, but she'll be good as new before you know it. Isn't that right?" she said, directing the question to Jeremy.

"It is," he said as he walked in and sat in an overstuffed chair. "She's going to be just fine. Did you know the bakery wants to buy her stuff?"

Rebecca smiled, although tears shone in her eyes. She was fighting hard to keep them in check. "They do?"

He nodded and saw Jake peek out at him. "You ready to go home?" he asked the boy. "You ready, Lucky?" he said to the dog, who stood up at once.

"You know," April May said, "that's a pretty sharp dog."

"He barked," Jake said to Jeremy.

"I know," Jeremy said. "I was glad to hear it."

"He went to protect Mama."

Jeremy nodded. It was hard to know exactly what to say. Everything he thought of to say seemed wrong, since the "bad man" had been their father. Maybe it was best not to say anything. "Let's go home."

"Jake—" Rebecca started with a sheepish look on her face.

She was about to say he'd wet the bed and had no clothes to wear. "Jake's fine as he is," Jeremy said, rising. He picked the boy up and Cessie made sure the blanket went as well. "He can get dressed when he's home. I don't want to wait." As Jeremy turned, he didn't miss the pleased expression on April May's face.

"I'll get our coats," Rebecca said, popping up.

He turned back to the ladies, who were rising. "Saying thank you isn't enough," he said quietly.

Cessie patted his arm. "It isn't necessary at all."

Lizzie was dressed and sitting in the kitchen, which smelled like cookies and freshly made coffee. Half a dozen gingerbread men were laid out to cool on the table. Jeremy set Jake down, and Rebecca and her brother stood frozen momentarily, taking in the black eye, cut lip, and bruised face of their mother.

"I'm not the prettiest thing," Lizzie said, "but I'm all right."

The children rushed forward and she opened her arms to embrace them, kissing one and then the other. Lucky tagged along, wagging his tail.

Jeremy got a cup of coffee and went to sit at the table.

Rebecca was wiping away the tears that embarrassed her. Lizzie had pulled Jake into her lap. "Who wants to decorate gingerbread men?" she asked.

"I do," Jake said.

Lizzie kissed him again. "After you get dressed."

He nodded, got down, and ran off.

"He wet the bed again," Rebecca said quietly. "And he had a nightmare and woke up screaming."

"It'll go away," Jeremy said. "It got better before and it will again."

Rebecca looked at him. "What happened to my father?" she asked guardedly.

"He's gone," Jeremy said solemnly.

"Is he dead?"

Lizzie stiffened.

"Yes," Jeremy replied calmly.

"Did you kill him?"

"Rebecca," Lizzie admonished.

"I did," Jeremy said. "We fought. He drew on me, but I drew faster."

Rebecca had locked her gaze with Jeremy's. "I think I'll call you Papa," she said.

He swallowed, surprised by the statement. "That'd make me proud."

"I'll check on Jake." With great dignity, Rebecca started for the door.

Lizzie watched in amazement. It felt as if her child had aged years overnight.

At the door, the girl turned back. "You're wrong about one thing, though," she said to her mother.

"What?"

"You are the prettiest thing ever."

Touched by the words, Lizzie smiled and Rebecca returned it. In fact, she glowed with it.

Chapter Fifty

"Shouldn't they be back by now?" Rebecca fretted for the fourth or fifth time. She and Cessie were sitting together on the sofa, putting a hem in the green and white gingham curtains that would hang in Rebecca's new room—which had been the room she'd shared with Jake. Jake's room would be where Jeremy had slept.

"Honey," April May said without looking up from the cranberries she was spearing for the Christmas tree garland, "they'll be here when they get here, but they will be here."

The fragrant, eight-foot tree was decorated with colorful, blown-glass balls that were placed around hand-sewn fabric ornaments. Sy and Livie Blue had liked a colorful tree, and so the Blue household had never known any other kind. The children's artwork had also been added this year. In the minds of Cessie and April May, it had never looked better.

"Why do people go on honeymoons, anyway?" Rebecca muttered. "You're going off to be together when you're already going to be together every day from now on."

Cessie and April May chuckled. "They didn't go far, you

know," Cessie said. "Only to Roanoke. It's just to be different. To have a different setting. It's romantic."

Rebecca rolled her eyes. "I'm never getting married."

"Maybe you will and maybe you won't," April May replied. "Although don't you think you might want to give it a few months before you decide for good and all?"

After a moment of consternation, a grin broke through on Rebecca's face. Jake was stretched out on the floor in front of the fire, playing an intense game with his toy soldiers, which, given his expression, must have been locked in an angry confrontation. The dogs were stretched out around him, mostly dozing. It occurred to April May how much these children, this family, had filled their lives.

Jeremy and Lizzie had tied the knot the day before yesterday. It had been a small ceremony with only the family and a few others in attendance. Of course, she counted herself and Cessie as family, and then there had been Emmett, Fiona and Wayne Jones, Doll Summers, Tommy and Em Medlin, and the Howertons. Gregory Howerton had purchased a majority holding of Number Six from Jeremy, and he and Jeremy were working together on plans to rebuild it better and safer than before. Emmett had brought it all about. In fact, the man had brought quite a bit about. He'd also taken a shine to Cessie. Cessie refused to acknowledge it, although it was fun to see her light up a little bit around him.

"What are you thinking about?" Cessie asked her sister.

April May looked at her. "I'm thinking life is good and I'm just awful glad to be alive and kicking."

"Alive and kicking," Jake laughingly repeated.

"Did those soldiers get their war worked out?" April May asked him. "It looked to me like they were going at it pretty hard."

Jake looked unsure for a moment and then he nodded.

"That's good. Peace is better than war. Especially at Christmastime."

Wags's head popped up moments before they heard the sound of a tinkling bell from outside.

"What's that?" Rebecca jumped up and hurried toward the front door before anyone could reply. Jake followed. She opened the door and saw a sleigh coming. "It's a sleigh! It's Mama and Jeremy," she said happily, "and they're in a sleigh."

Her mother saw them and waved, and they waved back. It had begun lightly snowing again.

Jeremy drove around the side of the house, and the children closed the front door and went running to the side door in the kitchen.

"Where'd they get the sleigh?" April May wondered aloud as she placed the strand she was working on in the bowl of cranberries and set it aside. She followed Cessie toward the kitchen as the door opened and excited greetings were exchanged.

As everyone was hugged, Jeremy and Lizzie seemed to glow, and the pink of their faces wasn't caused by just the cold. Snowflakes clung to their coats and hats.

"I didn't know it was snowing again," Rebecca said, wiping away the cold wetness from her face where a snowflake had fallen from Lizzie's embrace. "Until I saw you. We heard the bells."

Lizzie nodded. "Mr. Rice met us at the station and offered us the horse and sleigh for our ride home," she explained. "We drove him to Tommy and Em's farm and we'll go back for him in a few days." She looked at April May and Cessie. "We've all been invited for lunch the day after Christmas. Will you come?"

"Really?" Cessie asked. "Us, too?"

Lizzie nodded. "Yes, ma'am. Doll said to insist that you come."

"Well," April May said. "If she insists."

"We'd love to," Cessie said. "And you're still coming to Christmas dinner with us?"

"Of course. With my best rolls and carrot cake."

"And sugar cookies," Rebecca reminded her.

"Yes," Lizzie replied. "And sugar cookies."

"You ready to go home?" Jeremy asked the children.

They took off to get their coats without bothering to reply.

"Walk," Lizzie called to them.

"Thank you both," Jeremy said, looking from one to the other.

April May waved off the thanks. "What are grandparents and great aunties for? The question is, did you have fun?"

"It was wonderful," Lizzie said, looking to Jeremy, who smiled back at her adoringly.

"It was," he agreed. "Maybe we could all go in a few months. Take the train, eat in a nice restaurant, stay in a hotel."

"That sounds wonderful," Cessie said exuberantly.

Jeremy smiled with great affection and led the children outside once they'd hugged Cessie and April May good-bye and said thank you. They were eager for the sleigh ride, apparently their first.

Lizzie lingered. "This isn't your Christmas present," she said, pulling two small boxes from her pocket. She handed one to each lady; they were marked with their names. "And don't open them until I'm gone," she said with tears glistening in her eyes. "It's just, I want to say—" Her voice broke.

"We know," April May said.

Lizzie nodded. "I know you do, but I want to say it. I

want to say how much I love you." Tears spilled from her eyes, and Cessie stepped forward to wipe them away, despite the fact that tears slid down her own cheeks.

Cessie kissed Lizzie's cheek. "We love you, too."

April May stepped up and gave her a hug. "Now get on home. You got little ones out there who can't wait for a ride. In fact, I want one tomorrow."

Lizzie sniffed and laughed. "You've got it."

"And I plan on belting out 'Jingle Bells' at the top of my lungs."

"I'll join you," Lizzie promised as she stepped back. "Good night."

"'Night, darlin'," April May said.

Cessie's hand was pressed to her throat, her voice trapped within from raw emotion. "How did we ever do without them?" she said when she could.

April May held the gift up. "You ready?"

Cessie nodded and they opened the gifts at the same time. Inside were monogrammed gold lockets. Cessie's was rectangular, April May's oval. "Oh my," Cessie said as she opened her gift. "Look how lovely." Each woman had received a picture of herself as a young woman on one side of the locket, and on the other side, a photograph of the children. "How did she do that?"

"Mine's from the family picture," April May said with an amazed smile. "Damn, was I a nice lookin' thing. Let me see yours."

"How did they get it so small?" Cessie wondered. Hers was a smaller version of the photograph from her sixteenth year of life—the year before John passed.

"I'm glad I admired mine before I saw yours," April May grumbled.

Cessie smacked her lightly. "You're so silly."

Handing back Cessie's locket, April May noticed the

inscription on the back She read it and handed it to her sister with a smile that was strained in an effort not to tear up. Cessie read the inscription as April May read her own. Cessie's read, *To my dream mother with love*. April May's said, *To my favorite aunt with love*.

"That girl," April May said with a shake of her head and a swelling of her heart.

Chapter Fifty-One

Shortly before noon on Christmas morning, the hands at the Martin-Medlin ranch lounged around the parlor of the bunkhouse watching Caty's comical attempts at walking. Wood was on the floor, as were Hawk and Jeffrey. Doll stood watching with wry amusement, commenting frequently on "fully growed men sitting on the floor talking baby talk."

They ignored her.

Caty fell onto her bottom and Wood scooped her back up and put her back on her feet. "If at first you don't succeed," he said.

Emmett was also watching in bemusement, a cup of hot coffee in his hand. "I'm picturing the day she goes off to school for the first time, surrounded by all of you," he teased.

"I think it's a nice picture," Hawk replied as Caty made it to his outstretched hands. He lifted her in the air. "Don't you, Caty-did?"

"Stop calling her that," Doll scolded.

Hawk put her down and pointed her in the direction of Jeffrey, who clapped his hands in encouragement.

"Growed men," Doll said again with a shake of her head. "Pretty soon you'll start singing patty-cake."

"Only 'cause we learned it from you," Joey said from

the table where he and Edward were involved in a game of two-handed spades.

"You're only mad we took up the floor space first," Wood said to Doll.

"If I want to get down there, I will move you aside," Doll retorted.

Wood threw up his hands in concession. "Not going to touch that, because I want my Christmas supper."

Tommy and Em, meanwhile, strolled back to the house after a walk to the end of the drive. Every Christmas, they made their way to the welcome sign. Presenting it had been a meaningful moment for both of them, and they spent a few precious minutes each year in remembrance of that day and in appreciation for the blessing of their life together. After the mining disaster, their gratitude had a new dimension.

Although the sunshine was bright, the day was bitingly cold. Frozen snow glistened brilliantly as though countless diamonds were trapped within. Every step they took made the snow crunch. It was a breathtakingly beautiful day.

"I wonder if the hot mulled wine is ready," Tommy said as they got close to the bunkhouse. His breath fogged in the freezing air.

"Sounds good," Em agreed.

Nearly at the door, Tommy stopped and turned to her. "My nose is cold, but"—he leaned in to kiss her—"merry Christmas."

"Merry Christmas," she returned.

A burst of laughter came from within and they grinned and hurried inside.

* * *

Greg and Charity Howerton were still in their large, elegant bedroom, still in dressing robes, having a lazy morning. They'd slept late and enjoyed breakfast in bed, then exchanged gifts. Charity seemed reticent about handing over the last one, or perhaps she was teasing. He couldn't tell.

"It's not exactly for you," she said. "More for . . . which one of us needs it."

"Are you going to let me open it?" he asked, since she still had a grip on it.

She let it go and he tore off the wrapping paper. Opening the box, he saw white fabric. It was soft. He pulled it up and saw it was rectangular, like a small blanket, perhaps three feet by four. It was too large for a scarf, too small for a blanket. And she was watching him so strangely. "Give me a hint. Why would I . . . need this?"

"For the same reason you'd need this," she said, reaching into a corner of the box where something else was wrapped in tissue paper. It was a rattle.

He jerked his gaze to hers, and she laughed and nodded. And glowed. "You mean—" He was afraid to say it, but she nodded fervently. "A baby?" He had to know for sure.

"Yes. We're going to have a baby."

He felt delirious and dizzy and overwhelmed—and more gloriously high than he'd ever felt in his entire life. He dropped the blanket and wrapped her in his arms.

His reaction was exactly what she'd hoped for and she clung to him. She'd wanted to tell him her suspicion for over a month, but she didn't want to build his hopes up for nothing. The truth was, she'd worried she was too old to conceive. She was nearly thirty.

As he pulled back to look at her, the burning wood in the hearth popped. "It's the best gift I've ever gotten."

"Me too."

"When?"

"July or August."

He laughed in delight and pulled her back into his arms.

The Sheffield family climbed into the two-seat sleigh for the short ride to the Blues' for Christmas dinner.

"Ready?" Jeremy asked the children in back. They were sitting close together under a warm plaid lap blanket.

"Can Lucky come, too?" Jake asked.

"He'll follow," Jeremy said.

"No, we mean with us," Rebecca wheedled. "Please?"

Lizzie was about to say no when Jeremy whistled to the dog and Lucky jumped in, to the amusement of the children. It took a little coordination and a shuffling of the lap blanket, but then they were off. Laughing all the way.